LOVE ON THE WAIVER WIRE

BALTIMORE COBRAS
BOOK 1

ANNA NOEL

Love on the Waiver Wire: Baltimore Cobras book 1

Copyright © 2023 Anna Noel.

All rights reserved. No part of this publication may be reproduced, distributed, or transmitted in any form or by any means, including photocopying, recording, or other electronic or mechanical methods, without the prior written permission of the publisher, except in the case of brief quotations embodied in critical reviews and certain other noncommercial uses permitted by copyright law. For permission requests, write to the author at the contact form @annanoelbooks.com

Any references to historical events, real people, or real places are used fictitiously. Names, characters, and places are products of the author's imagination.

For more information about the author and her books, visit her website —https://annanoelbooks.com/

Book design: Anna Noel

Formatter: Anna Noel

Editor: Alaina Morris

Proofreader: Amber Letto

First Edition: December 28th, 2023

www.annanoelbooks.com

❦ Created with Vellum

Playlist

End Game by Taylor Swift, Ed Sheeran, Future

Wonderwall by Oasis

bad idea right? by Olivia Rodrigo

Sweater Weather by The Neighbourhood

Labyrinth by Taylor Swift

Till Forever Falls Apart by Ashe, FINNEAS

Feels Like by Gracie Abrams

Mirrorball by Taylor Swift

reckless driving by Lizzy McAlpine, Ben Kessler

Jackie and Wilson by Hozier

Iris by the Goo Goo Dolls

Dancing With Our Hands Tied by Taylor Swift

Ribs by Lorde

American Money by BORNS

Bejeweled by Taylor Swift

AUTHOR'S NOTE

Dear Reader,

Thank you so much for giving my little sports romance a try. I'm passionate about many things, and football has always been one of them.

Living in New York and being a Ravens fan was always an experience. Every time I wore my prized Joe Flacco jersey my grandparents bought me I'd hear someone say "Sacco Flacco" at least once. But honestly? It builds character.

The Ravens have always had my heart, and although this novel doesn't include any characters based off of real ones, I knew I wanted to base my little fictional team in Baltimore.

There is going to be a lot of talk about fantasy football in the first couple chapters. It'll stop fairly quickly, but if there is a word you don't know, it may be in the back where I've listed some definitions!

I really hope you all love these characters as much as I do.

CONTENT WARNINGS:

This is a much much lighter book than my others, with almost no triggers. There's on-page alcohol consumption,

AUTHOR'S NOTE

mild mentions of depression, and only a passing mention of a side-character's loss of a parent that happened years ago.

NOTE: NFL players are allowed to play fantasy football as long as they do not earn over $250. You can learn more about the NFL's gambling policy (and limits on Fantasy Football) from their official document here: https://shorturl.at/erVY4

To those who love slow burn and football players that are hot as hell and sweet as candy, this is for you.

Being perfect is not about that scoreboard out there. It's not about winning. It's about you and your relationship with yourself, your family and your friends. Being perfect is about being able to look your friends in the eye and know that you didn't let them down because you told them the truth. And that truth is you did everything you could. There wasn't one more thing you could've done. Can you live in that moment as best you can, with clear eyes, and love in your heart, with joy in your heart? If you can do that, gentlemen—you're perfect!

Friday Night Lights

FAN·TA·SY FOOT·BALL

/ˈfan(t)əsē ˈfo͝otˌbôl/
 noun

a competition in which participants select imaginary teams from among the players in the NFL and score points according to the actual performance of their players each week.

PRE SEASON

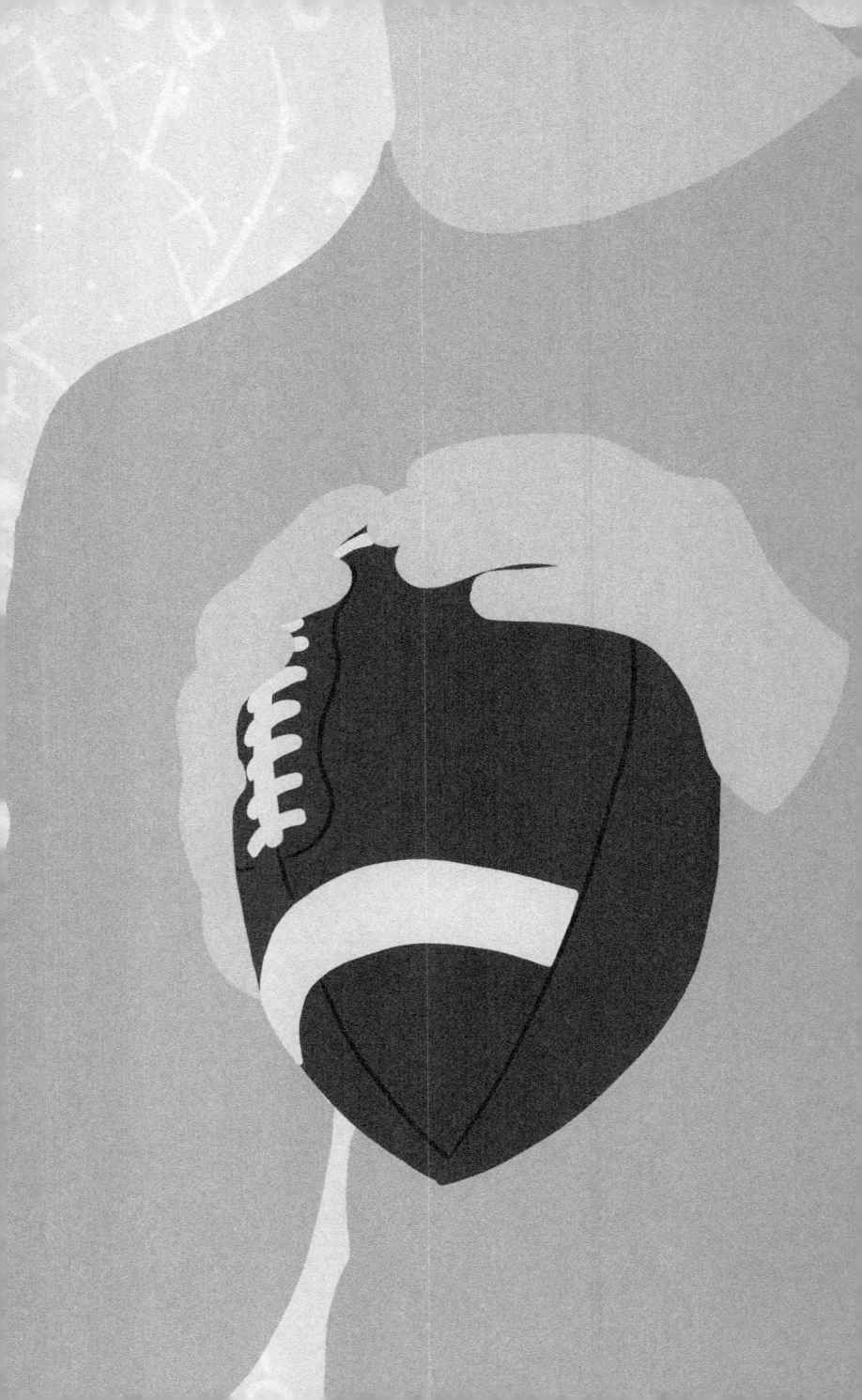

1

OWEN

When I get to Leo Warner's apartment, the last thing I expect to see is his neighbor outside of her apartment in just a towel, angrily turning her doorknob.

I stop mid-text as I watch her try one more time before letting out a defeated sigh, bringing her forehead to the smooth surface and resting it there.

"Lock yourself out?" I ask with a smirk.

She jumps, her eyes wide as she takes a step back, her gaze drifting over me lazily. "Yep," she says, tucking her wet hair behind her ear before crossing her arms over her chest and looking around the beige hallway.

I nod, whipping out my key to Leo's place and heading inside without another word.

The smell of sausage hits my nose instantly and I head to the kitchen to find Leo already stuffing his face with his favorite pizza, the setting sun casting a dreamy glow over the whole room as it reflects on the bay below.

"Your sister is naked in the hallway," I tell him as I take a seat.

His pizza drops hap hazardously onto the counter in front of him. "Excuse me?" he asks, his mouth still full.

I shrug. "Your sister. She's naked in the hallway."

Leo's green eyes bug out of his head, his neck turning crimson as he turns toward the hall leading to the front door of his fancy apartment, his shoes squeaking against the polished hardwood as he goes.

Leaning over the counter, I pick up a slice of the greasy monstrosity Leo loves and sit back in my chair, listening for what's to come.

The door opens.

"What the fuck?" I hear Leo ask.

"I got locked out of my apartment again," Isla Warner tells him, her voice sad.

"Why were you even out here to begin with?"

"I was sending home my latest hookup, obviously. God, Leo, it's like you have no life."

I know it's a lie. He knows it's a lie. We all know it's a lie. But it gets him worked up anyway.

"Isla you can't just be walking around the apartment naked."

"Actually I can," she cuts him off. "That's the entire point of an apartment. That you can walk around naked."

"You know what I mean. Shared common spaces are different."

"Okay dad."

"Don't call me dad. You have one dad and he's not here."

"You're right, my bad. Sorry, I just have to inform my date from last night that he's not my daddy."

There's a loud noise, and I can picture Leo's arm dramatically hitting the doorframe. I can't help but chuckle to myself.

"Jesus Christ Isla, I have your spare key just, I don't know," I can hear his voice get closer as he heads back inside, "chill out."

Leo stomps back into the kitchen, his hands scrubbing his

face as he pulls out his clutter drawer, taking her spare key out. I take a bite of pizza, feeling the cheese slip off in a particularly odious manner as the grease drips down my chin, and when his eyes meet mine, I can't keep down the chuckle.

"Shut up."

"Yes daddy," I say as I try to chew without gagging.

Deciding that a response would only make me push him harder, Leo heads back to the door once more, unlocking hers for her and letting her back in.

When he returns, he looks more irritated than anything else, his brows furrowed as he bites his lip.

"What's up?" I ask him, setting the slab of blubber down on the back of the pizza box in front of me.

"Zeke was traded," he says, crossing his arms in front of him.

I sigh, rubbing my temple. No matter how many years we go through this, it's always hard. In only a couple of days the official 53-man roster is due, and great players are always cut, traded, and demoted to practice squad left and right.

"He knew it was coming," I say, feeling that familiar sense of discontent waft over me. It's sad every time, but it's what we signed up for.

"He was so excited for our league this year though, man." Running his greasy hand through his dark hair, Leo pouts, looking out the window to the inner harbor, his lips pursed. After a minute, I swear I hear a sniffle.

"Leo the guy isn't dead. We're still friends with him." Leo was the quarterback at one of the most prestigious colleges in the entire country with one of the best football programs there is. He's most known for breaking down on camera as he held up a jersey with his coach's number on it. *"This win was for you coach. We miss you so much. God, I wish you were here for this,"* he cried into the microphone.

Was he dead? No. He was suspended for three games, a

league low, for a recruiting violation. He would be back the next game to watch them win by over 50.

"But the league."

I stare at him as he dramatically gazes at his pizza still sitting face down on his counter. "You know you're the commissioner, right? Like, you make the rules. You can change them if you wanted."

Leo's eyes slowly lift to meet mine before narrowing, his arm shooting out as his pointer finger makes contact with the counter. "The league's rules are written in stone, Crosby. You know this." He scoffs. "God, if we just throw out the rules for this what's next? The rules of football are changed? Then what?" He throws his hands in the air. "Ocean laws are tossed out the window?"

"What the hell are ocean laws?"

"The whales, Crosby. The whales." He rolls his eyes, heading for the fridge. I let it be, more confused than ever.

Which is, unfortunately, par for the course with Warner. The only time he makes sense is on the football field, thank fuck.

"What are we going to do? The draft is in three days."

Taking a swig of milk from the container, Leo shrugs. "I'll find someone to replace him. It'll be easy. Who doesn't want to be part of our league?"

Most people, I think. Most of the guys on the team have their own leagues going, and although everyone loves Leo—he is one of the best quarterbacks in the entire league after all—most don't have the time or patience to deal with his league. Although a lot of professional football players have their own leagues, it's hard to convince them to join yet another when there's no money involved.

Players are allowed to participate in leagues as long as they don't earn over two-hundred and fifty dollars from it, so to prevent any issues at all, Leo just gives out a trophy.

Leo's fantasy league is his baby. He's a little obsessive

about it, and although it's fun, it's a lot of work for a group of men who already have a lot of work.

Well, not Franklin. I guess he could be a good contender.

Except Leo's fantasy rules require all league members be active players of the Baltimore Cobras team at the start of the season, not management, coaching staff, or water boys.

Zeke was the only son of a bitch we could convince to join two years ago. We've been solid ever since.

"Well, that's a you problem," I tell him, getting up to get a beer. Pursing my lips, I turn back around to him. "So, your sister…"

"You know the rules, Crosby."

Look at my sister and you're dead. Yeah, I know it. I know it well.

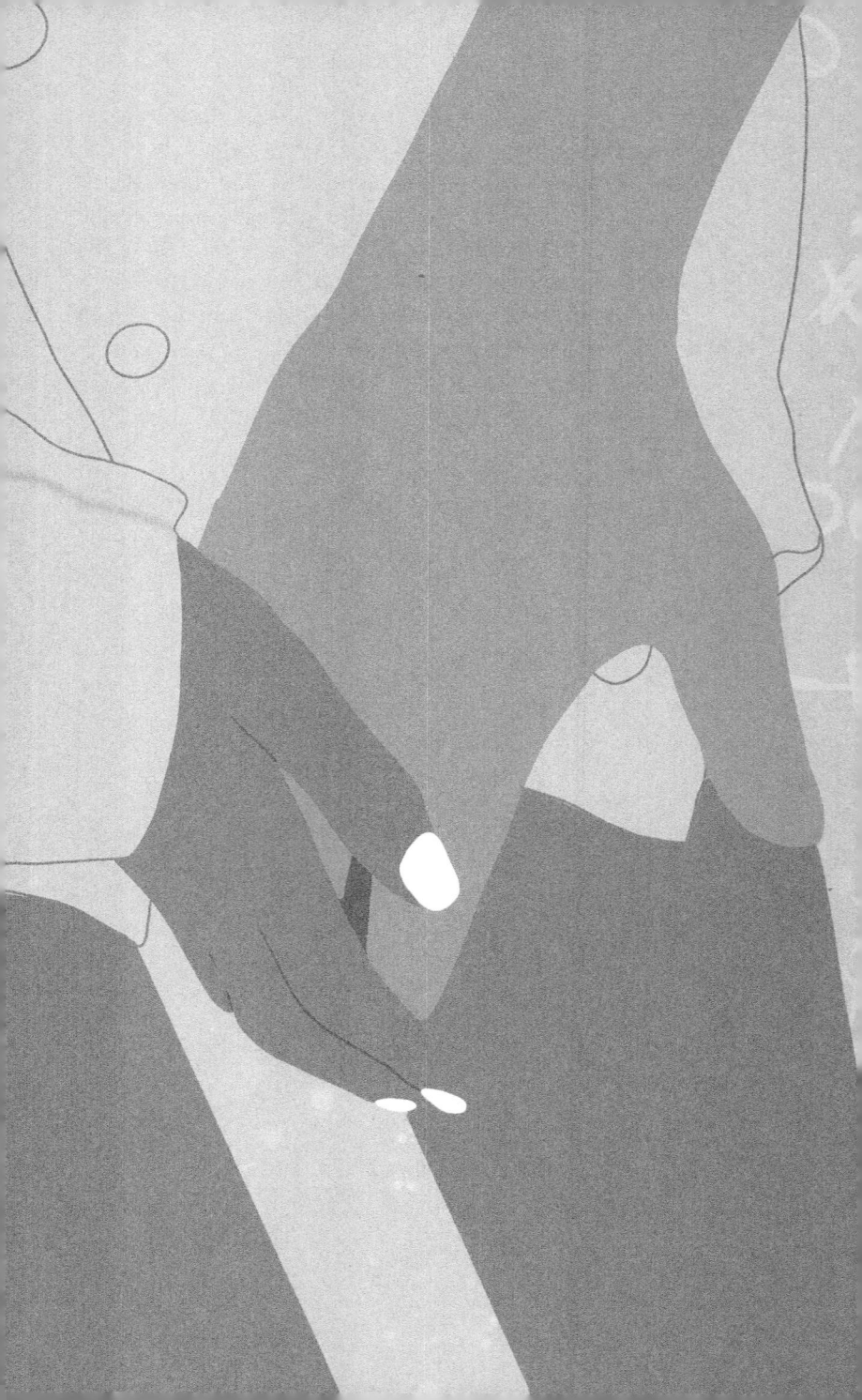

2

ISLA

Sometimes, I forget that my brother is adored around the country. He's just such a giant idiot I can't picture it. I love him, but he's so easy to rile up it's ridiculous.

"What happened?" Mila asks, her voice oddly soothing over the loudspeaker of my phone.

"Well, I took a shower and was getting ready to go back to work on this painting when I heard a knock on my door. I thought it was the food that I had ordered for dinner and went to answer it. No one was there, so I went to peek down the hall, and the door shut on me!"

Silence follows my words, and I put down my paintbrush before checking my phone to ensure I haven't lost her. "Hello?"

"You've done that what? Three times now? You're going to get yourself locked out and in trouble one of these days, Isla."

Rolling my eyes, I take a sip of wine before placing the glass back down on the sheet covering my floor, busying myself once more with toning my canvas. "I know, I know.

It's not going to happen again. I just hate that the doors lock themselves, you know?"

"I just worry about you. And I miss you here, if I'm honest."

I moved into this apartment three months ago, and I'm still getting used to it. Bought and paid for by my brother, I don't pay a thing; not that I don't try to give him what I can.

"I know. I miss you too. Do you want to come over sometime next week and we can watch dumb movies?"

"Hell yeah," I can hear the smile in her voice, and it relaxes me a bit. "We still have a couple of episodes of The Housewives to get through."

I wince, tossing my head back. "Oh, I thought you were catching up on it yourself," I grit out, chuckling guiltily.

"Fine. I won't subject you to it. I'll just watch it here, all alone."

As we finish our conversation, I start thinking, not for the first time, what I would do without Mila. My best friend since we were kids, we've been attached at the hip for most of our lives.

Which is why we both took it hard when I moved.

And I did feel guilty. I didn't have to move. But I also needed a bigger space to work on my art, and living here, with harbor views, isn't really a bad gig. I asked my brother if she could move with me, and he said yes.

She loves her little house and decided to stay. She just visits me... often.

When my canvas is completely coated with a thin layer of deep orange, I sit back and stare at it, trying to figure out what exactly I want to paint today. I have a small gallery showing in a couple of weeks, and I've been determined to put out my best. I've been looking for a big break.

After years of painting and being told I'll only get opportunities because of my brother, I'm done listening to the noise. I want my big break to be because of my work, even if I give my brother full credit for being the reason I can follow my dreams in the first place.

As much as I give him shit, he's one of my biggest supporters, and wouldn't take no for an answer when he offered to help me financially so I could focus on making that dream happen. He wanted it almost more than I did.

But no ideas are coming to me today.

Groaning, I uncross my legs, getting off the floor. Wiping my hands on my overalls, I cross the room to my oversized couch, flopping down before twisting to look out the large floor-to-ceiling windows behind it. The sun is almost set, the water glistening below.

I still can't believe I get to live here.

A moment later, my doorbell rings, and I cross my fingers and toes hoping it's finally dinner. I adore the little Italian place down the street, but they take a million years sometimes.

Opening the door, I catch the delivery man just as he's about to set the bag down on my doormat. I smile at him, thanking him before snatching it right up.

"Do you know who lives next door?" the man asks, chuckling a little.

I pause. "No, why?"

And that's when I hear it.

"No, you're not fucking doing that, Owen. You're not taking him, don't even start!"

"You can't tell me who or what to take, man."

"I can and I will."

"Rock, paper, scissors for him?"

The voices are muffled, but we can hear as clear as day.

The delivery man shakes his head, continuing his trek down the long hall away from me. I wait until I hear the elevator ding before heading back inside, placing my food down on my counter, *grabbing my keys,* and heading next door.

There are certain hours I'm allowed to use Leo's key, and this is not one of them. Anything past 6 P.M. is a danger zone. Luckily for me, I know he doesn't have a girl over.

The first thing that hits me when I enter the apartment is that the lights are down low, and I start to second guess what I heard.

"Stop it right now, God dammit the guy took Freddy."

"What a little bitch."

I walk into the large space to find my brother sitting on the couch, his laptop in front of him, his best friend Owen on the other end, his phone in front of his face. My cheeks warm without my permission as I remember him catching me in the hallway earlier. But it's not like he hasn't seen worse from other women.

"What's going on here?" I ask, my hands on my hips.

Owen's head snaps up, his eyes immediately on mine before he quickly looks at my brother.

Who looks pissed. "What time is it, Isla?"

"It's *don't bother Leo time,* but you guys are so loud that you have my delivery guy commenting on the noise."

"Did you hear anything in your apartment?" Well, no. No I didn't. I go to open my mouth, but he beats me to it. "No, of course you didn't. No one is hanging outside our apartments. Just say you're nosy."

He's got me there. I *am* nosy.

As nosy as a man who says he doesn't like drama.

"That's rude but fair," I sigh, rounding his couch and making myself at home in the middle.

"Hey! Hey, what are you doing? We're conducting important business here." Leo's eyes are wide, clearly amazed that I'd have the audacity to still be here.

"What are you guys up to?"

He frowns, his eyes darting to Owen before back to me. "If you must know, we're doing a mock fantasy draft."

I nod, suddenly understanding.

Fantasy football has always been huge in our house, but Leo has taken it ten times further than it ever needed to go.

It started with our dad, who somehow convinced Leo that being good at fantasy football was more than just luck. It had to do with football skill—*If you're not good at fantasy football, how do you expect to be good at actual football?*" he'd ask.

I still don't know how that works. I'm pretty sure he was just trying to make sure he'd play it with him.

But Leo believed it. Poor, well meaning, dense Leo. It's not shocking that that got him.

But it turns out he sucked at it. And he has continued to suck at it for the last decade. That doesn't stop him from forcing his friends on his team to play with him, though. The only thing that matters to him is that he doesn't lose every year.

I would never say it out loud, but I almost think that his team lets him win sometimes. It's the only thing that makes sense.

"And all the good players are being taken?" I ask, crossing my legs under myself. Leo watches the movement carefully, frowning.

"Obviously. Go home."

"I can't hang out with my brother?" I ask him.

"Not after six P.M. without permission, no."

I look over at Owen, noticing his eyes on mine. I look away, brushing my hair behind my ear.

He's always been, in my opinion, the most attractive player on the whole team.

"Do you want help?" I ask Leo, sitting up straighter as I become all too aware of the pair of eyes still on me.

"I don't need it but thanks."

"Leo, just let me look."

"No, Isla. I need to do this. This is do or die for me over here, okay? You should know this."

Slapping my hands on my knees, my mouth clamps shut

as I get up. "Alrighty. Well, I'm going back home and eat dinner and watch another season of Love Island."

Leo snorts. "Elsie was in my DMs a day before she went on the show."

I roll my eyes. "Of course she was."

His head jerks up from his computer once more, looking shocked that I wouldn't believe him.

But as I turn to leave and look at his apartment—the apartment that mirrors mine—I'm hit again with the realization that my brother *did, unfortunately,* possibly have a pretty influencer from Love Island in his direct messages.

Owen probably has had them in his, too.

But when I look back at him, he's simply rolling his eyes, probably also done with my brother's antics.

"Yeah, well, she's with Kevin, but he seems like a bit of a douche."

"I'll have to hit her up when she's back."

"Not if she finds love, Leo. Don't be that guy."

He scoffs, and as he's about to say something, his computer dings, and he holds up a finger, selecting his next player before returning his attention to me. "You don't go on a show like that to find love, Isla. You go on it to get brand deals. No couple actually lasts."

"You play fantasy football every single year and still never win. Isn't that kind of the same thing?" I shoot back, popping my hip.

"Oh fuck," Owen says under his breath, looking between us.

Leo rolls his eyes again, shooing me.

With one last look shared between Owen and me, I retreat to my apartment, warming up my food before settling into my couch, turning on my show, and relaxing for the evening. Finally.

3

OWEN

"Hey Ken, do you want to join my league this year?"

"Oh, I'm sorry, man; I have so much going on outside this and two other leagues; otherwise, you know I would."

"It's okay, bro; I'll forgive you."

It's been two days, and Leo has been freaking out. Two days of trying to convince anyone he can to join our fantasy league, and as I suspected, none of them wanted a part of it. Something about him being a bit of a psycho for the rules and loving punishments a little too much.

Don't get me wrong, I love a good fantasy punishment, but on a much different level than Leo. Leo loves them because he's a maniacal son of a bitch. I love them because they're fun to watch. I haven't had to worry about fantasy punishments for years, considering I've been consistently on top of the league.

Leo slams his shoes down, plops onto the bench next to his locker, and hangs his head in his hands. "I can't believe no one wants to be in the league."

I somehow manage to hold my chuckle in. "I'm sure it'll

be okay. Just choose someone who's not on the team. You're the one who made that rule; you can change it, you know."

He groans as he looks up at me, annoyance clouding his face. "You don't get it."

"What don't I get?"

"You just don't get what being the commissioner means. It's important."

I roll my eyes, grabbing my bag before leaving. I love Leo, I do. He's been like a brother to me for a couple of years. But some of the shit that comes out of his mouth needs to be studied.

"You leaving?" Leo asks as I turn toward the door. I look over my shoulder, nodding. "Wait up, I'll come with you."

Great.

I sigh, turning again to wait for him. I look around, watching the guys get changed. There are so many of us here, and every single one of us has put our bodies and minds on the line for a game we love. Sure, it pays well, but this isn't something you can do if you don't put your heart into it.

When I have moments to stop and think about my life and everything that's happened to get me here, I can't help but be thankful.

"Okay, I think I'm ready. And I think I have a plan," Leo tells me as he gathers his things and marches out the door. I follow him, wondering what this plan could possibly be. But he doesn't say anything.

"Are you going to fill me in on this so-called plan?" I ask, dodging a door he doesn't hold open for me.

"Nah," is all he responds, and I hold back the urge, not for the first time today, to choke him out.

It's the same feeling I get whenever he sends a hospital pass my way during practice.

"Okay, well, anyways," I start, rolling my eyes. "I can't wait to find out what you've come up with."

"It's all good. It's a brilliant plan."

I'm sure it is.

Practice was brutal today as the official 53-man roster was submitted. To no one's surprise, I made the cut. We spent some of the day going over some new plays that our offensive coordinator came up with and started talking about our first game of the season, which is always exciting.

And now I'm back at my apartment, looking out at the city in front of me as onions sizzle in a pan on the stove. A rush of peace and excitement run through me. These are the best months of the year, and I'm excited to finally see my parents for the first time, considering my mom works long hours and my dad is a lawyer. They're always busy.

All that matters is they're happy.

Buzz

Grabbing my phone out of my pocket, I open it as I down the rest of my water.

> LEO
>
> Okay broskis, we have a twelfth player. Jesus, I just had to type twelfth like five times to get it right. Why the hell is it spelled like that? Wild. Anyways, his name is Ian. He's pretty cool. Works for the team, but isn't on the team. I bent my rules and don't want to hear anything about it. You'll probably meet him someday but who knows. He's officially on the team, and will be drafting first. Sorry, I didn't make that rule. I just randomized it just now. I feel like they're going to pick me first overall, just a heads up.

Leo's texts are always a bunch of nonsense, but they're usually a little smoother than this one. Still, I shrug. At least we have someone else to complete our twelve-man league. Though I'm not sure I've ever met an Ian who works for the team. Maybe he chose someone random in the hallway and asked. I wouldn't put it past him.

> **COOPER**
> Sounds good. As long as we have someone it'll be fine.

Cooper Henry, our good friend and one of the best tight ends in the league, texts back.

> **LEO**
> It's more than fine. It's great. Trust me on this guys. Anyways, we're drafting tomorrow night. I'll have pizza, the uzhe. I'll send the drafting order in a bit when Ian changes his team name.

There are a lot of rules in Leo's fantasy league, but one of the biggest is we're not allowed to use any generic names. No *Owen's Fantasy League* allowed. No. We have to create the best team name we can possibly think of.

Heading back to my pan, I pour some wine in to deglaze it, leaning back against my kitchen island to scroll through my audiobooks before choosing one and connecting it to my speaker.

Tomorrow is going to be a long day.

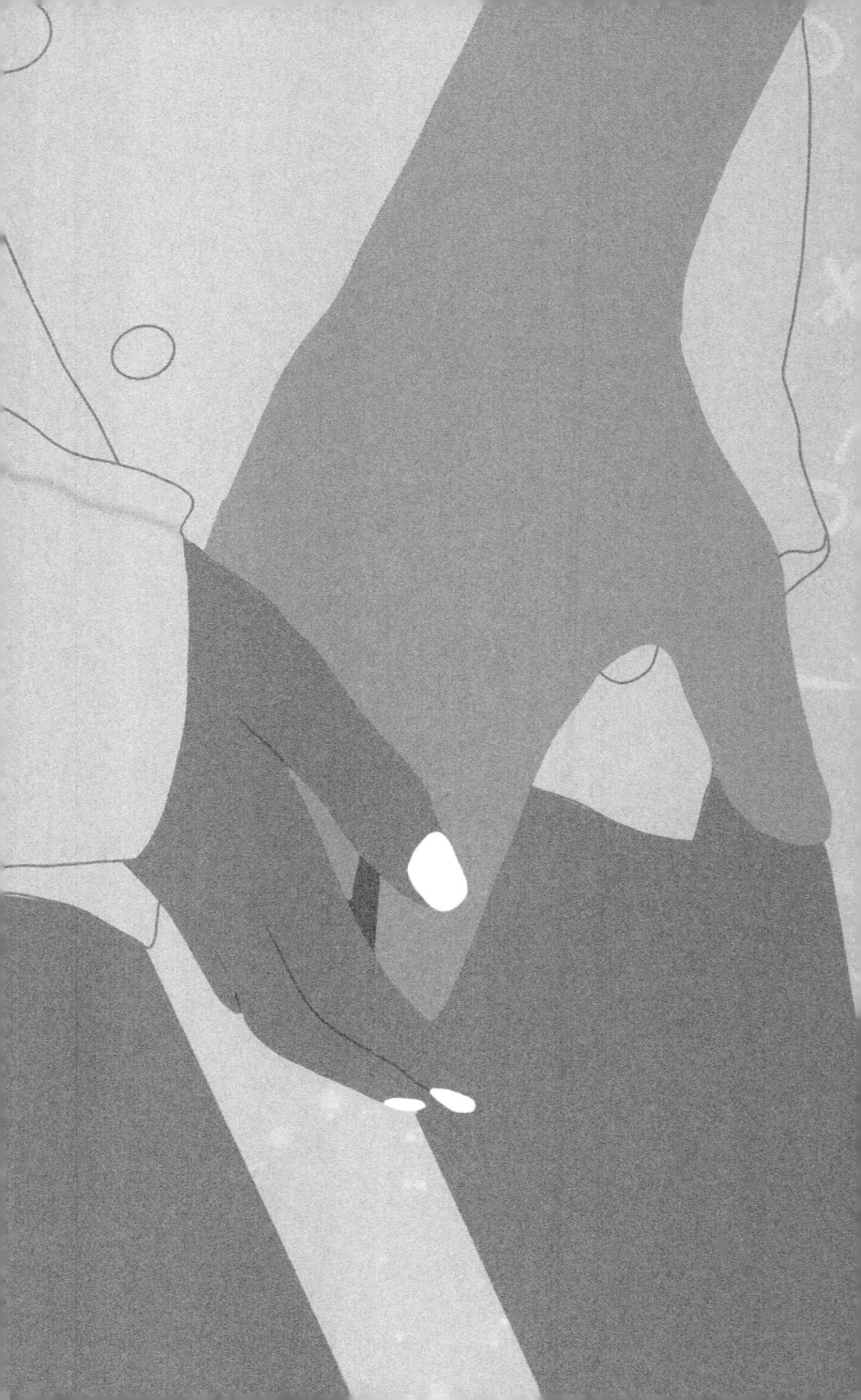

4

ISLA

I'm peacefully painting on my floor, the low hum of my favorite 90's band filling the room and my large candle casting a pretty glow across the room, when a loud bang on my door sends my paintbrush up as I flinch.

"Isla! Isla! I have a favor I have to ask of you," Leo practically yells as he barges in. He flips on the light, and I squeeze my eyes closed, slowly opening them one at a time so they can get used to the brightness. My brother's eyes are wild, his chest heaving. If you didn't know any better you'd almost think he wasn't a professional athlete.

I groan, shooting him a look before grabbing my wet rag and trying to get as much of the smudged paint as I can off the canvas. There's still a dark spot, but it's nothing I can't paint over.

And I was so focused…

"What do you want?"

"It's actually important, Isla, I swear."

I wave him on, hoping he'll get to it.

"I need you to join my fantasy league."

A laugh builds inside me until it comes tumbling out with

no restraint. I can't help it. That's one of the funniest things he's ever said to me.

"Isla, I'm *serious*."

"No, you're not," I tell him, getting up from the ground and heading for my kitchen to grab another glass of red wine. I fill my cup a little higher this time.

"Isla."

"Leo," I shoot back, meeting his green eyes.

Stressed, he wipes his hand through his hair, pulling at the ends a bit as he looks up, trying to think of what to say next. My brother is great at many things, but words are not always one of them.

"We need a twelfth person for the team. You're someone we can add. I need you. Please?"

"Leo, we had the family league years ago. Remember how that went down?"

He stares at me as if he doesn't, but I know he does.

Five years ago

The entire family sits around the table for dinner. My grandparents have been here since Christmas for an extended visit.

"So what's the punishment for losing again?" my grandfather asks as he takes a slow sip of his scotch.

"You have to do the hottest chip challenge," Leo tells him, crossing his arms over his chest.

"You're not making your grandfather eat that thing, Leo."

"Yes, I am," he throws back.

"Ellen, I'm fine, trust me. I'm old, not dead. I can take a spicy chip.

He couldn't take the spicy chip.

He's fine now, though, thank God.

"Isla, just listen to me, okay? Do this for me, and I'll give you whatever you want. Seriously. I won't bother you in here anymore. I'd give you the spare key, but apparently, you go into the hallway naked, and honestly, that concerns me, but otherwise, I would. I'll leave you alone, I promise."

Honestly, that kind of sounds promising…

"Do I have time to think about it?" I ask him.

His eye twitches before he looks down at the floor, his lips pursing. "It's funny that you should ask that, actually, because I already set up your profile. And, well, the draft is in about half an hour."

I gape at him. "I haven't even researched anything about the players this season, Leo."

"I mean, you're first overall, and I figured you'd pick me first like you used to," he states, walking across the room to take a seat on my couch.

"What kind of draft is it?"

"Snake"

"Leo!"

"What?"

I groan, throwing back my wine before filling the glass again. "You do know that means that I'm picking first overall in a league I've never played in, with players I don't know, and then I don't pick again until the twenty-fourth pick, right? That's a lot of time for me to just be sitting here at my laptop twiddling my Goddamn thumbs, right? I can't pick you in the first round."

"You used to!"

"Because we were playing with people who didn't know what the hell they were doing. Mom used to pick a kicker in the first round, Leo. The first overall pick made it all the way to the 8th round the last year we played."

He weighs my words, his arms folded over his chest.

"You're going to be okay with whatever you do, just please?"

The thing is, I know that I don't have any other option. When Leo asks something, he's persistent. He's annoying. He's like a little tiny pest under your skin, and he'll keep asking and asking until he eventually gets what he wants.

It's how it's always been.

"Fine," I tell him, annoyed, as I turn to grab my laptop.

"Yes! Thank you, Isla, you're seriously saving my ass." He gets up, ready to head back out, when he pauses, turning back on his heel to look at me. "I have one more thing to tell you," he says.

I nod, hoping he'll go on and stop looking at me with guilty eyes.

"Well, I told the guys your name is Ian. You work with the team."

Tossing back my head, I let out a loud groan. Why does everything he does have to be so complicated? Why can't things be simple?

"Why would you do that?"

"Because I said that all the players have to be on the team, and I didn't want to bend the rules that bad, but also because I don't want any of them flirting with you."

That's just—there's no reason he should be concerned about any of the players flirting with me. I've been around them plenty, and all I've felt is sibling love from them. Well, from almost all of them.

"Why do you care so much?"

He throws up his hands. "Because I don't want to deal with one of them hurting you and then having to play with them like everything is fine, okay? Not only would I be pissed at them, but I'd be upset at myself for not stopping it so that you wouldn't get hurt. Most of those guys are players."

"Like you?"

"Exactly like me."

"Well, don't worry because I'm not going to fuck your buddies." I open my laptop with a huff, pulling up the fantasy website before turning the screen to him. "Sign me in commish."

5

OWEN

Leo's apartment smells like grease and the strongest body spray you can possibly imagine. It always does when he has everyone over. Some of these guys haven't learned how to actually apply that stuff without overdoing it yet.

"Want some pizza?" Cooper asks from behind the counter as he passes out plates.

I look at the pale slice he's holding out and shake my head. "No thanks, I ate before I got here."

He nods, understanding. We've had several conversations about how disgusting Leo's favorite pizza is.

Leo claps his hands from the family room, rubbing them together like a supervillain. "Okay guys, everything is set," he says as he looks around. Baltimore Cobras players sit around the room, laptops open in front of them as they all log into the fantasy website to get ready for the draft. Leo has the prime seat on the corner section of the couch, while Dirwin sits next to him. Cooper rounds the counter and takes a seat on the other side where his laptop kept his spot, a plate of hummus in one hand while he uses his thumb to open the computer.

Tristen and Myles sit at the counter, and the other guys sit along the coffee table and are spread out around the room, leaning against walls. Some of them don't mind others looking at their screens, while others, like Emmett Gardner, would rather throw themselves off a bridge than have someone see what they're doing or their next move.

Which is honestly understandable, considering some of these guys are complete assholes and will absolutely steal a player if they think that you're going to take them next. But that's just fantasy football.

Sighing, I take a seat against the wall facing the others, opening my laptop to get ready.

"There's only eleven of us?" Cooper asks, his head tilted as he tries to count us again.

Leo's head whips up, his eyes a little wide. "Yeah, Ian couldn't make it. He's going to draft from home."

We never draft from home. It's one of Leo's stupid rules. It's a team bonding exercise, apparently.

Cooper looks as perplexed as I feel. It's been years. We've moved the draft completely before because guys couldn't make it. Two years ago a guy was kicked out of the league because there was no possible way he could make the draft, despite the fact that everyone is in town with almost open availability because of practice. It's not like the guy had much going on.

But for Leo to be okay with someone we don't know to not be here? It's a little suspicious.

"I feel like we should ask more questions," Tristen says as he spins on his seat at the counter, but not before closing his screen enough so no one can see. He cocks his head, his deep brown eyes staring daggers at Leo.

Tristen is one of the other wide receivers on the Cobras and one of the nicest guys alive. But he has always had a healthy dose of skepticism, which is something Leo has had to overcome with him. As a rookie he used to question everything, and it became a reasonable question of whether he was

LOVE ON THE WAIVER WIRE

coachable. He's learned a lot over the years, though, and is now one of the best on the team.

"For someone who got the first overall pick, it's wild that they're not here, but whatever," Christian says from the other side of the room, his massive frame looking hilarious, leaning up against a small pillar.

Leo freezes for a second. "We didn't have any other choice," he says as he scratches the side of his face. "We needed someone, I found someone, they're on the team, that's what's important."

The guys all turn back to their computers, though the amount of eye rolls I count needs more than one hand.

I take a look at the draft order, spotting Ian up top. *Cover 1, 2, 3, Let's Go B—*

Why does that sound so familiar? I wrack my brain for the reference but it doesn't come to mind. I'll think of it eventually.

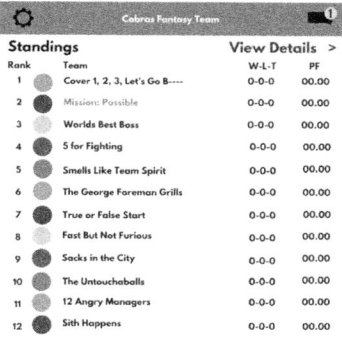

"Isn't it a little weird that there's a new guy first and then you and your best buddy are second and third?" One of the guys says.

Leo sighs loudly, groaning as he tosses his head back dramatically. "I was last last year guys; I'm not trying to screw anyone over. I take the job of commissioner super seriously. Anyways, the draft is starting in two minutes, time to get your shit together."

I have a list of picks I'd like to make on the side. I have the second pick, which means that I could pick myself, but there are better players than me available. Although I'm good and definitely a first-round pick, I'm not someone that most people would pick first-round, either. My ADP is around 6, and although that's really good, I strive to be number one.

But then again, apparently, there are people out there who would draft Leo first, which is truly wild. No one drafts quarterbacks in the first round, not even Leo, who picks himself if he's available every year.

At 9pm on the dot, the clock starts ticking.

Most of us are on our game and don't need the full two minutes to make our pick, but as the clock ticks down and there's under a minute left, the guys start looking at each other, trying to figure out what the mysterious Ian is going to do. Leo sits forward, his elbows on his knees, his hands clasped in front of his mouth as he watches the clock tick on his laptop sitting on the coffee table in front of him. He looks almost worried.

Ten seconds.

Nine seconds.

Eight seconds...

Ding!

I don't have time to read the pick before everyone's heads turn toward me.

"What?" Emmett asks, his face twisted in confusion.

It was me. The guy chose me. In the first round.

Honestly? I'm a better pick than Leo would have been, so that's a plus.

Still, it was unexpected. The best wide receiver by a longshot still sits untouched on top of the list.

I realize I'm on the clock when it flashes red, letting me know I only have a few seconds left to make my pick. I select who should have gone first overall to begin with, feeling excited.

"I don't know how that happened," I mutter, leaning back. Waiting 24 more picks to choose again sucks.

"I mean you're good man, but that man should have been gone first round," Cooper says.

I nod, shrugging. "You don't have to tell me that I can assure you that."

The room falls silent again as everyone focuses on making their picks.

About forty minutes later we're done. Everyone has full teams, and there weren't too many crazy moves other than Christian, our linebacker, snatching our defense a couple rounds too soon. Dirwin, our backup quarterback, even got picked as a backup by one of our centers. Whether that was a smart move is another story, but he was happy despite Leo's annoyance.

"Are you just inviting me to get an injury?" he had asked.

"Nah, bro, I just wanted Dirwin to have his time, you know?" Jason responded.

"Yeah man, Dirwin doesn't get picked first very often ya know?" Cooper throws in.

"If you bring Jessica up one more time I swear—" Dirwin starts.

Cooper throws his hands up in front of him. "I didn't say shit man, all I'm saying is that sometimes people pick others instead of you. No names were mentioned."

"Get fucked Henry," Dirwin said, turning his attention back to his screen.

Cooper snickered, selecting his pick. "I mean I did, thank you for that."

The two of them go out all the time and consistently fight over girls. I don't know how they're still friends, though I guess we should be lucky that they leave the drama behind them. Most of the time.

"Okay guys, I'll see you tomorrow," Leo says as he stands, shutting his laptop.

Everyone follows suit, packing up their things and grabbing last-minute pizza.

I stay for a couple minutes after everyone leaves, helping Leo clean up a bit before heading out. I give him a hug, patting his back before opening the door and stepping out into the hall.

Buzz

Taking my phone out of my pocket, my sister's name, Briar, lights up asking me if I can watch my niece Elara for a few days in a couple of weeks.

I stop and respond to her, and as I type out that I would absolutely love to as long as she's okay with her daughter staying at my place alone while I'm off at practice, I hear it.

The faint sound of a familiar song coming from the apartment next door...

A Taylor Swift song.

A memory flashes in my mind. One of my favorite memories, actually, of me taking my sister and her daughter to her concert only a couple of months ago. Briar had to explain to me why people were yelling little things between lines of songs.

And there was one in particular that I remember.

Instead of responding in a text, I immediately call my sister. It only rings twice before she answers, her voice low, likely trying not to disturb Elara.

"Yeah?" she asks.

"I have a question. But before that, yes she can stay with me. Of course she can stay with me. I'm going to have practice, though, but that's not a travel week, so we should be good no matter what. I assume it's okay she stays at the apartment by herself for a few hours?"

Briar lets out a relieved sigh. "Yeah, of course. Mom and Dad are going to be back home and Erick—"

"Erick is going to be off doing who the fuck knows what, right?" I roll my eyes. Her ex-husband is one of my least favorite people on this floating rock.

She doesn't say anything, but I can feel the nod from here.

"Anyways, that's sorted. I was going to ask you, does the phrase 1, 2, 3, let's go b mean anything to you?" If I'm remembering right, the b is for bitch, but that's all the team name has written.

Briar lets out a low chuckle. "Yeah, why? It's what people were yelling at the Taylor Swift concert."

Oh Leo, you dumb motherfucker.

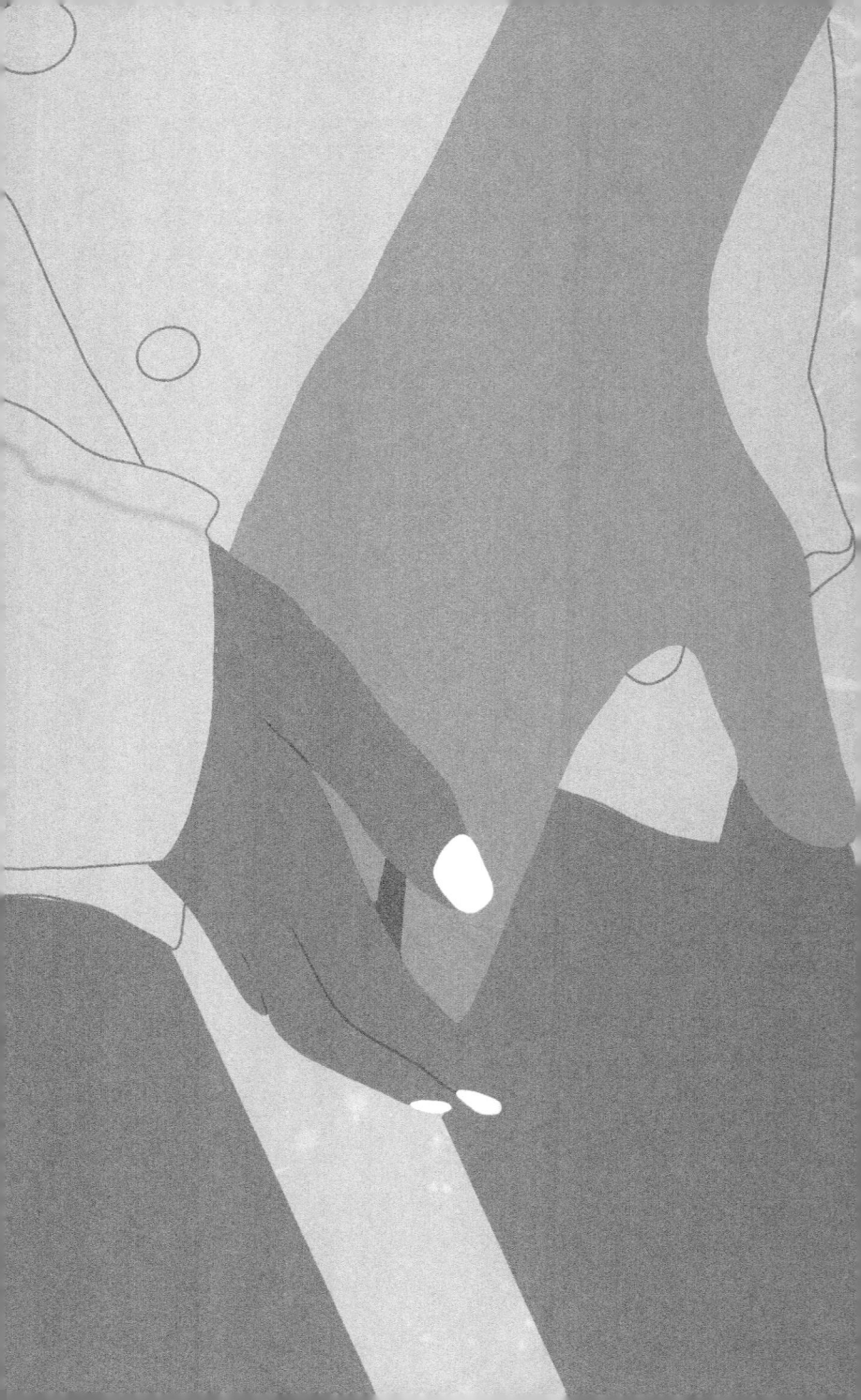

6
ISLA

There are only a couple of things I have to do to really make this apartment feel like home, and one of them is hang curtains.

It's one of the only things I don't like about fancy apartments like this. They lack the charm and character that so many other places have.

That being said, my brother bought this place with me in mind, knowing that I was struggling as an artist. As annoying as he can be, the fact that he wants me to do what I'm passionate about so badly that he's done this for me warms my heart.

"I think you've got it," Mila tells me as we attempt to drill the screws through the curtain rod holders. We've had to readjust it about five times now, and it's getting too frustrating. "Yeah, just hold it right the—"

My front door slams open, and I lose my balance on my ladder, falling to the plush rug beneath me. I keep my arms in, making sure I land on my back.

But still, it hurts like a bitch.

"What the actual fuck do you think you're doing?" Leo's voice thunders through the room.

Rubbing my back, I sit up, turning toward him and narrowing my eyes. "What are you talking about? And I thought you said you'd stop doing this."

"Doing what?" he asks.

"Barging into my place."

"I don't think I ever said that."

Sure.

I climb to my feet, plucking a small feather from one of my pillows off my black hoodie. "What do you want?"

"Your team name?"

"What about it?"

"Do you think a dude would choose that name?"

Mila climbs down from her ladder. "What's your team name?"

"Cover one, two, three, let's go bitch. But without the itch. The app wasn't a fan of that one."

"I mean, how many guys are going to know that's a Taylor Swift thing?" Mila asks, placing her hand on her hip.

Leo slaps his hand on his forehead. "It's a *Taylor Swift thing?*"

I reel back, throwing my hands in the air. "Who the hell cares, Leo? No one is going to know. It's a team name. It's cute. I like it. Lighten up a little."

"You're supposed to be a dude, Isla."

"Guys can like Taylor Swift too, you know."

"Whatever. Change it, okay?"

A tight smile spreads across my face as I stare at him, nodding.

He nods back, looking between me and Mila before opening his stupid mouth again. "Where did you get two ladders?"

"I needed them for an art project. Why? Want to help hang these curtains?"

He makes a face, turns on his heel, and leaves before I can

ask him for more help. He's usually the first one to offer, so he's definitely pissed off at me.

Oh well.

"What's with your brother?" Mila asks, her eyes wide.

"I don't know. He's always a bit odd."

"You know what they're saying about him in the tabloids?"

I scoff. "One, who the hell reads tabloids anymore, and two, absolutely not. None of us pay attention to any of that. He has his publicist, and they do their thing. We don't get involved, and I honestly don't want to know anything about my brother's sex life."

Mila smirks. "So you know it's about his sex life."

Okay, she's got me there. My brother has been in and out of the news online for the past few years. He's made a name for himself as quite the lady's man; I'll leave it at that. Women seem to find the himbo energy he exudes cute. I just find it obnoxious.

"I just don't want to know specifics. I know what he's usually in there for, that's all." I shrug.

"Well, let's just say he's not a lonely guy," she says before sitting down. I chuck a pillow at her before flopping down myself.

"I love him. I do. I just wish that he would let me have my own life here, you know? I mean, I do. He doesn't invade my space that much. But I'm tired of being nervous that he's going to barge in here for whatever reason at any time and just annoy the shit out of me. What if I have someone here? I feel like I'm allowed to have a dating life too."

Mila picks at the frayed edge of a hole in her jeans before flipping her sleek black hair over her shoulder. "You should get out there, you know."

"I don't think I have time," I tell her simply. Because I don't think I do. I have so many pieces I need to finish for this show, and then I need to get ready for the show, and then maybe, if it goes well, I'll book a bigger show, and then I need to get ready for that one. Between all that work, I have to complete several commissions for some of my favorite clients.

I look over at my stack of canvases, immediately finding a small spot that isn't up to par. I'll have to fix it later.

Although I love to paint just about everything, I've started to make a name for myself with the blend of modern and neo-impressionism styles. I haven't gotten far yet, but I've gotten quite a few clients around the country who commission me occasionally. In the future, I would really love to just paint whatever I'd like and sell at art shows. Maybe I'd end up in a museum someday like my brother will end up in the Hall of Fame.

Biting my lip, I realize I've been dazing out when my phone vibrates at my side. I dig it out of my hoodie pocket, confused at the notification.

MagicFantasy: New message from Mission: Possible

MISSION: POSSIBLE

Hey new guy, ready for the season?

I scratch my cheek, trying to figure out who Mission: Possible is. I can't ask my brother because he'll probably choke on air and yell at whoever this is, and I don't want that to happen. I feel like that would be more suspicious than me just talking to this person.

COVER 1, 2, 3, LET'S GO B—
I think so, you guys seem fun.

MISSION: POSSIBLE

I would hope so. Though I was surprised when you picked me first.

Ice runs down my spine as realization hits me. It's Owen. "Owen Crosby just messaged me," I tell Mila, my wide eyes meeting hers. She gapes, standing up quickly from her seat and rounding the coffee table to peer over my shoulder.

"Why"

"I think he's trying to figure out why I picked him first."

"Why did you?"

"I don't know I just didn't want to pick Leo this time."

"Fuck."

"Yeah."

"Tell him you panicked."

"I panicked and chose the person listed eighth and not the very first person on the list?"

"It's probably been done before!"

I stare at her, thinking over my options. There's absolutely no way I can tell him that I picked him simply because I think he's hot and wanted him on my team.

Nope.

Never.

"Why did I agree to this?" I groan, sitting back on the couch and throwing my head into my hands.

"I can't tell you that." Mila sits beside me, placing her small hand on my shoulder.

"Okay, I got this."

Picking up my phone, I breathe in deep as I open the app.

COVER 1, 2, 3, LET'S GO B—

> Yeah, Leo didn't give me a lot of time to research before and you were the first Cobra on the list. I thought why not.

"See that wasn't a horrible response!" Mila tells me, slapping me on the back.

MISSION: POSSIBLE

> Yeah, I can see that. Leo can be a little intense sometimes.

> COVER 1, 2, 3, LET'S GO B—
> Oh yeah, he sure can be.

> MISSION: POSSIBLE
> How did you meet him?

"He asked me how I met him," I panic, my fist tightening at my side.

"Did Leo tell you anything about the guy you're pretending to be?"

"The thing is, I don't think this guy exists at all. All I know is that I'm supposed to pretend to be someone who works for the team."

"Then that's simple; just tell him you work with the team and met him in the hallway or something."

"But what if he asks more questions? Or what if he told them how he met Ian, and it's not what I say?" My voice rises higher and higher as I go.

"Then that's Leo's problem, not yours."

She's right. I know she's right. But that doesn't make it any less stressful.

> COVER 1, 2, 3, LET'S GO B—
> We met at work. I dropped something in the hallway and he helped me pick it up.

That sounds so lame.

> MISSION: POSSIBLE
> He can be a good dude like that.

> COVER 1, 2, 3, LET'S GO B—
> Yeah, I bet.

> MISSION: POSSIBLE
> Well I'm looking forward to meeting you at some point. Nice to meet you, Ian.

When the conversation is over I let out a deep breath, allowing my shoulders to relax.

"That was stressful."

"And it's just the beginning," Mila adds, slapping my knee.

And she's right. It's only the beginning.

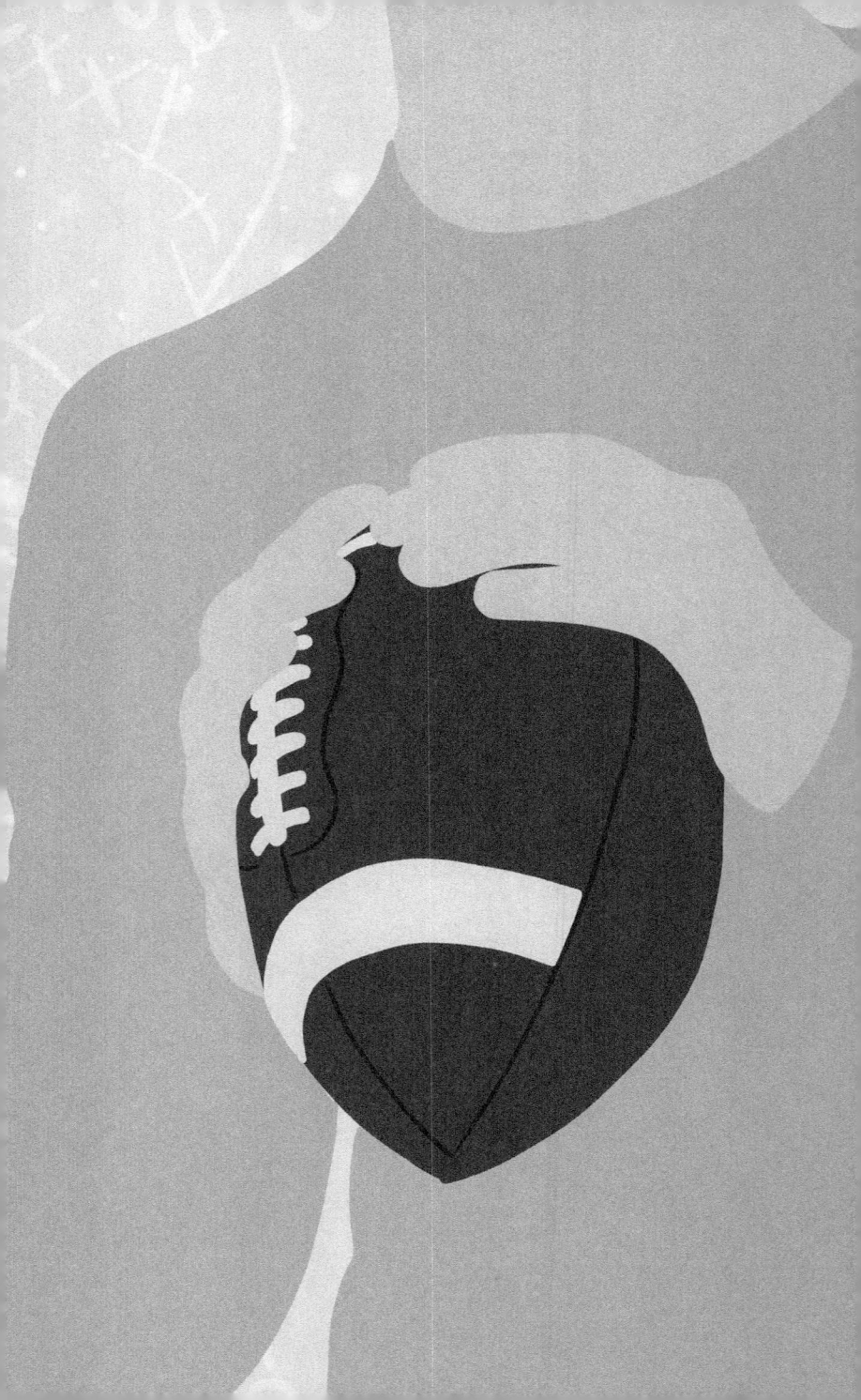

7

OWEN

The first game of the season is fast approaching, and practices have been intense.

In only a few short days we'll be hosting the Jacksonville Cheetahs, and although it should be one of the easier games of the season, you really never know. They've had a great off-season, got a few more pieces together, and their rookie quarterback was the number one draft pick this year. He may need a year or two to rise to his full potential, but everyone thinks he'll be a great franchise quarterback, us included.

We need to be ready for whatever comes at us.

I'm showering off when I start to think about my conversation with Isla from the other day. I'm not sure how to go about talking to her.

Sure, I want to respect Leo. But I'm also intrigued. I always have been, if I'm being completely honest. Isla Warner is someone you desperately want to know, no matter the cost. She just has that allure about her. She doesn't try. It's not something she puts effort into.

When I saw her naked in that hallway, I knew that I was a goner.

ANNA NOEL

I just think she's cool. And funny. And I'd like to get to know her a little better, whether her brother has an issue with it or not.

Grabbing my phone from my locker, I open the fantasy app.

> MISSION: POSSIBLE
> Hey! Are you working today?

I know she's not. She's not Ian. She doesn't even work here.

> COVER 1, 2, 3, LET'S GO B—
> Hey, no I'm not. Off day, sorry.

I'm pretty sure almost everyone important who works here is here today, so I'm not entirely sure what Leo thought he was getting away with.

But then again, I'm probably the only one messaging her.

I look around the room at all the guys pulling their shirts on, getting ready to go home for the day. To their girlfriends, wives, or, in Leo's case, his flavor of the week.

I watch as he digs in his locker for something, pulling out an old pair of socks before pulling them on. I don't want to know how long they were in there for. I don't need to know.

Well, a little part of me wonders.

But no, I know whatever the answer is will be disgusting.

> MISSION: POSSIBLE
> That's fair. I hope your day off is going well. Are you going to the game Sunday?

Let's see what she says to that.

> COVER 1, 2, 3, LET'S GO B—
> Yeah I'm probably going.

> MISSION: POSSIBLE
> Probably?

LOVE ON THE WAIVER WIRE

COVER 1, 2, 3, LET'S GO B—

I mean not probably, I'll definitely be there.

M SSION: POSSIBLE

Let's make a little deal.

I pause, looking up from my phone and running my finger over my lip. Is this smart? No. But am I going to do it? Hell yeah. Taking a deep breath and running my hand through my hair, I type out my message.

MISSION: POSSIBLE

I get the first touchdown of the season, and you tell me who you are. Does that sound okay?

She doesn't respond right away. In fact, I start packing up my things, getting ready to leave before she answers.

COVER 1, 2, 3, LET'S GO B—

There's nothing to disclose, but that sounds like a deal.

MISSION: POSSIBLE

Do you promise?

COVER 1, 2, 3, LET'S GO B—

I never break a promise.

WEEK ONE

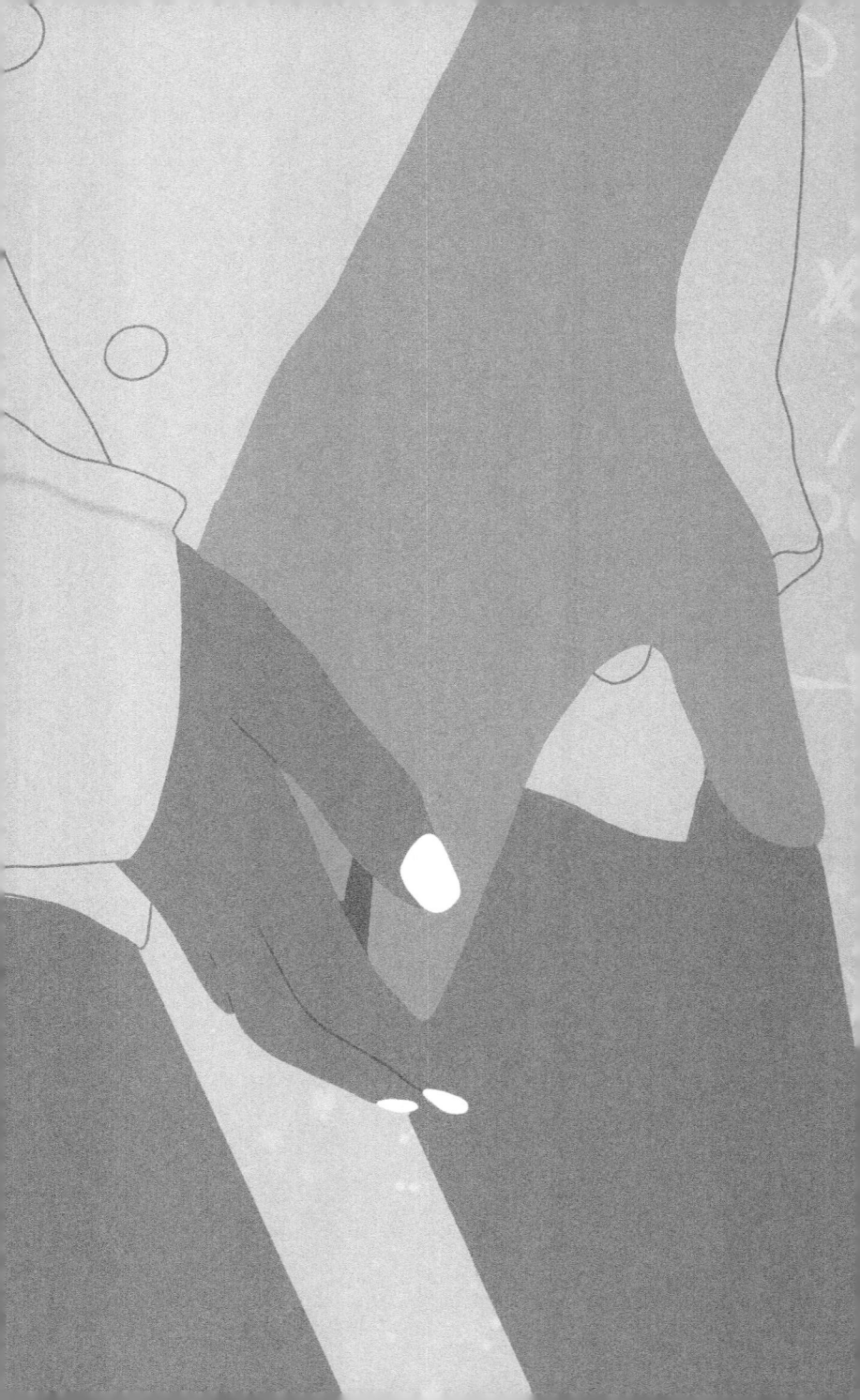

8
ISLA

"Isla honey, you look so good!"

The second I open my door, I'm bombarded with hugs. My parents are here, and although they're staying with Leo, we met at my place to get ready for the game together.

They want to get there early to take full advantage of Leo's box and the food the stadium provides there.

"I love that color jersey on you; I swear it makes you glow," my mom tells me, wrapping herself around me again.

"Thank you, it's my favorite of theirs too."

I'm wearing my favorite Warner jersey, the number eight sitting proudly on both sides of it. No matter how annoying my brother can be, I'm proud of him.

"I can't believe how far your brother has come, can you?" Mom asks as she digs around in her purse for mints.

"I can't either," I say, but I can. Leo has always been the golden child. The one everyone thought would get far in life no matter what. He was destined for greatness while I was stuck in his shadow.

Not that I blame him for being great. I'm happy for him. I am. I just get tired of hearing about it sometimes.

"You guys ready to go?" my dad asks from his spot near the door. He's dressed from top to bottom in Cobra gear, the purple looking a bit out of place on him.

"Yeah, one sec." I grab my purse, meeting them at the door. Since it's not that long of a walk to the stadium, we're doing just that. Walking.

My parents decided that when I left for college, they would take full advantage of their empty-nest status and travel the world. Although they got a couple months into their worldwide party, my mom became obsessed with Scotland, and they ended up staying. She had dual citizenship anyway.

I talk to my parents about how their trip over was and how the cows are doing back home as we pass hundreds of people in purple and, every once in a while, someone in blue.

"Oh, you have to come visit us and see them, Isla. They're just the cutest little guys ever. I wish I could have brought one home for you."

"I don't think their owners would have liked that very much, Mom," I tell her.

"Well, of course not. But I still wish I could have. They're just the happiest little things you'll ever see. I just love it there."

"I think your mother was meant to live there all along," my dad says.

I can believe it. My mom's grandmother immigrated here from Scotland and going back there was always super important to her. We grew up learning about it; my mom daydreamed about the day she could afford to travel and visit again.

Then, Leo found his love of football.

It started out small. He played in high school, and as a family born and raised in Pennsylvania, high school sports aren't as big as they are the further you travel south. It was a fun extracurricular activity for him but nothing anyone thought would go that much further.

It really started when he led his Division Two team to a title. It was the first one they had in twenty years. He eventually had a highlight reel made and was offered scholarships to at least a dozen universities around the country. He'd practice harder than ever there, eventually going on to win the Heisman and a championship.

From there, Leo was invited to the NFL Combine and would later be drafted first overall. We grew up Baltimore Cobras fans, so it was exciting for us all. He could stay home and do what he loved.

Everyone was so happy for him.

I was, too. Really. I was. And I'm forever proud of him. He's worked incredibly hard to get where he is now. It's just an enormous shadow to live under, and I've been striving every day to climb out of it and not be Leo Warner's little sister but Isla Warner, an artist who's also pursuing what she loves to do.

My parents try their hardest to acknowledge my accomplishments, but when you have one of the best NFL players in the league as your brother, sometimes it's hard to see anything else.

When we get to the stadium, we go through security and are escorted to our box, and we're just in time to watch the guys on the field warming up.

Family and friends crowd the room as time goes on, and the chatter in the stadium gets louder and louder. When Leo runs across the field, everyone screams, and I can't help but smile.

There's something about a crowded football stadium that just makes you feel at home. The fact that you're here, in this place, with thousands of people who are just as passionate as you are about something is beautiful.

About an hour later, the game is set to begin.

And begin it does.

The Baltimore Cobras have been on first for the last couple of years, but they've been missing a few key pieces to their offensive line to make a real Superbowl run. This year, they finally got those pieces, and their new right tackle allows Leo the time to throw to, well…

To Owen Crosby.

Running up the side of the field, Owen catches the ball easily and has a clear shot to the end zone as the Cheetahs' defense gets tied up.

He drops the ball, jumping in the air and pointing to the crowd. The cameras zoom in on him, and his dumb, handsome face smiles into them, winking as he dances away with his teammates.

The guy did it.

He really freaking did it.

MISSION: POSSIBLE

That catch was for you, new guy. Pay up.

I've been dreading the message all night.

My parents and I left the stadium after the big win and went right to dinner, where they had their fill on crab cakes before they have to go back to the land of haggis. While they talked about the game and the small farm my mom apparently wants to buy, all I could think about was how pissed Leo is going to be at me for ruining the secret the very first week.

Because Owen would tell him, right? They're best friends. He has to. There's no reason he wouldn't.

"Hey, your little sister screwed up again," he'd tell him.

But I try to keep myself calm. We've barely spoken over the years other than in passing. Owen is a reasonably quiet man compared to my brother. Maybe he's cool.

And here I am, in my pajamas, curled up on my couch, stressing about what I'm going to paint next when I hear my phone go off.

I don't know; I don't think the touchdown was fast enough. I type out, but stop. That sounds an awful lot like flirting.

I hit send anyway.

MISSION: POSSIBLE

I took the opportunity, that's for sure.

I put my phone down, thinking about it all once again. I don't want to do this. I don't want to tell him who I am because that invites Leo to criticize. Not that he does it often, but my brother can be weird about me talking to men.

Especially his teammates.

On one hand I get it. On the other, I'm a 24 year old woman who can make her own decisions.

MISSION: POSSIBLE

You there Ian?

Fine.

COVER 1, 2, 3, LET'S GO B—

I think you know Leo better than every single one of those guys on that team. I feel like you clearly know who I am, Owen.

I expect teasing. I expect maybe a threat to tell my brother I came clean. I expect, well, I'm not sure, actually.

But what I absolutely didn't expect was a knock on my door.

For a split second, a shot of fear runs down my spine. Was he with my brother? Was it a setup? Some kind of sick and twisted sibling loyalty test?

But when I get up and look through the peephole, I find Owen.

Positive it's not a serial killer waiting on the other side for me, I crack my door open, peeking out at him as he stands in the middle of the beige hall looking, well, anything but boring and beige.

His skin is tan from the hours of practice outside in the September sun, his light brown hair streaked with gold under the fluorescent lights lining the hall. His brown eyes twinkle as he flashes a smile at me.

Owen Crosby is the kind of handsome that can put you on your knees in a second. It's not because he's perfect, no. It's because he wears his flaws so confidently that they don't really seem like flaws.

His nose is slightly crooked, and while some people with millions at their disposal would get it fixed, Owen wears it like a badge of honor. I've always wondered what the other guy may look like.

He's beautiful, broken bones, scars, and all.

"So you did know," I state dryly, opening the door a little wider.

Although I'm fine that he's here, I wasn't exactly planning on him showing up. My place is a bit of a mess, and if I'm honest, I'd rather not open the door to one of the hottest men in the NFL wearing an old baggy pair of paint-covered sweats and a ratty t-shirt, and I really would rather not have to talk to him with my hair looking how it is.

In any other circumstance, I think I would panic a little more. Right now, all I can think about is him knowing that Leo lied. I failed the mission.

"It wasn't tough to figure out. A Taylor Swift reference as your team name? Really?"

I shrug. "I figured why not, you know? I didn't think anyone would figure it out."

He leans against the doorframe, his grin widening as a

dimple appears on his right cheek. "I don't think you accounted for my sister and my niece then."

Of course. "No, definitely didn't account for that."

His eyes look me up and down, assessing my attire, and when I think he's going to leave, he cocks his head to the side. "You think you could let me in?"

My lips thin as I scratch my head. "Are you really sure that's a good idea?"

He shrugs. "Why not?"

"Is my brother home? Wouldn't he be upset?"

"Well, I think he'd be more upset if he came out here right now and saw us talking, but if you must know, he's out with the boys celebrating. He'll probably be back in a bit but too intoxicated to care about what you're doing."

That makes sense.

Stepping out of the way, I gesture for him to come in, closing the door quietly behind him. My neighbor across from me loves to slam their door at night, and although I've desperately wanted to be petty back, I've refrained for the other neighbor's sake.

Heading back into the family room, I watch as Owen looks around my place curiously. A part of his confidence has waned, and he looks almost unsure of what to do as he places his hands deep in the pockets of his dark jeans. I hate how my eyes zero in on the way his bicep moves when he does so.

"Are you going to tell my brother?" I ask him suddenly, frozen in the middle of the room.

He makes a face, looking over me, perplexed. "Why would I do that?"

"I don't know. I just know he can be a little—"

"—Intense," Owen finishes for me.

I nod. "Yeah."

"I'm not going to tell him. I don't have a death wish. As long as you don't tell him that I know, either. Just easier that way."

I walk to the couch, sitting on the edge as I stretch my legs out in front of me, placing my hands between my thighs as I look up at the massive six-four man in front of me. "Then why did you want to know who Ian was so bad?"

He runs a hand through his hair. "I knew who you were the second I left his apartment that night, Isla. I just thought it was a little fun making you sweat."

Heat rises to my cheeks as I look down to the ground.

"It was cute," he adds as if picking up on my discomfort.

My head whips up as I meet his eyes. "I don't like being played with, Owen."

"I play enough games for work. I don't want to play games with you, Isla. I can assure you that."

Something in me knows he's telling the truth, even if my brain tells me he's not. He's best friends with my brother, after all. King of ripping hearts to shreds.

"Okay."

"You paint?" he asks suddenly, gesturing to the pile of canvases leaning against a corner wall. The question seems weirdly intimate to me. I make a mental note to file that into the growing list of new things to talk to my therapist about.

"My whole life," is all I say, looking at the canvases for the hundredth time today. Every time I do, I find something new I have to change. Maybe I should just put the ones I think I'm done with in the studio.

He walks over, bending over to take a closer look. I try not to look at his ass. I do. I promise. But it's there, in front of me. How can I not?

God, I'm no better than Leo sometimes.

Looking down, he runs his sneaker-clad foot over the drop cloth beneath my canvases.

"Don't you have like three rooms here?" he asks, looking around. I'm confused for a second, but Owen and Leo can be inseparable. He was probably here when Leo closed on it.

"Yeah, but the natural light from these windows is better

during the daytime. I keep everything in my studio, but I paint out here most of the time.

He nods, shrugging.

"Leo may be home any time now," I blurt out before I can stop myself.

"Yeah, probably."

"My parents are next door. I'd rather them not hear something going on here and come asking questions."

A sly grin slowly makes its way onto Owen's lips, and I quickly curse myself.

"Isla, as much as I'd be honored, I'm not here on that kind of visit."

Rolling my eyes, I groan, flipping him off. "You know what I mean. And Leo would be furious if he found you here."

"Leo doesn't have me on a leash."

"Do you like being on a leash?" I ask without thinking. The second it's out of my mouth, I mentally slap a hand over it to keep me from saying anything else.

"For the right person, I think."

9

OWEN

There's a reason I'm known for being quiet, and it has nothing to do with me having a calm mind.

It has to do with the fact that every time I open my mouth I feel like something dumb comes out. Especially around women.

"That was dumb," I tell her, all of a sudden feeling way too hot despite my thin blue t-shirt.

"It was," she agrees, but I'm relieved that her tone is playful and not upset. I shouldn't have said that.

"Well, thank you for confirming what I already know. I look forward to playing against you, Isla."

What the hell is that now? I think. *You say something stupid, and you turn into some old-fashioned stuck-up weirdo?*

"Yeah, me too," is all she says as the awkwardness settles around us.

As I get to the door, I hear a commotion outside as Leo likely tries to unlock the door drunk. I'm not sure if he has someone with him, though I hope to God he doesn't for his parents' sake. Not that I'm staying around to find out.

The second I hear his door close, I open the door without a

word and leave, booking it down the hallway in case someone decides to peek out into the hallway.

Nah, that's not why.

It's because I needed to run away. Like a loser.

Why can't I just keep my damn mouth shut like a normal person? It doesn't happen often. Or at least, not as often as Leo blurts out stupid shit. But it happens often enough that I actively think my words over multiple times before I say them sometimes.

Breathing a sigh of relief as I get to my car parked down the street in a different garage not owned by the building—the last thing I need is Leo asking why my car is there—I quickly put it in drive and head home.

Monday nights are for partying.

Leo and I met up in the parking lot of the training facility Monday morning for our usual Monday lift. Since we won yesterday, all we have to do is stop in and lift.

"I think we did really well yesterday," Leo says as he tosses his bag over his shoulder.

I nod, watching the ground as we make our way into the building. We're here early, and most of our other teammates were out late. They probably won't roll in until around eleven.

"I think winning by thirty points counts as really well."

I can feel Leo's grin before I see it. "I think this is our year, man," he says excitedly, his nose scrunching at the prospect.

"I think so, too."

"You doing okay?"

I sigh. "Yeah, just ready for tonight," I tell him simply, hoping he won't pry too much.

"Tonight's going to be amazing," Leo says without a care in the world. "I think I'm inviting Victoria out."

"Weren't you with her last week?" I ask, thoroughly confused.

"I can see a girl for multiple weeks, you know," he shoots back.

He can. He has before. But often? No.

"Who are you and what have you done with Leo?" I chuckle.

He laughs back. "It's a brand new me."

We change and get our lift in before talking to our coach for a couple minutes. He congratulates us both on the win again, letting us know that if we can keep it up, he can see us going all the way this year.

As we're leaving, Leo asks me what my plans are. "Are you just meeting us there?"

"I think so," I tell him. "I need to get some things done at home. But I'll be there when you guys are."

With a wave, Leo gets into his truck, quickly backing out of his spot and racing down the road.

All I can do is hit my head against the back of my seat, thinking about how screwed I am that all I can think about is his sister.

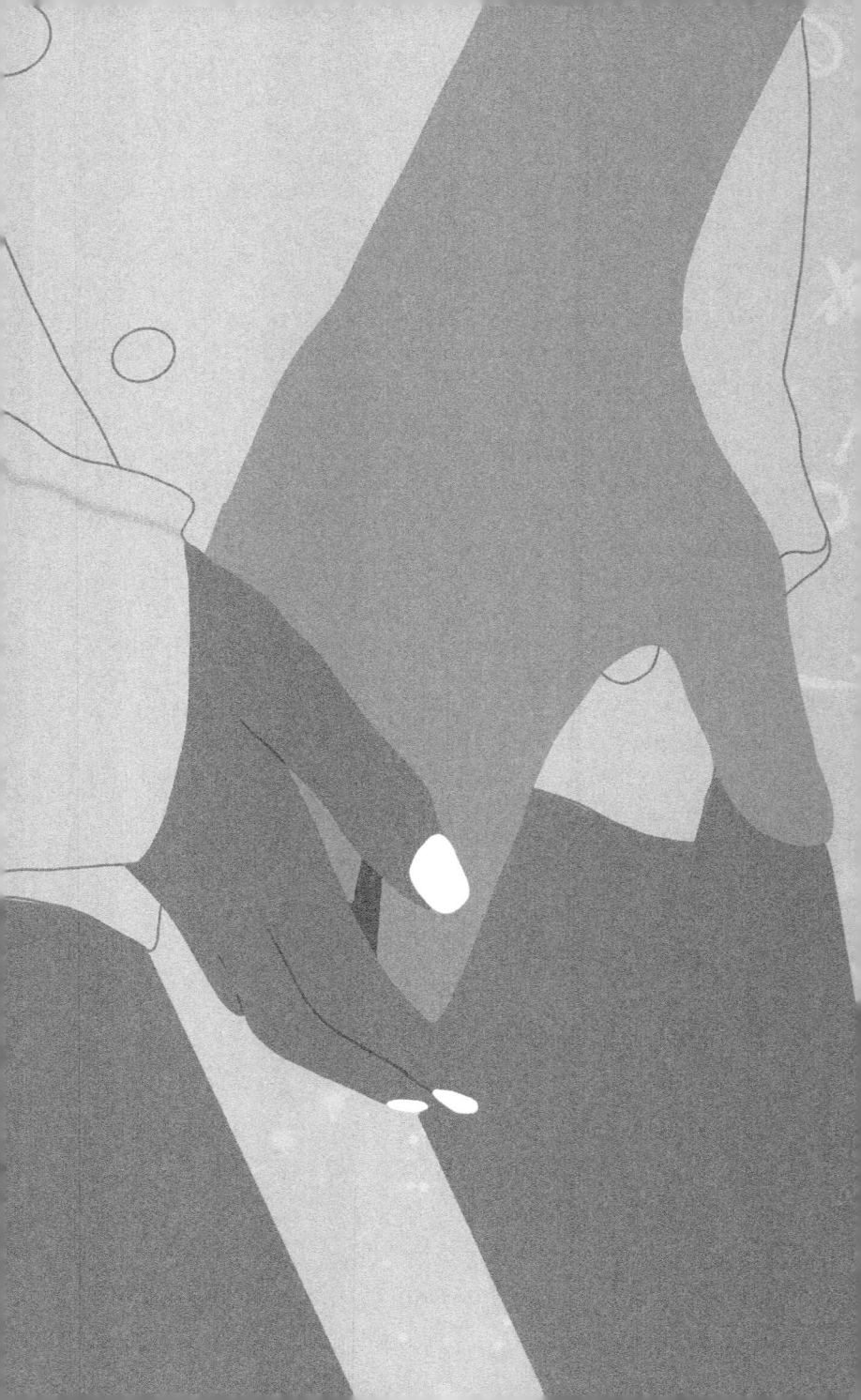

10

ISLA

"Can you pass me my brush again?" Amara asks me as she fluffs her hair in my bathroom mirror.

"Yeah, here you go." I hand it to her before going back to lining my lips.

"It's been a while since we did this," Mila mutters from her place perched on the toilet as she watches us.

"I think last time we went out like this, Amara ended up passed out on a bathroom floor," Heidi chuckles.

"Yeah, that was one time after I broke up with Josh. Of course, that happened. Am I ever going to live it down?" Amara snaps, rolling her eyes.

I can see Mila making a face from my peripheral, but I decide not to chime in and annoy Amara even more. She's had a short fuse for as long as I can remember.

But Mila is right. We haven't really had a real night out in years. We used to drive into the city on Monday nights specifically to go to Lulu's, but as we got older and they went off to college in different states, we stopped.

The four of us have been friends since middle school. We've seen each other go through every phase of life, whether it be losing their virginity behind the bleachers like Amara or losing their dad like Heidi.

No matter where we were in the world, we have always been there for each other, no matter how irritating we can get.

"Are the guys going out tonight?" Mila asks, brushing her fingers through her hair.

I shrug, grabbing my lipstick. "I'm not sure. I haven't heard anything."

Which is true. I haven't heard anything from my brother or Owen, actually.

If I'm being honest, I've been waiting for the sound of the fantasy app all day, but nothing has come. Nothing at all.

Since the team usually has off on Tuesdays, the guys like going all out Monday nights. And there's really only one club that's worth going to on Mondays. Lulu's.

The reason we've always gone? Women get in free on Mondays. None of us have normal jobs, so why not? And even if one of us did—Amara worked an office job for about a month before deciding that being tied to a desk wasn't exactly her thing and got her old job at the old pub back—we would always make time for Lulu's.

"Well, maybe we'll see them." Mila gets up from her seat and heads out of the bathroom. I watch as she grabs her dress, slipping it on over her shorts and sports bra. She's been asking more questions about the team lately, and although I know that she doesn't like my brother like that, I can't help but wonder if she has her eyes on someone else.

Mila had a crush on my brother in high school, which quickly dissipated when she saw him chase a ping-pong ball around a room.

When Amara and Heidi are done with their hair and makeup, we all get dressed. Nothing fancy, but not sweats either.

And finally, we're on our way, and all I can think about is how happy I am that we're all back together.

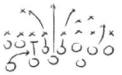

"Is that your brother over there?" Heidi asks, peering through the fog filling the room as lights bounce around at an almost dizzying rate.

"Is he bigger and taller than almost everyone here?" I ask. It's pretty easy to spot my brother. We're a tall family, with him coming in at six-five and me at five-eleven.

"He has a whole gaggle of women around him."

"Then that's probably him." I nod, rolling my eyes. Nothing changes with him.

When I finally spot him, he's jumping up and down, a beer in his hand splashing all over the people around him.

As the four of us grab drinks at the bar, I scan the rest of the room for Owen. Maybe I should message him first? He left my apartment in a rush the other night, and I don't want him to feel like he upset me. It was awkward, sure, but it was also funny.

Maybe he's not as quiet as I thought he was.

Still, I hate how much I desperately want to hear from him.

"Are all the usual suspects here?" Mila asks as she brings her vodka cran to her lips.

"I think so. Cooper is over there." I point to the left of Leo, where Cooper sits in ripped jeans and a white t-shirt, sipping his drink as he watches the dance floor. "and Myles is against the back wall talking to someone, I think." All I can see is a bright blue suit, which he's worn out before. How many bright blue suits can you see at a club?

Mila nods, her eyes locking on something in the distance, but the room is so crammed that I can't tell who exactly she's looking at.

"You guys want to go dance?" I yell as the base gets louder. The three of them nod, and we head into the crowd.

As the alcohol hits my system, I feel less and less stressed about life and boys. Not that I have much to stress about in that department. My conversations with Owen have been the most I've talked to a man in a long time. After some truly awful dates, I've sworn off dating apps, and I'd rather hell swallow me whole than Leo play matchmaker.

The three of us sway to the beat and lose track of time, taking turns going back to the bar and grabbing more drinks. Mila is the first to leave the group, accepting an invitation from someone to dance. I don't recognize them, but I know that with the guys around, we're all safe.

Because I know for a fact my brother's eyes have been glued on me since we hit the dancefloor, waiting for someone to make a wrong move so he can come in like a knight in shining armor to rescue us.

Which isn't a bad thing. I appreciate him keeping watch. He can just be a little overboard, like with everything.

Heidi grabs my arm, her shoulders hunched as she squints through the dim light. "I met someone at the bar I think I'm going to go dance with, okay?" she yells. I nod, taking another sip of my drink before watching Amara prance off without a word. "Our usual plan?" she asks.

"Yeah, if you guys want to leave at any point, let me know."

No matter what we do when we're out, we always leave together. No exceptions. It's too dangerous out there for us to leave each other. If someone wants to go home with a guy, that's one thing. I trust their decision-making. But if we're just out and about, none of us leaves the others behind.

She nods, turning back around to meet whoever she's been talking to.

Sighing, I down the rest of my drink and head to the bar myself, taking one of the few vacant seats.

"Can I get two waters?" a familiar voice says from beside me.

"You," I say simply, my eyes narrowing.

Owen doesn't look at me, instead keeping his face forward. "It is me," he chuckles. When the bartender hands him his waters, he carefully slides one over to me.

"I don't need it, but thank you."

I can see Owen's eyes roll from the side as he brushes his thumb across his lips. "You think I haven't noticed how much you've been drinking tonight? Drink up."

"Are you trying to tell me what to do, Mr. Crosby?"

"Are you trying to get me in trouble, Ms. Warner?"

I can feel my stomach start to warm at his words, and I take the water, downing it before slamming it down on the bar top and gesturing for the bartender.

"What do you want to drink?" Owen asks, eyeing the man in front of us as he takes other orders.

"I'm good on my own, but thank you."

"Why are you so frustrating?" he shoots, eyes still on the bartender, who hears him. Turning, his eyes widen as he realizes he's being watched like a hawk.

"Why are you so frustrating?" My hand balls into a fist in my lap.

"I just want to make sure that you're being safe," he says, sending a pang of fury through me.

"I don't need anyone to make sure I'm safe. I already have Leo for that, but thanks."

"Isla—"

"Are you okay?" the bartender asks as he approaches us.

"Yeah, I'm sorry, I'm not talking to you." Owen winces, handing him a hundred-dollar bill.

"Okay, I wasn't sure—" the man drifts off as Owen continues to stare at him. "Can I get you anything?"

"Whatever she's having, we'll have two."

The bartender turns to me, but not before shooting a look of confusion Owen's way.

"I'll have a rum and coke," I tell him, sitting back in my seat.

He nods once before looking back at Owen, only to find his eyes still on him.

"Are you okay?" the bartender asks him, leaning against the bar.

"You see that pretty girl right there?" Owen asks, taking a sip of his water.

The bartender looks at me before Owen snaps, directing his attention back to him. "Her brother is big and scary and across the room watching to make sure we're not talking. She's doing her best to screw that up for me though."

The man nods, understanding finally dawning on him. I look forward too, annoyed. "He's not going to kill you, Owen."

His eyes finally shift to me, his head unmoving. "You have no idea."

"Where did your friends go?" he asks when the bartender sets our drinks down.

"Dancing with people."

"And you're not?"

"No one to dance with."

"I'm sure you could find someone."

I take a sip of my drink. "Why didn't you message me today?" I blurt, losing my impulse control.

"Did you want me to message you?"

"I figured you would."

"Isla Warner, I think you want me to message you." his lips tip up at the corner as his eyes crinkle, and my lips tighten as I look straight ahead.

"I just figured you'd want to recover after whatever the hell happened last night."

"That's true. I wasn't exactly smooth, was I?"

I shake my head.

"Well, I'd love to make it up to you at some point."

I consider that for a moment, but the room starts to spin a little, and suddenly, the barstool feels too unstable. "Mm, I'll consider it," I tell him simply before hopping down, shaking out my legs. My jeans aren't tight, but they're starting to feel suffocating.

Without another word, I head to the dancefloor, swaying to the music by myself. It's not long until I feel a pair of hands on my waist, pulling me into them. I don't have to look behind me to know it's Owen.

"I think you have a death wish," I throw over my shoulder.

Hot breath hits my ear as he lowers his head. "I think you're right, but your brother left with someone."

"You act like you're not Owen Crosby." Even if my brother left, there are people everywhere with phones. My brother seeing him dancing with me plastered over social media is the last thing either of us needs.

Instead of responding, Owen grabs my hand, leading me to the other end of the club. A bouncer greets us with a smile, and when he sees it's Owen, he opens a door, letting us into a separate room. It's lighter, and it takes my eyes a moment to adjust. Instead of smelling like alcohol, the room smells like cigar smoke. There are a couple of men sitting around socializing.

"I don't think I've ever been in this room before," I grumble as he pulls me along to the other end of the room.

"That's because it's private. No phones."

I nod, still confused. I've been coming since before I could legally get in, and I never knew this was here.

"Do the others know?" I ask.

"Yeah, they know. They just don't use it. Here, I want to show you something."

Around the corner from the main room is a darkened

room with neon blue lights running along the ceiling. In front of us stands multiple ski-ball machines, and to the left, there are various arcade games. On the right sits even more arcade games.

"Oh wow," I say, walking into the room further.

"Want to play a game?"

"I'm not sure you want that," I chuckle.

"Why not?" he smiles, his teeth so bright under the neon lights, and I'm not sure if it's the alcohol or a wish, but I just want him to touch me.

"Competitiveness runs in the Warner gene," I tell him, pressing the button on the ski-ball machine for it to dispense balls. When it doesn't, I stand, looking at him with confusion.

"It may be a special room, but they still want your money," Owen chuckles as he pulls out his wallet, grabs a dollar bill, and inserts it into my machine. He does the same with his, and they light up, the ski-balls sliding down the ramp.

"I'm a champion at this," I say more to myself than him. I haven't actually played in forever, but I want nothing more than to beat him at his own game.

Owen grabs a ball, aiming it for a moment before letting it go. It flies into the top hole, and the screen flashes with a large "fifty."

Wanting to one-up him, I take another second to aim, letting the ball fly up the ramp. It barely misses the one-hundred hold, instead sliding down into the ten.

"Oof, good attempt." Owen smiles, grabbing another ball.

By the time we're done, my ass is thoroughly whooped, and Owen has the biggest smile on his face.

"I'm glad I can be a source of amusement for you," I say, trying to sound annoyed. But I'm not. For as annoyed as I am that I sucked, I'm just enjoying this time with him.

"Me too," he says simply as he moves to one of the arcade games.

"Have you played this before?" he asks.

"I don't think so," I lie.

Owen inserts fifty cents into the machine before positioning himself behind me, coming in close. "So you're supposed to run at the enemy knights. You see them? You're going to want your lance higher than theirs to win."

His hand covers mine as he helps me navigate the game, taking down a couple of enemy Knights before he moves beside me, his arm still touching mine. The connection feels warm, and it sends a shiver through me, heat pooling in my lower belly.

"You ready?" he asks as he inserts change into his side and grabs the joystick.

I nod. "I think so."

And I continue to absolutely obliterate him.

"I thought you said you didn't know this game!" he says, throwing his hands up at the end.

"Leo was obsessed with it as a kid. We used to go to the old cinema a town over just to play it. He beat me over and over, but then I got good." I shrug.

Owen laughs, his eyes lingering on mine for a beat too long to not feel intentional.

I look around, exhaustion settling in as I fight back a yawn. "Do you want to go home?" Owen asks. My eyes widen and I'm about to fire back when he adds, "Not with me."

Looking down at my shoes with guilt, I nod. I don't want to hurt his feelings.

"I need to text the girls. We all leave at the same time." I check the time, realizing that two hours have gone by and none of them have texted me. I always hate being the first one to call it, but I'm about to pass out.

I shoot them a text before letting Owen lead me out of the room and back into the main club.

11

OWEN

I'm not sure what to think of it.

I know that I shouldn't be hanging out with Isla. I'm smarter than this. And yet, something inexplicable draws me to her. Like some type of force of nature. I don't know.

One second, she's flirting with me, and in another, she's treating me like we've been friends our whole lives.

"Want to wait outside?" I ask her as we make our way through the thinning crowd. It's late, and although Lulu's is open until five A.M., people start to head out around three most of the time.

She nods, her head lolling to the side a bit. I can tell she's exhausted, and I feel bad for keeping her out for so long.

"I just heard from Amara. They'll be out in a few," she tells me, her hand rubbing her neck as we exit the club.

The second the cold air hits me, I feel my mind start to clear. Everything that happened tonight—well, nothing happened tonight. Literally nothing.

Except it feels like something did.

"So I was thinking about something," I say suddenly.

Isla leans against the building and crosses her arms in front of her. "Yeah?"

"Yeah. I think it would be a little fun to challenge each other every week."

Her head tilts to the side a little, and her eyebrows furrow. "What do you mean?"

"In fantasy. I think we only play each other once," I say, hopeful that she doesn't pick up on the fact that I checked. "But each week, one of us has to get lower points than the other, right?"

"Mm."

"So whoever wins the week gets to determine the punishment. Or we can discuss a punishment before the week."

She considers this, her curled brown hair falling over her shoulders as her green eyes meet mine. "Is that normal to do?" she asks.

I weigh my options. "Some people do it." It's not exactly a lie. Some people do do it. But I never have.

"Doesn't Leo have other stupid weekly punishments?"

"Yeah, but you probably won't have to deal with that."

"Why not?"

"Because your team is really freaking good. You're already leading everyone in points this week."

She purses her lips, debating.

"I think it could be fun," she says finally, and I smile, suddenly excited.

"Then we have a deal."

She nods, and a second later, the door to the club opens, and three girls walk out, all in different states of drunkenness.

"Did you get the uber?" Heidi asks.

Isla pulls out her phone to book one, and I quickly hold up my phone. "I got one for you guys."

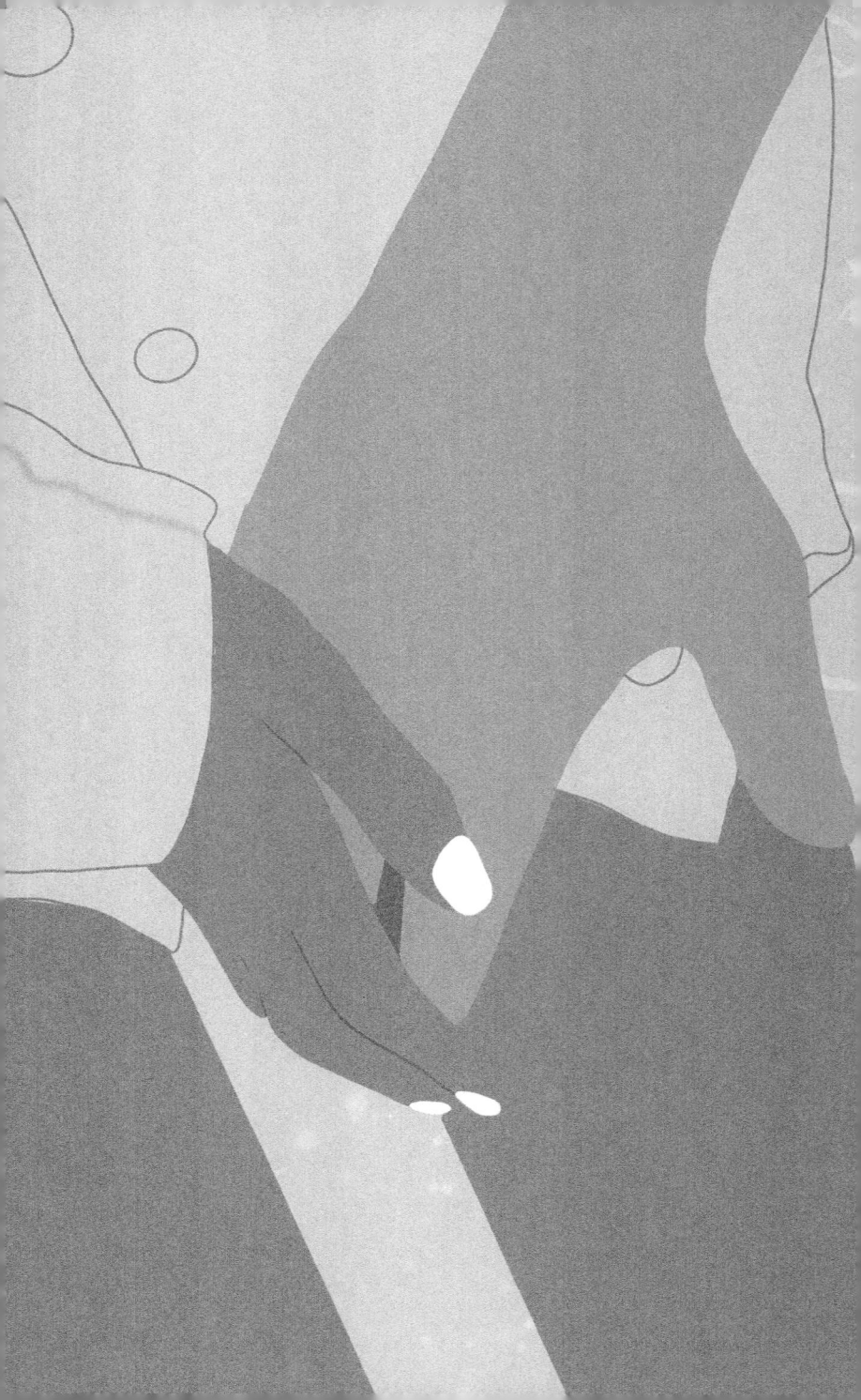

12
ISLA

"Are you serious?" I ask him as he holds out his phone.

"Yeah. Let me add a couple of stops. What are your addresses?"

"Well, they were going to stay over at my—"

"I think we're all super tired and want to go home," Mila says, her brown eyes wide as she nods toward the others. Heidi looks confused at first, putting her hair up into a high ponytail, a single red curl falling out and blowing in the gust of wind. I pull my arms around me a little tighter, shivering.

And I'm not sure if I'm imagining it, but I think Owen moves just a little closer to me, his arm practically touching mine as the girls give him their addresses. He puts them in, and we wait a couple minutes for the SUV to pull up.

Owen is the first to move, opening the door for us to get in.

Mila looks at me from the corner of her eye, tilting her head slightly as if to say, "We'll be talking tomorrow."

The problem is that I don't know what's going on. This whole night has been confusing.

Settling into my seat, Owen slides into the front seat. No one talks over the soft hum of whatever 80s hairband music plays over the radio, and before we know it, I realize we're headed out of Baltimore to drop the others off.

I'm last.

Butterflies take flight in my stomach, and I fold my arms over myself again, trying to get them to settle down. Does this mean he wants more time with me? Do we have more to talk about?

I really am tired, and I really do want to just go to bed.

And we also shouldn't be doing this.

But God, does it feel right.

It's only been a few days, and Owen Crosby has easily taken over my thoughts.

When the other three are dropped off, Owen directs the driver to my apartment, telling him that he can drop him off there, too.

"Are you sure?" I ask him quickly, wide-eyed.

"My car is around the corner, and I only had a beer. I'll just get home that way."

So he had his car near my place and still wasted his own time making sure we all got home safe?

The second we get out of the car, we stand awkwardly, not entirely sure what to say or do. "Thank you for a nice night," I tell him, watching my shoe as I kick a pebble around.

"Thank you for kicking my ass at Joust," he replies, the light from the building behind me twinkling in his dark eyes.

"I'll kick your ass anytime you want."

Did I just say that?

His smile broadens before he lifts his hand, running a finger over his lips. He looks away.

It's all or nothing. "Do you want to come up?" I ask suddenly, tucking my hair behind my ears as I look up at him.

His head swivels back to me, his eyes wide. A silence settles between us for a few moments as he juggles his options before he finally says, "I'm not sure that's a good idea."

I nod, my lips thinning. "I get it, it's fine."

"Not because I don't want to hang out with you, but because we should really think about this first, okay?" he says, his voice low as his head dips to meet my eyes.

I nod, only a little embarrassed, and turn to head into the building before his hand grabs mine, pulling me back in.

"I really had a great time tonight, Isla."

"I did too."

My room is spinning as I watch Owen's touchdown over and over again. Not only was it incredibly sexy, but the camera gave us an absolute gift by zooming in just as he turns around, giving us the perfect view of his butt in those football pants.

Most importantly, though, is that the meaning of this touchdown is different now. He knew it was me the entire time. Maybe before tonight I would just say he was being an ass, but I'm not sure anymore.

And as I finally manage to drift off to sleep, the realization hits me.

He pointed after rolling into the end zone.

He pointed right at me.

13

OWEN

Leo Warner's little sister has taken over my thoughts, and I'm only a little mad about it.

I don't want Leo to hate me. I know that I'm treading in dangerous waters. Riding with the girls to get them home? Going into the private section with Isla? Anyone could say anything. Anyone could grab a photo and plaster it over the internet. What is Leo going to say when he sees that? What would I tell him?

The truth, of course. I wouldn't lie to him if he ever asks me.

But I know he'll be furious. But I just can't help it.

The only time I'm able to get my thoughts away from her is when I'm lifting in the training room. It's Tuesday, our day off, so I head to my gym for a lift. While some of the guys just take the whole day off, many of us try to at least get something done to ensure our minds stay in the right place. And I need that more than ever now.

"You're looking good, man," Cody, my strength coach tells me as he comes up behind me, studying my form in the mirror before us.

"Thanks," I say simply, wiping the sweat from my forehead before grabbing my water.

"Want to head into the mini hurdle bounds?"

Absolutely not, is what I want to say, but instead I nod, stretching my shoulders before following him.

I train for about an hour more and grab a protein shake, heading home.

I haven't heard anything from Isla since last night, and the second I step into my apartment I feel overcome with the stifling feeling of loneliness.

> MISSION: POSSIBLE
> I hope you're feeling okay today

I'm not sure if texting her was the best decision, but I don't know what else to do today.

> COVER 1, 2, 3, LET'S GO B—
> No hangover here; thank you for asking

> MISSION: POSSIBLE
> What do you have planned for today?

Am I being too forward?

> COVER 1, 2, 3, LET'S GO B—
> Nothing much. Just getting some paintings done for a showing in a couple of weeks. Nothing too interesting.

> MISSION: POSSIBLE
> I think that's really interesting, actually.

> COVER 1, 2, 3, LET'S GO B—
> Not really.

> MISSION: POSSIBLE
> Would you be upset if I came and watched?

> COVER 1, 2, 3, LET'S GO B—
> Leo will kill you.

I take a deep breath. I know he will. But what he doesn't know won't hurt him, right?

> MISSION: POSSIBLE
> Leo doesn't have to know.

COVER 1, 2, 3, LET'S GO B—
He has a nasty habit of barging into my place.

> MISSION: POSSIBLE
> It's a good thing I know his every move.

COVER 1, 2, 3, LET'S GO B—
Oh please, you do not.

> MISSION: POSSIBLE
> Is that a yes?

COVER 1, 2, 3, LET'S GO B—
Yes.

I'm at her door an hour later, and it only takes a second for her to whip open the door and pull me in.

"He's not home," I tell her with a chuckle.

Her head tilts to the side, her green eyes wide. "What do you mean he's not home? I heard him in the hallway just a bit ago. I thought he was coming back from something."

"Nope. Headed out. He has some very important business to attend to."

Her brows furrow but she doesn't ask any other questions, which is probably a good thing. Leo's extra-curricular activities can be quite concerning and I'm not entirely sure she's ready to hear about them.

I'm not ready to hear about them and yet I'm subjected to it all the time.

She suddenly looks down, realizing what I have in my hands. "Are those peach rings?" she asks, confusion in her eyes.

"Yeah, I brought them for you," I tell her, handing them to her.

She takes them, examining the package before looking back at me. "Why would you get these for me?"

It's my turn to be confused.

"Your brother and I went Christmas shopping two years ago and he bought like fifty bags of them. He said that he was filling your stocking with them because they're your favorite."

She stares at me for a second before looking back down, tucking a strand of her hair left out of her bun behind her ear. "I like to eat them when I paint. Helps me concentrate." She pauses. "Thank you."

"No problem. I just want to watch you."

She studies me for a few more moments before accepting that this is what it's going to be and heading back into the room. She stands in front of her current piece before looking behind her one last time, watching me sit on her couch.

Her place is beautiful, and much more homey than Leo's, that's for sure. While his place has been kept a little stale, all greys and hard lines, Isla has made a significant effort to make this place warm.

Her couch is deep and cushy, a deep green color, while the walls are cream. She's wallpapered a couple of the smaller walls, creating a statement. A cozy plush rug covers a large portion of the family room.

Her kitchen is both tidy and chaotic, with colorful mugs, plates, and kitchen equipment lining the counter. A vase of flowers—an assortment of white and yellows—sits at the end of her marble kitchen island, and I make a mental note to get her the same kind at some point. Maybe a lot of them.

But I'm getting ahead of myself. This may not even be anything.

But the more I think about it, the more I watch as she takes the clip out of her hair, letting the chocolate brown tendrils loose before picking them up once more and clipping them a different way, the more I realize that I think I've felt something for her since the very first moment I met her when she came to watch our practice with her parents.

Isla Warner has always been off-limits. Always been like this shiny prize that I can't possibly get. Better than the Superbowl. Better than one of the most prestigious awards.

I had a chance of winning those.

I never had a chance with her.

Being here now, watching as she dots her canvas with precise strokes of the most beautiful blue, feels like a dream.

And even though it's early, even though this is totally stupid, I can't help but feel like I'm free falling.

I sit there for hours as she goes about her business. Her headphones are on, and I wonder what she's listening to. Her face is a mask of concentration as she works on one corner of her painting. A beautiful landscape of an ocean, a boat floating in the distance, the beautiful pinks and blues of the sun setting on the horizon reflecting on the water.

Does she only do landscapes?

I want to know more, but I can't interrupt her. I want to be invited back, and interrupting her peace while she's focusing isn't the way to ensure that.

Suddenly she opens the bag of peach rings beside her and pops one into her mouth, tilting her head as she looks at her work from a new angle, using her finger to smudge two colors together.

I don't know much about art, but the style looks familiar, but all hers at once.

She sits up, taking out one of her headphones, but she doesn't turn, instead adding some small white lines to the waves.

"Why now?" she asks suddenly.

It takes me by surprise, and I take a moment to respond. "What do you mean why now?"

"Why are you talking to me now?"

I shrug, aware she can't see it. "I don't know. Sometimes things just have to feel right."

She turns, biting her lip. "And now feels right?"

"I think it does."

She nods, going back to work.

Thirty minutes later, she turns to me again, spinning on the cloth that lines the floor, placing her paintbrush in a mug of water beside her.

"We can't do this," she says, and my heart sinks.

"Why not?"

"Leo will kill us both. I don't think I can risk that."

"Leo would forgive it."

She shakes her head. "He'd hold it against you. He's protective of me. A little overbearing. I just don't want to do that to you. He would forgive me but I'm not sure I can say the same for you."

I consider this, but I don't think she's right. "If you're worried about the team, we're professionals. All either of us want to do is win. He would never ever let any issues with us come between the game."

She purses her lips, looking down at her hands. "I just don't want to hurt him."

"Sometimes you need to put yourself first."

She nods.

We're quiet for a couple of minutes while she thinks. "What is the punishment for this week?" she asks suddenly, changing the subject.

I smile.

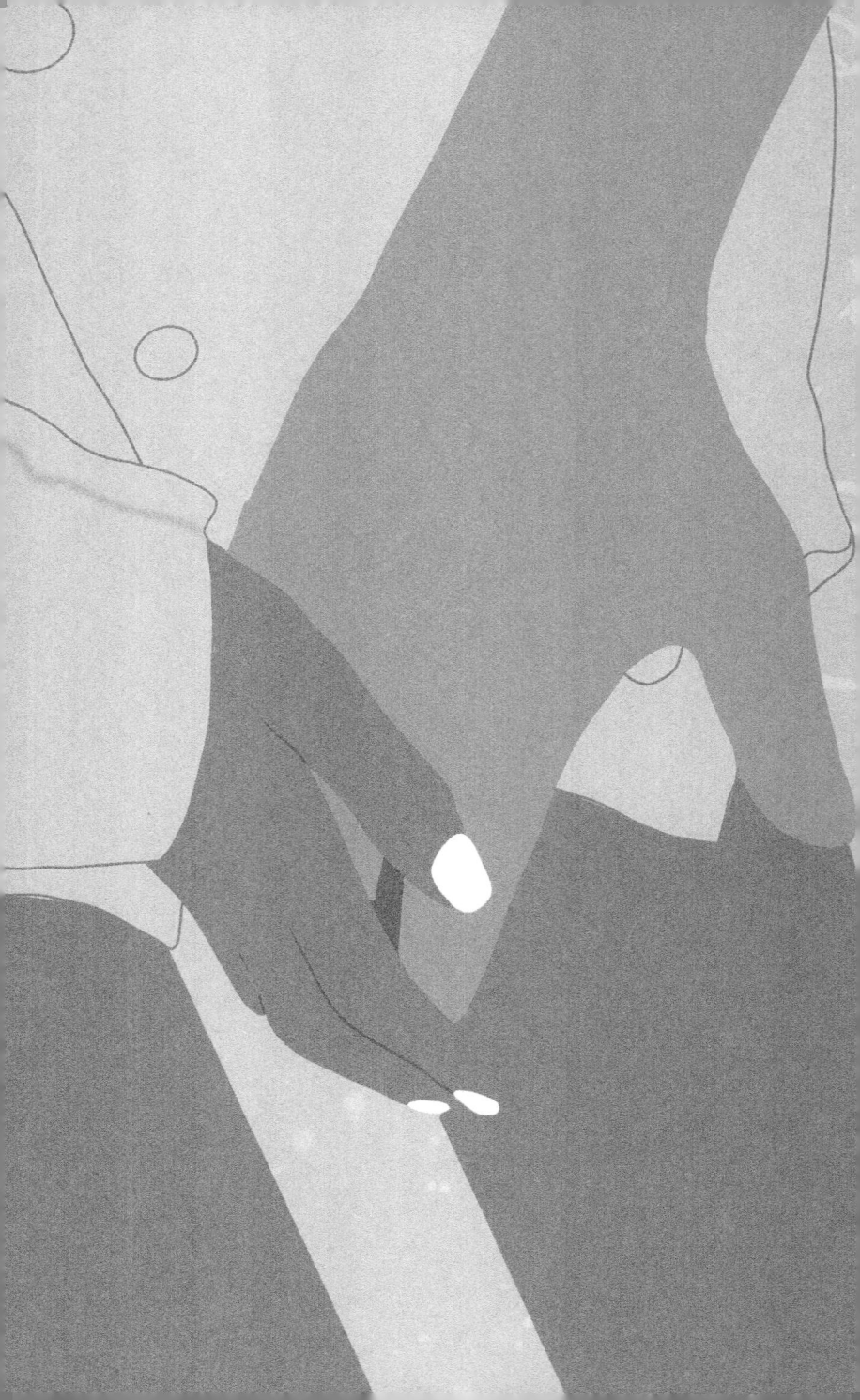

14
ISLA

There was a shift on Tuesday. One I can't completely explain.

I spent all of Wednesday thinking about it. Around dinnertime I asked him if he wanted to stay, but he said he had to go and take care of things before work Wednesday. I know from Leo that Wednesdays can be intense for teams, and they usually start early. So I got it.

He left, telling me that he liked watching me paint and would love to do it again.

I spent the night finishing off my peach rings, grabbing some real food, and sitting on my couch watching corny reality TV in order to shut my brain off. Sometimes that's necessary.

I was able to get a lot done as he watched me, actually. I'm not sure what it is, but I've always been able to focus a little bit more when someone else is around. Not always, but a lot of the time.

Sometimes you just want to be alone, and that's okay.

But his presence was nice. I didn't feel embarrassed or annoyed and he didn't bring attention to himself. He just let me be.

I'd be fine if he watched me all the time.

It's Thursday now, the beginning of the second fantasy week. I started off the season strong, scoring the second most points in our league. Owen scored the most, so we're sitting comfy at the very top. Leo lost, but from what I hear, Leo loses in this league a lot.

I went into this not really knowing what to expect, but after the first week, all I want is to win. It sparked my competitive edge, and there's nothing I want more than to take it all.

Isla Warner winning her first year with the league against a ton of big scary football players? I'll take it. Not that there's anything to win other than bragging rights and a trophy…

Leo is a lot of things but he's not stupid enough to get money involved.

Owen texted me earlier today to let me know that practice is ending around three P.M. He wants to come over again to hang out, but I'm not sure. I still don't completely understand where this is going to go, and I'd rather take things easy.

But how much easier is him just hanging out here? We don't have to do anything. We've barely touched each other.

We're just friends enjoying each other's company.

I've been working on a different piece for my showing, this one of a field of daisies, when I hear my phone ding.

> MISSION: POSSIBLE
>
> I know your brother is home, I don't want to knock and have him come to the door.

I quickly get up, brushing my hands on the smock dress I have on and go to answer the door.

Just like Tuesday, Owen stands in the doorframe with a big grin on his face, a bag of peach rings in his hand.

He holds them out for me as I step away to let him in and slowly close the door.

"Your brother is having some of the guys over for the football game later," he says, stretching one arm across his body. I can't help but watch his muscles bulge. "So I'm going to have to head next door around 8 if that's okay?"

He looks at me expectantly, as if he's hoping that I'll say no. "Of course," I tell him. It's the only acceptable answer. No matter how much I like his company I'm not going to take time away from my brother.

Especially if it's a team activity.

He nods, taking his shoes off before heading to the couch. He sits in the same spot he did before, and I smile to myself. I like the look of him there.

The sun streams in through the large windows behind, and we both turn to watch the water silently.

"You know, this has been nice," I say simply, taking my place in front of my canvas.

"What has?"

"Just having someone here."

"Don't you have your friends?" I don't turn around, but I can feel his confusion.

"Obviously. But they all have their own lives and I'm not going to ask them to just come here and sit with me while I work. Heidi does sometimes. She's a wedding photographer, so sometimes she comes and hangs out with me while she edits photos."

"That sounds like a fun job," he replies.

"I think she likes it, but it's stressful. It's definitely over forty hours of work per wedding usually."

"Really?"

I pick up my brush, dipping it in the muted green I mixed a bit ago. "Yeah. I mean, you have the wedding, and that's usually a whole day's event. And then she goes home, edits a couple photograph to send the couple right away, and then she has to go through hundreds and hundreds of photos and delete ones she doesn't like, edit them all, sometimes edit people out or things into images, and then do other things. It's a ton of work. She's stressed out a lot."

"If she's that stressed why doesn't she find something else?"

The question annoys me for a second, but I have to remember that these guys play football for a living. Although there's something romantic about sports, it's not a super creative job, no matter what Leo will say. We're both passionate about what we do, but the passion for sports and the passion for creative arts is different.

Same... but different.

"The same reason you get upset and annoyed at your job and don't quit," I tell him simply with a shrug as I look over my shoulder. Some hair falls out of my clip, and I place my brush down before re-clipping it. "It's the same reason I don't quit my job either."

He doesn't reply.

I'll admit I've been extremely lucky. I would never be able to do this without my brother, and I love him endlessly for allowing me to follow my passions. He's one of the best people on the planet, and we've always been incredibly close, no matter how annoying he can get.

He knows how I feel about living in his shadow, and all he's wanted is for me to be comfortable and do what I love.

Leo Warner is a big softie, and I would absolutely love for him to settle down soon.

"Besides, she just loves love."

Owen doesn't say anything for a long time, and when I turn, I catch him watching me intensely. "I get it," he says before leaning back, his hands clasped behind his head. My eyes go to his muscles again.

God, the man is art.

I grab my headphones and am about to put them on when Owen says, "What are you listening to?"

"Do you want to listen?" I ask, suddenly feeling embarrassed. I should have asked last time. I'm not sure what he does while watching me, but it's probably awkward sitting there in silence while I have my headphones on.

He nods with a smile.

"Okay."

Grabbing my phone, I hit play on my favorite playlist before connecting it to a speaker I have in my home. The low hum of some 90s alternative rock fills the space, and I hope he's a fan.

"This is what you listen to?" he asks in surprise.

I swivel in place. "Yeah, why?"

"Just surprising is all."

"Why?"

"I just didn't expect you to like divorced dad rock."

And I can't help it. I burst out laughing, which causes him to follow.

"It's not divorced dad rock!" I tell him, feeling a big smile stretch across my face.

"This? This most definitely is. How You Remind Me? Peak divorced dad rock."

He's got me there. "Okay well it's a 90s alternative rock playlist." I roll my eyes. "It's just this one in particular."

"I'm pretty sure this came out in the 2000s," he deadpans, the corner of his full lips twitching.

"It's definitely the 90s."

He shakes his head, whipping out his phone and typing something in. "It's from 2001 Peaches."

I rear back at the name, my eyebrows drawing together. "Peaches?"

"You eat a lot of peach rings." He shrugs.

My lips thin, unsure of how I feel about him calling me that.

It almost feels like a pet name.

"What's another song on the playlist?" he asks, moving on

without a second thought. He can move on, but I'm still thinking about it.

I open the app on my phone, scrolling through my list. "Well, the next one is Semi-Charmed Life."

He nods, snapping before pointing his finger at me. "Third Eye Blind. See? That song's in the right playlist."

I just smile, shaking my head. "Okay whatever. Anyways," I say, abandoning the painting for now. I spin in place, facing him. "How do you think you're going to do this week?"

"The team or fantasy?"

"Fantasy." We already know they're going to kill it this weekend. They're up against the Cincinnati Bobcats. Although it's a big rivalry team, the Bobcats have sucked for the last couple of years.

"I think I'll do okay," he says, scratching his chin. "I'm up against Myles. His wide receiver already got hurt week one." Owen winces. I'm sure talking about tragic injuries means a whole lot more to the guys who are actually playing.

"That's good."

"How about you?"

"I'm not sure. I don't really have any expectations to be honest. I did well last week but we'll see about this week." I pause, looking him up and down. "If I'm honest it comes down to how you do on Sunday."

He smirks. "I'll try to do my best for you, Peaches."

WEEK TWO

15

OWEN

"Your parents are here?" I ask Leo as we practice before our game.

"Yeah, they decided to stay longer and visit some old friends. They'll be here for almost the whole season, actually," he says as he throws to Tristen.

"That's cool," I say, surprised. I bend down, stretching my legs. "Where are they staying?"

Leo shrugs before catching a ball thrown at him. "They got a small place to themselves outside of the city. Something about the city being too much for them now."

Honestly, if I lived in a small town in a foreign country, I'd probably feel the same way about a city.

I start doing some drills before catching some passes, and we finally head to the locker room before the game kicks off.

I'm smart enough not to ask Leo what I'm really wondering though—is Isla here with them.

I caught two touchdowns, Leo ran into the end zone for one of his own, Tristen got one, and one of our running backs also got one. We ended the game thirty-four to fourteen. Our defense was a little rusty tonight for some reason, but we'll work on it this coming week.

We won, and that's what's important. Well, and no one got hurt today.

The energy in the room is great as we pack up to leave, and although all the guys are talking about hanging out, I can't help but only think of Isla. I take out my phone, opening my texts. We exchanged numbers finally the other day.

To make sure Leo doesn't have a fit if he sees my phone, her contact name is *Peaches*.

> I hope that was enough points for you

Finishing up my packing, I grab my water and head out, passing Leo and his parents on my way, almost missing Isla behind them, looking at her phone.

"Hey!" I call out to the Warner parents. They've always been nice to me. Sure, am I mostly going over to get Isla's attention? Yeah. But I do also want to say hi to their mom and dad.

"Hey man, great game," their father, Ted, says.

"Thank you so much sir," I say, enveloping his hand in mine for a firm handshake. "I'm happy you guys have been hanging around."

"Well, we figured we've been gone for a couple of years and haven't really had an extended stay. Gotta spend time with the kids." Fiona, their mother, says.

I nod in understanding. My parents don't live close, and it would be nice if they could come visit. But my parents had me young, and they both still work. My mom's a nurse and can't take much time off at all.

Briar and I make do, though.

My phone vibrates in my hand as Isla looks up at me. I won't check it here, but I smile at her. "I hope you guys all enjoyed the game. I gotta head home, but I hope you guys have a great night." Leo slaps me on the shoulder before calling out to another teammate, but I hold Isla's gaze for a beat too long. Nodding at them, I turn, heading out.

"He's so handsome, isn't he Isla? What was up with the way he was looking at you?"

"Mom, stop. Please for the love of God not here," I hear her hiss quietly.

I can't help but smile.

The rest of the day is a blur. I went home after the game, hanging out on my couch to watch the night games.

PEACHES

I hope you did. Won't know until tonight

I look at the text before opening the fantasy app. She doesn't have any players playing on Monday, so she's done for the week after this next game. But her opponent has a player—a kicker. She's currently far enough ahead that I don't think she has to worry.

I think you'll be fine. How's dinner?

Leo told the guys that he couldn't go out with them because the family was going out to dinner. I really am glad that they get time with their parents.

PEACHES

It's good. Leo ate the entire appetizer. But then ordered three more for the table.

> I bet he ate one of those three too, didn't he?

How'd you know?

> Psychic.

I bet. When's your birthday by the way?

> April 27th, why?

Oh you poor, poor fool. You should know better than to give a woman your birthday.

> Why?

No reason. What time were you born?

> 3:11 in the afternoon... why. I'm scared.

You should be.

> I'm shaking.

The texts stop after that, and I know they're probably eating.

I wish I was there with them.

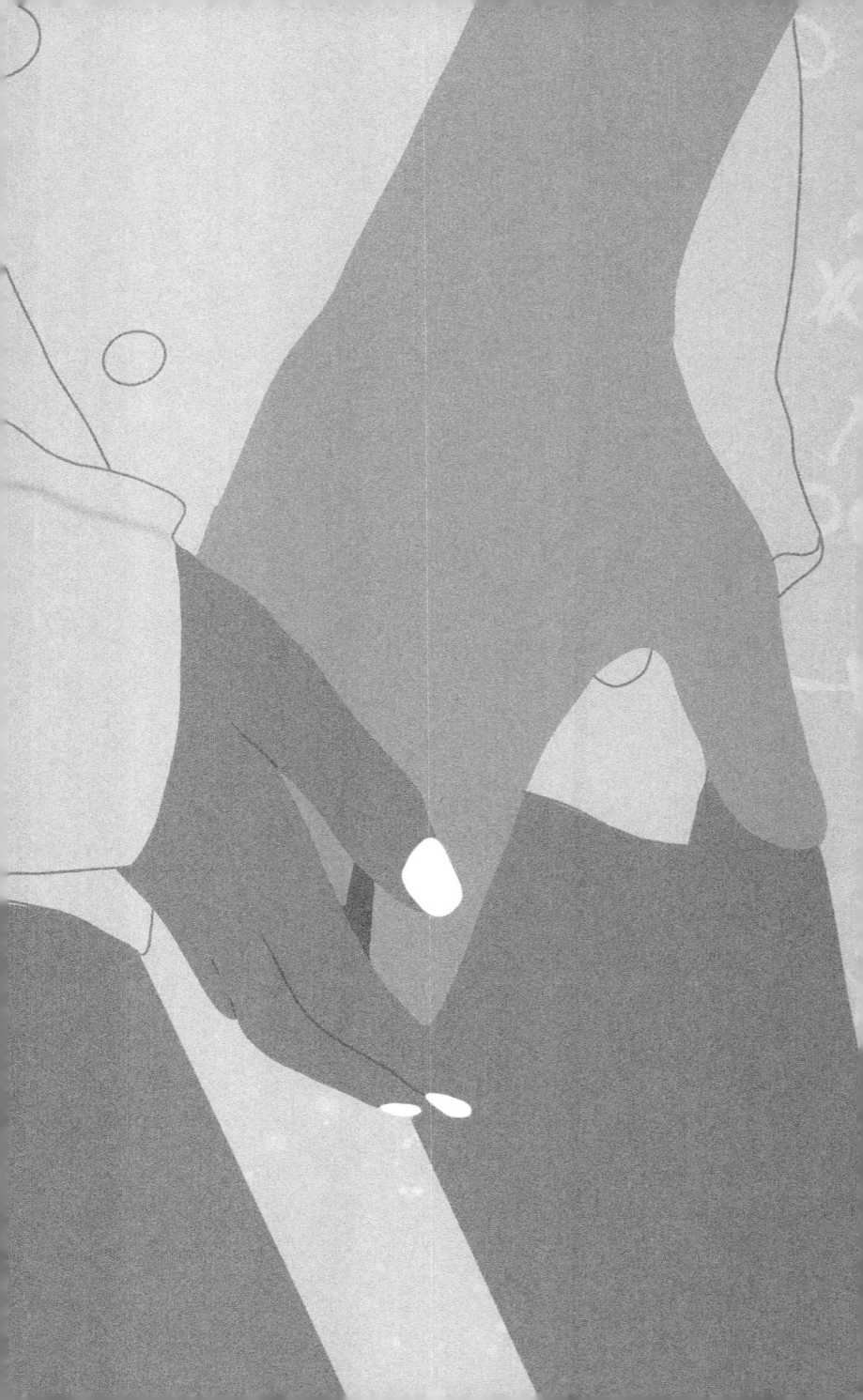

16

ISLA

I haven't heard much from the guys today. It's Monday, and I know that Leo said he had things going on, but I haven't heard much from Owen either. I busy myself with my paintings, finishing my fourth for my showing, starting to feel a little less stressed. I'm starting to actually like the paintings I've been finishing, and although I think I'll always be a bit overly critical, I'm genuinely happy with these.

Around four in the afternoon Mila texts me asking to hang out, and I let her know I have the night open. I'm just going to be watching the football game.

I hurriedly clean the main living area, making sure everything is tidy. Mila wouldn't care, but I do.

When I'm finally done, all I can do is think about texting Owen.

ISLA

> Hey, I hope you're having a nice Victory Monday

The second I hit send I feel butterflies erupt in my stomach, and I flop down on my couch, annoyed with myself.

How did I let myself get this attached?

OWEN CROSBY

> Hey Peaches, I'm doing okay. Just having a day out and about with my niece. Sorry I haven't texted you, I hope your painting went well today.

The text is accompanied by a photo of him with a little girl, her hair almost the same color as his, her toothy smile infectious as she sits in a booth, a large sugary milkshake in front of her.

The text didn't help the butterflies at all.

I can't help but wonder if he knew exactly what he was doing with that photo.

> She's adorable!

> She's a little demon, don't let her cuteness fool you. But she's the best.

> Well I hope you guys have a great night

> I hope you do too. It looks like I may win this week

> In your dreams, Crosby

"I'm not sure how you watch hours and hours of this," Mila says as I cheer on my last remaining player in my lineup.

"You get used to it." I shrug. I've been watching hours upon hours of football for as long as I can remember. It's natural for me.

"I bet, I just don't know if I can ever get to that point." She sighs, grabbing a handful of popcorn from the large bowl propped between us.

"I just need that guy to get three more touchdowns," I tell her, opening the fantasy app on my phone. I'm winning my game, but I'm not beating Owen yet. His team did crazy numbers, once again in the lead.

"I'm certain yelling at the TV will get through to him," she chuckles, and I just roll my eyes.

My guy's team is losing, down by 24 points in the third quarter, and I'm losing hope. One of the other wide receivers was injured, being carted away on a stretcher, and I cross my fingers for a big comeback.

And surprisingly, I get it.

The team kicks a field goal, and now I just need the guy to somehow get three more touchdowns.

And then the guy catches a 60-yard pass, running right into the end zone.

My points skyrocket. It's only up from there.

At the end of the game, I'm beating Owen by two points.

I jump up, pumping my fists into the air as I do a little dance around my coffee table as Mila watches me, her brows furrowed and lips pursed.

"What did you have riding on this game that you're this happy?" she asks.

"Nothing," I say innocently, scrolling through everyone's scores.

"I think you're lying to me, but I'm sure I'll find out soon enough." She flops back onto the couch, taking a sip of her coke.

"It's just a fun game," I shrug, not ready to tell her about my little game with Owen.

She's already been suspicious since last week when he got the Uber for all of us. I don't need to show her all my cards yet, because I know she'll never let up. It'll be all she asks me about for the next couple of weeks.

I've never dated. Sure, I've went home with people. I've gone on dates in the past, but I've never actually had a long-term relationship. Nothing that actually meant something. Mila has been on me about dating for as long as I can remember.

But as the friend who had to nurse all her friend's broken hearts, I was never quite sure it was worth it.

I'm not against it, I'm just not going to go out and force anything just to have a relationship.

It's the same with Owen. Do I like him? A lot. I've found him attractive for years. But is this going to turn into anything? I'm not sure. I'm not going to rush it, even if my heart wants me to.

Sometimes you just have to sit back and enjoy what's happening.

> You win, Peaches. I'm surprised.

Speak of the devil…

> Thank you, I knew I'd pull through.

> No you didn't, but nice try.

"Who are you texting?" Mila asks, sitting up and stretching. I look at the time. She has work in the morning and is probably heading out.

"My brother," I lie. "He didn't do great this week."

"Does he ever? I feel like whenever you've ever talked about him playing fantasy it's always been to talk about how much he sucks."

She has a point.

"He's been doing better I think, from what it sounds like."

"Are you still named Ian?"

I nod. "I don't think any of the guys have figured it out.

I'm honestly not sure how much they care. It's just some stupid rule Leo decided to make."

Mila gets up, putting her long hair in a bun before getting up to grab her shoes.

"Well I hope all of that works out because I can't imagine how irritating your brother would be."

I can.

My phone buzzing wakes me up in the morning. I roll over, staring at the grey-blue wall in front of me. If there's one thing I don't want to do today, it's get up and do much of anything.

I have two commissions to finish and ship out today, one of which has been from a nightmare client, the other for an older woman in California who somehow found me online. Both pieces have been fun to paint, but one client is definitely easier to work with. I'm nervous about sending the difficult client a message to let her know that the painting has shipped, because I know I'm going to get ten emails back right away asking how it was packaged—carefully, wrapped in multiple layers of paper and bubble wrap, and then put in a wood-enforced heavy-duty box—what to do if there's any damages—there never has been any issues but if there are, there is insurance on the package—and if I know when it's going to arrive—the tracking number sent with the email is super useful, but it says it'll be there Friday.

I close my eyes again, my phone vibrating once more. I groan, reaching for it on my side-table, almost pushing off my jade-colored lamp and a couple of books stacked up.

OWEN CROSBY

Are you taking advantage of your win today?

Maybe. What time are you free?

Anytime after three.

How about you meet here for six? I'll order food. Bring snacks.

You got it.

Rolling out of bed, I go about my morning routine getting ready, throwing on a sports bra and loose pair of overalls. Pinning my hair up, I grab my mug of water, brew a cup of coffee, and sit down on my floor as the morning light streams through my windows, casting a golden glow on my canvases.

These paintings are meticulous. I love the challenge of commissions, because when I paint for shows, it's from my heart. When I paint commissions, it's something the client wanted. I love doing both. The relaxation that comes from painting whatever comes to mind, and the challenge that painting something that may not come as easily to me.

It keeps my brain working. Coming up with new ideas. Not settling for comfort. It allows me to broaden my talents and learn new things.

Pulling out some gold foil, I add it to the sunset behind a city skyline, brushing off the excess.

Before I know it lunch rolls around, and I go about my day as I normally would, but all the while all too aware of the warm and fuzzy feeling in the pit of my stomach about what's to come.

Owen is at my door at six on the dot, a bag of peach rings in hand despite me not painting tonight. He sits them on the counter, letting me know they're for my workday tomorrow.

I had changed into a pair of shorts and an oversized sweater I'm pretty sure I stole from my dad moments before he texted me, and the way he looks at me makes me wish I put in more effort.

"Are tacos okay for you?" I ask him, filling a glass of water.

He places a bag on the counter, pulling out a variety of other snacks as I push the glass to him before grabbing one for me. "I'm always down for tacos," he tells me with a smile. "So what are we doing tonight?" he looks around, noticing that I moved the couch around so that the ottoman is in the center, fluffy blankets stacked on top. More pillows line it too, a couple of candles lit around the room. "Whoa, I didn't think we were there yet," he looks at me, his eyes wide.

I smile, shaking my head. "We're watching tv."

"What?"

I shrug. "I thought it would be a great punishment. Guess what we're watching."

"Is it a movie?"

"No."

He thinks for a minute, running his hand through his shaggy hair as he tilts his head back. "Okay I don't know."

"You, my friend, are watching the Real Housewives with me."

His face twists, but he tries to hide it. A smile spreads across my face as I watch him start to fidget. "I just want to tell you that this was your idea you know. You were the one who wanted punishments."

He looks around, almost as if looking for a way out. "Yeah, the Real Housewives is kind of like torture though, isn't it? Cruel and unusual punishment? Yeah I think it counts as that."

I round the counter and smack his arm, and as I pull away, he grabs me, pulling me into a hug.

It's the first hug we've shared.

And his body is so hard.

His chest and arms I mean. Though I wouldn't be completely opposed to checking if the other part of him is too.

His cheek comes to my head as I stand stunned. "I hope you had a good day," he says, pulling me tighter. It's like I can feel every muscle in his body. His strong arms wrapped around me, the scent of him—a woodsy scent that feels almost out of place on him—enveloping me in a cloud of euphoria.

"I hope you did too," I say quietly, finally returning the hug. He pulls away, heading to the couch.

"Did you order dinner yet?"

I shake my head. "Not yet. I was waiting to see what you wanted."

"I'm good with anything."

"Okay well let's go with this. Steak or chicken?"

He only has to think for a second. "I think steak."

"Do you want any sides?"

"I'd be down for some salsa."

I nod, adding everything to my cart. "Alright, it'll be here in thirty minutes." I inform him, grabbing my water and heading over to sit beside him. "Let's get the show started!"

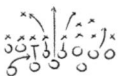

"Wait so what happened between those two?" Owen asks, pointing between the two women on the TV.

"One of them told everyone else that the other has an alcohol issue."

"Does she?"

I shrug. "I think they all do to be honest. Whether they admit to it or not."

He nods, scratching his cheek.

We finished our tacos two hours ago, and since then we've just been binging the latest season of the Real Housewives. It's my guilty pleasure show, something I never thought I'd ever get wrapped into. But God, the drama is just too good. Way too good.

"I feel like all of this would be resolved if any of them could just communicate," Owen mumbles as three of the women start screaming at each other over dinner.

"Well yeah, but that wouldn't make for good TV."

I watch his face as he considers this, his eyes never once leaving the fight happening on screen. "I guess that's true, but none of this is real, right?"

I grab a few pieces of popcorn, popping them into my mouth. "If I'm honest I have no idea. I think a lot of it may be fake. Or I assume it is. I can't really believe anyone lives their lives like this."

"They probably get paid a lot though."

"Probably."

"I wonder why those two also hate each other."

"That storyline is from season thirteen."

"SparkNotes version?"

I shake my head. "No can do. It's a lot."

He purses his lips, watching me.

"Hmm," he mumbles as he turns back to the drama in front of us. I smile. I just know he's going to go home and look it up.

Men love to pretend they don't like drama, when in reality they live for it. They crave drama more than women most of the time, they just won't ever admit it for some weird reason.

"Do you watch this often?" he asks suddenly. He sits up, scooting even closer to me, which I didn't even think was possible. We're touching now, and without thinking, I drape my left leg over his.

He puts his hand on the blanket covering my thigh, keeping it there as he watches me expectantly.

And it feels like the most natural thing in the world. There's no awkwardness, neither of us froze. It's like he was meant to be here.

I need to stop thinking like that.

"I used to watch it more when I was living with Mila. She loves it. But I've been left to watch it on my own."

"That's sad."

"Ehh, it is what it is."

A commercial break ends, the show returning. Owen quiets down once more, sinking into the cushions and leaning his head back.

Owen watches three more episodes, our eyes getting heavy as the hours drag on.

"Don't you have practice tomorrow morning?" I ask, my voice groggy.

"Yeah, but I wanted to be here."

"Why?"

"You won."

"Oh."

He freezes, and I want to know what's going through his brain. "I appreciate you doing this, even if it's a punishment."

"You can punish me any time, Peaches," he says simply, and I simply choose to ignore the innuendo in that.

"I'll keep that in mind."

Finally, at midnight, he stirs, checking his phone for the first time in hours. By this time my head is resting on his shoulder as one of the wives brings up shit from the past again. "I should probably go," he says quietly, patting my thigh.

"Probably," I mumble, internally pouting a bit.

"Would it make you feel better to know that I would absolutely watch this with you again?"

I perk up, not expecting that. I mean sure, I figured he'd probably look stuff up about the past seasons maybe out of morbid curiosity, but I didn't think he would actively suggest we watch it again.

"Are you that desperate for my attention, Owen Crosby?" I smile.

"Are you being an asshole, Isla Warner?"

My smile only widens at his words, and I stand, stretching my arms above my head.

"That's what I do best," I reply finally.

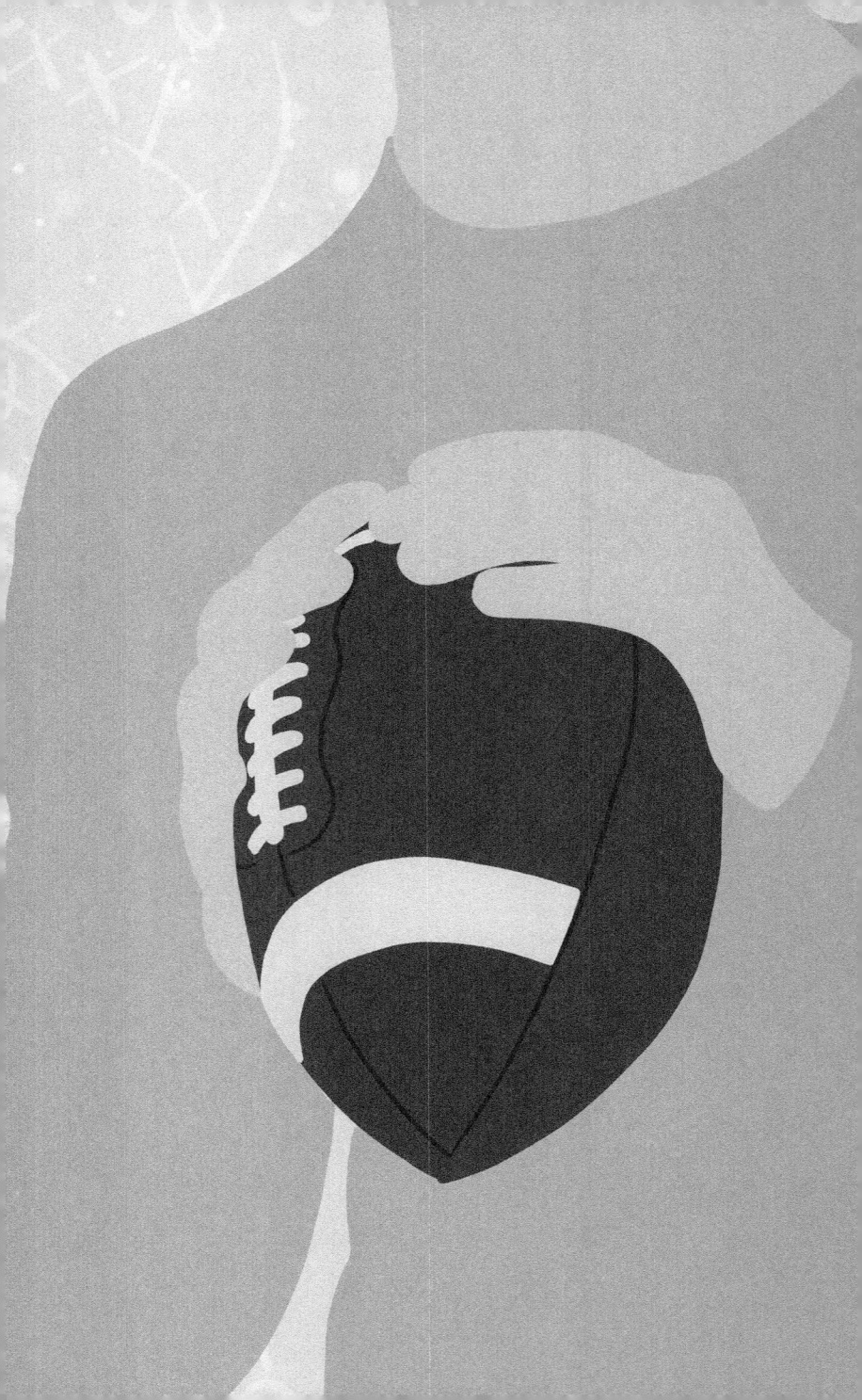

17

OWEN

"Cooper I'm not dating anyone you set me up with. I don't trust you after last time." Leo shivers in his seat, shoveling chicken into his mouth.

"I've apologized for that a million times, man. Let it be. I'm serious, there's a couple of really nice girls I met the other night."

"And I'll meet them myself and make that judgement call," he says with a shrug.

We're taking a break from practice for lunch, and the two have been at each other's throats all day. I'm not sure why.

"I'm always open to being set up," Emmett says, pushing his salad around his plate.

"Why would I set you up? You have no issues getting girls."

"You're saying I do?" Leo asks, slamming his fork down on the table.

"I'm saying that you're a man whore who should settle down."

"Says you," Leo says under his breath as he stabs his chicken, shoving it into his mouth as he looks away dejected.

"Why are you guys fighting between yourselves when the

perfect candidate is sitting right across from us?" Dirwin asks, motioning to me.

I shake my head, drinking my water. "I'm not looking to date right now, sorry," I tell them.

"We're not asking you if you're looking to date, we're telling you that you're a great candidate. Cooper is trying to set everyone up."

"Cooper should worry about himself," I shoot back, officially joining the argument.

"Cooper is worrying about himself, thank you very much. In fact, he has his sights set on someone," Cooper says, rolling his eyes and shimmying his shoulders.

"Who?" Emmett asks.

"None of your business," he shoots back.

"Says the one trying to get into everyone's business," Leo mutters.

"I'm not saying you guys have to actually date anyone, I just think it would be cool if we all got into relationships and then our girlfriends could hang out."

"Why the hell would that be any different than now? And what if one of us breaks up with our girl? Then what?"

Cooper thinks for a moment, his nose scrunching in concentration. "Then we deal with it as it happens," he says finally, sighing. "All I'm saying is that I watch these guys with their wives and they all look so cute. And I think that I'm in a place where I want to settle down."

"And why are you making that all of our problem?" Dirwin asks, scratching his dark beard.

"Because I love hanging out with all of you. One of us gets tied down and we won't be talking as much. Women are social creatures. They'll want to hang and then we get to hang."

"I'm pretty sure we can just, I don't know, make an effort to spend time together," I tell him, pointing my fork at him.

"But how much fun would it be if we were all in the same place in life?"

I shake my head. "That's never going to happen, man. Sorry."

"Owen just think about it. Have you ever even touched a woman?" I stop chewing and glare at him, the crease between my eyes deepening every second.

"Yes, I have touched a woman, thank you."

"Well all I'm saying is it doesn't seem like it. You're always holed up in your apartment or at Leo's. Which, if that's a thing," he leans back in his seat, his hands out in front of him. "I'm here for it, I promise. I'd be so here for it, actually. I could see it."

Leo smacks him on the back of the head.

"I had a girlfriend before I started playing," I inform him, propping my elbow on the table, my cheek resting on my fist.

"And then?"

"And then she moved. Nothing more to it."

"Well that's stupid." Cooper rolls his eyes. "Anyways, can we start planning our touchdown celebration this weekend?

"No, that's Andrew's job."

"Then I'll ask him." Cooper scoots his chair out, getting up to go ask one of our special teams players if he can come up with the touchdown celebration moves for this week. Andrew has enjoyed making them, mostly because he has the best ideas out of us all. He doesn't get to do them with us, but he likes watching.

"What *is* going on with your dating life?" Leo asks, his eyes pinning me with daggers. I freeze, not knowing if he knows something.

"I don't have anything."

"You don't answer texts as fast as you did."

"I didn't know there was a timeframe I had to get back to you in."

"There's not. I just think something's up."

I shake my head. "Nope, nothing is up." I look down, busying myself with the food in front of me.

"You know you can tell me anything, right?" I nod, but I know that's not true. There are certain things that I simply can't tell him, this being one of the biggest. Not yet, anyway. There will come a time, hopefully, when we have to, but I sincerely hope that we can keep it between us for as long as possible.

I love Leo, I do, and I get why he's concerned, but he shouldn't be.

"So how did the loser punishment go?" I ask him to change the subject. The person with the lowest fantasy points each week gets a punishment to do. Something that's definitely much worse than simply watching the real housewives, snuggled up with a beautiful woman.

I could deal with that punishment all day every day.

No. These are evil punishments, meant to inflict pain. Physical, mental, and beyond.

"I haven't done it yet," he says quietly, despite the others right next to us.

"You mean you haven't painted your toes and put them up on craigslist yet?" I ask loudly, making sure to get everyone's attention.

"Yeah, I actually don't remember a photo being sent to the group to show it was completed," Dirwin says.

"You need to get that done, man," Emmett adds.

"What are we talking about?" Cooper asks as he sits back down.

"Leo still hasn't put his feet up online."

"Leo, my guy, what are you doing? It was supposed to be done within 24 hours."

"It'll be done," he grumbles.

"It better be. We want to see those piggies." Cooper tells him.

"Please stop."

I barely survived the rest of the day with the guys. I'm not sure what got into them today, but they decided to annoy the shit out of each other.

Suddenly, my phone lights up. I pick it up, stretching out on my couch as season 1 of the Real Housewives of whatever city plays in front of me. I wasn't sure which one it was and I was too much of a wuss to ask, so I looked through the women in each city to find the ones I was looking for. The drama from the very first season has been immaculate.

PEACHES

Hey, are you picking the punishment for this week?

I have an idea.

Does a girl get to hear?

If she's good.

I can be good.

Although I didn't intend for it to sound suggestive, it's where my mind goes the second she sends that reply, sending all my blood south. It's been getting harder and harder to think about her as just a friend. Not that I was trying very hard in the first place.

But I've wanted to move slowly. I know she does too. It's beneficial to us both.

But I just want to hold her.

I'm sure you can, Peaches, but I'm not sure if I can tell you.

> Why can't you?

It's not a super fun punishment like the last one.

> Oh you thought that was fun? I'll have to try harder next time.

It was fun because it was with you

> Noted. No punishments that include me.

That's punishment enough.

> You're a smooth talker, Crosby.

I try sometimes.

> You succeed.

Alright, I'll tell you. Just keep showering me with compliments, alright?

I smile, typing it out. Now I just have to pray I win.

WEEK THREE

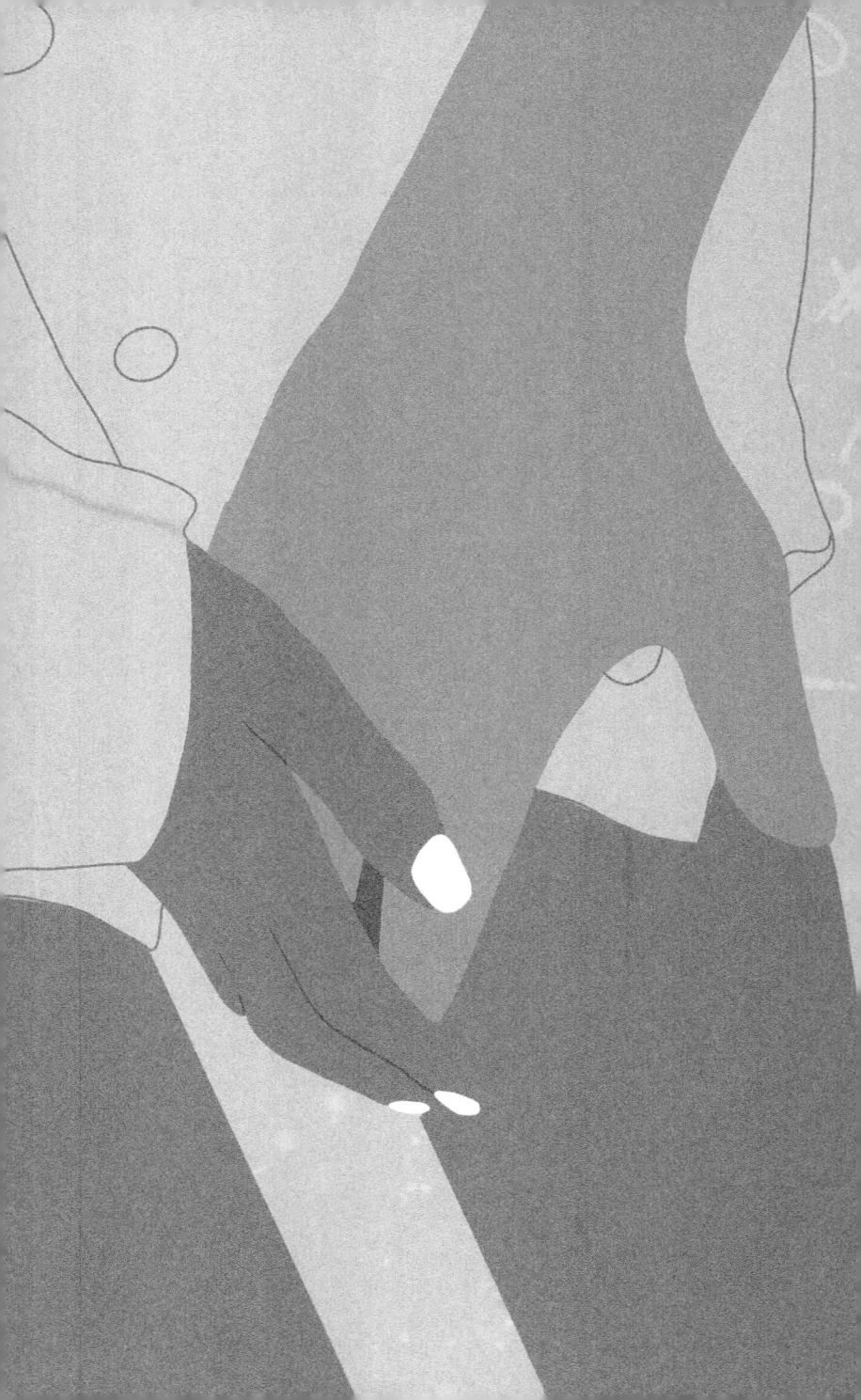

18
ISLA

The Cobras are away this week. Their first away game, a primetime spot on Monday Night Football, and they're sucking.

I mean really sucking. Horribly… sucking.

Leo can't keep the damn ball in his hands, and he threw a pick-six in the first quarter. Owen dropped a couple of passes, and the others haven't been much help either.

Thankfully Owen is the only one from the Cobras I have, but no one on my team has done well this week. Not a single one.

My defense, one of the best in the league, ended with negative two points.

I groan, rubbing my eyes as I spread out on my couch, watching the horror go down on the TV.

I'm so screwed. So royally fucked, even.

I've been complacent. It's only been two weeks and I was sure that I was the best in the league. A definite winner. I would skyrocket to the top, taking everything from these idiots.

But that's not the case. There are bad weeks, even at the start, and this is one of them.

I'm going to have two punishments to do.

I don't even know how that's going to work. How am I going to send proof of me doing whatever I have to do to the group?

I wasn't even told what the punishment is. Leo has a group chat with all the guys, but he has a dummy number in there for Ian. I have no idea what he's been doing if one of the guys texts me, though I'm not sure why they would.

He doesn't want me accidentally getting lose lips and letting them know who I am.

But he also doesn't tell me anything.

So now I'm going into the end of the week, probably losing, and having two punishments under my belt. The one I can deal with. Sure, it'll hurt like a bitch, but if I don't even know what the other is, I can't prepare for it.

It feels like a special kind of torture.

I know he's playing and won't see it for another hour or so, but I shoot a text to my brother.

> Text me when you can

Laying back on my couch, I watch as Owen gets another target, barely keeping it between his butter fingers before he gets tackled from the side, the ball falling from his grip where someone on the other team's defense scoops it up. He's immediately tackled, but the ball is officially the other team's.

It's been a long time since I've seen them play this badly.

The Cobras defense finally does something, and a second later flags fly, a holding call being announced.

I'm so ready for this game to be over.

The men look frustrated. Understandably so.

The game is so stressful, in fact, that I can barely appreciate Owen's ass every time they show it.

When the game finally ends, the score is straight up embarrassing. I'm not sure I want to watch the post-game interviews, since I'm sure there will be some words thrown about.

The men trudge off the field, their heads hung low, their helmets hanging from their hands. Leo looks pissed, but I know it's only because he screwed up. He knows when to admit that something was his fault, and although everyone played horribly, Leo would place most of the blame on himself regardless.

I debate texting Owen, but I refrain. I'm not sure where we're at. I'm not sure, still, what this is. I don't want to overstep a boundary by asking him whether he's doing okay after the game. Men can be emotional, and I don't want to be shocked by him being short with me. I know myself better than to do that to myself.

I'll let him come to me.

***

"What do you mean I have to get a nipple pierced?" I ask, my jaw hanging to the floor.

"That was what the punishment was this week."

"You can make an exception, though."

Leo shakes his head, leaning against my kitchen island. "I can't, sorry."

"You do realize that I'm your sister, right? You're telling your *sister* that she has to *get her nipple pierced.*"

He looks concerned for a moment before whatever part of his brain is responsible for his incessant desire for chaos files the thought under "does not care."

"I'd rather you not remind me of that, but it's the rules. You have to."

"You do know that I have boobs, Leo, right?"

He closes his eyes, looking away as I point to my chest. "Can you not?"

"What do you mean *can you not.* You're asking me to get my fucking tit pierced, Leo. My boobs. My C-cup boobs. And then I have to send it to the group."

Realization dawns on him then, and he looks troubled as he watches the waves out the window behind me, trying to figure something out.

"I don't really know what to do," he confesses, throwing his hands up.

"You went into this thinking that I would be one of the worst, correct?" he meets my eyes then before casting them downward, guilt clear in the way his shoulders slump just a little.

"I didn't think that you would be the worst but I wasn't thinking that you would do super well either."

"So you added me to this knowing that at some point I could be the one with the weekly punishment, and yet you were also totally fine with this particular punishment?"

He tosses his hands up, bringing them down onto the top of his head, pulling his brown hair at the tips. "I don't know what I was thinking obviously, I'm sorry. But it can't be changed. You're just going to have to figure it out."

"No, no, no," I hiss, shaking my head. "You're going to figure this out, Leo. This isn't on me, it's on you. This is on you, you hear me?"

"Do you know how many messages I got from old men asking if they could suck my toes last week? I'm still getting them, Isla. I took the photo down but I'm still getting messages on that craigslist account. It's traumatizing. Trust me, if I could change something I would."

Wait. Toes? Sucking? Craigslist?

"What are you talking about?" I ask him, sitting back.

"Last week's punishment!"

"You don't *tell* me the weekly punishment, idiot."

He rolls his eyes, folding his arms over his chest. "I had to paint my toes and put feet pictures up on Craigslist."

I sit for a moment to process this. Our eyes are locked, his jaw ticking.

And I laugh.

And laugh.

I can't stop myself. I go on for minutes. Hours. Days.

Okay, probably just two or three minutes. I'm not sure. I completely lose track of time as I picture Leo in pretty red nail polish, posting his hideous athlete feet on the internet.

"Can you stop?" he finally asks, annoyed.

"Did you make any money?" I ask as I choke on my laughter.

"I was offered five hundred."

Oh damn. I may have to get into that. "What did they offer that kind of money for?"

He throws up his hands again, clearly on the verge of losing it. "To suck my toes, Isla! Oh my God do you listen? The man wanted to suck my toes."

And I can't help it. I'm taken over by another intense wave of laughter.

"You suck," he mutters before heading to the door.

"Where are you going? We're not done discussing this."

He doesn't look back at me. "Yes we are. You need to figure it out. I don't want to see your nipples in my group chat."

"Technically I'm not in your group chat, so I would actually have to send my boob photo to you before it's sent to the guys."

That stops him in his tracks. "Get someone else to do it."

"Who the hell am I going to convince to get a nipple piercing?"

"Find a random weirdo on the street. I don't know. Maybe they already have one."

"Leo—"

"Isla—"

It's clear I'm not getting anywhere. Not only am I going to have to do Owen's punishment but I'm going to have to get my nipple pierced.

"This is the dumbest shit I've ever heard," I mutter, going back to my phone.

"Yeah well, the guys are going to start asking questions if it's not done by Wednesday night."

I flip him off, watching as he retreats to his apartment.

I sit with my thoughts for a moment before opening up my texts.

> I have to get my nipple pierced.

The response is almost immediate.

> Only one?

I roll my eyes.

> It's only for the fantasy punishment.

> Oh yeah. He's still making you do that?

> Yeah. I don't know what to do. I have boobs.

> I've noticed.

My cheeks grow hot.

> And I also have to do your punishment.

> Yep, you do. Want me to come over tonight?

> Yes.

"Are you trying to do something weird?"

"What does that even mean?"

"I mean are you trying to get yourself or something? Are you trying to drag my team down so I'll make the trade?" I cross my arms over my chest, my eyes narrowing at Owen as my hip makes contact with the counter.

A look I can't quite place flashes across his face. "What are you trying to say?"

Throwing my hands up in exasperation, I grab my phone, opening the app. "I'm saying that you sucked. Royally. I lost this week because you only completed one catch."

"You lost this week because of a lot more, for one," he says, placing his hand on his chest as if he's wounded. He frowns. "Two, I wouldn't ever intentionally suck to force you to trade me to me. Though I will say, seeing you this worked up is one of the only silver linings to having one of the worst games of my career." My scowl deepens as I take in his words, feeling bad for a moment. "Plus, if you want me to do better for you, tell your brother to throw better."

And have him kick me out? I'm certainly not doing that.

His comment sobers me. "I'm sorry, I shouldn't have said that," I say, slumping down in my seat. "I just don't want to do this."

"I can imagine."

I groan, tossing my head back.

"You need to get your nipple pierced for me," I tell him suddenly, sitting up so quick I almost give myself whiplash.

"Excuse me?"

"I said what I said. You're my only hope. I need you to get your nipple pierced."

"You know those guys see my nipples every day, right?"

"You can take it out right after."

"No." He shakes his head, crossing his arms over his chest.

"Yes, you have to. Please?" I sit forward, tucking my arms between my legs as I bat my lashes at him.

"That's not going to work on me."

"I'll do just about anything."

"No."

"Owen please."

I can see his resolve starting to break as he looks me up and down. When he pinches the bridge of his nose, I know I got him.

19

OWEN

The day has come. I've made a stupid decision for a woman.

I honestly thought the day would come sooner, if we're all being honest.

"I can't believe I'm doing this for you," I grit as the piercer places small dots on both sides of my nipple, the marker freezing.

"They're not wanting to come out, that's for sure," the woman says. "Are you okay if I blow on them?"

"Excuse me?"

"They should be hard. Is it okay if I blow on them."

My jaw hangs.

"Listen sir, I need your consent. Just trying to give you what you want."

"Fine." I tell her, my eyes shutting hard.

I feel a breeze on my nipple, and it hardens after a couple of minutes.

"I'm just going to flick it once or twice, okay?" she says.

I nod, groaning.

"It's almost over Owen!" Isla cheers from beside me.

I open one eye, scowling at her. "This is your fault."

Her smile falters, but she keeps it up. "And I will owe you forever for it."

"I'll be taking you up on that."

Finally happy with how my nipple looks, the woman gets her piercing kit ready. I shut my eyes tight again, ready for the pain.

"This is going to hurt for a second, but it'll be fine after," the woman says, as she presses the needle to me. I take a deep breath…

And the worst pain I've ever felt rips through me before it quickly dissipates.

That really was fast.

I look down, watching as she screws the small silver ball onto the other side of the bar.

"See? Not bad!" she admires her work.

Isla is quickly in front of me, her camera out. "Okay, now we just need a photo."

The woman looks between us, confusion clear in her eyes as Isla snaps a couple photographs from different angles.

"Why do you need so many photos?" I ask her.

"I don't know, why not?"

Hmm.

Finally, she turns to the woman. "Okay. Now can you take it out?"

Her brows furrow even more as she looks at me. "I'm sorry," I tell her.

"We'll pay for two nipples," Isla assures her.

"Two full nipples," I say as I hold up two fingers, my vision starting to get a little hazy. Isla notices, snapping her fingers in front of my eyes.

"Why did you get it done in the first place?" the woman asks.

"We were contractually obligated to for a," Isla pauses, her eyes shooting up as she thinks of a good excuse. "a thing," she says, unable to come up with anything.

"Yeah, we just had to get a photo of it."

"You got your whole nipple pierced just for a photo? You know there's fake piercings out there, right?"

We freeze, my eyes slowly, very slowly, making their way to Isla, who's looking anywhere but me. "I actually didn't know about that at all," she says, fidgeting.

"Yeah," the woman nods, her lips thin.

"Hmm." Isla doesn't meet my eyes, but instead looks at my nipple. A second later, her eyes lazily move up to finally find mine.

"I *do* think it's cute." She cocks her head to the side, examining it.

I'm a big man, and I'm not sure how a nipple piercing could possibly look on me.

Isla brings her phone up to her face once more, and I can see her taking another photo of me from further away.

"Okay, well if you're still paying for it I'll take it out," the woman says, hovering over me once more. "It may hurt a bit coming out though. And you're still going to have to make sure it closes up well. Though it won't take long."

I nod, holding my breath as she undoes the ball, sliding the piercing out.

"Is it done?" I ask, opening one eye. Isla grins, holding two thumbs up. I scowl at her.

"You ready to check out?" the piercer asks.

Instead of saying yes right away, Isla looks at me for a moment before turning her attention back to the woman. "I think I actually want to get mine pierced. For real. I'll pay for four nipples."

I feel the blood rush from my brain.

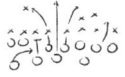

"Are you telling me that you made me get my precious nipples pierced for no reason?" I ask her as we drive back to her place.

"No, I still wasn't about to send a photo of my boobs to my *brother,* Owen."

I roll my eyes. "But you acted like the thought of even doing that was horrible."

She shakes her head. "No I didn't. The thought is okay. I'm fine with getting them done. In fact, I've wanted to for a long time now. They're cute. The perfect accessory to any outfit, really. But I still wasn't about to send a photo of them to my brother. And then from my brother to a group chat of ten other men."

Okay, she has a point, no matter how much I don't want to see it.

"Fine." I say, not as annoyed as I should be.

Damn her.

"Listen. I know that was a little traumatizing, and I really appreciate you helping me. I owe you one, Crosby."

"Yeah, you do."

Isla took her piercings like a champ. Not that I saw it go down. I'm not sure I could watch, but I wasn't about to make her feel uncomfortable watching her get topless in the middle of the tattoo and piercing shop.

So, like a gentleman, I went to the front of the store, watching as she and the piercer talked about aftercare.

Only a few moments later, Isla was swiping her card to pay for *four nipples,* and we were leaving.

She rubs her chest a little, putting pressure on it.

"You doing okay?"

"Yeah. I just need a more supportive bra. Deborah said that it'll be more comfortable if they're held up, you know?"

I don't know. I don't pretend to know. I don't need to know.

Or do I?

"Okay," I say, coughing.

"How is your nipple doing? He was a trooper."

My head whips over to her before looking back at the road. "Please don't talk about my nipples like they're their own person."

"Why not?"

"Because they're nipples, Isla."

She rolls her eyes, sinking in my passenger seat.

And I can't help but find it cute. God, I can't stand that I think it's cute. Why?

"Whatever," she says, flicking her hand over to me.

This woman is going to be the death of me. But she's been opening up to me over the last two weeks. This is as carefree and happy as I've seen her, and it makes me smile. I've adored her from afar, but Isla when she's comfortable with you? How can you not fall for her.

Fall for her? I shake my head. There is no falling yet. There's very strong like, which I'm not even letting her know. But there is no *falling*.

Get your shit together, Crosby.

"Do you want to get your second punishment done and over with when we get to your place?" I ask her.

She nods, fiddling with her phone. "May as well get them done and over with."

I nod. "Alright. I brought the pepper."

"What kind is it?" she turns to me, her eyes wide as she tucks her phone between her thighs, done with whatever she was doing.

"Habanero."

She snorts.

"What?"

"That's nothing. Give it to me. I'm ready."

I'm confused. "It's nothing?"

"Yep. I love them. I've had a whole one before. I got this."

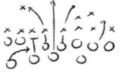

She did in fact have it.

In one swift move, Isla eats the entire hot pepper. Sure, it's clearly spicy to her. She definitely chugs a whole glass of milk. But it's not as bad as I thought it would be.

I was actually going to tell her she only had to take a small bite, but she had other plans. Before I cold tell her, the entire pepper was in her mouth.

I'm not going to say that watching the whole thing *wasn't* one of the hottest things I've ever witnessed. And I was just with her when she got her nipples pierced.

She took it like a champ.

She stands in front of me, finishing off her glass of milk in just a pair of shorts and a tight sports bra she threw on after we got back, sticking her tongue out to show me that the pepper is gone.

Before I can stop myself, the words are out. "God I wish you were on your knees doing that."

Her cheeks immediately pinken, but she doesn't move. Instead, a smirk plays at her lips as she watches me from under her lashes. "Yeah?"

I wipe my face with my hands. "I shouldn't have said that." I check my watch. "I should probably get going."

"You know you can joke with me, right?" she says, crossing her arms over her chest. I refrain from watching as her chest is pushed up in her bra.

"Yeah of course," I say, but she cuts me off before I can say anything else.

"I'm not made of glass, and I'm not Leo's innocent little sister. You can joke with me however much you want."

I nod, looking at my shoes. It's not that I see her as innocent, or just as Leo's little sister. I want to tell her that's so far from how I see her. But if I make a move there's no going back for me.

I know myself. It's why I haven't hooked up with anyone in years. Since my last relationship, to be exact.

The girl in front of me has been actively in my life for the last three weeks, and yet she's taken over my whole brain. I don't want to think about how I'll think when—if—anything ever happens between us.

And I have no idea what to do about any of it.

WEEK FOUR

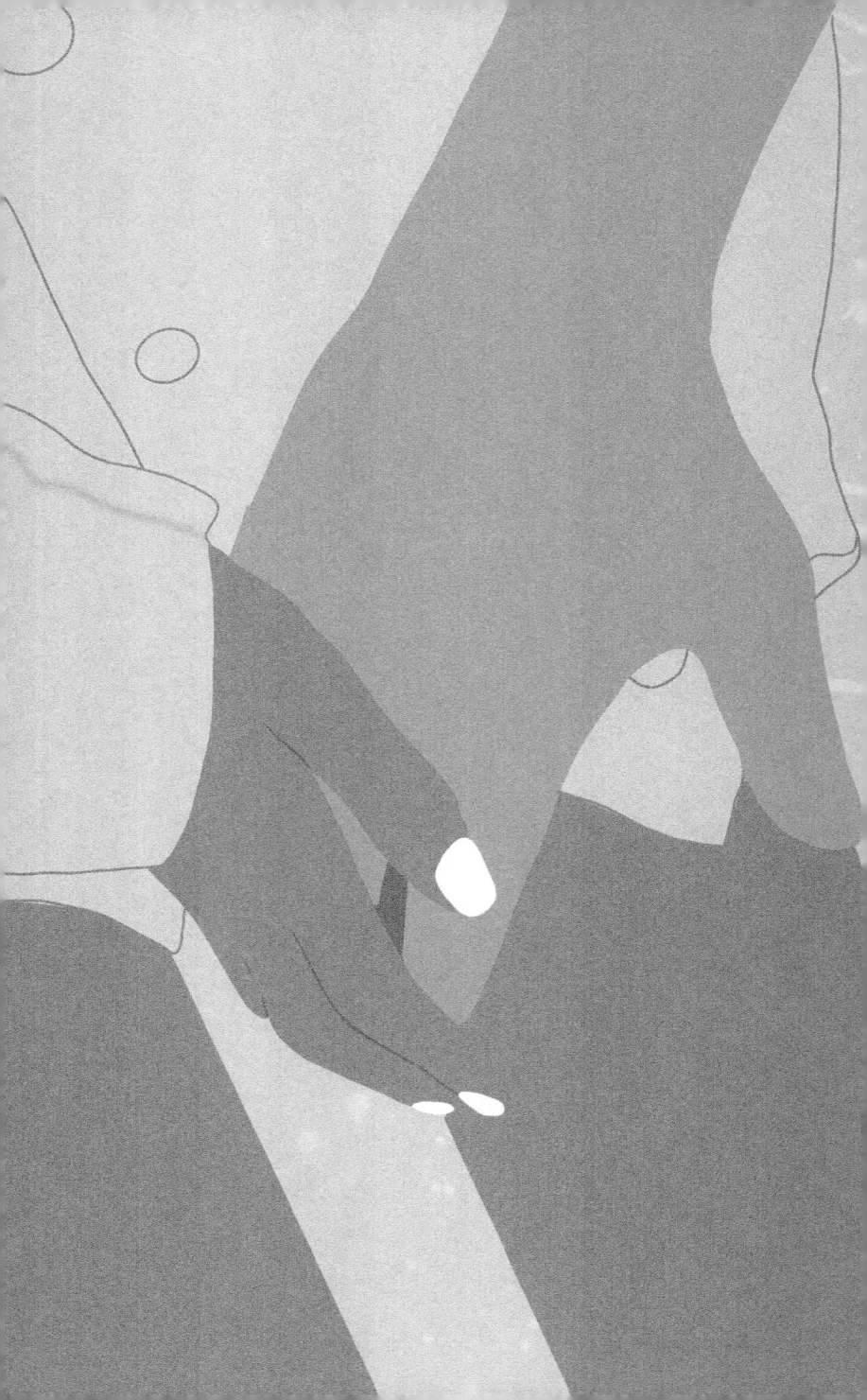

20
ISLA

"You know how to play the guitar?"

I nod, bringing the guitar to my lap. "Of course I do."

"I could never learn," Owen says, watching as I strum a few notes.

I shake my head at him. "It's easier than it looks. I think you could. You could definitely play Wonderwall."

"Is it easy?"

I chuckle.

"It's one of the easiest songs to play. There's that joke that men will bring a girl home and just play her Wonderwall. It's like the first thing that a lot of them learn to play and they're always so proud of themselves but it's so funny."

Owen looks at me skeptically. "How easy?"

I shoot him a look. "Very. And I'll teach you."

I hand him my guitar and watch him fumble with it, not sure how to hold it. I help him, positioning it on his lap as I place his hands where they need to go.

"It's only six chords," I tell him, and realizing he should probably see it before trying it for himself, I grab it back.

I strum the beginning, tapping my foot in time as I

encourage him to do the same thing. He awkwardly does, nodding his head in time with me. I go on a little longer, making sure he watches my fingers.

And I start singing.

When the first verse is up, I hand the guitar back to him.

"How are you good at everything?" he asks, and my cheeks heat up.

"I can assure you I'm not," I tell him with a smile. "But I was always an artsy kid. I went to college for art at Towson. Took some music classes. I had already learned guitar and piano as a kid."

"I think you're impressive," he says, strumming a little tune that's definitely not Wonderwall. Or anything, for that matter.

"And I think you're impressive. In fact, the entire country thinks you're impressive," I fire back.

"There's certainly some haters," he says, watching his fingers as he fools around with the strings.

"There's always going to be haters. But we're passionate people, and passionate people get really good at what they love to do. I love art and music. You love football and fitness."

"I like other things too," he nods.

"Oh? Do tell."

His cheeks flush. "Well, I love fitness and football of course, but I have other hobbies I'm passionate about."

He stops, and I raise an eyebrow when he looks at me, encouraging him to go on.

"I love cooking. I'll cook at home any day rather than eat out. I actually hate my diet during the season because it's often too simple for most meals. I can still cook a healthy meal, but that's not what we're told to eat a lot of the time."

"I'm sorry."

He shrugs. "I still do it of course. But yeah. I love cooking. I've taken a bunch of classes."

"Maybe you'll have to cook for me." I feel bold, but the

words are out of my mouth before I can consider them. His dark eyes snap to mine, a boyish grin spreading across his face.

"Peaches, are you asking me out?"

"I'm saying I want to see what else those hands do," I shoot back. It's only when I see his neck grow red that I realize the other meaning behind that.

"I meant like, cooking. Not, not that."

He nods, clearly not believing me. "Yeah, I'm sure that's not what you meant."

"It isn't!"

"Whatever."

Owen starts nodding as I did, and when he gets a chord right, he looks at me expectantly. I nod, encouraging him to go on.

After about thirty minutes, I think he's got it.

I clap my hands together, placing them around my knee. "Okay now, here's where the punishment comes in."

His head whips up as he stares at me.

"You're going to film yourself playing Wonderwall and you're going to post it to the internet."

"Isla that's evil."

"It's funny as hell."

He scowls at me, the muscle in his bicep bulging as he shifts the guitar. "I'm not even playing it well!"

"Owen, you're Owen Crosby. You post that to the internet you're going to get more DMs than you know what to do with from a million different women."

The thought makes me want to vomit, but I'm not going to say that.

He shakes his head. "I don't want a million women messaging me."

"Well then it'll just be funny."

He groans, looking around. "Let's get this over with. Where can I go to do this?"

I point to an empty white wall across the room. I already prepared for this, even getting out my super old guitar so it looks generic enough that Leo won't question it.

Owen sits on the floor, his legs crossed as he strums the chords a couple of times again, messing up a few before getting the hang of it once more.

I prop his phone up, hitting the record button.

And he does it. He sings the song.

He closes his eyes in the beginning, focusing a little too hard on what his fingers are doing instead of just feeling it. But after the first verse he opens them, his eyes piercing mine as he smiles.

I can't help but smile back.

I stop him halfway through, telling him he's good. I end the video, handing his phone back to him. "Now you just have to post that to youtube," I tell him.

"And then I'll be done for this week?"

I nod.

Owen and I curl up on my couch watching the comments roll in on his latest youtube video. Turns out, he used to post some cooking videos, but stopped about a year ago. He says it was for no reason in particular, but I feel like there was a reason.

He got a lot of hate for it. The better you get at football, the more hate you get. From opposing teams, from your own team. Everyone feels entitled to tell you their opinion of your playing, whether you're doing well or not.

Being on the internet can suck for athletes, and posting content that isn't football related is just welcoming rude comments.

But we're here, snug against each other on my couch, watching all the positive comments roll in.

If he was horrible, I would have told him to forget it. I wouldn't have done that to him. But he was actually pretty good, and four-hundred people already think the same.

"That was fun," I tell him, yawning. "You know, that band is my roman empire I think."

"Roman empire?" he asks, confusion clouding his eyes.

"Yeah. Like, something you can't stop thinking about. Like, how many times do you think about the roman empire?"

He thinks for a second. "Like never."

I nod. "Well apparently most men think about it daily. But I'm pretty sure most men are also liars. So thank you for the honestly, sir." He smirks, and I keep going. "I just mean that I think about that band constantly."

"Why are you constantly thinking about Oasis?"

I'm shocked. "Why wouldn't you think about Oasis all the time? Don't you know what happened to them?"

"No?"

"Exactly. No one knows what happened to them. They split up after some argument in the late 2000s. The brothers hated each other."

"Why would you be in a band if you hate the other person."

"I have no idea. But the Gallagher brothers are genuinely my Roman empire. Liam, the singer, and his brother Noel who played guitar for the band had been feuding for years. At their last concert, I think it was in Paris? I'm not sure, don't quote me on that, they got into a massive fight and they broke up."

"That's insane," Owen says, and I'm not sure if he's actually interested or just pretending to keep me happy. "That was years ago, right?"

I nod. "It was, but the feud is still going, Owen. Still. As in, just this year Liam has been saying he wants a reunion. But want to know something? His brother just befriended some guy that said something horrible about Liam. The guy is a comedian I think. It's insane. I desperately want to know what went down that day."

Owen chuckles, wiggling in closer to me. "Okay I'll admit that *is* interesting. I'd be curious too."

We settle into a comfortable silence before his arm brushes mine, his finger absentmindedly resting on my thigh. His thumb starts rubbing circles on my skin, and for a moment, I forget to breathe.

And I miss what he says.

"What?" I shake the fog off.

"Do you have any other Roman empire things?"

I think for a moment, realizing that I actually have a lot.

"Yeah. You know Edgar Degas?" I ask. He nods. "Okay, you know his Little Dancer statue?"

I watch him as he tries to recall it before I just pull it up on my phone, showing him. "Oh yeah, I've seen that around before I think."

"Well, long story short that's actually a cast of the original. Degas and a couple of other artists were actually viewed as insane by the art community for a long time. There was this huge shift in the art world in the late eighteen hundreds. Mostly in Paris."

"I feel like that makes sense."

"So there were these painters who wanted to embrace more modern forms of art, but then the others wouldn't consider that art. At the time most artists only really respected sculptures made in marble, and Degas created her out of beeswax and just, well, things he found around his home. Her hair was human hair. No, I don't know where he found *that.* But anyways, he got so much hate for it that he ended up keeping it in a closet for years upon years. It was his first and last sculpture to be shown to the public.

"But the guy ended up having a studio with impressionist legend and overall badass Mary Cassatt—one of my heroes—and was asked by a guy if he could buy it. Even though he had it in a closet he refused to part with it. When he died his family decided to get it casted in bronze. A lot of other sculptures were found, too. He just never showed them publicly. They're gorgeous.

"But anyways, back to the Roman Empire part of this, right. The skirts change! They replace it every once in awhile to update it, which I personally think is beautiful. They could keep it how it was, or they could update it every couple decades to update it. To modernize it a bit, almost. I think that's beautiful and so true to him, you know?"

I've been rambling for far too long, but whereas most people tell me to shut up or get to the point by now, Owen has been watching me intently, actively listening. No phone in sight, not looking elsewhere. Watching me with fascination. Even if he doesn't personally fine it that interesting, he's interested in it because I'm talking about it.

My chest tightens when I look into his beautiful brown eyes, and I can't help but melt.

"I never thought about art that way," he says, his lips quirking up. "But I'd like to know more sometime."

I return the smile. "I promise you I can talk about art all day. I was really inspired by the impressionist movement and use a lot of what I learned about those artists in my own art. But those artists are as badass as they come, let me tell you. Well, there's been more intense art movement of course, but the impressionist movement really made waves in Paris, which was huge. My favorite artist, Jean Clemment, he does some of the most beautiful art I've ever seen."

"Is he alive?" Owen asks.

"Yeah, he's only about ten years older than me."

He nods.

"Do you have any Roman Empire facts?"

He thinks for a minute. "I'm not sure. I think about a lot of things often but not that frequently. I used to be super into the Egyptian Gods actually. I still think about them pretty often."

"Oh yeah? Which one is your favorite?"

"I feel like Anubis is pretty cool."

"That's such a dude answer."

"It's true! He's deeper than what people think." Owen places his hand on his chest.

"Yeah, sure." I smile.

"He is!"

"Anything else?"

"You."

21

OWEN

Why did I say that?

Isla barely flinched, but she also didn't lean into it. I'm not sure what I was expecting her to do though, so it's not her fault.

That woman has more passion and love in her pinky finger than anyone I know, and it's fascinating to watch. It's remarkable to watch her speak about the things she loves.

I want her to talk about me that way, too.

If she were mine, she's all I'd be able to talk about.

We talked for about half an hour more before I snuck out of her place, careful not to make too much noise before heading down the street to the garage I keep my car in.

For the first time since we started talking, I check my phone.

And realize I have about a million messages.

"When did you start playing guitar?"

"Dude that's so weird. Just say you need to get laid. I got you."

"I need you to tell me if you're about to spiral out of control. You feeling okay?"

"Hey, I'm not saying you need it, but let's say, well, let's say you may need to get some help? I know a good therapist I swear."

Well, that video spread quickly.

But I don't even care.

The second I get into my car I hit my head on the back of the seat. I'm so incredibly screwed. More screwed than I've ever been in my life. Royally, terribly screwed.

I like Isla way more than I've ever been able to admit, and I really have to up my game.

WEEK FIVE

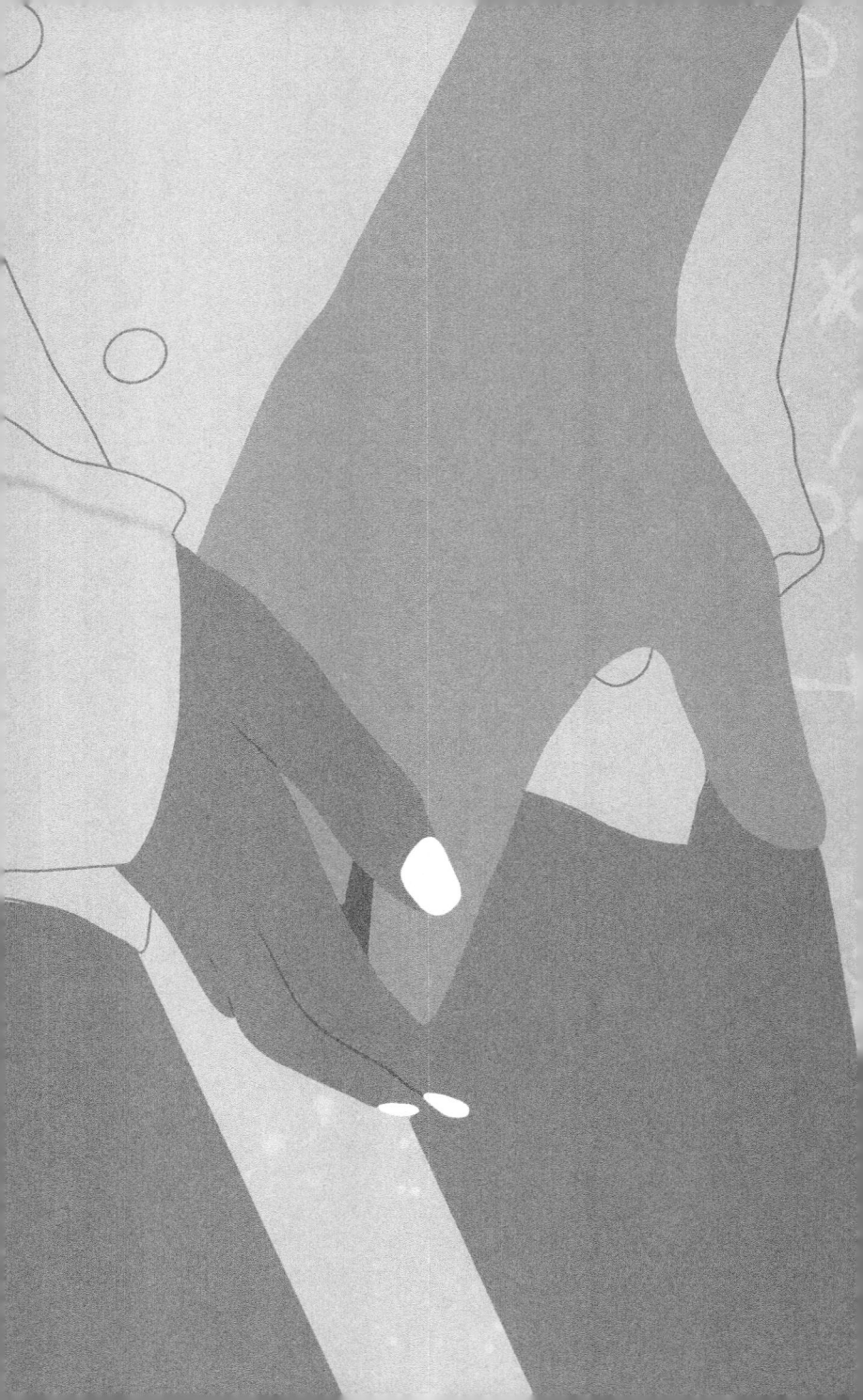

22

ISLA

It's the end of week five, and I'm kicking ass.

Okay, maybe I didn't that one week. But every other week? I've been on point, at the top of the league with only Owen next to me.

I've avoided embarrassing punishments while also winning against Owen most weeks, picking out most of his punishments.

If I wasn't super aware of his competitiveness, I'd almost think that he was letting me win. But I know he's trying to crush me.

> **OWEN CROSBY**
> What's it going to be this time, Peaches?

I smile at the text. The Monday night game just ended, and his player wasn't good enough to surpass my numbers.

> I think I want you to take me apple picking.

> Out in public?

I didn't think about that.

It's not as simple as just going to another state. I sometimes forget that Owen is famous, too. We've gotten lucky when interacting with people thus far. The piercer had no idea who he was, and there hasn't been any news in the media since, so I think we're good.

Still, we've been living dangerously, and unfortunately the thrill is exciting.

> We can wear disguises.

I think that's easier for you

> A baseball cap and sunglasses, my guy.

Can I wear a fake mustache, too?

> Please for the love of everything wear a fake mustache.

The things I would do to see that man with a real one, phew.

Only for you.

"This mustache is itchy," Owen says, scratching the side of his nose.

"You don't have to wear it for hours, just enough time for us to pick apples."

"I really hope we don't bump into anyone we know here," he mutters as he turns into the apple orchard.

It's a little late in the season, so a lot of the good apples are probably gone, but either way, they're apples and they're yummy.

And most importantly, I get to watch Owen reach up and

grab apples for me the entire time. A drool-worthy sight I wouldn't miss for the world.

I make a mental note in my mind: *Make Owen reach high things more often.*

Oh, I'm sorry Owen, I have no idea why the peanut butter is on the top shelf of my cabinet that I can't reach. Crazy how that happened. Can you get it for me?

And men love being useful, so he won't even know it's because I've become a little thirsty over him.

A little too thirsty, if I do say so myself.

I've never opened up to anyone the way I have with him. Not since my friends years ago. I normally stick to myself, choosing to stay home and paint all day and night. Opening up to someone new has been hard for me, and it hasn't happened until now.

And I feel like that little piece of myself that I lost years ago, that smiley, happy girl I left in the past for no reason other than needing to grow up, is back.

She's giddy. She jokes. She feels good about herself. She's confident.

I haven't seen this side of myself in years, and that counts for something, right?

Getting out, Owen pulls a hat over my head. Although I'm not as recognizable as he is, I don't want to risk anyone recognizing me from Leo's Instagram. It's a long shot, but it's happened before.

It's always weirdest when it's grown men who decide to ask about my brother's performance.

"Let's go, Peaches."

I tell myself I don't like the nickname, but I think I'm also lying.

I think I love it deep down.

I get out after him, and when he grabs my hand to pull me along, my heart skips a beat.

We get to the main stand and he pulls out a fifty dollar

bill, handing it to the woman in exchange for a bag. She goes to hand him back some change but she shakes his head, telling her to keep it.

She points us toward the best apples they still have, and we're off.

"I'm sorry there's not that many anymore," he says looking around. "I should have thought about this sooner."

"It's fine, I should have thought about it too."

We go around and pick a bunch, but at one point, they're way too high for me to grab.

"Can you help?" I ask innocently, hoping he'll step up and grab them so I can watch.

But instead of doing that, he dips down, lifting me easily on his shoulders. I let out a small scream as I try to gain balance—I'm not a short woman by any means—and he grabs my hips, keeping me stable.

"Can you get them now?" he asks, and although I can't see it, I can tell he's smiling.

"I think so?" I say, reaching up. His hands tighten around me as I go.

"You got this," he encourages me. I grab a couple, tossing them into our bag on the ground.

"Everything looks so tiny from up here," I tell him. "It's crazy."

"It's definitely nice being tall."

"I mean I'm tall too."

"You're tall for a woman, sure."

I tap his head once, chuckling.

Keeping me on his shoulders, Owen dips down and grabs our bag of apples, slowly moving us to another tree.

"Have you carved pumpkins before?" I ask him as I eye the patch across from us.

"I don't think so actually," he says, placing the bag of apples in the trunk of his car.

"Do you want to?"

He looks me over, almost unsure of the answer before grabbing my hand once more, pulling me to the patch. He takes out another fifty, handing it to another worker, still refusing the change.

"Now let's find the biggest fucker here, shall we?" I ask, rubbing my hands together.

He laughs, helping me as we go from pumpkin to pumpkin, from row to row trying to find two of the most perfect pumpkins we can find.

Across the way a small child points to one, and his mother tells him they can't carry it, it's far too large.

I can tell that Owen really wants to help by the way I see him listening, glancing over at them every couple of seconds. But in the spirit of not being caught, we decided that we need to keep to ourselves this whole time.

And for good reason, considering his mustache is peeling off.

"Psst," I hiss at him, trying hard to get his attention without getting other attention. "Mission Possible!"

He shoots me a weird look. "What?"

"I don't want to stay your real name and I don't have a nickname for you. Figured your fantasy team name would suffice."

He doesn't look convinced.

"Anyways, your mustache is coming off. You can't go help them."

He sighs, knowing I'm right. I want more than anything to watch Owen carry a giant pumpkin for a small child, but I also know that if anyone thinks it's him it'll probably be all over the local news and Leo will skin us alive.

When the family leaves, Owen goes over to it. "It's perfect," he tells me when I meet him there.

And it is. It's ginormous. Perfect for a giant man. "Okay, we'll get that one, and then I found another over there. I'll pick that one."

And just like that, we have a car full of apples and squash.

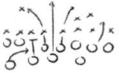

"What are you carving?" Owen asks as he puts the apple crumble in the oven.

The second we got back to the car, the fake mustache and hat were off. "That feels so much better," he breathes as he runs his fingers through his light brown hair.

"You don't like hats?"

He shakes his head. "I'm fine with hats usually, I just take them off every once in a while. We wear helmets for hours at a time, and sometimes even baseball hats feel suffocating.

It makes sense.

The ride home was silent but nice. A peaceful silence.

Owen dropped me off at the door to my building and I grabbed the apples, lugging them all the way to my place. Since he parked down the street, Owen wasn't sure what to do with the pumpkins, opting to only bring one to my place, considering he took the back stairway to make sure he doesn't bump into Leo.

He immediately went to work on some apple crisp, asking me where a couple of important tools were.

Watching him so at home in my kitchen makes something deep inside of me stir.

"I'm actually not quite sure," I respond, looking at the pumpkin in front of me.

I started trying to carve a generic cat, but I'm not quite

sure what it is anymore.

"It kind of looks like the Cobras logo," he says, coming up behind me and pointing. It does, actually.

"Maybe I'll do that," I say, getting back to work.

About forty minutes later, I'm done. It's as good as it's going to get.

My art skills don't exactly translate to pumpkin carving.

"That smells so amazing," I say, taking a deep breath in, the smell of cinnamon and spice filling my kitchen.

"It's almost done," he says, checking it.

A minute later, it's out cooling on my stovetop.

Pushing away from the counter, I hop down from my stool and round the island, reaching for a plate, but Owen has the same idea, coming up behind me, his chest right up against mine.

"I can get them," he says quietly, grabbing two before closing the cabinet. He puts them on the counter but doesn't back away.

I try to turn, and he gives me some room to do so before moving closer again.

"You okay?" he asks, a smile playing at the corner of his lips.

"Why wouldn't I be?" I ask, unable to look away from his lips, just mere inches from mine.

"You seem a little frazzled."

I take a second to collect my thoughts. "I don't know what this is."

"What do you want it to be?" His hands rest above me on the cabinet, his face moving back, and I miss the proximity.

His dark eyes watch me with curiosity.

"I want this to be real," I murmur, peeling my eyes from his lips to meet his eyes. "I don't want to hurt Leo, but I want this to be something."

I can feel Owen's breath on my cheek, and I close my eyes, letting him wash over me. Or maybe I just don't want to look into his eyes anymore. Don't want to analyze. Don't want to ask myself questions.

"I want this to be real too," he responds, moving away. My body turns cold as I realize how much I miss his warmth.

"Then what do we do?"

He grabs the plates, digging into the apple crisp.

"We keep doing what we've been doing."

It feels like ice water was dumped over my head, disappointment swirling in my stomach.

"And not because I don't want something more. God, I want something more," he puts the spoon down, turning to me. "But we both respect your brother. I'm fine with him hating me. I'm fine with him punching me in the face, even. I'm fine with it as long as we make this work, Isla."

"I want it to work," I whisper.

"I do too Peaches," he reaches for me, pulling me into a hug. I feel his lips on the top of my head, and I sink into the feeling, wishing it would swallow me whole.

"I want to make sure that we're both serious about this before we jump into it, okay? It'll all be worth it. Every single argument your brother and I will have. Everything he'll send my way. But I just," he sighs into me. "We need to make sure that we're not jumping into something neither of us can sustain. This needs to be for the long-haul, okay?"

I shake my head, understanding despite desperately not wanting to.

Leo is sensitive. No matter how much he likes to pretend he's not, he is. And he's always been protective of me. He doesn't want anyone to hurt me.

If Owen and I started seeing each other and it ended badly? It would ruin him. And we both know he would be loyal to me over Owen, no matter how professional my brother would act on the field.

But I can't help but wonder when our breaking point will be.

WEEK SIX

23

OWEN

The Baltimore Cobras haven't had a bad week since that one away game, I'm winning in our fantasy league, and Isla Warner texts me every single morning to say she hopes I have a good day.

Things are better than good, they're great. Truly.

And this week, I finally beat her.

I'm making her dinner.

Quite the punishment.

I go to the store to get all of the ingredients I need and a bottle of wine, lugging them up the back steps to her place.

Leo and I have been hanging out a little more this week, and he's still suspicious about why I haven't been around as much. Cooper and Emmett too.

But I still don't think they suspect this, and the longer the realization can be put off, the better.

I text her before I come out into her hall, and she's waiting for me with the door open, a smile on her beautiful face.

"Oh I love that wine," she tells me as she takes it from my hands, grabbing her wine opener.

"I hoped you did."

"I'm so excited to see what you have up your sleeves."

I smile, unpacking my bag. The sun set about an hour ago, the days getting shorter and shorter. The bay out the window looks beautiful as the moon cast an angelic glow.

Isla went all out tonight at her place. The light is low, candles lit around the large room. If I didn't know any better, I'd think she's challenging me. Trying to test how good I can be.

There's nothing I want more than to kiss her right here, right now.

Isla lifts her hair up into a ponytail, and my eyes immediately zero in on her chest. She's gone braless, her pert nipples poking through her thin shirt, the balls of the bars through them making my mouth dry.

Fuck.

"Isla Warner, are you trying to seduce me?" I ask simply, smirking as I pull a couple onions from my shopping bag.

Her eyes widen, her mouth hanging open. The things I could do to that mouth—

"I would do no such thing." She shakes her head, her hair already coming loose.

I look around the room again, raising an eyebrow at her as my eyes drop once again to her chest.

"But it sounds like that's all you can think about." The minx smirks at me, leaning back in her seat, her shirt tightening across her even more.

"I think it's a reasonable thought," I reply, going back to making dinner.

"If it happened I don't think I'd be upset," she says quietly, examining her paint-splattered nails.

"How much wine have you had before I got here?"

"None."

"Are you lying to me?"

"I would never ever lie to you, Crosby." She looks up at me from under her lashes, a seductive smile spreading across her lips.

"I don't believe you."

"You don't have to."

She takes a slow sip from her wine glass, her eyes on me the entire time.

I can feel myself harden, straining against my pants, and I press myself against the counter to hide it. I don't need her to use that as ammunition right now, no matter how much I may want her to.

To distract her, I ask her about her day.

"It was okay," he says, taking another lazy sip. "I got one piece done finally, and another is making good progress."

"When is your show?"

"Three weeks."

"It's coming up fast."

She nods, twirling her glass in her hand.

"I'm ready for this one to be over though. I've only done a couple, but for some reason I feel so much pressure about this one. I feel like it could be my moment. Like I can finally make a name for myself, you know?"

"Of course," I say, starting to cut up everything I need.

She settles, slouching against the counter.

"How has your week been?"

I shrug, watching her as I chop a pepper. "It was okay. We've been working on a lot going into this next week. We think we really have the pieces we've needed to make a Superbowl run. It's too early, of course, but we're on our way. They've been more intense about studying tapes and making sure we're ready."

"Tennessee is a good team, too. You guys ready for it?"

"I think so. Coaches seem to think so too."

"That's good."

"Yeah."

She shifts in her seat, her eyes following the movements of my knife before drifting up over my chest and arms. I smile, trying to get a peek at her while also not chopping my finger off.

"How do you do that?" she murmurs, watching my hands.

"With a lot of practice." I've taken a lot of knife skill classes in the past couple of years after I accidentally chopped the tip of my finger off when I was a teenager. I said that as soon as I could pay for them, I'd learn how to cook for real. Not just random recipes I thought of off the top of my head or found online.

Not that there's anything bad about those. I still make my own recipes sometimes.

But there's something about knowing how to cook and how to do it confidently, which includes how to use a knife.

I grab the onion I brought from the counter, placing it on the cutting board before cutting it in half, peeling the outside layer off. From there, I curl my fingers as I hold onto the top, bringing the knife down in even, fast strokes.

Isla shifts again, taking a slow sip of wine before her eyes drift over my arms, making their way to my face.

"You okay?" I ask, smirking.

"I just never considered that to be hot before. But it is."

Her cheeks are pink, her eyes wide and innocent. "What's hot about it pretty girl?"

The name just flusters her more as she leans in to watch even closer. "I'm not sure. Just something about a man being able to control a knife like that."

"Yeah?"

"Mhm." She takes a strand of her hair, wrapping it around her index finger watching me. "I don't know, just sets me on fire a little bit."

My smirk morphs into a grin, watching her get drunk off of wine while I cook for her. I want to do this for the rest of her life.

"It's the hands," she says finally, watching as I work on

the other half. "The way you control the knife and the onion. It's precision. Skill. You, Mr. Crosby, have excellent hands."

It's my turn to blush, but I can't deny that watching her get turned on by me doing something I love doesn't do something to me, too.

"Hands are a weird thing to be attracted to, aren't they?"

"I mean they aren't the only thing I'm attracted to." Her voice is breathy now, taking everything in.

"What else then?" I push.

"I think your butt is pretty great if I do say so myself. And your face isn't too bad either. And your thighs, I'm a bit of a thigh girl."

She presses her chest into the counter, leaning in more as she becomes visibly more and more flustered, her teeth peeking out to bite her lower lip as she looks up at me from under her lashes.

And I want to just take her right here.

Fuck Leo. Fuck our expectations. Screw taking things easy and slow. This? Yeah, I want this for the rest of my God damn life.

A sniffle interrupts my thoughts, and I quickly look back at her.

"Are you, are you *crying*?"

"No," she says, sitting back in her seat and wiping her eyes.

"Open your eyes, Peaches."

I can tell she doesn't want to, but eventually she does what she's told. I reach across the island, grabbing her chin between my fingers and bringing her face closer. Her eyes are bloodshot and watery, her nose red from the alcohol. The freckles that dot her small nose stand out against her flushed skin.

"You okay?"

"Yeah," she sniffles. "I don't know. God that was so hot. Like, I'm so incredibly turned on, kind of hot."

I chuckle. "Then why are you tearing up?"

"Owen you're cutting onions."

"We've discussed."

"Do you seriously not tear up while cutting them?"

I look down, realizing what she's talking about. I've never had an issue with them personally, but I know my sister hates them.

Letting go of her, I hang back, scraping the onions into a bowl and covering them with the board. "And here I thought you were tearing up because of how hot and turned on you were getting."

"Honestly I was getting pretty emotional." Her voice is low as she wipes her eyes, her mascara smudging.

"Okay pretty girl, I'm going to start the actual meal while you tell me why you're going through a whole bottle of wine, alright?"

She nods, her eyes holding a guilt I can't quite place.

As I busy myself sautéing the onions and getting a big pot of water boiling, I give her some bread. She takes a chunk, smearing butter onto it before popping it in her mouth.

"I didn't give you that so you could make yourself busy. Spill it."

She sighs, shooting me a look before going back to fidgeting with her hair.

"I'm just stressed about this show. I'm stressed about life, and I'm stressed about us."

"There's a lot to stress about," I nod. I can be a serial stressor too; I know how it is.

"I just want this show to be over, I want Leo to not be as overbearing as he always is, and I want things to be figured out. I'm tired of stressing over what this is," she gestures between us, her eyes flashing to mine before looking back down at her hands.

I want to tell her not to stress, but I know that's a load of crap coming from me. I'm stressed about it too.

"If it makes you feel any better, I'm also having a hard time figuring it out."

She shakes her head, her waves cascading down her back. "That doesn't make me feel better. It makes me feel worse."

"I'm sorry."

She huffs, and within a second, her hand is around the wine bottle once more, pulling it toward her. I intercept it, carefully pulling it back to me. "Why don't we save this for when we actually eat?" I ask, setting it down.

While she's amusing me, I can tell I'm mildly irritating her.

She doesn't say anything, just sits back and watches me some more.

"Are you going to tell me why you're dressed the way you are?" I probe after a few too many minutes of silence.

"No."

"Why not?"

"I think it's obvious."

Finishing with the pasta, I turn back to her, leaning against the counter as I watch her glassy eyes widen. "You thought I would come here with the intention of making you dinner and eat you instead, pretty girl?"

Her face is instantly five shades of red deeper, her mouth opening as her breathing becomes a little more labored. "I never said that."

"You didn't have to." My eyes drift down to her chest again, the piercings like a giant invitation to look.

"I just like them."

"You like the thought of me pushing you back on this kitchen island more though, don't you? My head between your thighs—"

Her hips shimmy in place as she tries to get comfortable, her eyes looking anywhere but me as she licks her lower lip. "We're both adults, Owen. It's been weeks of this back and forth. This weird tension I can't figure out. Of course, I want you to fuck me," she says suddenly, her steely gaze meeting mine at last.

If I thought I was having trouble not getting hard before, I've failed now.

"I want that too," I say, shifting uncomfortably. "We just have to figure some things out."

She rolls her eyes, huffing as she props her head up on her fist. "Well then let's stuff our mouthes with pasta then, why don't we."

WEEK SEVEN

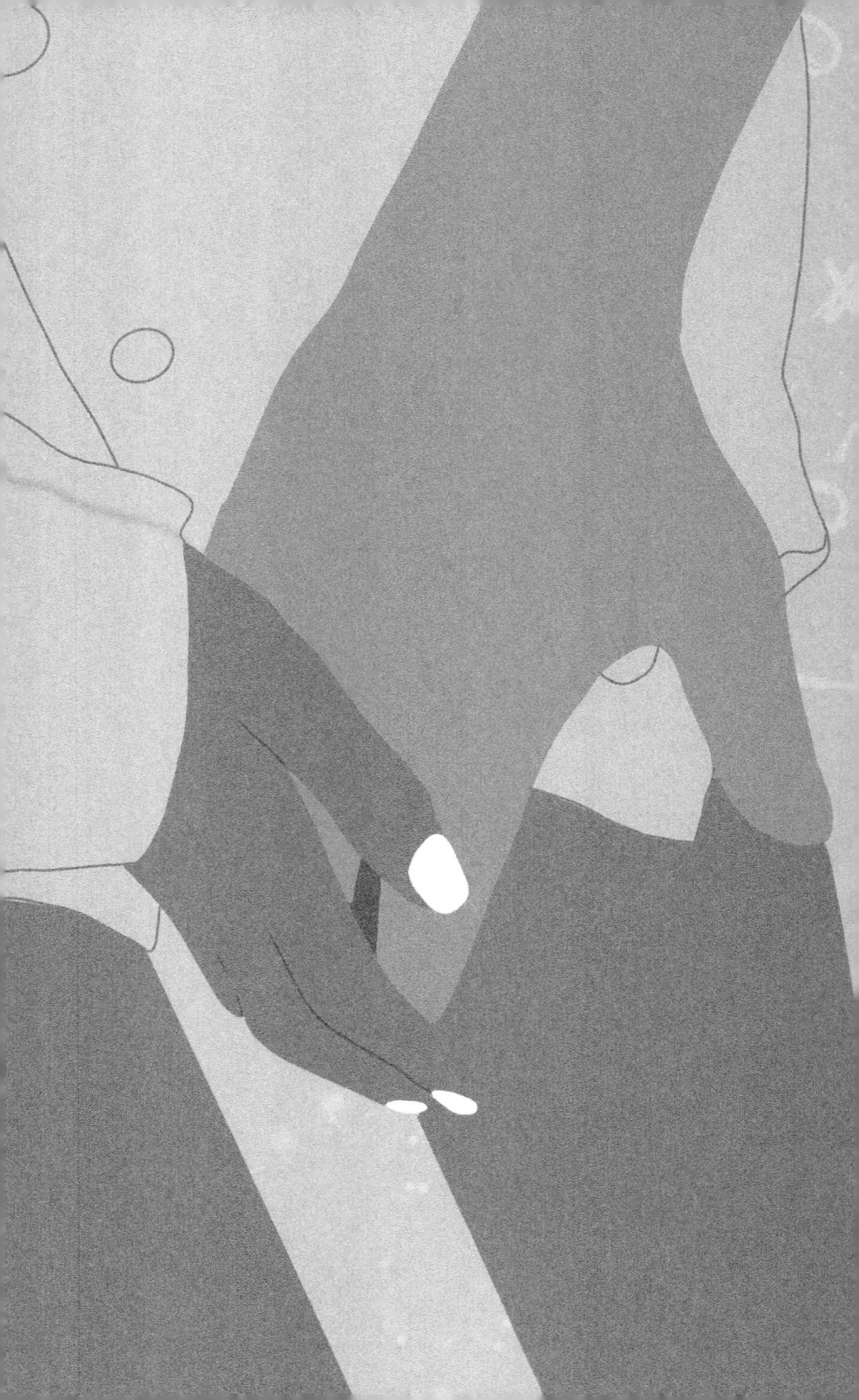

24
ISLA

Things have been weird between Owen and I ever since that last night we were together. He's been busy ever since, although we've been texting back and forth almost every day.

I really did want to see how far we could go that night, but he has better self-control than I do.

Watching his arms work as he cut those onions, the way his fingers curled as the knife chopped next to them; that control was something I can't possibly imagine having.

But now it's week seven of fantasy, which means it's week seven of the Cobras' season. So far they've only lost one game, and the fans are starting to get excited about the possibility of them going all the way this year. It's been a long time coming, and the hopeful, boisterous energy is palpable in the air as the whole stadium erupts in screams and cheers when the boys run out of the tunnel.

"This is so exciting!" Heidi yells as she looks around, her cheeks red in the chilly October air. She pulls her purple Cobras hat down over her ears a little more, taking in the crowd. It's her first Cobras game ever, though I'm not sure how. She's never been one for sports, but when I asked my three best friends if they'd come with me to this game, they all surprisingly agreed.

"You can go back in the box for a bit if you want, I think there's coffee in there," I tell her, pointing behind us. We're in our usual seats, but I opted to sit in one of the rows outside of the box today.

"I'm good, Mila will keep me warm, right?" She looks at our friend, also bundled up to the nines despite it being not *that* cold.

"Mhm, this is perfect." She shoots me a thumbs up, and something about the spark in her eye makes me think that it is not, in fact, perfect.

"Well if you guys need anything let me know."

"I think coming here is worth it just for the butts," Amara keeps her voice down low as if embarrassed to have said anything at all.

I nod, completely agreeing with her.

The Cobras win the coin toss, and the game officially starts.

Leo is doing well today. It's like he found his confidence again after that one bad game, making sure to never repeat it. He's only sacked once, although it looks like it hurt, and he doesn't throw any picks.

They're up by two touchdowns in the third quarter, but with five minutes to go, one of our corners gets injured, taking him out of the game.

"That looks like it hurt," Amara says.

It takes the wind out of our guys, and balls are starting to get dropped.

At the two-minute warning of the fourth quarter, the teams are tied.

The crowd comes alive, screaming as our defense breaks through, the visiting quarterback sacked at the fifty-yard line. The ball flies out of his hand, picked up by Emmett. He shoves past the other team's center before their tight end grabs his legs, sending him down.

The guy is like a bulldozer.

With only about a minute and thirty seconds left, I know they can do it.

"So they just need to get a touchdown here to win it, right?" Heidi says, her eyes round as saucers as she watches the field.

"Yeah, but they're probably going to run the clock down just a little. If they score right now, a minute twenty seconds or so is plenty of time for the other team to do something wild and tie it again."

She nods, bringing her thumb to her mouth and biting her nail as she leans forward, worried.

The guys take as long as they can, and when the clock flashes under a minute, Owen runs forward before turning to his left, catching a pass from Leo perfectly. He barely manages to dodge one of their safeties, but when he does, there's nothing but field in front of him.

With twenty seconds to spare, Owen jumps into the end zone, winning us a game.

"Does the other team really think they can do something in twenty seconds?" Heidi asks.

"Probably not, but it's worth a shot."

Her head tilts, the pom-pom of her hat shifting to the other side of her head. We watch as the other team snaps the ball, but they can't get a completion.

The clock quickly runs down, and we officially win the game.

Smiling, I hug my friends as we cheer, watching the guys high-five each other and the coaches.

The stadium fills with smoke as fireworks shoot up above and people start filing out.

"So we're still going out tonight, right?"

"Of course. When do we ever miss Halloween night."

"Never," Amara shakes her head.

"You guys are coming back to mine to get ready?"

"Always," Mila smiles.

"I can't believe you got your nipples pierced and you didn't tell us," Mila deadpans as she looks at me.

"Are they that noticeable?"

"You're in a skintight outfit of course they're visible."

"I put pasties on!"

"Well they're not working great," she responds.

"I think you look fine. It's hot," Amara assures me, slapping my back. She looks back into the mirror, putting her mouse ears on.

"Heidi what are you being, anyways?" I look her up and down. She wears pink stockings, the tiniest green shorts known to man, and a pink bodysuit.

She turns, her mascara wand in her hand as she shows off. "I'm Patrick Star, duh."

I blame my parents for not allowing me to watch it growing up.

"Ahh," I say, turning my attention to Mila. "Who's attention are you trying to get tonight?" My eyebrow raises as I take in her thigh-high boots, fishnets, and black leather bodysuit. A tail hangs from her lower back and she wears a black mask complete with cat ears.

"I'm not looking to impress anyone," she says matter-of-factly, examining her long red press-on nails she just put on. I'm willing to bet any amount of money they don't last the night. She's always ripped them off hours after.

"Don't even lie Mila," Amara says, rolling her eyes.

"I'm not lying, I'm just going to have fun," Mila snaps.

Not wanting to be caught in the middle of a cat fight, I help Heidi with the rest of her costume, careful not to get any makeup on mine. I may regret wearing this later.

When they're finally ready to go, we hop in a cab and we're at Lulu's in no time, watching as we drive past the line wrapped around the block.

"I wish Leo was here," Mila slumps in her seat, and quirk a brow at her.

"I don't want to fuck your brother, Isla don't worry. I just wish he could get us in. This line sucks."

"You should have brought a coat," Heidi says, holding up the hoodie she brought.

"It's Halloween, I'm not bringing a coat to a club on Halloween."

Heidi shrugs.

We get out, thanking the driver before getting in line. About twenty minutes later, Cooper walks by. Not that I recognized him at first in his batman mask. In fact, if he hadn't been animatedly talking to the man next to him—my guess is Emmett in a full long, blonde wig and dress, his massive frame looking absolutely hilarious as the dress sways.

"Cooper!" I yell, not sure if I'll get lucky enough to catch his attention. He turns, spotting us.

"Hey! What are you guys standing around here for?"

I shrug. "Trying to get in!"

He shakes his head, grabbing my arm. "Come on ducklings, follow me."

Cooper drags me behind him before he realizes I'm two seconds away from tripping. The other three are close behind, huddled close together.

When we get up to the front of the line, Cooper flashes a toothy smile at the bouncer, lifting his mask. "I have four guests here," he motions behind him, and with only a short once-over, the bouncer waves us inside.

"That was easy," Mila whispers.

Lulu's is busier than any Monday night we've ever been to, but it always is on Halloween. Everyone is packed in like sardines, only some spots in the back have real room to breathe. But there's something about the DJ blasting Halloween music, the green and blue lights bouncing off of spider webs and fake blood spatters, that just makes it all worth it.

It also helps that we *do* get special treatment. If you hang out with the team, you always do.

"Are the rest of the guys already here?" I ask Cooper, looking around.

"I think they're in the back," he yells over the music, pointing toward where Owen had taken me a couple of weeks ago.

"There's a back?" Amara asks, her hand to her chest.

"There's a back," I nod.

"Come on, Barbie will lead the way," he says as he pushes Emmett in front of us. We form a line behind the two men, happy we don't have to push and shove our way through the thick crowd.

When we reach the back, we turn down the small hall and are let in by the second bouncer. The main room of the back is also packed, but much less so than the actual club area. There's a couple seats free at the bar, and we make a beeline for them, the four of us crowding around two stools.

"What can I get you tonight?" the bartender asks as I hand him my card to start a tab. The other three are great about sending me money for their drinks at the end of the night, so I never mind.

"Rum and coke please," I call over the music, moving aside for the other three.

A couple minutes later, with our drinks in hand, we head for a corner, watching as people file in.

"What is this room even used for?" Heidi asks, looking around.

"I think it's just for like, famous people."

"We're famous?" Amara gasps.

I take a sip of my drink, smiling. "My brother's annoying ass has to have some perks, right?" The second I say it I feel guilty. "Well, he has a lot of perks," I nod, correcting myself.

Leo does a lot for me. I never want anyone to think I'm ungrateful, no matter how annoyed I may be with him.

Cooper and Emmett shimmy their way through the crowd, coming to a stop in front of us once again. Clinking their beer bottles, they both turn to me.

"Haven't seen you in a long time," Cooper says.

"I've been busy," I reply.

Cooper is the one teammate my brother doesn't have an issue with talking to me. We've been like siblings since the day we met, constantly bickering. He's a good dude, and one of my favorite people one the team.

"How did you end up Barbie?" I ask Emmett as I take in his outfit.

He doesn't say anything at first, looking at Cooper as if asking permission to talk to me. I hate that he feels that way. "You can talk to me, Emmett. You're fine."

His lips thin but with an elbow from Cooper, he speaks. "Lost last week," he says with a shrug.

"Fantasy football?" I feign shock, not wanting them to know that of course I know.

"Yeah. It's been awful this year. I mean, Owen is always on top. Always. So that's no shock. But your brother found some weird dude off the streets."

"Off the streets?" I pretend to be shocked.

Emmett nods. "Yeah. Just straight off the street. No one knows him. Leo says he works for the team but I don't think a single one of us believes him."

Cooper shakes his head as if to agree.

"That's wild," I say as Mila pinches me in the butt. I can feel her laughing behind me at my performance.

"Yeah. But oh well. Owen got to pick the punishment this week and he said I had to be the Barbie to his Ken."

I'm momentarily sad that I wasn't the Barbie to Owen's ken, but I shake it off quickly.

"That's wild," I say. "Where are the others, anyways?" when Cooper's eyes shoot to mine, I add, "I wanted to say hi to my brother."

"They'll be in in a minute. I think they were talking to friends out in the other room."

The six of us stand huddled in the corner, the boys asking my three if they liked the game.

"It was so fun!" Heidi smiles from ear to ear, somehow having more energy than she did earlier.

About ten minutes later, Emmett is tapped on the shoulder from behind, and when he moves out of the way, I choke.

My brother stands in front of me in a nude morph suit cut at the neck. The only thing keeping his bits from being clear as day is the brown scrappy fabric around his waist. The suit looks like he rolled in dirt for an hour before coming in here.

But it's the bald cap that makes me lose my mind. My brother—known for his beautiful hair—is bald, with only a few strands of scraggly dark hair hanging limply from it. He has red lining his eyes, and his face, as everything else, looks dirty.

"What the hell?" I ask, looking him over. At the same time, I reach behind me, grabbing Heidi's sweatshirt from her hands. Bringing it in front of me, I hug it to my chest, knowing that if he's not too distracted, he'll have a fit about what I'm wearing.

"I'm sexy Smeagol," Leo says, looking down at himself.

I shake my head. "There's nothing sexy about him, Leo."

"I would hope it wouldn't be sexy for you, dumbass."

"I think it looks good!" Amara says, and I look back at her, amazed that she had something nice to say to him while he looks like some type of decomposing elf.

"You've never seen Lord of the Rings?" she asks, shocked.

I shake my head. I'm not sure I have.

"Well that's our next order of business," Amara tells me, taking off to get another drink.

"Did you lose a bet?" I ask Leo.

"Nope," he says, crossing his arms. "I've been planning it for months."

"Well it's certainly something."

"Thanks. Hey, what are you guys up to?" He quickly turns to Cooper and Emmett, his eyes narrowing at the later.

"We got them in earlier so they didn't have to wait in the cold," Cooper tells him, quickly realizing Leo is being weird about me. "Was just keeping them company and protecting them from any weirdos in bald caps."

Leo high-fives him. "You're the best."

Mila and Heidi are busy laughing behind me, and I down the rest of my drink. I ask them if they want anything else and make my way back to the bar after handing Heidi her sweatshirt back. I'm not going to steal it all night. If Leo wants to be an ass than he can be an ass.

I'm only there a minute before I feel a hand on my back. "We've got to stop meeting like this," a deep voice says into my ear, his breath tickling me.

"I think I'm more concerned about how you knew it was me."

"You think I don't notice your butt when you walk around your place in those tiny shorts? Peaches, please."

I let out a chuckle, grabbing my new drink and turning to Owen.

And I stop. Again. For the second time tonight.

Owen is a cowboy. A very shirtless cowboy. A cowboy wearing a pair of tight shorts and assless chaps.

"Jesus Christ—" I breathe.

"It's good, right?" he asks, spinning around.

"A cowboy?"

He motions back to the corner I came from. "Technically cowboy Ken. Emmett's my Barbie."

I nod, still trying to process the image in front of me.

Which is when he actually takes in my appearance, too.

"Pretty girl are you Padme?"

"I think you need to pick one nickname and stick with it," I tell him with an eyeroll.

"I like both."

"I like neither."

"Don't lie to me, Isla. I've seen how flustered you get."

Ignoring him, I decide to lean into his compliments. I spin, showing off the whole outfit. "You like it?"

He nods, biting his lip. "I always preferred the Padme white outfit over the Leia one."

"It's because you're an ass guy, isn't it?"

He smiles, the dimple on his right cheek deepening, and it takes my breath away.

"I must be drawn to the force, because yoda only one for me," he says, his voice low.

It's so stupid I can't help but burst into laughter.

"That was bad," I tell him, placing my hand on his muscular chest, his bare skin searing mine. I watch as goosebumps form at my touch, feeling his body lurch slightly as he shivers.

He looks down, and when he looks back up, his eyes are darker. More sultry.

I shake my head. "My brother is right over there and he's going to kill you."

"I think it would be worth it, don't you?"

25

OWEN

Isla's hair is braided into a bun at the back of her head, the white costume fitting her like a glove. Her light makeup is perfect for her, and although I think she's pretty no matter what, I love when I can see her freckles.

And I really like that I can make her laugh.

I watch as she looks curiously at where my chest and her hand meet, and am about to ask her out for real this time when I feel a hand come down on my shoulder, the slapping sound loud in my ear.

I turn, immediately nervous as Leo's bald little head comes into view.

"What's up?" he asks, his eyes narrowing at his sister. I just hope he didn't watch as her hand fell from me.

"Nothing much, just getting a drink," I say as I hold my cup up.

He looks suspiciously between us as Isla shoots him an awkward smile.

"What are you wearing?" he suddenly says, and before I can respond that I'm clearly wearing assless chaps, I realize he's looking at his sister.

"I'm Padme," she deadpans, already knowing that this is going to be a fight she doesn't want any part in.

Leo raises his hand, covering parts of her from view.

"Yeah, you gotta go put something over that. Now."

She groans. "Leo for the millionth time, you're not dad. I'm an adult. I can do what I want." Her eyes flicker to mine.

"You're here at this bar because of my friends, Isla. I don't need you here practically naked."

"This literally covers my entire body, Leo. My *entire* body."

"Not enough," he fires back.

"It's not up for you to decide!"

"It is when I'm here looking out for you!" Leo's voice raises, and a couple people start to glance over at us.

"You're not looking out for me, you're being misogynistic."

"I'm looking out for you like I always have," Leo says, clearly annoyed.

"You know what? Get fucked, Leo." Isla doesn't look at me once. She simply turns on her heel, flashing her middle finger at her brother, and walks away toward her friends.

He watches her go, making sure she's safe with her friends and not somehow kidnapped on her short walk.

And then he turns to me, his eyes shooting fire. I feel like I'm being roasted on the spot.

"And what the fuck are you doing, man? What have I told you? What's my one rule?" He starts walking toward me, trying to intimidate me.

He could, possibly. If there weren't exactly three hairs on top of his bald little head.

I hold my hands up. "I'm not doing this with you."

"You are doing this with me. Answer."

"No."

"Crosby."

"Warner."

I level him with a glare, my chest puffing. I can feel the rage building deep within me, and for a brief moment, I hate him.

I don't really hate him. But I hate this. I hate how much he adores his sister. I hate how much he cares for her. And I mostly hate how he can't see how anyone would be good for her.

"Are you just going to keep her holed up in that apartment for the rest of her life?" I ask, throwing my hands up. "Not allowing her to talk to anyone at all? Or live her life?"

Leo's eyes narrow even more, and before I know it, he's pulling me toward the back door.

"What the fuck man?"

"We need to talk."

Leo bursts through the back door, grabbing a hundred-dollar bill from under his brown skirt around his waist—I'm not sure I want to know what he has under there—to hand to the person manning it so we'll be let back in.

Pulling me a little down the alleyway, I've never been so sure I'm about to get the shit beat out of me.

But instead, Leo pushes me onto a bench, sighing as he plops down beside me, tossing his head back to get his little hairs out of his face. They fly back, blowing in the wind.

"What's going on with you?"

"Nothing."

"Don't bullshit me, Owen."

"We're just friends," I assure him, crossing my arms over my freezing chest. The bench is frigid under my ass.

"I didn't think what I asked was that hard."

"You can't control her life like that, Leo."

A silence settles between us as he leans forward, clasping his hands in front of him. Rubbing them together, he looks at me, his eyes sad. "Do you know why I do?"

"Why you control her?"

He shakes his head. "I'm not trying to control her. I'm trying to protect her."

"She's a grown woman. She doesn't need you to protect her."

Leo takes a deep breath. "Isla used to be the golden child. Straight-As, awards for her art, passionate about the things she loves. I loved that about her. I was the one who didn't take things too seriously."

"Why does this matter?"

He flashes me a glare and I quiet down.

"When I found football, it took over our lives. She was always a fan, but now she spent her time traveling with our parents to watch me. She spent time helping me practice however she could. My parents, though supportive of both of us, only saw me.

"Isla's accomplishments were celebrated, sure, but they were on the backburner compared to mine. My games and practices came before celebrating her birthday. Before anything that mattered to her. It was like the family, including Isla, decided that my hobby would get me somewhere, and hers wouldn't."

A pit settles in my stomach as I look down at my feet, seeing where this is going before he has the chance to say it.

"Isla eventually fell into a depression. And it was bad. She threw away years and years of work, Owen. Years of it just gone. She stopped eating. Just stayed at home and wasted away. I came home one day after a game to find her curled in a ball in her bed, sobbing. She couldn't tell me why.

"I vowed that day to make sure I never made her feel that way ever again. I've always supported her. Always wanted her to follow her dreams just like I am. But I get it. There's more appreciation in this world for what I do than what she does. And that's not fair to her."

I nod, humming in agreement.

"No matter what we may wish our lives are like, we're

professional athletes. Professional athletes on one of the best teams in the league right now. We go to a different grocery store than normal and there's photos of us everywhere."

He's right, and I hate that he's right. The memory of Isla and I at the apple orchard flashes in my mind, and I have to force down a smile.

"She gets involved with one of our players, that's all the media is going to talk about. It's not going to be her talents, or how much she loves art, or her showings. It's going to be how she's dating someone on her brother's football team. If you break up," his eyes narrow at me, "that's all they're going to talk about. That's not fair to her."

I get it. I do. But on the other hand, I feel as though Isla should be able to decide for herself what's fair or not.

But he's right. And I hate that he is.

WEEK EIGHT

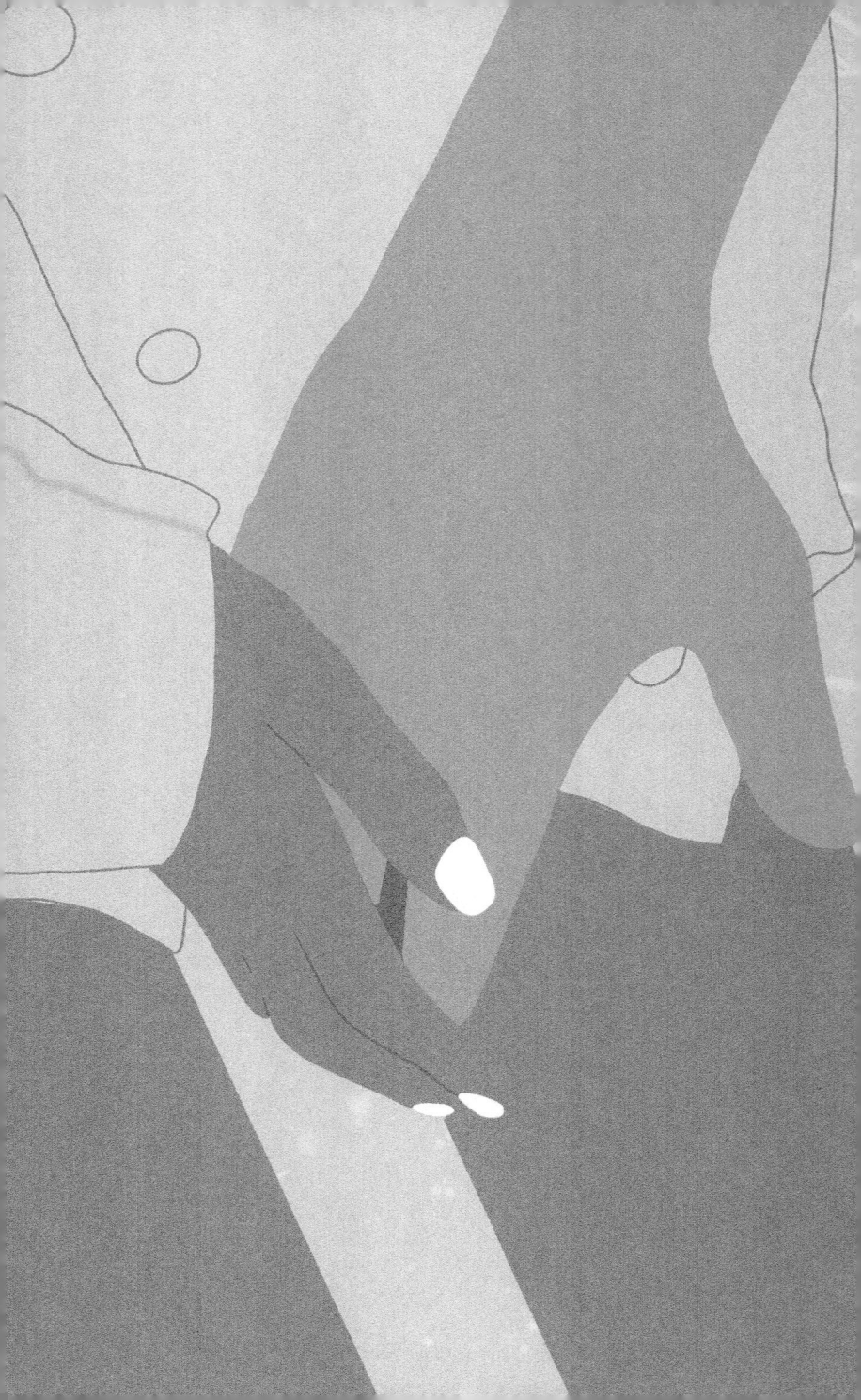

26
ISLA

Monday Night Football came and went. I lost this week. I never got a text about my punishment.

All I've done is sit on my floor painting, feeling sorry for myself over a stupid boy.

A stupid boy who apparently lets my brother dictate his life.

Leo tried to come by my place on Tuesday, but I slammed the door in his face, not interested in talking to someone completely unwilling to listen to what I have to say.

And now it's Thursday, and I haven't gotten out of bed yet.

But I've come to the realization that this isn't me being dramatic over a boy. No. It's me being livid over not being able to make my own choices.

I liked someone. I liked someone for the first time in a very long time. Liked them enough to let them in and actually allow myself to feel hope that it goes somewhere.

But that's not enough for Leo. There has to be rules and regulations to what I'm allowed to do and feel.

I look around my apartment, taking in the home I've created for myself here in only a few short months.

I'd give it all away if I could just be free.

So maybe I should.

But a much bigger part of me feels as though I'd be the most ungrateful bitch in the world if I did. There are people without homes, and here my brother is, giving me this beautiful place.

Don't get me wrong, I make enough to afford a comfortable life. My commissions make quite a bit. But being able to use that money to invest in new supplies, new tools, and booking gallery shows until I hit the jackpot and get invited somewhere?

I can't put a price on that, and that's the problem.

Sometimes if you love something enough, you'll breathe all it's air, suffocating it.

And Leo is suffocating me.

Owen has been my peace for the last eight weeks. An unlikely pairing, if I do say so myself. But a welcome one. And I miss the morning texts. I miss the good night texts. I miss him grabbing my thigh in his car.

And we haven't even kissed yet.

I turn over onto my side just as a loud knock echoes through my place. Groaning, I kick my blankets off me, the feeling of the sheet getting stuck on a toe filling me with silent rage.

I don't bother looking in a mirror or even changing out of my sweats and ratty old t-shirt. It's probably going to be Leo anyway.

Swinging the door open, I come face to face with three people I don't expect.

"We're worried about you," Amara says as she holds out a box of pancake mix. Heidi lifts syrup into the air, a large smile on her face. Mila pops up behind them, a bottle of orange juice in one hand, and a bottle of champagne in the other.

"Brunch! Brunch! Brunch!" Amara chants, and the others dance around her with their various items.

No matter how hard I try to remain cold, my heart melts.

"Who called you?" I ask, my eyes brimming with tears.

"Your brother," Amara shrugs, pushing me aside as they make their way to the kitchen.

"Plus I asked you something about art two days ago. You still haven't responded. I knew then it was an emergency."

I think back, but can't recall her text. I haven't wanted to check just to realize I have none from Owen.

As happy as I want to be, I've dealt with bouts of depression for the last ten years of my life. Nothing serious, I don't think. But once in a while I'll have my moments, and I'll take a week to just keep to myself and sit in my feelings.

Eventually the fog lifts, and I'm okay again. It's not bad enough that I've been concerned about getting help, despite what my friends think.

I don't talk about it often. I'm well aware that my life is good. I have it easy compared to so many that chug through the day, getting everything they need to done despite their circumstances.

But as Leo told me one time, the chemicals in my brain are to blame, not my life.

I'm allowed to feel how I feel.

I just don't want to push the burden on anyone else.

The three women in front of me have always been instrumental to getting me out of my funks. Somehow, they always know, no matter what, when I'm starting to slip, and they come barging into my life whether I like it or not.

"You have that stash of chocolate chips still, right?" Mila asks, invading my cabinets.

"Top left," I tell her, perching on a stool, curling my knees into myself.

Amara pulls a large bowl out, immediately pouring pancake mix in before taking it over to the sink and adding water, no measuring cup needed.

Heidi finds my speaker, plugging her phone into it. She

scrolls for a few minutes before finding our favorite playlist and hitting play.

The three dance and twirl around my kitchen without a care in the world, and after a couple of minutes and a shared look between Amara and Mila they try to hide from me, Amara spins around the island, making her way over to me. Her hands are in the air as she sings to the song playing, a large grin on her face as she grabs my hands, pulling me gently off my stool.

It's not that I don't want to dance. It's that I can't. I'd never intentionally act like an asshole when my friends are doing this for me.

But they know that.

Amara firmly grabs hold of my hand, holding it above our heads as she spins. When the next song comes on—an even more upbeat pop song—Mila abandons the pancakes on the stove, holding the spatula to her mouth as she dances over to us. Heidi follows closely behind, a mason jar filled with mimosa in hand. They circle me, jumping up and down to the song, and I can feel myself break.

When my lips tip up, it's not because I'm forcing it. It doesn't feel physically painful to do so.

It feels a little bit like happiness.

Heidi's eyes find mine as she sings, and she knows it. Her smile broadens as she grabs the other mason jar from the island, handing it to me. Amara sees and quickly grabs a whisk, passing it to me too.

And we just sing.
And dance.
And yell.
And I'm happy.

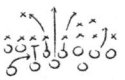

"So, what's going on this week?" Heidi asks as she pops a piece of pancake into her mouth.

The first three Amara had made were absolutely burnt to a crisp. I mean absolutely charred.

I made a joke about them spending time on Mustafar, but I always forget that Amara has never watched Star Wars. I keep meaning to force her to.

At least Mila appreciated it.

More pancakes were on the stove in no time, and we barely dodged a blowout fight between Mila and Heidi over what the standard size of a pancake should be.

If there's one thing I've learned from being so close to the three of them, it's that there are large pancake families and small pancake families. I much prefer small pancakes, but there's nothing bad about large pancakes.

I take a sip of orange juice, pushing my last bite around my plate absentmindedly.

"I'm not sure," I shrug. And I really don't know.

"Why do I have a feeling that this has to do with a boy?" Mila asks. Amara flashes her a scowl while I hear Heidi slap Mila's leg under the table. She jumps at the contact.

Whenever I've needed this, they've always gone to great extents to make my day feel completely normal. This means no talk about why I may be feeling the way I do, or negative things. If I want to talk about them, I can bring them up.

They're not positive to be positive, and they don't force me to just *look at the positives,* so to speak. They just want everything to feel normal. Safe.

I always end up telling them on my own time.

This time, I shrug. "I can't really talk about it," I tell her, not bothering to look back up. "It's complicated."

I know they'll be pissed at Leo, and I have no idea what Owen told him. With Mila's temper, I don't need her marching next door and giving Leo an earful and getting anyone in trouble.

"Well we're here for you whenever you need, you know that."

I nod, letting a little smile free.

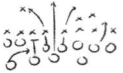

My friends left about two hours later, after more laughs, another forced sing-along, and Heidi pelting Mila with chocolate chips.

And although I feel better, I still don't feel like myself. I know the only thing that can pull me out of it is time.

Buzz.

My phone vibrates in the pocket of my sweats, making me jump. I take it out, my heart stopping as I read Owen's name flash across the screen.

OWEN CROSBY

> Loser of this week brings the other to the aquarium. Sound good?

A feeling I can't quite describe settles in my stomach. A twisting feeling that makes my head spin and my gut drop.

Why is he reaching out now? Why was there silence for days?

Why is he now suddenly wanting to go out in public with me?

I don't respond for hours as I zone out to my favorite movie, my eyes growing heavy.

It's not until I'm climbing into bed that I respond.

> Okay.

27

OWEN

We won our Sunday night game in Ohio, and the plane home is loud.

Cooper has been dancing around, hyping everyone up, and our coach has been coming around to talk to us about how proud he is of us. We're on the right path, and if we keep it up, it looks like this could be our year.

Leo and I have spoken on and off in the last week, but I've mostly given him space. After our talk a week ago I haven't wanted to push anything, much less talk to him about the idea of me still perusing Isla.

I can't not.

I can't take not talking to her. Not seeing her. Two months, and all I can think about is her when I'm not playing. How to win her back and how to make her happy. How to make her brother happy. How to make him okay with me seeing her.

There's nothing I want more. I know that.

When I got her simple "okay." my heart dropped. I'm not sure if it was the period included or if I could just feel it through the phone, but I know she's upset. I know I messed up. I know I should have reached out to her after my talk with her brother.

But I didn't.

And I don't want to do that to her ever again.

It's a day after our game, an hour before the Monday night game kicks off, and I'm at home on my couch, my fantasy app pulled up.

I'm winning my actual game this week. By a lot, with only one more person to go.

Isla is close, but she only has her kicker to go. If I were to guess, the guy will get only about four or five points.

My finger hovers over the option, unsure about whether I should do it. Will the guys call me out on it? Probably. But I could say that it was a mercy call, right? That I just didn't want to run it up on our poor corner, one of the worst teams in the fantasy league.

"Fuck it," I whisper to myself as I move the guy down to my bench, instead putting their other wide receiver in. The one currently injured and not playing.

The guys will know I already had him in my Injured Reserve spot, so I'm not sure they'll believe that I just simply didn't see it. But maybe they will.

They can be dense sometimes.

"I can't believe I'm doing this," I mutter to myself.

Immediately a text comes in.

PEACHES

You have an injured player starting.

Isla.

So she's been watching.

I feel a smile creep onto my lips as I look at the clock. It's almost eight. The game is almost starting.

I wait until 8:01 to text her back.

> What? Dammit I could have sworn I saw he was okay. Thank you for telling me, nothing I can do now

I add a shrug emoji to the end for full effect.

She doesn't answer me, which is slightly concerning.

The kicker misses his first two kicks. Of course he does. Isla is only a couple points below me, but kickers don't tend to score that many fantasy points.

It's not until the third quarter that we get lucky.

When the game ends, she has exactly one point over my score.

> Congrats on your win

I sit back in my chair, watching the post-game reporting.

> That was hardly fair.

> I think it's fair enough

> Okay.

The okay with the period again. I swear it'll be the death of me.

But I'm not sure what to say. I don't want to say anything over text, and I also don't want to go over there right now before I have the chance to really knock her socks off.

I knew that I was going to lose to her this week no matter what. Isla isn't stupid, she knows what I did. Doesn't mean I wouldn't have done it.

> I'll be at your place to pick you up at 8 P.M. sharp tomorrow. Look cute.

> Okay.

ANNA NOEL

My Tuesday started with a workout, followed by driving over to the aquarium to pick up the NDAs my agent and I had all of the nighttime employee's sign.

I want to give Isla a night to remember without the fear of photos or news getting out. After all, it's a big deal to rent out the entire National Aquarium.

True to my word, I'm at her place at eight, dressed in my best jeans and a comfortable button-up shirt, I take two steps at a time up to her apartment.

I don't need to knock or send her a text, either. The second I'm at the door, she opens it, her eyes immediately dialing into the bouquet of yellow and white flowers in my hand.

Without a word, she steps aside, letting me in.

Isla looks beautiful as ever in her low-cut black long-sleeve and green skirt. Her chocolate hair falls in waves down her back, her red highlights catching the light as she moves around. She grabs her boots from her shoe rack, pulling them on. They make her about two-inches taller, the top of the boot ending around her knee.

"You look stunning," is all I can say. She looks up, her lips pursed.

"Thank you," she says finally, taking the flowers from me.

"It's awful late to be going to the aquarium, isn't it?"

I shake my head. "Nope. They were more than accommodating."

She narrows her eyes as she stares up at me. "Please tell me you didn't pay a fortune."

I shake my head. She doesn't need to know those numbers.

"Are you ready?" I ask her.

She doesn't answer, instead grabbing a vase under her

counter, filling it up half way, and sticking the flowers in it. She studies them for a moment. Through the tough exterior, I can tell she loves them by the way her eyes light up, her finger brushing a petal as if testing how soft it is.

Her lip twitches, and she finally meets my gaze, giving me one curt nod.

She grabs her bag as I grab her hand, leading her to the elevator. Her brother is off with his new girl, so I know we won't bump into him.

I don't want her to have to walk down so many stairs in heels.

When we get to my car, I open her door for her. I wait a moment to close it to make sure she's comfortable before rounding the car and climbing into the driver's seat.

"You settled in okay?" I ask her as I press start, the car humming to life. I took the fancier one today; the one that normally sits in my garage. She looks around, pulling her seatbelt around her. She nods, but after a couple moments of struggle, she looks at me apologetically.

"Is the buckle stuck? I don't think I've ever had anyone in the passenger seat of this thing," I tell her as I reach over, grabbing the seatbelt. I dig for the buckle, pulling it up and clicking it into place. My head rests near her chest as I do, and I can feel that she's stopped breathing.

She looks around once more as I'm pulling out of my spot. "What is this thing?" she asks, her fingers gliding over the smooth material of the dash over to the screen sitting in the middle. She pauses, looking at me for a moment before swiping through the music options listed.

"It's a Mercedes-Maybach S Series," I tell her simply. "I only got it because my financial advisor told me I needed to look into some new investments."

She pauses, her brows furrowing. "Aren't cars known for being absolutely horrible investments?"

My lips twitch as I run my hand through my hair. "Yeah,

that's what he said when I came back with what I bought. Gotta say, I thought he was going to be super proud of me."

From the corner of my eye I can see Isla struggle to keep a straight face, her lips quivering as she tries not to laugh.

A second later, she coughs.

Great cover, I think.

"My brother has mentioned buying a fancy car, too."

I shake my head, chuckling. "Your brother wants to buy an eight-hundred dollar Aston Martin Supercar. Hundreds of thousands of dollars more expensive than this baby here."

She cracks a smile at that. "Yeah well, my brother is an idiot."

"A very rich idiot," I nod.

Leo's rookie contract is up at the end of the season, and it's been a push to get him to sign a new one. There are options, of course, that the league can take, but he's already one of the richest rookies in the league. A number one pick of his draft, Leo signed a four year, thirty-nine million dollar contract, one of the highest ever.

He's set to make history with his new one, but he's weighing his options. Over money, fame, and fortune, Leo really does value the game and winning overall. Taking a bit of a cut would help the team pay for better players, stacking the team and ensuring we're good for the next couple of years.

On top of that, Leo really does donate a lot of money on top of helping his family.

I hate the bastard sometimes, but he's a good guy.

Regardless of how much the contract ends up being, it's going to be a sum of money that many people can only dream of. More than enough to get his dream car.

"You know we could have walked, right?" she asks, watching as we round the harbor. While her apartment is on one side, the aquarium is on the other.

"We're going to be walking around the aquarium all night. I'm not making you walk there and back, too."

And I wanted to impress you, my brain screams.

But I know Isla isn't impressed by fancy things. She may be curious, but she's not impressed.

Swallowing, she leans back in her seat, settling down finally.

We park outside of the aquarium, making sure it's locked before heading inside.

The city around us is alight, the moon hanging high above. It's beautiful, and so is the woman in front of me.

"Have you come here often?" I ask her as we head in. It's one of the most beautiful aquariums in the country, and she has a view of it from her apartment.

"I did when I was a kid. I heard it's changed a lot since the last time I was here."

It has changed a lot.

"Then I'm excited for you to see," I tell her, gently tugging her along.

There's a guard waiting for us outside, and they open the door for us as we approach. I smile at him, thanking him before following Isla though the main entrance, past the giant waterfall from the exhibit above.

We pass a couple more people, all of whom greet us with a smile and a nod, letting us know they hope we have fun on our visit.

Isla looks around, her eyes wide as she takes in everything we're seeing.

We turn right into what's one of my absolute favorite parts of the whole place, their reef area. A wide-open space, the reef is full of the most beautiful fish.

"Oh my God," she breathes beside me, pulling my hand as she goes to the edge. "That ray is huge."

We watch as their whiptail ray swims past us, its spots shimmering in the light above us.

Isla is entranced as she watches the fish swim past, but she seems particularly in love with the zebra shark.

"He's beautiful," she says as she leans over the edge, watching him closely. "I mean they're all beautiful, but he's gorgeous."

I stand next to her, my hand on the small of her back, and when she turns, I'm closer than she thought. Her chest pushes up against mine as I look down at her.

She casts her eyes downward, and I pull her in closer, kissing the top of her head as I run my fingers through her hair.

"We have a lot more to see, are you ready?"

"I don't think I can pick a favorite," she says as she leaves the tropical rainforest exhibit. It was darker than it usually is, but looking around and watching the city lights outside was something special. Making our way down to the Atlantic coral reef exhibit, we take our time. My favorite is next.

Catching sight of it, Isla is the first to say something. "Are these the sharks?" she asks, her eyes shining with excitement.

I nod, smiling back.

"She takes off, making her way down the ramp.

"They're beautiful," she says as she steps up to one of the viewing windows, watching as a nurse shark floats by.

I come up behind her, wrapping my arms around her shoulders and pressing my lips to the back of her head. Breathing in, I close my eyes, feeling so at peace I never want to leave. The scent of vanilla fills my nose, and when she grabs my arms, holding them to her, I know I'm a goner.

Isla opened up more and more as we walked around, getting comfortable. I'm not sure if it's because of me or because she's excited about what's going on around us, but I'm not going to complain.

"Thank you for this," she whispers so quietly I barely catch it.

"Hmm?" I ask into her cheek, my face right next to hers.

She turns slightly, rubbing her cheek along my jaw, her eyes closed. When she opens them, they're darker. Dangerous. Clouded with desire.

The girl in my arms doesn't care about consequences.

And neither do I.

Within a second she's turned in my arms, her lips on mine.

A guttural growl escapes me, a sound I didn't even know I was capable of making as I wrap my fingers around her hair, her hands running up my chest to my neck. I run my tongue across her bottom lip, and when she parts them, we're a mess of gnashing teeth, desperate to somehow get closer to one another. It's like I've been without water for months, and I'm finally getting my fix. Like I can't get enough.

The taste of her tongue, the smell of her, the feel of her body in mine; I can't get enough.

I grab her waist, pushing her gently into the railing behind her as I desperately seek skin on skin contact. I pull up on her shirt, slipping my hands underneath.

I don't want to do anything extreme. I just want my hands on her. To feel her skin under my fingertips. She clings to me as I trail my lips along her neck, and the moan she lets out has me desperately wanting to take her right here.

After what feels like hours, we pull away, her forehead resting against mine.

"What are you doing to me?" I ask, my nose grazing hers. Her eyes close, her breathing shallow.

"This is going to hurt," she whispers, opening them once more.

I pull away a bit, my brows furrowing in confusion. "What do you mean?"

"You're going to decide you don't want this at some point, Owen, and it's going to tear me apart."

I shake my head. "Peaches, I don't think you understand how long I've been waiting for this."

Her lips clamp shut, her hand coming up to fix her hair.

"Hey," I say, grabbing her chin. "I want you more than you can ever imagine. But in every way, you hear me? I want your mornings. I want your nights. I want your bad days and your best days. I want you."

Her eyes brim with tears, shining in the dim blue light. "What if that's not enough?"

My head tilts to the side.

"What if you need more than that? You have your whole career. You have my brother. I can't deal with the fallout of coming second to my brother again, Owen."

I nod, understanding.

I sigh, stepping away. "I can't promise that there won't be bad times. That I won't disappoint you at some point. But we work together on that, okay?"

She looks me over, her tongue peeking out to swipe over her bottom lip. When she slowly nods, I grab her hand, leading her down the rest of the ramp.

After a minute, I can feel her shoulders relax.

"What's that?" she asks, looking around.

"What?"

"That sound?"

I smile, pulling her further into the underwater viewing room at the end of the exhibit.

"Did you seriously have them play Taylor Swift down here?" she asks, walking further into the room.

She walks up to the wall of glass, watching the fish swim in front of her. Bathed in the blue hue, Isla looks like a vision. And when she smiles at me?

I walk over slowly, watching as her eyes linger on my movements. My fingers fumble with the sleeve of my right arm, rolling it up my forearm carefully. When I'm finally done with both, I reach out for her, grabbing her hand as the song changes to a slower tune.

Pulling her into me, I grab her hand, swaying to the beat as I rest my head on her forehead.

And I can feel myself falling every second that passes.

WEEK NINE

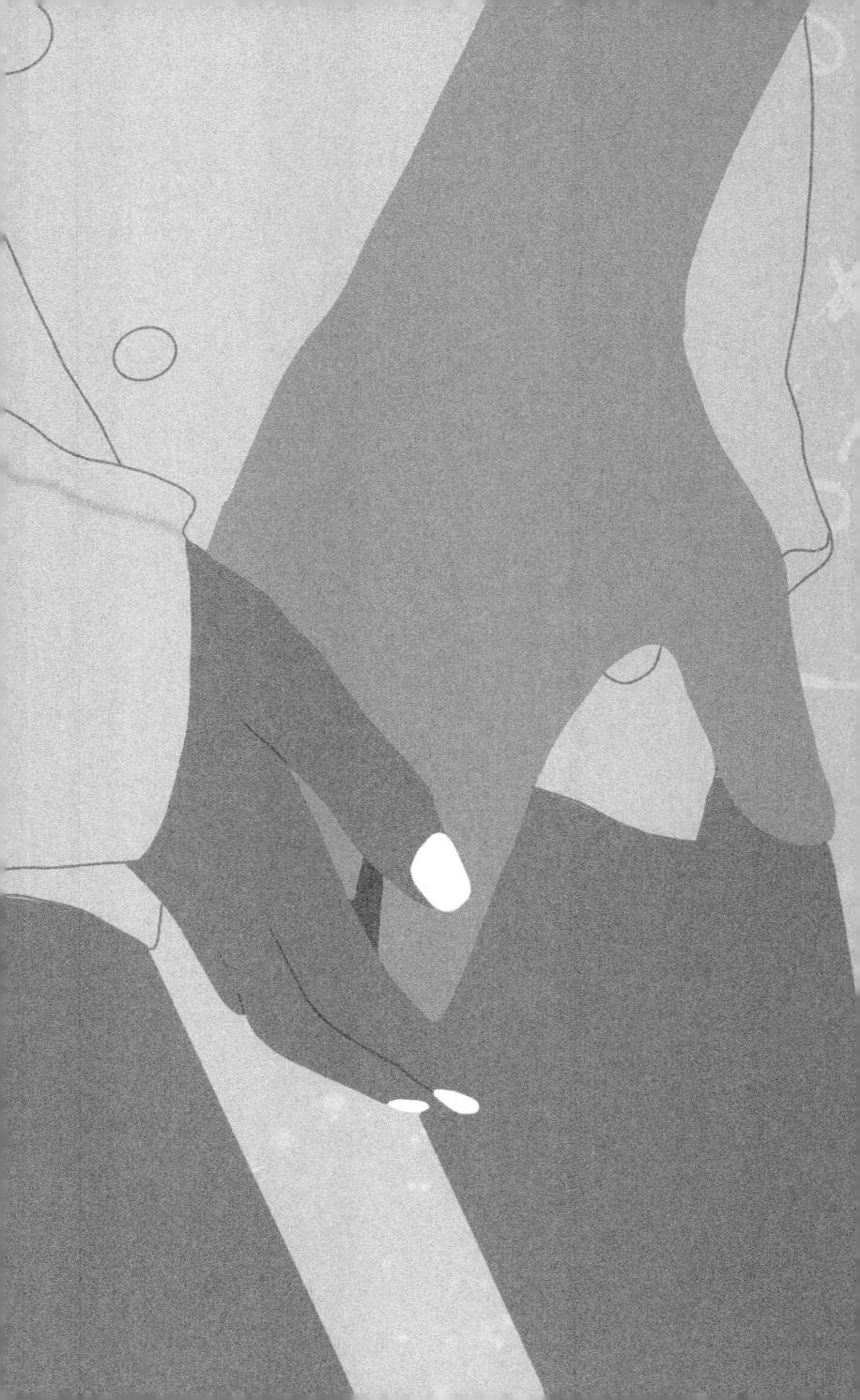

28
ISLA

It's been three days, and I can't stop thinking about Owen's lips on mine. I don't think I've ever felt more comfortable in someone's arms, and as cheesy as that sounds, it's true.

But it's gallery day, which means that I need to focus on different things.

Nerves have been eating at me for the last two days, which is why I'm here at the gallery hours before I should be in shorts and a t-shirt making sure everything is hung up in the right spots.

I'm dusting one of the displays one more time when I hear a knock on the glass, finding Amara with her arms full of boxes.

"I got your snacks!" she exclaims as I let her in. She sits them down on the table with a huff, unstacking them to reveal one large box of grazing board items, the other various wines.

She looks at them, her head cocked to the side. "Hmm. I think Heidi is bringing the wine glasses."

"I think they have some here," I tell her, heading to the back to look.

I come back with a whole box of them, and she texts Heidi to let her know we don't need them.

"Thank you for the board," I tell her, hugging her firmly.

She waves her hand at me. "Don't even mention it. You're helping me. I think I want this to be my new venture."

I look over her things, watching her unload different crackers, fruits, and other items to spread along the table. Amara has never talked about making grazing boards before, so her words come as a bit of a shock.

"Yeah?" I ask, watching her work. "When did that happen?"

"When did the business happen?" She shrugs, stacking her cheeses. "These go in the fridge until about half an hour before doors open," she tells me with a wave. "But yeah, I'm not sure. It feels like a calling."

"To, to make cheese boards?" I ask again, gathering the various cheeses in my hands.

She nods vigorously. "Yeah. I mean I love a good grazing board. I love working for myself. Boom. There."

I nod, a little concerned for my friend.

But then again, who am I to talk? If she wants to do it, she should try.

Which is exactly one of the reasons she's here today.

"I've got glasses!" comes a call from the front. I walk back to find Heidi with a box of glasses.

"Oh! I thought Amara texted you! We've got glasses covered," I tell her, gesturing to the box. She purses her lips, looking down at her box.

"I did text her! I'm sorry I didn't do it sooner," Amara apologizes, continuing to line crackers on the brown paper she laid out.

"No that's my bad," Heidi smiles. "Can I just put these in the back? I don't feel like lugging them all the way back to my car down the road right now."

"Yeah, just stick them right back there."

The three of us continue setting up, occasionally being dropped in on by the gallery owner. She's a very nice older woman who's owned this place for decades. She always makes it a point to let me know that she caters to smaller artists, and that some day I won't be able to show here.

You know, because I've made it big.

It always makes me smile, despite how unsure I am about my current career path. I mean, maybe I'll get enough commissions to make a great living. But I'm not sure if I'll ever be good enough to show my art at more prestigious places.

An hour before opening, Mila dances through the doors, looking more chipper than she has in months. I send the other two questioning looks, but they look just as perplexed.

"You look happy," I say slowly, watching as she tosses her shiny hair over her shoulder.

"Sometimes you just have a good day, you know? What can I help with?"

I point her in the direction of the broom, wanting one last sweep. Amara definitely dropped a couple crackers on the floor.

A half an hour after opening, there's only been three visitors. Three visitors who looked a little more interested in Amara's grazing board than any of my paintings on display.

I've changed into a pretty blue lace dress, put my hair up in a messy high pony, and threw on some makeup about ten minutes before we were set to open, but the first person didn't enter until about ten minutes after that.

"That painting is so beautiful," an older man says as he stands in front of one of my paintings of the city.

"Thank you, it's one of my favorites," I tell him as we stand next to each other, looking at it.

I'm not super confident in a lot of my work, but there's a few pieces that I really love with my whole heart.

Maryland is the state that raised me, but Baltimore shaped me into the woman I am today. There's nothing more romantic than this city to me. Not even Paris.

"A lot of people hate this city you know," the man mutters. "But it's been my home for the last sixty years."

I nod, smiling. "It's a beautiful city, no matter what anyone says," I agree.

How can you not be romantic about Baltimore? The people, the baseball team coming back to take it all two years ago, or the football team led by my big brother. There's hope here.

Sure, there's a lot of things that need to change. I acknowledge that looking at the city as romantically as I do comes with privilege. But one day I want to have enough money to give back. To make a difference.

I know my brother has donated to social programs, but at some point I want to go bigger.

When I look at Baltimore, I see a place for everyone to love, no matter what.

"I'll take this one," the man says, turning to me suddenly with an outstretched hand. I stare at it for a minute, wondering if he's joking. "If you don't shake on it I'm going to have to walk out," he chuckles.

A grin takes over my face as I grasp his hand firmly in mine, shaking it. He cuts me a check right then and there. "Are you going to ship it to me or can I take it now?"

I look around. A lot of artists just mark a piece as sold, shipping it to the buyer afterwards or holding it for pickup so that other people have the chance to see it, but there's not really anyone here.

"If you want I can have my friend help you box it up?" I ask, gesturing to Amara.

The man smiles, nodding. I take the painting down, heading to the back with Amara in tow.

Grabbing the painting, she makes quick work of it. We bring it back out front, sending the man on his way.

"Congrats!" Mila yells, hugging me. I can't stop smiling. There's usually one sale at showings, but it's usually smaller pieces, not the big ones.

A few more people drift in, some of whom planned to be here and some who were just walking by and got curious. They're all super friendly, but none of them seem super interested in buying right now.

I'm talking to a young woman who ventured in to escape the cold when the doors open, loud voices carrying through the small space.

Looking behind me, I find my brother and what must be half the Cobras team.

On one hand, I find it sweet, my brother showing up for me.

But as I watch everyone in the room turn to them, their eyes wide as they start whispering to themselves, taking out their phones, I feel myself slump.

More people follow them into the gallery, and when my brother comes up to hug me, a few people snap photos before interrupting us.

"Will you take a picture of us?" a teenager asks. He's not here for my artwork, he's here to meet the football team.

My smile falters, but I plaster it back on, nodding as I grab his phone and snap a few photos for him.

I look around, trying to find Owen before spotting him in the corner. He doesn't look happy, and when he sees my face, his own drops even more.

I can see the apology in his eyes.

My lips thin as my eyes sting, watching person after person filter in to take photos with the team.

I know what Leo was doing. I know that he was trying to do the right thing. To show support.

But this is exactly what he's been trying to protect me from. It's the same exact thing.

Me coming to his games is not the same thing as him coming to mine. I wish I could appreciate it, I do. But this? It's one of the worst feelings.

Mila, Amara, and Heidi all find me, questions in their eyes. I know that they'd kick them all out if I asked, but then who would be in a newspaper as the local artist who kicked the football team out of her showing?

Maybe people wouldn't care. But maybe they would.

Instead, I grab a glass of wine, bringing it to my lips as I head to the back.

I know my friends will keep an eye on the rest.

My brother tries to talk to me on Saturday. And Sunday, asking if I'll be at the game with mom and dad.

I won't be.

Owen has texted me too, but I let him know that I just needed some time alone.

I'm not upset with him. My brother told me it was his idea and he forced everyone to come. He thought it wouldn't be a big deal.

But of course it was.

The Cobras were gathered in a small gallery where anyone could step in and meet them.

"Isla please talk to me," Leo says outside my door.

I don't answer.

And I feel like a giant asshole.

He was just trying to help. He's doing his best. From the outside, it's one of the sweetest moves. Any sister should love a brother like him.

But from here, in my shroud of solitude and overthinking, I'm mad.

I'm mad because he wants to dictate my life to protect me, and yet he doesn't think through his own actions sometimes.

I'm mad because he thinks that telling me not to talk to his friends is the only way to make sure I don't live under his shadow.

I'm mad because he cares so damn much yet doesn't use that big brain of his to think past what he thinks may be good for me in that moment, to hell with the big picture. To hell with every single thing he's preached at me for the last few years.

And there's something so damn lonely in that.

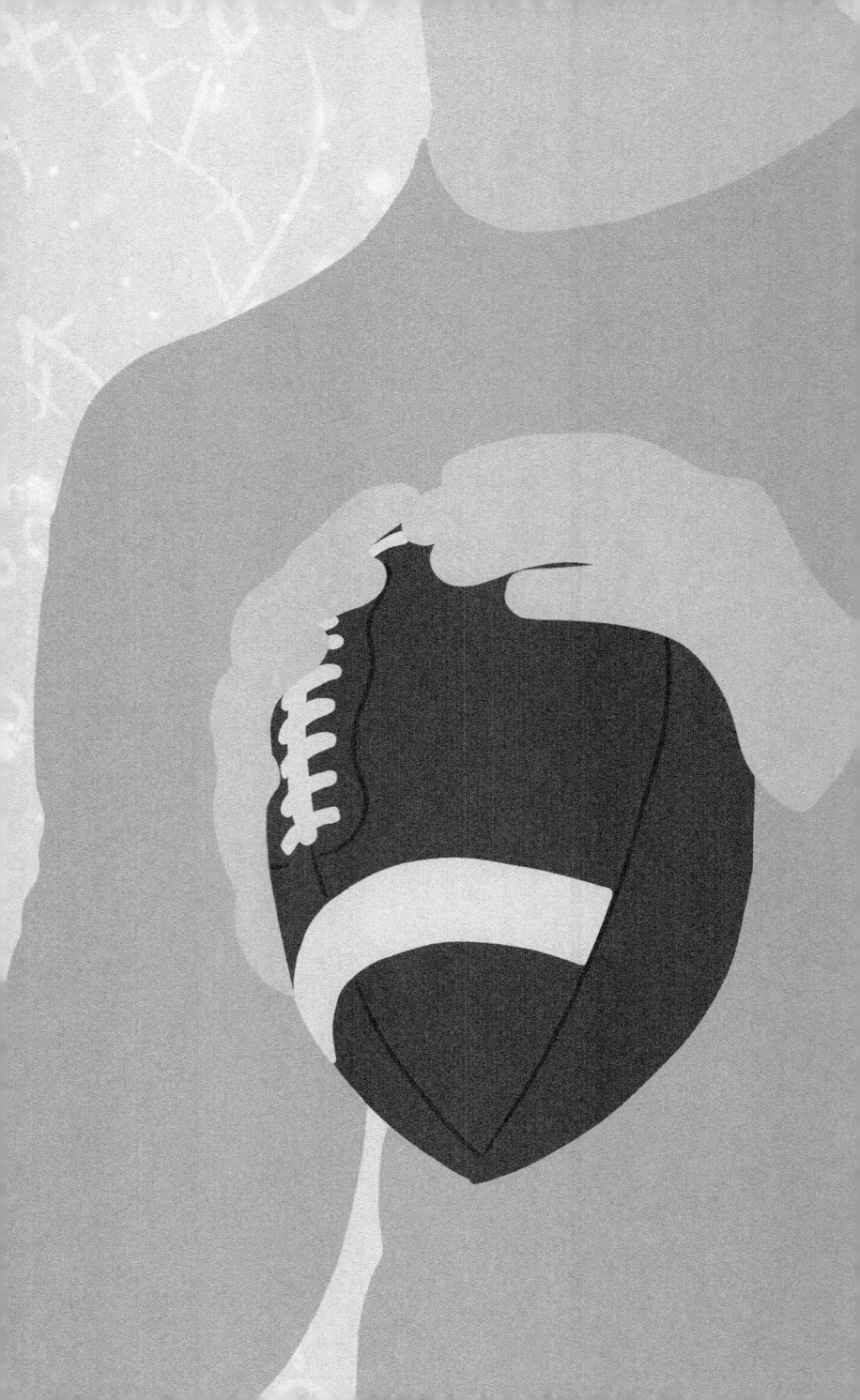

29

OWEN

Isla hasn't talked to either of us in days. Leo hasn't shut up about it, and it's bothered him enough that he's been screwing up at practice with one of our bigger games coming up this week.

He'll admit he's wrong, but he still won't admit that he's done exactly what he didn't want for her. Exactly what he was concerned about me doing.

And if I say it, I'll be the bad guy.

"You doing okay?" Cooper asks him, clapping him on the back.

Leo nods, dropping to the ground where he lays, his arms outstretched.

"You okay?" a game coach calls, his face worried. I wave him off and shoot him a thumbs up. "He's fine! Just dramatic!"

Leo scowls at me.

"Man you fucked up. You just have to own it." I shrug, not feeling sorry for him.

"I just don't know how to make it better."

Before I can stop myself, I say, "maybe you can let her make her own choices for once."

"Don't even go there, man," Leo growls, and I'd take him seriously if he was any threat to me at all down there.

"Just think that you have some thinking to do," is all I say before running off to practice some new routes.

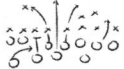

Isla made it clear that she wasn't upset at me, but it still makes me upset that I was involved in something that hurt her.

So I've made it my mission to cheer her up.

> Hey Peaches, check your door in about ten minutes, alright?

> Owen I really don't want to see anyone right now...

> It's not me, I promise. But I'm here whenever you need it.

Ten minutes later, she sends me a photo of her doorway, stuffed to the brim with the most beautiful yellow flowers I could find right now along with a giant bag of peach rings and a Van Gogh teddy bear.

"You didn't have to do this," she tells me over the phone. She sounds sad, but I can hear the appreciation in her voice. Which is enough for me.

"But I wanted to."

It's Thursday, and my package finally came.

Despite everything that went down at the showing, Isla sold quite a few paintings.

While some of the guys were forced to buy a few when Leo realized he fucked up, I handed Isla's friend Mila a check, asking her if she could mark my favorite to be shipped to me. I didn't have room to lug it home with me then.

She had nodded, curiosity twinkling in her eyes. I could tell she wanted to ask something more, but the girl has restraint.

And I got it today.

The thing is huge, and when I unwrap it, it's as beautiful as the first time I watched her sit in her living room painting it.

I walk around my apartment to find the perfect place to put it, finally deciding on one of my many blank walls.

I've been here for two years now and I still have barely decorated. I haven't felt the need to until now.

But now I want a home filled with paintings just like this.

No, I want a home filled with a few paintings like this, and stocked full of Isla's most favorite artists. Not prints. The real thing.

I want her with me, surrounded by the things she finds most beautiful. The things she loves the most.

Have I always been this gushy?

I'm careful as I hang it, making sure it's even before I snap a photo in front of it.

And I hit post.

For the first couple of minutes the only comments that roll in are women and men telling me how handsome I am and fans telling me I need to do a little better this week or we're going to lose, as if I don't know. Watching them come in, lead settles in my stomach. Maybe I did the wrong thing. Maybe this is me pulling a Leo and making her art about me.

But then it happens.

Who painted that? a comment reads.

I wait a little longer, and there's a few of them. The first comment has twenty likes.

So I comment her name, tagging her Instagram she uses to post her art.

In only a few short hours, Isla has a couple thousand more followers, and when I check her site, all of her prints are sold out.

PEACHES

Thank you, Owen.

WEEK
TEN

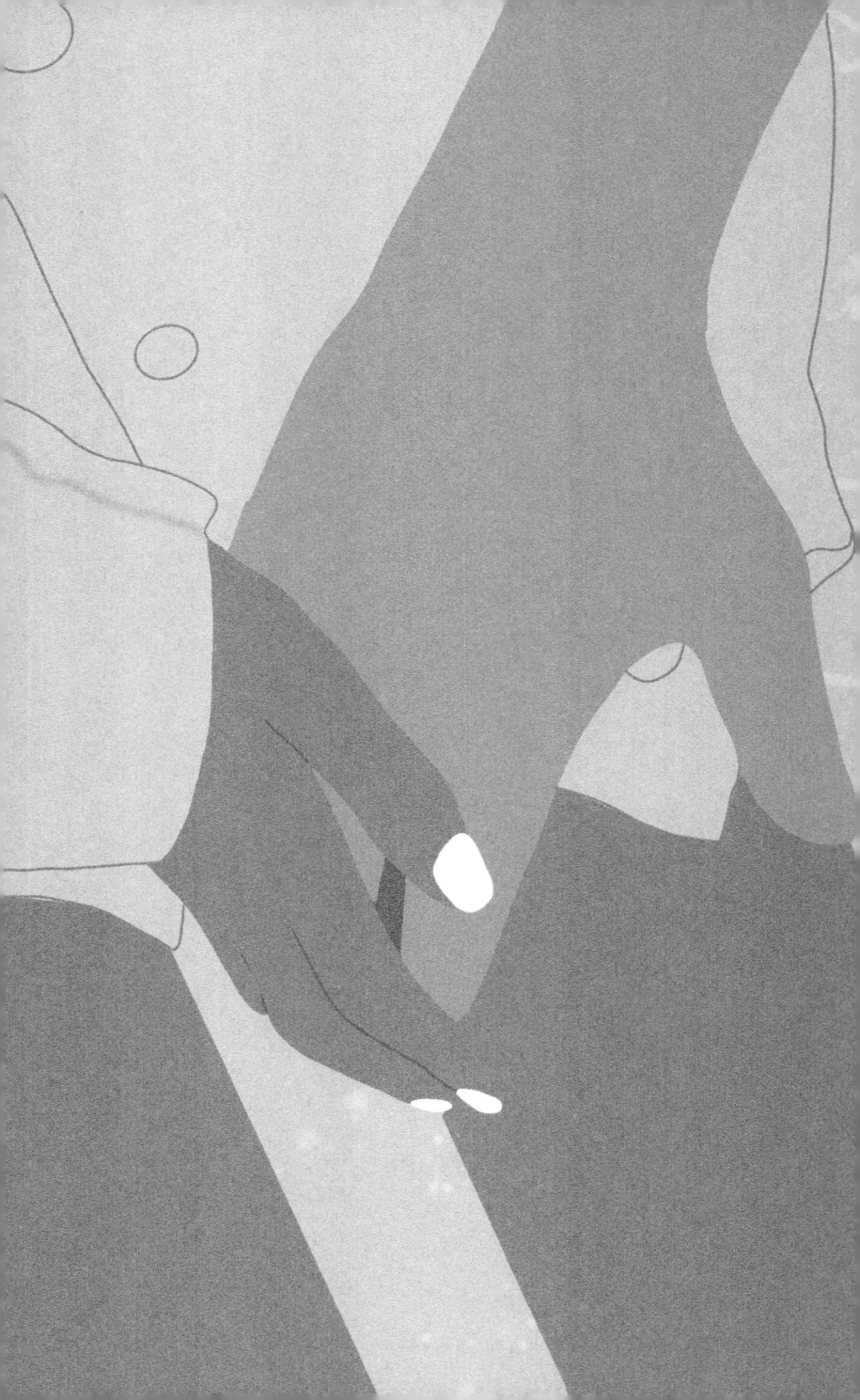

30
ISLA

I've barely spoken to Leo, and I'm starting to feel bad about it.

"I feel like you should answer his calls at some point," Amara says, which is honestly scarier than the concept of talking to him about the whole situation. Amara isn't the biggest fan of my brother, so her telling me I should forgive him feels like a stab.

"I know I should," I say, bringing my iced coffee to my lips. "I just don't feel like explaining why what he did sucked so much, you know?"

Mila nods, slipping an olive onto my plate as her face twists with disgust.

I grab it, popping it into my mouth. "And what, exactly, is the reason you're so pissed about it?" Heidi asks, dipping her sandwich in her soup as she looks between the other two.

"I feel like you guys know," I deadpan, taking a bite of pickle. It's extra juicy, the snap sending a splash of juice onto Heidi's face. She wipes it away with a gag.

"What? Us? We know nothing," Amara says with a smirk.

"Okay John Snow," I roll my eyes. "My brother wants to control my whole life for one reason, and it's, in his opinion, to protect me. He doesn't want me to live in his shadow. Which, that makes sense, okay? It does. I get it. I appreciate that. But what I don't appreciate is the fact that he doesn't allow me to make my own choices. You know, like an adult."

Mila nods her head enthusiastically, giving me a little golf clap. Heidi snaps her fingers next to me.

"And what is this very adult decision you're trying to make?" Amara asks, and I can see Mila's eyes flash to hers.

"Guys seriously stop. You know it's Owen."

"Oh my God, *Owen?*" Heidi smacks her hand on the table, her jaw hanging open.

"Guys."

"Seriously Isla? Owen from the *Baltimore Cobras?* That Owen? I can't believe this. This is... this is *unbelievable.*" Mila throws her hand to her forehead.

"I know right? I never saw that coming at all. I would have thought she'd fall for Ian before Owen. This is shocking. The shock of the century, actually."

"Ian literally doesn't exist."

"Oh my God you're killing us with these secrets, Isla! What do you mean he doesn't exist?"

"You guys done now?"

"I just can't believe it. Owen Crosby. Who woulda thunk it?"

I hate them.

"Okay I'm sorry for not opening up about him before."

"Why didn't you?" Heidi asks.

I shrug, trying to find the words. "I'm not sure. I just wanted something to be mine."

"And he was? Yours, I mean?" Mila asks, her stormy eyes narrowed.

I contemplate the question. "I think so."

"Did you guys hang out? Or was it just a flirtation?"

"We hung out," I say simply as I reach for a chip.

"Her neck is turning red," Amara whispers.

"Yeah you dirty dirty bird. What happened between you guys? Is hanging out some sort of code for something else now? I can never keep up with the lingo today."

"Heidi you're twenty-four."

"Okay?"

"Okay," I interrupt them. "We haven't done much at all. We've kissed."

All three of the women in front of me gasp.

"Oh you whore!"

I smile at that, weighing whether I should continue. "We haven't gone any further at all."

"And when was that?" Mila quizzes.

I pause. "Umm, you remember that night a bit ago when I said I couldn't hang out and you guys thought it was because I was spiraling again, and then you guys tried to break into my apartment and I wasn't answering my phone? And I called you guys at like one in the morning letting you know I was just out?"

Mila's eyes fill with irritation from the memory as she nods.

"Well," I shrug one shoulder. "We were on a date."

"Tell us every detail and maybe we'll forgive you." Amara says.

"You already have."

"I'm getting angry about it all over again. Now spill."

I tell them about how he rented out the entire aquarium for us, and how beautiful the place is.

I felt so happy there that I just couldn't continue to be angry at him anymore.

"See that's your problem though," Heidi says, placing another olive on my plate. "We're never too happy to be mad at men. Stay mad. Stay livid."

We giggle, and when I tell them about Shark Alley, their jaws drop.

"So did he just like, grab your hair? Or did he like, *grab your hair?"* Mila grabs Amara's hair and gives it a good yank, causing Amara to slap her hand away.

"Grabbed," I confirm, making a fist and dragging it downward.

Mila's mouth hangs open as her eyes go wide, looking to the side.

"What?"

"I don't know how you didn't fuck him right then and there, if I'm honest."

"We were in public!"

"After hours!"

"There's still cameras everywhere, Heidi."

"Then you should have asked them for a copy to keep for your records!" Amara chimes in. "I don't watch porn but I would have paid to watch that."

I shoot her a questioning look.

She puts her hands up in front of her. "Look. I'd never hook up with you, you know that. But you're hot. He's hot. It's just a fact. Two hot people getting freaky in an aquarium in front of the sharks?" she shrugs.

"Honestly I probably would too," Heidi nods, and Mila hums as if confirming she would also buy my sex tape.

"Well I'll keep that in mind. Thank you for the support," I say with a chuckle.

"You're fucking welcome." Mila smacks the table, her plate rattling against it. A few people turn to stare, and I become all too aware that I've been talking about the possibility of me having a sex tape in the middle of our favorite brunch spot.

"And then," I say, getting them back on topic. "we go down into this underwater viewing area and you know what he had set up?"

They shake their heads.

"He had them playing some of Taylor Swift's most romantic songs."

"I think you need to marry this man," Heidi says, and I know coming from her she means it.

"I don't know about marry but fuck definitely," Amara nods.

"Guys I'm not having sex with him yet."

"Why? It's been what? Two months?" Mila asks.

"Like two and a half I think?"

"The man rented out an aquarium for you."

I sigh. "I mean, there was one night it could have happened."

Heidi finishes her iced coffee, swirling the ice around the bottom. "That night?"

"No, before that. He made me dinner and I just remember his knife skills were just—" My eyes roll back in my head at the memory.

"And you didn't have sex with him right then and there?" Amara gapes.

Mila nods. "Knife skills are one of the sexiest things on a man, let me tell you."

"I didn't think it was that hot until I saw him cutting that onion."

"Then why didn't you make a move?" Heidi asks.

I cringe, biting my lower lip. "Well, funny you should ask. I drank a little beforehand, and then he brought wine, and I drank some of that, and then as I was getting too horny from the alcohol the onions hit me like a bus."

"Isla Warner did you seriously cry because you were too horny?"

"No! I'm serious! He was chopping onions right in front of me!"

The three look between each other, looking skeptical.

"I promise on my life I did not cry because I was drunk and horny. It was the onions."

"I'll only believe you if you film him the next time he chops things. I want to see what you're working with."

ANNA NOEL

MOMMA WARNER

I haven't seen you in weeks honey, why don't you come to the game today?

I'm not feeling great

That's funny because I saw Mila post a photo of you from brunch. Come to the game today, please? We're not going to be here forever.

I mean I'll see you next week at Leo's holiday party!

Come to the game.

Yes ma'am.

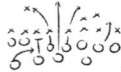

I'd rather be almost anywhere but here at the stadium today. The guilt eats at me, deep in my core.

Leo and I have always gotten along. We've always been best buds, so us not getting along really sucks.

"Have you heard from your brother recently?" she asks in that tone that tells me she knows exactly what's going on and she just wants to weasel her way into the middle of it.

"Nope," I respond simply as I take some popcorn from my dad, tightening my coat around me.

"Well I think you should."

I don't respond, instead focusing on the game.

My mom shifts in her seat. "Ted, what did Leo say his agent mentioned about the new contract the other day?"

My dad, popcorn half in his mouth, just looks at her, trying to figure out what she's asking.

"When you guys had that talk yesterday. What did he say his agent said?"

"Oh, yeah, that talk. Umm, I think he said that there's a small possibility that he won't get the deal he wants." He nods, taking another handful of popcorn in his fist.

The thing is, I know my brother. I know that he'd take literally anything they offered him.

"It's a shame if that happens," my mom shakes her head solemnly.

I roll my eyes.

I'll talk to him eventually. I may even talk to him soon.

But that's for me to decide, not them.

The third quarter starts and this game is a struggle. They're down by six and the other team's defense has been playing out of their minds. I check my fantasy app, realizing that I never swapped out one of this team's players for another. I never want to root against the Cobras.

But the guy has twenty-two points already, so I guess that's enough to settle down a bit.

On the first drive of the last quarter, Leo throws deep, and miraculously, Owen happens to be there.

Leaping up, Owen grabs the ball, hugging it to his chest as he gets tackled to the ground at his waist. He lands hard on his back, but it looks like his head didn't take too much of a hit.

The minutes are ticking by and the pass to Cooper is incomplete. They have one more chance to get the ball in the endzone before they end up just settling for a field goal.

Leo passes up the side of the field and Owen is right there, barely catching it off the tip of his fingers. He manages to pull it into himself, seems almost surprised he caught it, and he runs it into the endzone, just barely managing to dodge a massive man running into him at full speed.

Screams erupt, the stadium coming alive as lights above flash. Owen stands there, his arms spread as he turns to the crowd, and after a moment, he turns toward where our box is, pointing right at me.

I sink in my seat, trying to hide my smile.

And a couple of things happen simultaneously.

From the corner of my eye I watch as my mother stops clapping, looking from Owen to me, while I watch the camera pan to Leo, who also looks from Owen to our box, following his finger.

Earth, please swallow me whole.

My mom shakes her head, a small smirk on her face as she settles in her seat again, pinching my dad's arm. He jumps, looking at her.

All I can think about is how excited I am to leave.

31

OWEN

The second we get into the locker room I'm met with a towel to the head.

"What the fuck?" I rear back, holding my head. I can feel the headache start. This game was brutal and my entire body is killing me. I just need an ice bath.

"Knock your shit off," Leo hisses as he walks by me to his locker.

"Why don't you?" I ask, seething.

I'm done. So done.

"Because I'm her family, Owen. I know what's best for her."

I scoff. "You clearly don't. Let her make her own decisions, man," I wave him off, heading in the other direction. I don't want to be around him anymore.

I round the corner, almost walking straight into our coach. "Good job out there, Crosby."

"Thank you, sir," I manage, hoping he'll just keep walking.

"What's going on between you and Leo?"

"Nothing is going on, sir," I try to wave it off.

He places his hands on his hips was he looks over me.

"Yeah I don't buy that. Your performance is fine, but I can tell there's something up. I want it fixed before playoffs, yeah?"

"We'd never let anything come between the game, coach," I assure him.

He shakes his head. "I don't care about that, Crosby. I care that my team is a family."

"Families fight," I state, getting frustrated.

"They do, but then they work it out. You guys have plenty of time to do the same. Make sure it happens."

Coach walks away, leaving me in the middle of the hallway half naked and annoyed.

Monday night football is almost over and I text Isla to congratulate her on her win for this week.

The two of us have consistently been the top two, a pretty even pairing. We haven't played each other yet, but we are next week.

PEACHES
Thank you, but it's not over yet.

It's basically over.

If you say so, boss

Boss?

I figured why not?

You could have called me just about anything else, kid.

Oh my god yeah do not under any circumstances call me kid please.

LOVE ON THE WAIVER WIRE

> Boss sounds like you're talking to an old man.

I mean...

> Shut up.

Yes sir.

> ...

That better?

> You can call me that any day.

Good to know.

> About this week's punishment. What are you thinking?

I win, you come over Wednesday night and make pies for my brother's party.

> You got it.

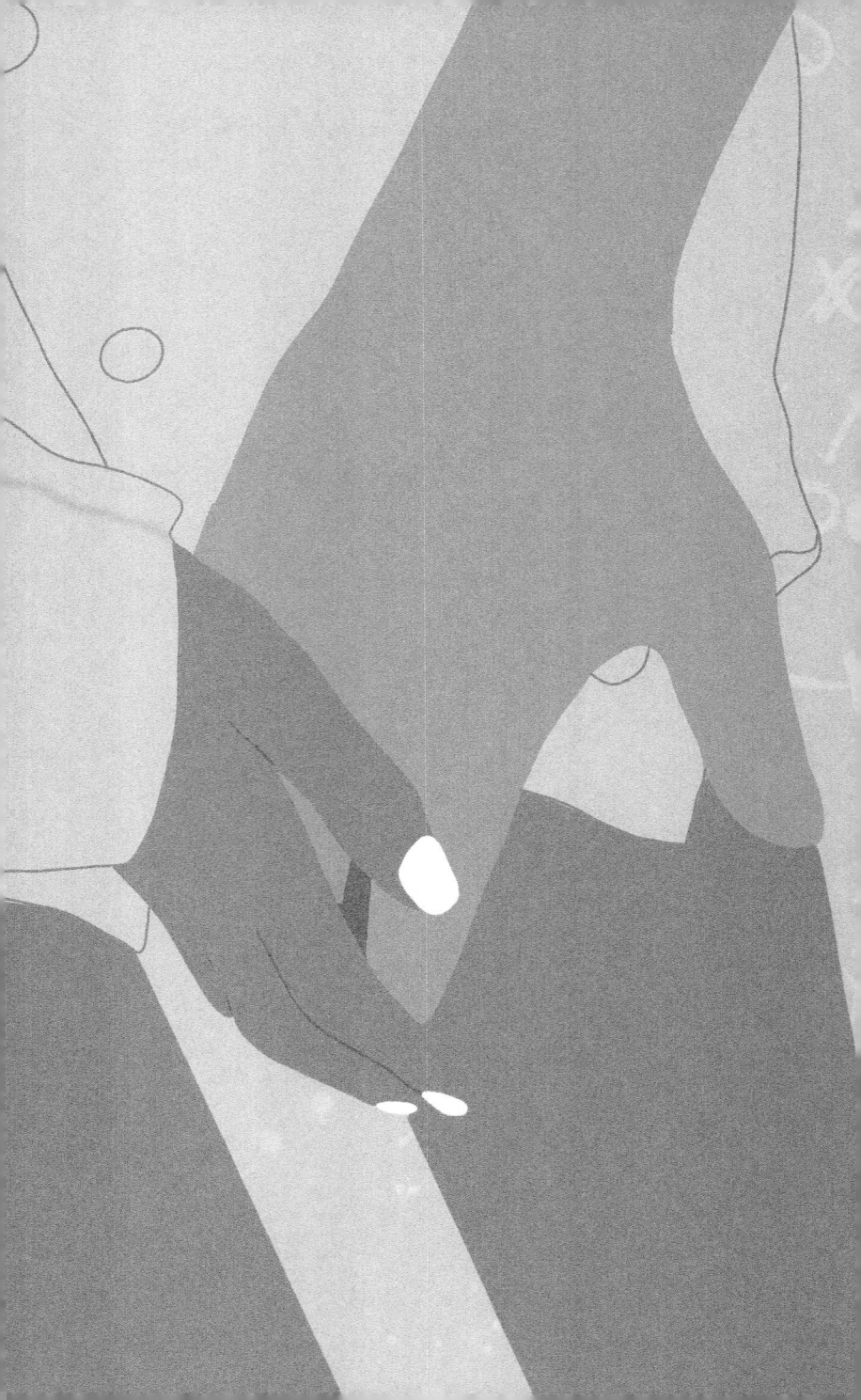

32

ISLA

"Hey," Leo says as I answer my door. Crossing my arms over my chest, I lean against the frame, calm enough to listen to what he has to say but not in a place where I'd like to invite him in.

"Hi."

"Can we talk?"

"I'm not sure."

"I'm sorry."

I shake my head, and he groans, his shoulders slumping. "I don't think you are, Leo. You've been a real dick."

"What can I do to make it better?" he pouts. "I don't like this fighting we're doing."

"And I don't like you controlling everything I do."

"I know, and I'm really, really sorry. I can't even describe how sorry I am, Isla."

I sigh, walking away from the door.

"Am I forgiven?" he asks.

"It's a start."

Most of the guys on the team had to pick up their lives and move here on a whim. And because of schedules and games, most of them can't go home for Thanksgiving.

Considering my parents usually aren't even in the same country, Leo throws a giant Thanksgiving party for the whole team. Everyone who wants to is more than welcome to come. There's always plenty of food, a questionable turkey, and plenty of carbs to go feed a revolving door of professional athletes.

There are some traditions that come with this. Leo tries a new turkey recipe every single year despite having no luck cooking said turkey, for starters. He spends days huddled over his computer trying to find the perfect recipe for the year. Then he goes to the grocery store to find the largest turkey he could possibly find, and then he buys several others. You want to know how many turkeys one singular athlete can eat? One. Depending on the size of the bird, I've seen these grown men absolutely house one.

"Yeah, that one belongs to James," Leo pointed out one year.

"Like, just James?" I had to clarify.

"I mean yeah, what else would he eat?"

I look around at all the other dishes stacked around the island. "Literally anything else. Like, I don't know, a normal person."

"James isn't eating carbs right now Isla, remember? He's trying to make those gains. Pure protein, man."

Two years ago, Leo decided that he wanted to try frying the bird. Which, as many may know, is extremely dangerous.

After a hefty donation to the closest firehouse, Leo asked

them to very politely come oversee him fry said turkey in the parking lot.

The place didn't burn down, but the turkey was questionable at best. I'm ninety percent sure that turkeys aren't supposed to be as pink as that one was in the middle, but my brother insisted that it was perfectly cooked.

Last year he was upset that their coach wouldn't make them their very own turducken, so he took it upon himself to make three for everyone.

It was a massacre.

One teammate brought his son, who proceeded to cry.

A second tradition is that I make the pies. I don't know why he doesn't allow anyone else to make the pies, but I'm the only one allowed to touch them.

He specifically sends out his invitations asking people to not bring pies, because we have them covered.

I don't like making pies.

Something about having to roll out the dough, the flour getting everywhere, and the science of the baking just isn't exactly for me.

I'm an okay cook, but I'm a lousy baker.

Every single year there's someone mumbling under their breath that they could have made a better pie. And I believe them. I'd like them to. Please.

But no. Every year when I ask to get out of it a couple days beforehand, Leo tells me that in no way could I ever ditch the pies before informing me that if I possibly stopped making them, it would ruin their entire season. It would throw the mojo off, and there would be too many injuries and they wouldn't have enough guys to even finish. Aliens would visit and kidnap the team.

It's always some random, dramatic excuse.

But God, I really hate making pies.

So every single year, the day before the stupid fucking

holiday party, I amble around my apartment preparing myself mentally to bake a handful of pies.

I never know how many specifically until the afternoon, when Leo gets an official headcount of who's still around.

But Isla, can't you ask your friends to help?

That's a great question. Yes, I can. And they've come to help before, sure. But all three of them usually travel somewhere else for thanksgiving, which means they're usually not home.

It's just me and my demons... and the pies.

But this year I have something else.

Owen.

The text comes at exactly six P.M.

I open my door quickly, worried about Leo ambling into the hallway, and pull Owen and the bags of groceries into my place. Leo has been great at not barging into my apartment lately, and I'm praying on my life and Owen's that he doesn't start.

I'm hoping him knowing I'm still pissed does helps me out.

"We have to make nine pies," I tell him.

Owen's eyes open wide as saucers, looking around the kitchen. "Nine?"

"Yeah. Nine. Nine pies, Owen."

"You do this every year?"

I roll my eyes, nodding.

He starts taking ingredients out of bags as he watches me smash pie dough together. "I have two questions," he asks, and the glimmer in his eye makes me stop what I'm doing, concerned. "First, what the hell are you wearing?"

I look down at myself, not seeing anything wrong with it. The ovens are going to be on all night, and it gets hot in here every year. I simply pulled on a pair of shorts I don't mind getting coated in flour and sports bra, and on top of that, I have a simple black apron.

Turning to face him, I turn right and left, letting him check my apron out. "It's a basic piece of cloth you use while cooking. Super great invention if you ask me," I tell him with a smile.

"You know what I mean," he says, throwing a stick of butter.

"Just you wait, you're going to be begging to strip off those jeans later, Crosby," I warn, throwing the butter back.

"We'll see," he says simply as he catches the butter with one hand without even looking, setting it on the counter with the other sticks.

Heat swirls in my belly, and I mentally scold myself.

No! Not right now! Nope! This isn't' happening. We are baking! Baking isn't a sexy activity!

We could challenge that though, couldn't we?

I shake my head. I'd rather not.

Baking is serious.

"Okay second question," Owen starts, interrupting my inner monologue. "is why you have to make homemade dough? Why not get a bunch of pre-made stuff?"

My lips tighten into a straight line as I look at him coolly. "Have you met my brother?" I ask.

He nods.

"I feel like you can answer that question yourself. You're a smart man."

"He really makes you bake all of these every time?"

"Yep."

"That's cold."

"Yep."

The two of us get to work making more pie dough. By the time we're done, we've gone through multiple bags of flour, I don't even want to know how many sticks of butter, and half a bottle of vodka.

"Vodka?" Owen had asked when I started pouring it into a cup.

"Makes the pie dough extra flaky," I inform him. It's a recipe Leo has been obsessed with since he learned about it.

By the time we're done my fingers are dead, my head hurts a little, and I never want to look at another pie.

"We have enough to make a little pie for tonight, want me to throw it in there?" Owen asks as we line the unbaked pies up in a line, ready to be thrown in when the others are done.

"Why the hell not," I shrug. May as well try it. Owen made the fillings this time, so maybe they'll actually be good.

"Cool. Throwing it in now before this next one and we can eat it as we wait for the others."

I watch as he slides the pan in, his shirt sticking to his skin from sweating.

It's hot as hell in here.

"Thank you for making these with me," I mutter, laying my head on my hands.

"I'll make them with you every year if you want me to, Peaches."

"I appreciate it."

Owen pours us two glasses of wine, pushing mine over to me as he gets to work cleaning the kitchen. I object, but he shuts me up quickly, telling me it's the least he can do to make up for the previous years of me making an ungodly amount of pies to feed them all.

I let him.

"It's nice that he does this," he says, and I agree. It is nice.

"It is. I just wish he wouldn't be as psycho about things as he tends to get."

"Reasonable."

We fall into a comfortable silence as I down my wine, filling the glass halfway up again. Owen scrubs the caked-on butter and flour from my counters, and before I know it, the whole thing is spotless.

When the alarm for our pie dings, he retrieves it and

LOVE ON THE WAIVER WIRE

places it on the counter. "You know what this calls for?" he asks as he looks down at it.

"What?" I lean in, smelling the most delicious scent I've ever encountered.

"Whipped cream."

I shake my head. "I don't have any. Leo usually gets a ton of cans and stocks the fridge."

But Owen goes into my fridge, retrieving a container of heavy cream. "That's why we can make it ourselves."

"Doesn't that take forever?"

"You have a hand mixer, right?"

I nod, directing him to the drawer it's kept in. When he finds it, he comes back, pouring some cream into a large bowl before adding some sugar and some vanilla.

He starts to mix it, and I get up from my spot at the counter and come up next to him, watching the magic happen.

"It's really that simple?"

"Yep."

When he's done, he quickly washes off the mixer and puts it away before returning to the bowl. "Have you tried it yet?" he asks, scooping some with his finger.

"No, I was waiting for you."

He grins, scooping some more up and holding it up for me.

I'm not sure what goes through my mind, but in a split second I decide to have some fun.

My tongue comes out, licking up his finger slowly before taking the whole thing into my mouth, my eyes never once wavering from his.

Owen shifts, a hunger settling in his gaze that I've only seen twice before.

"You like it?" he asks, his voice low and gravely.

"Loved it," I whisper, taking my finger and dipping it into

the mixture myself. I hold it up, examining it for a second, all too aware of his eyes zeroed in on me.

I look back at him, making sure our eyes are locked as I bring my finger to my neck, smearing it up the side.

"You know, I'm so clumsy," I say, throwing my hands up. "that was meant for you, I'll just go clean up—" I go to move for a paper towel, and like I hoped he would, Owen stops me, his control slipping from his grasp.

I can see it in his eyes. It's been almost eleven weeks, and yet all he's been is a perfect gentleman.

I don't want a perfect gentleman right now.

"Hold still," he demands as he runs his fingers up the back of my neck, digging them into my hair and curling them to keep me in place. Pulling my head to the side, he exposes my neck more.

Without a second thought, his head dips down, his tongue darting out to lick my neck clean.

A shiver runs down my spine as my mouth parts, a soft moan escaping.

When he pulls away, Owen looks feral.

In an instant I'm pinned against the counter, his mouth next to my ear.

"I want you to tell me this is a bad idea," he says as he leans even closer, the spicy scent of his cologne enshrouding me, my head spinning.

As much as I want my mouth to form the words, I can't bring them to. Seconds pass as his dark eyes stare into mine, and when his eyes flutter to my lips, his teeth peeking out to bite them, I can't take it anymore.

"This is a bad idea," I whisper, unable to meet his eyes. "It may be a horrible idea, actually."

I look away, a strand of hair falling from where it was clipped up. In the moment of weakness I'm happy to have something to shield me, but when his fingers leave my waist and grab my chin, forcing my eyes back on his, I feel like the world stops.

When his fingers move up the side of my cheek to tuck my hair behind my ear, I feel the ground beneath me drop.

"Tell me this is a bad idea," Owen's voice drops, "and mean it this time."

Instead of answering, I kiss him.

Hard.

It's not a nice kiss.

Not sweet.

Not loving.

It's gnashing teeth and bitten lips. Tongues mingling, fighting desperately for dominance in a hungry display of need.

It's Owen pushing me harder into the counter as I shove back, challenging him.

And when he's had enough of me fighting him, it's Owen fisting my hair, roughly pulling my head to the side, and devouring me.

He starts from my shoulder, making his way up my neck before licking the shell of my ear, his tongue following my jawline before he captures my bottom lip between his teeth, pulling at it.

It's the hottest thing I've ever experienced in my life.

My breathing becomes labored as I reach up, tossing my apron away before clawing at Owen's shirt.

33
OWEN

I feel what little control I have left disappear as I grab my shirt, tugging it over my head like she asked for. I've been sweating up a storm in this God damn kitchen, and my pants are so tight from being so Goddamn turned on that I can barely take it.

But I don't have to worry about taking them off myself, because Isla hurriedly fumbles with my belt, practically ripping it off before pulling my jeans off. My dick springs free, tenting my briefs underneath.

But I don't want to worry about that right now. For now, it's her.

It's always been her.

Catching her hands before they can do more damage, I run my hands up her arms, watching the goosebumps appear as I go. I can feel her watching me, trying to figure out my next move.

When I reach her shoulders, my fingers play with the strap of her bra, my eyes finally lazily meeting hers.

She nods, and with her permission, my fingers find their way under her bra, grabbing the bottom and tugging up as she lifts her arms.

Fuck.

I've never seen a more perfect sight in my entire life.

Isla Warner, topless, her pierced nipples hard from my touch.

My fingers reach out to them, running over one gently as I watch her reaction to see if it hurts. Her eyes roll back as she lets her head hang, and I grab her hair, carefully pulling her hair clip out so it can fall free around her.

"Do they hurt?" I ask.

She shakes her head, her chin dropping low as she looks up at me. When she tries to fall to her knees, I grab her, instead throwing her on the counter.

She lets out a squeak as her back hits the cold stone, and when she tries to get up, I push her back down.

"What—"

"I've been waiting to taste you for months, pretty girl, just let me have this first, okay?"

Her eyes are giant and look more black than green as she watches me hook my fingers into her shorts, pulling them down slowly. Propped up on her elbows, Isla watches my every move.

Grabbing more whipped cream, I bring it to her belly, trailing it down to her gorgeous cunt.

Lowering my head, I run my tongue down her, licking and kissing her burning skin, her face flushed as her breathing speeds up.

"Please," she moans, leaning back and covering her face.

"Please what?" I say with a sly smile. "I need you to use your words."

"I need you. Please."

I watch her for a minute more, trying to get myself thinking straight.

"Tell me to stop," I tell her breathlessly, painfully aware of how her legs wrap around me, my dick pressed to her core through my briefs.

"No."

"This is your last chance, Isla, I don't know if there's going back after I taste you."

Her legs tighten around me, pushing me into her harder.

"Don't stop," she whispers.

And I hear her loud and clear.

I'd make her beg, but I've waited long enough for this moment.

Grabbing her legs, I force them apart, moving them up to my shoulders where she crosses her ankles around my neck. Dipping down, I press my tongue to her clit, lazily dragging it upward before sucking on it.

She lifts her hips, crying out, and while something deep within my brain tells me I should quiet her down, the bigger part of me doesn't care.

My tongue flicks against her clit again before exploring the rest of her, kissing her lips before diving into her center, watching her lose control under my touch.

She moves one hand to grip my hair, tugging at the ends as her other runs up her body, pinching her nipple between her fingers and rolling it.

Her mouth hangs open as she pants, her back arching off the island as she pushes into me. I pull away just a bit, running my fingers over her, taking in how wet she is just for me.

"You taste so fucking good Isla. So wet, so mine."

I can barely get the words out before I dive back in, this time sliding my fingers into her, feeling as she clamps down around me.

I want her to come on my tongue more than anything I've ever wanted before.

Hooking my fingers, I find her g-spot, focusing on working it as I suck her clit into my mouth, flicking it with my tongue as she works her perfect nipples.

When her moans grow louder, her thrashing more forceful, I pull away for a moment, continuing to work my fingers inside of her.

"Are you going to come for me, Isla?" I ask, desire clouding my vision.

She cries out, pinching herself harder, pulling on them as I dive in one final time, and when I scrape my teeth across her, she comes apart at the seams.

Isla Warner's screams of pleasure will be my ultimate demise, I'm sure of it.

I helped Isla clean up after, not wanting to go any further tonight.

Despite our mutual loss of control, we both agreed that we should try to keep level heads, making sure this is absolutely what we want.

And it is. I want it more than anything. But I want to make sure she's okay. That she's ready.

That she's not going to have any regrets once it happens.

We spend the rest of the night waiting for pies to cook and watching the latest Real Housewives episodes as I fight for my life not to make comments that give away that I've watched the entire show from the very start.

And when all the pies are done, I realize it's getting harder and harder to leave.

WEEK ELEVEN

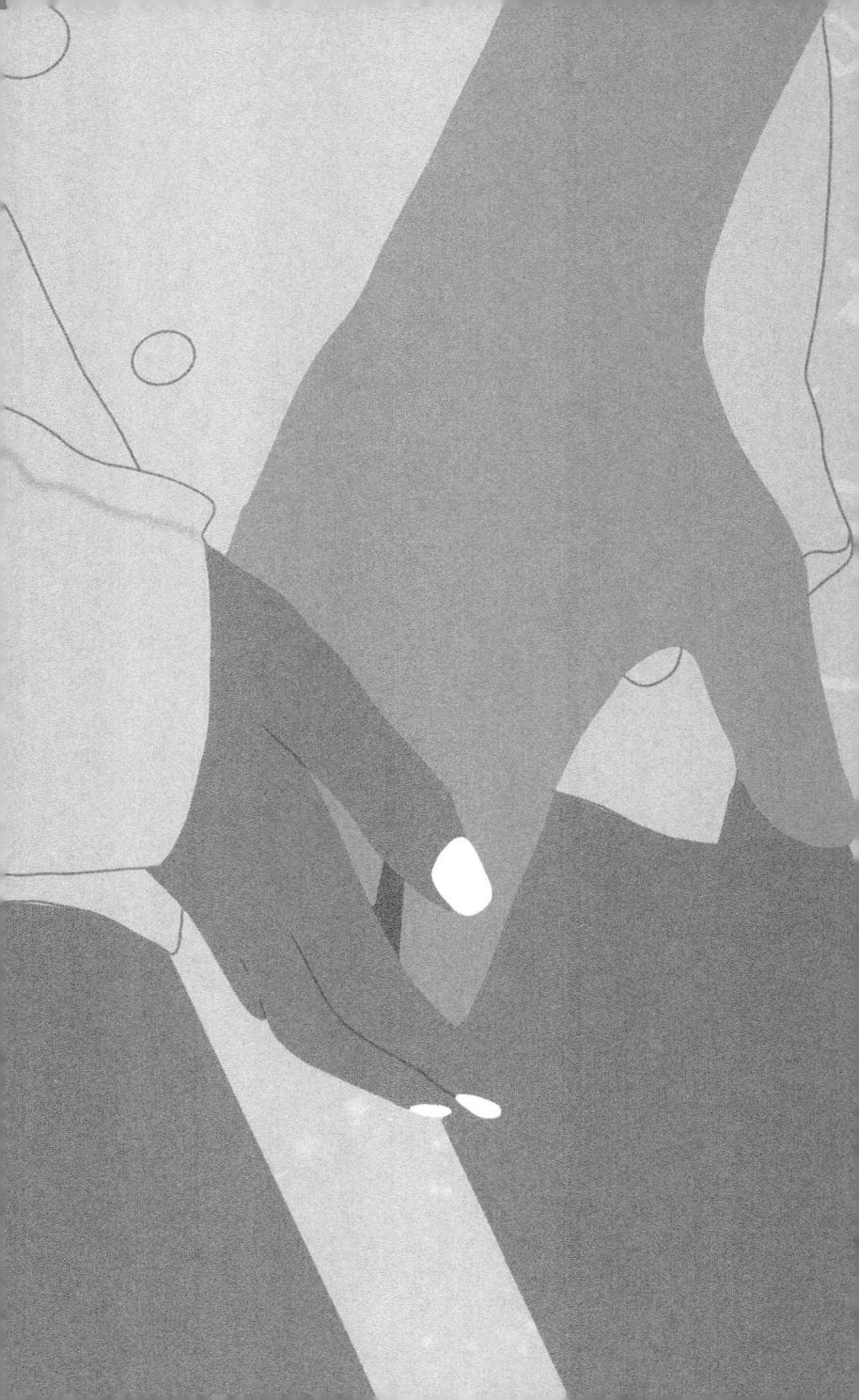

34

ISLA

The third Thursday is Thanksgiving, sure. But more importantly it's the start of week eleven of the football season, thus week eleven of fantasy football.

And what's special about week eleven?

Owen and I play each other, and I can't wait to see him get obliterated.

Owen has been number one in the league for almost the entire season. I managed to tie him at one point, but then he managed to slip past when I lost to Cooper one week.

But tonight is also my brother's party, and it's definitely going to be something, alright.

I spend the day cleaning my apartment, trying not to think about Owen's head between my thighs last night. If I think about it, I don't think I've ever experienced an orgasm orally before. Just not something anyone had interest in waiting for.

But with Owen it was almost automatic. He controlled my body with force, taking what he wanted only after making sure I was okay with it.

I've had a soft spot for that man for years, and yet nothing compares at all to coming undone under his touch.

Like any woman, I struggle with being self-conscience

about how I may smell or taste. I can hear him telling me how good I taste on his tongue randomly throughout the day, and each time I do, I end up dropping whatever I'm carrying, flustered out of my mind.

And giddy. I don't remember ever being so excited about someone before. No matter how new, no matter how promising, I don't remember having a permanent smile plastered across my face.

And when I close my eyes I can almost feel him there.

I can't help but feel butterflies when I think of seeing him at the party tonight, and even though we've agreed to still keep it quiet, I want nothing more than to run into his arms and claim him as mine.

Mine.

Is he though? We haven't talked about that specifically.

Around four in the afternoon I start getting ready, throwing on a pretty black dress and a pair of black heels. I curl my hair, securing sections on the side behind my head with a large black bow.

I keep the makeup simple. Light makeup, small, winged liner, and red lipstick.

The necessities for any holiday.

We're going slow, but that doesn't mean I can't remind him of what he wants every single time he lays eyes on me.

Around five, I start to bring the pies over to Leo's. I juggle three at a time, kicking off my heels for the time being so I don't end up falling flat on my face.

My brother has been missing in action, despite a whole host of workers coming in and out of his place. If he hired a private chef for a lot of the sides, it means there's going to be an ungodly amount of people here tonight.

I can't for the life of me think of what the hell my brother has up his sleeve, but the longer I don't see him, the more nervous I get.

Finally, about ten minutes before the party is set to

start, Leo walks through the door, six large men right behind him carrying turkeys. They filter in after him like they're following their mother duck, and when he points to a spot on the kitchen island, two of them put their turkeys down before Leo looks around, stroking his cheek as he tries to figure out what to do with all of the other turkeys.

"Do you need to put them in my place?" I ask him, examining the birds. They're a deep golden brown, and their skin looks crispy. He did something, alright, and I'm not sure I want to know what went into cooking so many large turkeys this way.

"Yeah actually, that would be great."

Directing the men to my apartment, I let them in. My island is big enough to fit them all, but just barely.

When we return, there's already a couple people arriving, bottles of wine with little purple bows in their hands.

"Isla, are these all the pies?" my brother suddenly asks, looking around.

"Crap I left some in my fridge. I'll go get them now," I assure him before he loses his marbles.

My feet are already killing me in the heels, and I'm praying I don't have to run back and forth all night. Leo has a key to my place and I'm more than happy to give someone mine if they want to do it.

Heading back I pass the army of turkeys and grab the remaining pies, but as I do the memory of Owen caressing my cheek floods my mind. I take a moment to sit down and clear my head.

I know Owen is going to be here tonight, and I want nothing more than to completely forget what happened last night simply so I don't have to lie to my brother when he eventually asks if something is really going on.

I could lie to him when it was simple flirting. I could lie to him when we went on a not so simple date. But lying to him after Owen had his head between my legs last night? I can't do that.

There *is* something going on. Clearly.

Sighing, I head back to my brother's apartment.

Taking a deep breath, I open the door to find the place even more packed.

Half the Baltimore Cobras team fills his large space, a whirlwind of men and their significant others laughing and carrying on. Several kids run around with what looks to be rubber chickens, and my mom and dad arrived while I was gone, huddled at the back of the room with one of the water boys my brother invited who couldn't make it home for the holidays.

When I catch myself scanning the room for one man in particular, I kick myself, shaking my head before heading to the kitchen to put down the goods.

"I can't wait to taste that, but I'm sure it's not better than what was on your lips last night," a familiar voice whispers in my ear as his breath warms my cheek.

I can feel my body warm, lust settling at the pit of my stomach.

"I'm positive it's not," I whisper back, not turning around as I feel his large hand settle on the base of my spine.

I can feel him breathe in as he reaches around me, grabbing one of the pies and repositioning it to make himself look busy.

"You look stunning tonight," he whispers, his breath tickling the shell of my ear. I resist the urge to lean backwards into him, my eyes shutting as his woodsy smell envelopes me.

Just as I'm about to respond, Leo stumbles up to us, nearly bulldozing into a small child as they run past, their screams both adorable and infuriating. Owen's hand quickly disappears.

"What's up guys?" he asks, his eyes flipping between the both of us.

"Just making sure everything is organized." My lips thin into a tight smile as I turn toward him. Instead of continuing the conversation, I run.

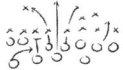

"I just really think that soup shouldn't count as a meal."

"Excuse me?"

"It's more of a beverage, you know?"

"You need to stop talking, man."

"You know it's true."

It's been two hours and all I've done is walk around Leo's apartment, making small talk with some wives and girlfriends and eavesdropping on conversations between grown men that make me shake my head.

But most importantly, I avoid Owen.

At least, I try.

I can feel his eyes on me the entire night, and the first time I dared to actually sneak a look at him, I felt myself melt.

He looks absolutely mouth wateringly beautiful.

His black slacks hug his giant thighs in the most perfect way. They were made for him. I've never seen a pair of pants fit anyone better.

He wears a dark red button-up shirt, the sleeves rolled up just a touch, the first couple of buttons left undone.

His dark-honey colored hair is slicked back, his beard shaved close.

His eyes glimmer in the light as he talks to a couple of teammates, sneaking looks at me the second they look away.

And his smile?

It lights up the whole God damn room.

My stomach swirls with the anticipation of feeling his hands creep up my waist again, and when I think about it for a beat too long, the anxiety of my brother finding out.

"Honey, how's your holiday going?" my mom asks as she wraps me in a hug. I've barely talked to my parents all night, too worried about dodging Leo.

I shrug. "It's been okay." I tell her, looking at my shoes.

"Have you gotten anything to eat? It looks like the turkey is almost gone."

"That's like the fifth turkey, and there's four more at my place," I assure her. "Cooper has the key, they've been grabbing them all night."

My mom's head tilts, her eyes scanning mine. "You didn't answer my question, sweetie."

I sigh. "No, I haven't eaten yet but I will in a bit."

She puts her hand to my forehead, feeling for it I have a temperature. "Are you feeling okay? This isn't like you."

I shake my head. "I'm fine mom," I assure her, my eyes flickering to Owen across the room.

A little too obviously.

My mom follows my action, and when I look back, she's still looking, catching his eyes flicker to mine, a slow smile spreading across his lips.

She looks back at me, her eyebrow arched.

"Honey, you need to go get that boy."

I rear back, shocked that she would say anything. "There's no one to go get."

Her face twists in annoyance, and I know I'm caught. There's no backtracking. "I'm not stupid, Isla. I see the way that boy looks at you. You need to go get him."

I shake my head. "Leo is going to kill me, mom."

"Leo will get over it. Your brother has always been a bit difficult when it comes to what he believes to be right and wrong. You need to pave your own path."

I cast my eyes downward, not wanting to meet hers.

"What if he kicks me out?" I whisper, realizing that that's one of my biggest fears. I like where I am right now. It feels comfortable. And as much as I want to do what my heart tells me I should do, I have to admit that the fear of losing the stability I thought I had plays a major factor in how I feel about this entire situation.

"Then I'll beat him," she winks at me, her dark hair swaying with the motion.

She would never really lay a hand on either of us, but Leo has always been worried about letting her down. It's not a stretch to say that if she told him she would be disappointed in his actions, I'd be alright.

But I also don't want to lose Leo.

Don't want to upset him.

"Honey," she places her hand on my forearm, her other hand reaching out to grab my chin, forcing my eyes on hers.

"You need to do what's best for you, and if what makes you happy is that boy over there who looks at you like you're the only person in this whole room, then you need to do that, do you hear me?"

I nod, but I'm still not quite sure if I believe it.

An hour later and I desperately need to have some time to myself. I can feel my anxiety creeping into my chest, my hands shaking as I try desperately to hold conversations I have no interest in being a part of.

I search for Cooper but can't find him in the sea of people, which feels like it should be impossible with his height, but I come up with nothing. Getting my key back isn't going to happen anytime soon, so instead of stress about it, I quickly make my way down my brother's hallway to one of his guest rooms, shutting the door quickly and hoping no one saw me and follows out of curiosity.

Walking over to the bed I take a seat, my feet screaming in pain from my heels.

Closing my eyes, I lean back, flopping down on the mattress and breathing in deep.

But a second later, the door creeps open quietly, and I can feel someone slip into the room with me.

Sitting up quickly, my eyes wide, I watch as Owen quietly closes the door, his massive frame seeming to take up the whole thing, before he turns, his hungry eyes devouring me from across the room.

"You okay?" he asks, taking a step closer. Despite his concern, it feels a little bit like a predator stalking his prey.

My head starts spinning, heat swirling in my belly as I watch him.

But anxiety takes over.

"I don't know if I can do this," I spit out, my eyes filling with tears.

The hunger in his gaze is quickly replaced by curiosity and panic, his steps become faster as he makes his way over to me.

"What's going on Peaches?" he asks.

I shake my head. "I don't know. I don't know if I can deal with all of this."

"All of what?" the lines between his brows deepen.

I motion between us. "All of this, Owen. All of it. It's so much, and I just don't understand what it is. I don't understand why I feel the way I do, and I don't want Leo to hate me. That's my biggest thing."

"He's not going to hate you Pretty Girl," he tells me quietly, kneeling between my legs as he runs his warm hand along my chin.

"He may. He may hate you, too. And I can't do that to

you. I can't do that to him either." I don't tell him about what my mom said. It's not worth it.

"Isla, we're both adults. Grown adults, okay? Whatever is happening between us is between us, not between us and your brother. However he feels is his own issue, not yours, not mine, not anyone's." His eyes are intense as they stare into mine, keeping my gaze captive as he runs a thumb across my lips.

"I know," I whisper, trying to look away. He brings my face back.

"I want you to know that it's okay to feel the way you do, but just know that these feelings aren't stupid. They're not something that'll pass for me, and you're not going to ruin anything, you got it?"

I don't want to nod. I want to tell him he's wrong, and then go home, lock myself in my room for a couple of days, and only come out when my heart feels like it's been put back together again.

Whenever that happens to be.

But that's not what I do.

Instead, I nod.

35

OWEN

It hurts to hear that Isla is so worried about us, because she's all I want right now.

Sure, my career still comes first. And I know that she would understand that. That's just being a professional athlete. That's just being someone passionate about what they do.

But this relationship? It's real, it's intense, and it's something I so desperately want.

The other part of being a professional athlete is we don't let distractions get the best of us. If Leo gets mad at me for my relationship with Isla, he's not going to risk a game to show his annoyance. I'll still get targets, I'll still play the best I can.

Our relationship isn't going to hurt anything, and if it does, then that's Leo's issue, not mine.

"I promise Pretty Girl, you have nothing to worry about, okay?" I whisper as she struggles to look away.

Her beautiful green eyes lock onto mine again finally, and after a couple seconds, she nods. It's faint, and if I weren't looking for it, I could have missed it. But it was a nod regardless.

"That's my girl," I whisper, snaking my hand behind her

neck and drawing her close. "I don't want you to be scared of anything, okay?"

"Yeah," she says simply, and although she hugs me back, her body is stiff.

I hold her for a couple of minutes, my face buried in her hair as her vanilla perfume makes my head spin.

But she pulls away suddenly, her eyes unsure.

"I think we should let fate decide."

My face twists in confusion.

"What do you mean?"

"I mean that we should let fate decide whether we continue this. You've been first in fantasy for weeks, right? I've been almost there but not quite. I win, we keep this up. You win, we don't. You just can't touch your lineup for the week unless someone is ruled out."

I look at her like she's crazy, because what she's saying is.

"I can easily just go insane this weekend," I tell her with a shrug.

"Then I'm dropping you."

"What?"

"I'm going to drop you." She whips out her phone, opening the fantasy app and clicking on my name.

"You realize that I'll go on waivers and get picked up by someone else, right? You can't get me back if you drop me."

She nods, her eyes large and intense. "I want this Owen, but I don't want this if it's going to end. If there's an expiration date of any kind. I don't want this if it's not meant to be. Do you believe in fate?"

I haven't. Not really. But the longer I think about it, I think I believe in it sometimes. I think that everything happens at certain times for clear reasons, and not a second sooner. That counts as fate, right?

"I think so," I tell her, still unsure.

"Okay." And before I can stop her, she hits the drop button.

My phone buzzes in my pocket, and I check it to find the notification letting me know her team dropped a player.

Me.

She dropped me from her team. Me, one of her best players, guaranteed to get her points, right before one of the most important fantasy weekends of my life.

She wins without me, as a team who consistently came second to myself, and we can try this. We can continue what we've been doing. We can work on us.

But if she doesn't win, if I continue to be on top, we don't.

And what happens then? We pretend like none of this has happened? I can't do that.

I breathe out, anxiety gripping me like a vice.

"I can't believe you just did that," I whisper.

She shrugs, and I can see it in her posture that her mind is completely made up. "Fate has always directed me down the right path. Just believe in it now."

I nod, closing my eyes. I agreed that I somewhat believe in fate, but I'm second guessing myself now.

I think she overestimated how much I did.

I overestimated it.

Maybe I should have been honest with my thoughts about it.

The dread in my stomach only intensifies as I focus on her face, trying to prevent myself from pushing her back and kissing her senseless. Will this be my last opportunity to?

Her small hand strokes my cheek, her forehead coming to rest on mine. "You need to trust me, okay? This is for the best."

I nod, not so sure she's right this time.

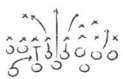

Isla and I stayed in the room for a couple more minutes before making our way to the party. I go first, and the second I walk back into the main room, I know we're fucked.

The entire fantasy league stands around, their phones out as the low hum of chatter silences. They look over at me, their brows furrowed.

I stop, my excuse running through my head at a million miles a minute.

And then Isla walks out. She does a double take as all eyes land on her, people realizing that it looks like we came from the same place, but she keeps going, disappearing into the crowd, desperate to get away.

And I'm really glad.

"Why would this guy drop him?" Tristan asks, scratching his big head.

"I'm not sure man, but maybe Owen knows."

Cooper turns toward me, grabbing me and pulling me to the rest of the group.

"Is there some kind of weird deal going on right now?" he asks, his eyes narrowed.

"What do you mean weird deal?" I ask. Yeah, there kind of is a weird deal going on right now, but it's nothing they have to know at the moment.

"You've checked your phone, right? The new guy dropped you. Why would he drop you?"

I shrug, pretending to be shocked but unconcerned. "Who knows. I've been a little disappointing the last couple weeks."

"You've been consistently one of their top performers," Tristen deadpans.

"I don't know guys, you'd have to ask him."

"We text him all the time and never hear anything back. Ever. The guy hasn't answered a single one of us once. We've actually tried to propose different trades with him. Nothing."

That doesn't surprise me. Isla has said that her brother had a number for her, but she isn't actually in the groups. She doesn't get messages at all. It does surprise me, however, that Leo doesn't answer them and try to enact some kind of weird plan to get ahead.

But I think he also knows that he'll never live it down for as long as he lives if he did. Having his sister secretly be in the league is one thing, pretending to be her and making deals with people as the commissioner is a whole other thing.

And entirely unfair.

"I don't know guys, it's not really for me to be concerned about."

"Who has first waiver priority?" Cooper asks.

Tristen scrolls through his phone, finding the list. "Leo. He's barely done anything all season. He hasn't picked anyone up for weeks."

"Shit. Did he see the notification?"

"I mean I would assume."

"Dammit. Fuck. He's going to get him."

I roll my eyes, half annoyed and half happy that it's a fight to pick me up.

But my chest squeezes, upset that she dropped me, and more upset that I agreed to leave this thing up to fate.

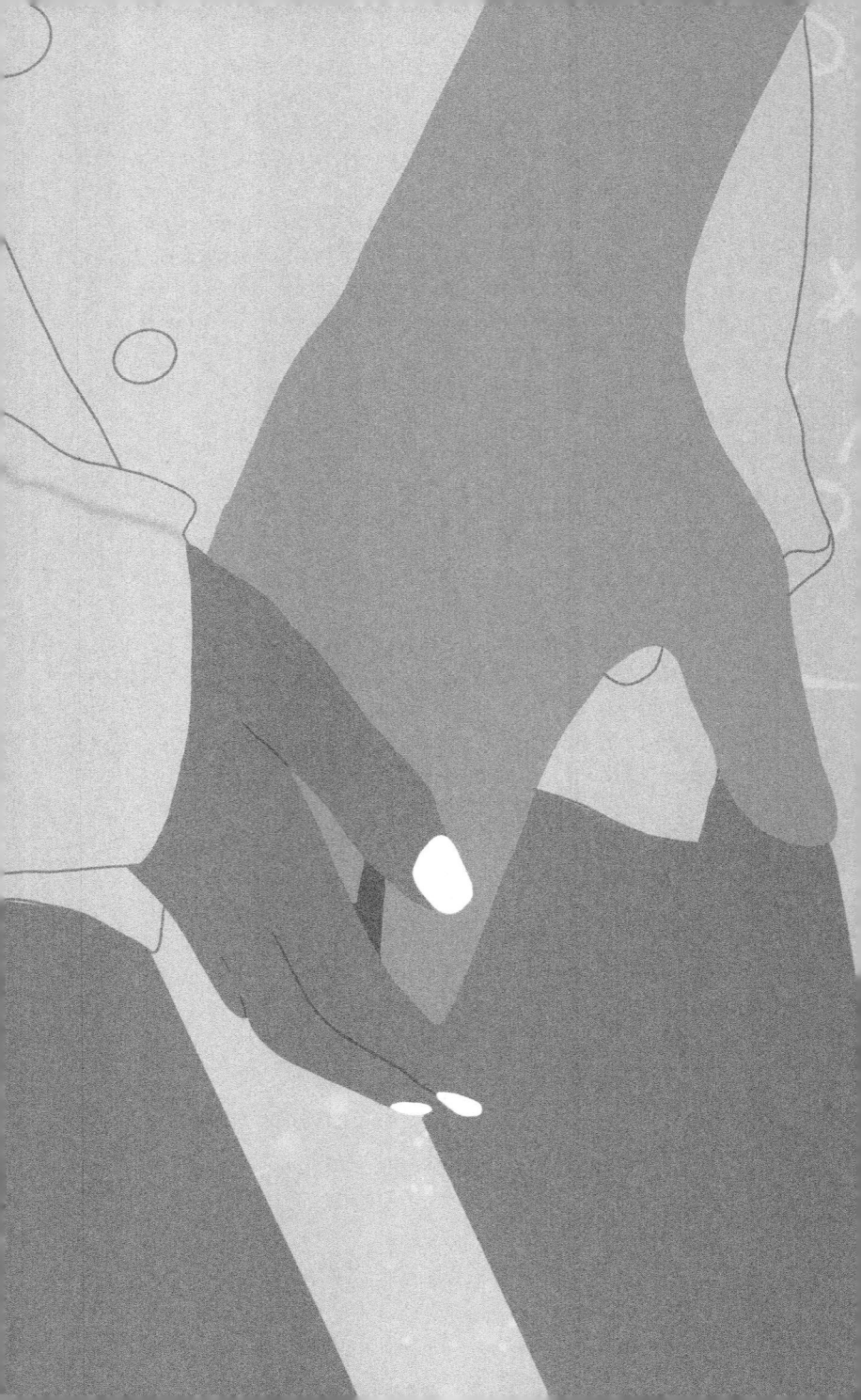

36
ISLA

I don't know what I was thinking when I decided to leave this up to fate.

Actually, I do. I wasn't thinking. That's the only answer. I wasn't thinking at all.

And it may ruin everything for me.

Once again I let my rash decisions possibly cripple everything I've cared about, and I'm terrified.

I know that all of the guys had a lot of questions about why I dropped Owen, but thankfully they all still think it was Ian. If I got any messages, I don't know. They all text, and for some reason not a single one of them other than Owen has had the brains to just message me through the app.

I replaced Owen with one of the other wide receivers on my bench, and so far they've done pretty well. I have one more person playing tonight and Owen has two, and our fates will be decided.

And it's terrifying.

Regret swirls within me as I watch our scores at the start of the Monday night game. I'm behind, and the player I have left is my kicker while Owen has a receiver and his defense.

It seems like a slam dunk. I'm going to get the shit kicked out of me, losing in the process.

And this loss is going to hurt a lot more than any other loss I've ever had in this stupid game.

I kick myself once more.

I mean, I could go back on it, right? But then I would be admitting that fate doesn't mean shit. Nothing matters, and that I'm wrong.

But, I could definitely be wrong. I could absolutely be wrong. I don't have to pull a Leo. I can admit when I'm wrong.

I groan, dropping back into my pillow on my couch, wrapping my blanket around me tighter.

The first quarter goes by without a hitch. My kicker gets a few points, but nothing crazy, and Owen's defense is doing really well, allowing his receiver to spend more time on the field, gaining points on me.

And then it happens.

The second quarter is a bloodbath. I'm not sure what changed, but the other team comes back with a vengeance, beating the crap out of the other. Their defense pulls off sack after sack, and seven minutes in they get a pick-six. My kicker strolls onto the field, kicks a field goal, and heads back.

Their defense demolishes the other team once more, their offense returning to the field once again.

And once again, only a minute or two later, they score.

My kicker gets more points.

In the fourth quarter my kicker has twenty points, which is almost unheard of unless you're one of the best in the league and desperately trying to kick from far back in an attempt to get points on the board to win.

I was still behind until Owen's defense's team dropped to negative two points.

And at two minutes to go, I'm winning.

Somehow, by some miracle, I'm winning.

The clock ticks down, and the second it reaches zero, I check once more.

And I won.

I stand, looking around. I don't even know how to process what just happened.

I had a nine-percent chance of winning going into this game. A nine-percent chance. That was all. And I won.

A knock on my door rips me out of my stupor and my head whips in the direction of it. It's probably Leo coming to ask me something about the game, right?

I head over to it, preparing to tell my brother to go home. I'm too tired to talk to him tonight. Too nervous about what this means.

But when I open the door, I'm greeted with the biggest smile I've ever seen on the most handsome man.

And my stomach drops to my feet.

No words are said between us. Instead, Owen pushes me inside, closing the door gently behind him before he grabs my face, his lips instantly on mine.

And they're not gentle. Or nice. Or sweet.

Instead, Owen's fingers tangle in my hair, pulling on it as he pushes himself closer to me, his teeth scraping my lips, his tongue fighting mine for dominance as I moan into him, pressing myself up against him as if I can't get close enough.

We pull apart for a second, our breath mingling as we catch our breath, our eyes locked into each other's, his fist tightening around my hair.

He doesn't have to say a single thing.

I nod, giving him permission.

In an instant I'm swept up into his arms, carried to my bedroom.

Owen's arms feel like home and safety, and through the dizziness of my head, through the lust running through my veins, part of me just wants to curl up within them and sleep.

But I can do that after he fucks me, right?

Owen flips on the light when we get inside before tossing me on the bed, but I don't have any time to process the action before he's on top of me, his hands roaming my body as he lifts my shirt, ripping it off my body in one go. His mouth is instantly on my chest, kissing, licking, and biting at my skin as I arch my back into him, trying to get closer and closer to his touch. To feel him better, if that's possible.

He reaches behind me, fiddling with my bra for a second before he successfully unclasps it, pulling it from me.

And he sits up, watching me as I shiver.

He's seen me naked. He's had his head between my thighs, his tongue buried in my pussy.

And yet this feels so much more intimate somehow. A shiver runs down my spine at the memory, my breath speeding up.

My arms come over my chest, all of a sudden feeling way too exposed.

Owen shakes his head, grabbing my wrists before pinning them above my head.

"Don't hide yourself from me, Pretty Girl," he whispers as his head dips, his mouth hovering over my pierced nipple as his tongue peeks out, flicking it.

I throw my head back, a feeling I can only describe as ecstasy flowing through my body with a fury.

I've never felt anything like this. So much passion. So much lust.

I want all of him.

And I want it now.

Kicking into gear, I push into his hands, trying to get up. He lets me, and when my hands are free, they instantly fly to his shirt, lifting it off his torso.

I've never seen a more beautiful man in my life.

All hard muscles, perfectly sculpted just for me. Pushing him over, I climb on top, and his eyes watch me curiously as I settle above his hard cock, the heat of our desire warming me. His hands grab my chest, his thumbs rubbing against my sensitive nipples as I arch my back closer to him.

Grinding into him, I take the chance to kiss up his chest, running my tongue over his abs before up his neck, kissing along his jaw, and biting his lip.

Owen growls, the most delicious, sexy sound, and all thoughts disappear from my head.

"I want you now Owen."

"Then take me."

I sit up, kicking off my shorts as he kicks off his. My muscles are tight with anticipation, my head fuzzy as I climb back on top of him without a care in the world about how big he is.

Because he's fucking huge.

But I don't have time to marvel at him. I don't have time to wrap my mouth around his cock this time.

Maybe next time.

But this time, I want him. I need him inside of me more than I need to breathe.

"Go slow Is—"

In one quick movement, I slide down on him, feeling him fill me completely. And it hurts.

But it also feels so damn good.

"Fuck," I breathe, squeezing my eyes shut.

"Are you okay?" he asks quickly, his fingers caressing my cheek the way I love.

I nod, breathing through my mouth as I lift up slowly, bringing myself back down on him.

"Fucking look at you," he whispers, his hands making their way down the sides of my body before grabbing my hips. "Taking me so fucking well. You look so fucking pretty taking my cock."

My eyes roll to the back of my head at his words, letting

them wash over me. Letting them make me feel pretty. Letting them make me feel sexy.

"God I've been waiting for this for so long," he says as I rise again, dropping myself back on him faster this time. His fingers dig into my skin before one hand makes it's way to my hair, grabbing it at my scalp and pulling it back to expose my neck, my spine bending to his will.

"You like that?" he asks, panting.

I moan in response, my nails digging into his chest as I drag them down. When they reach my body, I bring them up my torso, pinching my nipples between my fingers as I feel him watch.

"Just like that, Isla, fucking look at you."

I bring myself down faster and faster as his words are replaced with moans of pleasure, and before I know it, Owen hooks his leg around mine, turning me over in one swift movement as he hovers above me.

"I'm not sure how long I'm going to last here, Isla. Are you on anything?"

I nod. "I have an IUD."

"You want me to fill this pussy up?" he whispers as he sucks on my neck, dragging his teeth along my jaw.

"Please Owen," I whisper, gripping his ass in my hands as he pulses inside of me.

"Beg for it."

"Fucking please, I want nothing more," I cry as I'm pushed over the edge.

My whole body is set on fire, my whole body contracting against him as I scream his name, not even worrying about who may hear.

He keeps slamming into me for another moment before he moans. "I'm coming Isla," he says as he slams into me once more before his arms quiver around me, his head dropping to mine as I feel him fill me.

He stares at me, our eyes locked as our breath mingles between us, the smell of sweat and lust filling the room.

"I think I believe in fate a little more than I did yesterday," he whispers before kissing my nose.

"I do too."

WEEK TWELVE

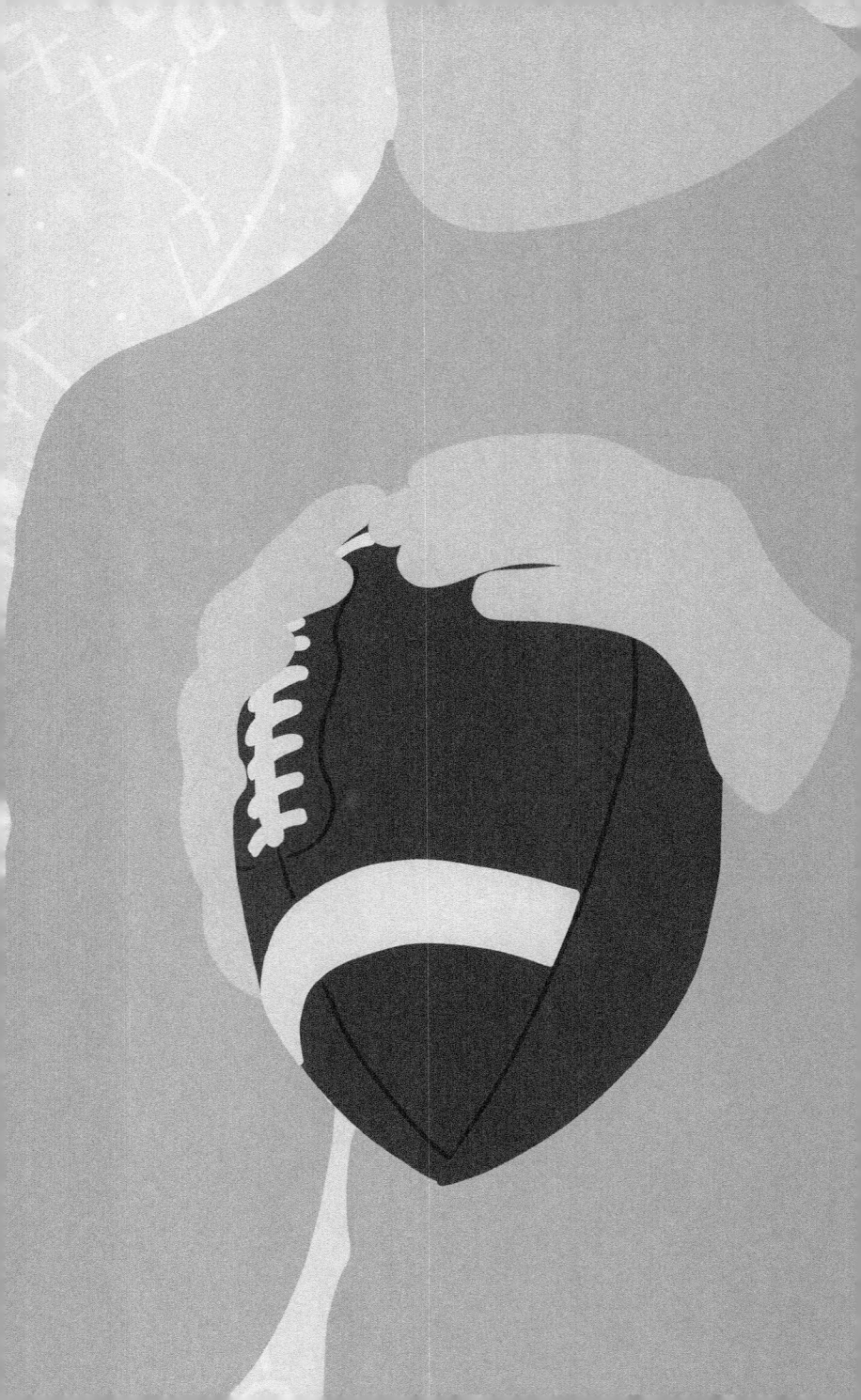

37

OWEN

Isla and I spent the entire night wrapped up in each other, our bodies intertwined, my mouth on her skin.

By the morning, we're both exhausted, our hair a mess, our eyes bloodshot.

I pull her into me, her ass grinding against my steel hard cock, my lips curving upward against the back of her head.

"How are you ready to go again?" she groans, her voice groggy from the hour of sleep we got.

"Just something about you," I whisper against her, my hand carefully dragging down her body.

"Mmm."

Silence settles between us again, and for a moment I think that she passed out.

"What are we going to do now?" she asks suddenly, turning onto her back so she can look at me. I keep my arm draped over her body, propping my head up on my elbow.

"What do you want to do?" I ask her, putting the ball in her court. I want her to be comfortable, and I'm willing to go at whatever pace will make her comfortable and happy.

"I don't know," she shrugs, her eyes examining my face. "I want this to be between us for awhile longer."

I nod, completely okay with that. The longer I get her all to myself, the better.

"We can do whatever you want," I assure her, running my fingers through her hair.

She smiles at me, closing her eyes as she pulls the blanket back up around her. "Don't you have to go to your workout?" she asks sleepily.

I look at the time. I'm usually getting there around now, but the workout today can happen at any time.

I shake my head. "No, I'm comfortable right here for a little while longer."

I get up about an hour later, heading to her kitchen to make some breakfast. Finding eggs in her fridge, I whip up some French toast and eggs, laying them on a plate as I hear her exit her room, sleep still in her eyes as she yawns, my t-shirt riding up her legs as she stretches.

It's a sight to behold, and one I want to see every morning going forward, even if I know that's not possible right now.

"Good morning Peaches," I tell her, watching as her eyes flash to mine playfully. I'm sure the nickname still isn't her favorite, but I know she still loves it.

"Morning," she says as she jumps into her seat, watching me as I pour her an orange juice before sliding it over to her. She grabs her fork as I fix my plate, not waiting to dig in.

"Can't imagine why you're so hungry," I chuckle as she sticks her tongue out at me.

I take a seat next to her, and we eat in comfortable silence.

"You know, next week is our bye week," I tell her as we finish up.

"Yeah?"

"Yeah. Your brother is going to Mexico with one of his girls."

Isla rolls her eyes, her face twisting with disgust at the mention. She told me at one point that she doesn't get involved with any of his girls, because they're never going to last. And I get it. If I didn't have to hear about the girls he hooks up with, I would be a happy man. That's just, unfortunately, not the case.

"Good for him. Maybe you can spend the week here?" her eyes light up.

"Well, I was thinking about something else," I tell her, spinning her chair as I take her hand.

Her face twists in confusion, her eyebrow arching. "What do you mean?"

"Will you go on a trip with me?"

"Like, a trip trip? Like to somewhere outside of the state?"

I nod.

"Where?"

"New York City."

"What the hell are we doing there?"

"Does it matter?"

"Owen it's New York City. You know how many people live there?" I stay silent. "A lot. Like, I'm not sure how many but I know it's a ton. That's a lot of eyes that can recognize us. Do we want my brother to die from a heart attack on his vacation?"

"Well I have a feeling your brother isn't going to be doing much on his phones the whole week," I say, and Isla makes a gagging sound as she turns away. I turn her back toward me. "but I want to go away with you. We can wear disguises. Again. I'll get a new mustache. One that stays on better this time."

Isla examines my expression, trying to find out if this is a trap or not. It's not.

"I want to go away with you," she says as she looks down. "I'm just nervous."

"Trust me, okay?"

"Okay."

"Whoever wins this week gets to decide what we do, alright?"

She nods.

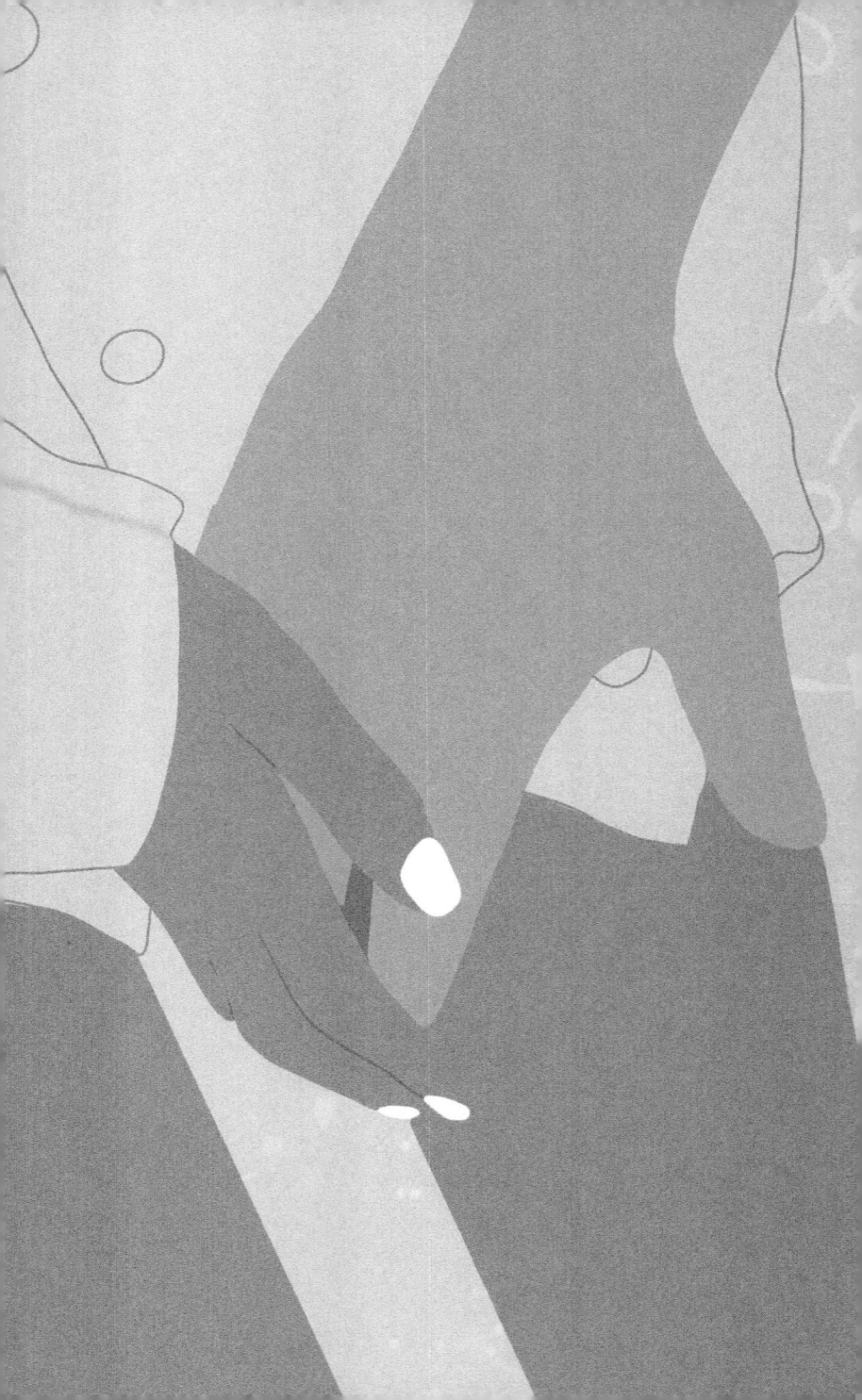

38

ISLA

Owen left around ten in the morning on Tuesday morning, but returned around eight at night.

"I brought you tacos," he tells me as I open the door, pulling him in.

"You know me so well," I tell him, grabbing the bag from his hands and setting it on the counter. We eat, but not before he fucks me up against a wall, both of us unable to contain our feelings.

It's been twelve weeks of feelings growing. Lust building, with nowhere for it to go. Sure, I took it out on my vibrator a couple of times, but that hardly counts in my eyes.

We settle onto my couch, the new episode of the Real Housewives on, when we hear it.

"Isla!" a knock on my door comes, and my back stiffens, my eyes round as I look to Owen, the same look on his face.

"Go, go!" I shoo him. He jumps over the couch, settling behind it as I try to collect his tacos before Leo walks in.

But I'm too slow.

My door swings open without me responding to him, my brother's body filling the doorway as he looks at me.

"What the fuck are you doing?" I ask him, pulling my blanket around me. I'm clothed, but hardly.

He looks me up and down, his eyes suspicious before they land on the two plates of tacos on my coffee table.

"Is someone here?" he asks.

I shake my head. "Mila was just here, but she just left."

"Oh good," he says, his eyes flickering with skepticism before whipping out his phone. "I need your help, and she would be great too. I'm calling her to see if she can come back."

My spine stiffens more, my pulse racing as he hits call, putting the phone on speaker.

"What do you want?" she answers, already sounding exasperated.

"If you just left Isla's, could you come back?"

There's silence for a moment. "No, I can't come back. I left because there was an emergency," she tells him, sounding annoyed.

His eyes narrow at me as if upset he couldn't catch me in a lie. "Thanks anyways," he says simply as he ends the call.

I gesture to the tacos, thankful that she wanted out of whatever my brother has in store enough to not only know to cover me, but to also give her an excuse to not come over. "See? She left her tacos. She was in a rush."

"Mhm."

"What do you need help with?" I ask.

"I need you to tell me if a couple of these outfits look dumb on me."

"You have half a week to go before vacation, can we not do this another time?"

He shakes his head.

"Okay well can you send me photos?"

He thinks about this for a second, his attention moving to my TV.

"What the fuck are you watching?"

"Reality TV. Now can you answer me? Can we please do this over text."

"How are you going to know what it looks like all around?" he spreads his arms, twirling in front of me.

"Take videos."

He contemplates this. "Maybe."

"No not maybe, yes. You interrupted me again, Leo. You told me you wouldn't do that anymore." He rolls his eyes. "Can I please finish dinner? Just send me videos. Better yet, send them to mom."

"Whatever," he tells me with a wave as he turns, heading out the door.

Fucking finally.

When I hear him open his door and head inside, I tap the back of the couch, letting Owen know it's safe to come back out.

He peeks up, looking around before standing fully.

"Does he do that often?" he asks.

I shake my head. "He used to, but not lately. He said that he would stop."

"We need to get you a lock," he says as he rounds the couch, taking a seat before taking another bite of taco.

I nod. We do need to get me a lock.

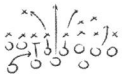

Wednesday night Leo and Owen fly out to their game in Texas. I watch them the next day as they get the win from home, curled up on the couch as always.

They're home the next day, and around 5 in the afternoon, Owen is at my door, dinner in hand.

"How did I get so lucky?" I ask.

"I think it was fate," he smiles, shrugging his shoulders.

He comes into the apartment, setting the bag on the counter before digging into it, producing a lock.

"What's that?" I ask, my eyes wide.

"It's a lock for the inside of your door. If you leave it won't lock you out, but when you're here you can flip it so that anyone from the outside can't get in, even if they have a key. So Leo has to leave you alone."

Anxiety creeps up my throat as I look at it, watching Owen rip it from the package, grabbing a screwdriver from the drawer I keep random tools.

"You okay?" he asks before he installs it.

"Yeah. I just hope that he's not angry that I put it on."

"Isla, if your brother is angry at you asking for a little bit of privacy, then there's a larger issue," he tells me.

And he's right. I know he's right. I know even my mom would back me up. But I just still don't want to find out.

Owen installs it, and we spend the rest of the late afternoon on my couch talking about his time at the game. They did great, and they're still really sure that they could go all the way this year.

"Has Leo been weird about anything?" I ask him.

Owen shakes his head. "I don't think so. I mean, he's weird about a lot of things. But he's been fine with me, if that's what you're asking.

"Did he say anything about me dropping you?"

Owen makes a face. "The guys naturally asked him what was going on with Ian. He said that he didn't know and he thought that he did it on accident," he says.

"But it wasn't on accident. Who picked you up?" It dawns on me that I didn't check.

"He did," he says with a smile.

I roll my eyes. "Of course he did."

We continue talking about the trip and what we're going to bring to New York City when Owen starts looking outside, taking in the beautiful moon high above.

"This place really is gorgeous," he says, pulling me into him.

"It is," I agree.

I get up, rounding the couch to stand in front of the large windows, watching the cars drive by outside as the waves roll in, reflecting the moonlight.

Crossing my arms over my chest, I rest my forehead on the glass. I do this a lot at night. It's peaceful. Serene.

A minute later, firm hands grab my waist.

"Ever since I got here I've been having these thoughts," he says, his fingers brushing the waistband of my shorts.

"Yeah? What kind of thoughts?" I ask, my back already arching into him.

"There's so many people down there."

"Mhm."

Owen spins me around, and we're face to face, his dark eyes practically black as his mouth comes crashing down on mine, my back pinned against the cold windowpane.

"I think I get what you're insinuating," I whisper between kisses.

"You do?" he asks as I pull his shirt off.

I nod.

I'm instantly turned on, the heat pooling in my lower belly as I drop down, pulling his shorts down with me. Owen grabs my controller that sets the lights and turns them down a notch, and we're bathed in soft light.

His cock springs free from his briefs, and I spend a few moments to really look at it this time.

And I can't believe the whole thing fit inside of me as it did.

He's huge. Standing at attention in front of me, his cock is bigger than I've ever seen. I look up, meeting his eyes as he looks down at me, trying to figure out what I'm about to do.

So I lick the tip, watching him as his eyes close, a slow hiss exiting his mouth as I grab the base, pumping once slowly as I take it into my mouth.

Owen backs me against the window, the cold from outside running up my spine, my nipples hardening as the shiver runs through me.

"That's it," he murmurs as I take him in deeper, my fingers rotating as I pump him a couple of times.

He rests his head against the window, watching me from above as I take him the best I can, spit falling from my lips between my legs as I gag.

"Fuck, Isla," he moans.

When he can't take it anymore, he grabs me, lifting me up and ripping my shorts down, his fingers going between my thighs as he feels me.

"So wet from sucking my cock," he says into my neck, pulling at my sensitive skin.

"Please, Owen," I moan, reaching for him,

He spins me, pressing my front to the window. My piercings ring against the window each time they hit it, a wave of pleasure running through me each time.

He pushes my back in, my butt shooting out for him as he dives into me, his right hand wrapping into my hair just like I love him doing as his other grabs my breast, holding it firmly.

"You like the thought of all those people down there seeing you being fucked?" he asks, and I feel myself near release at just his words.

"Yeah," I pant as he slams into me, crushing my chest against the cool window as his left hand moves down to my hip, pulling me into him.

"Anyone could look up here and see us, can't they?" he says behind him, his voice strained as he continues.

"Yes, Owen yes," I breathe, not sure what else I can even get out.

"Fuck Isla, watching me take you in the reflection is so God damn hot," he moans.

I reach down, touching myself as he slams into me, my back arching more and more to get the perfect angle. I get up on my tiptoes to bend over even more, and when his dick hits the right spot, I lose it, my body coiling intensely before coming completely undone at his touch.

"That's it, come for me pretty girl. Just like that," he calls, pulling my hair back.

A moment later he follows, his lips on my neck as he groans, pumping in and out as he finishes, filling me up.

My brother leaves for vacation on Sunday, but Owen has a meeting on Monday so we decide to leave for New York City on Tuesday, staying until Thursday. We're driving so that we don't have to deal with not being seen at an airport.

There's no way my secret is unraveling because of the fucking airport.

So when Owen tells me to be ready early Tuesday morning, I'm at my door the second I get the text that he's here to pick me up.

WEEK THIRTEEN

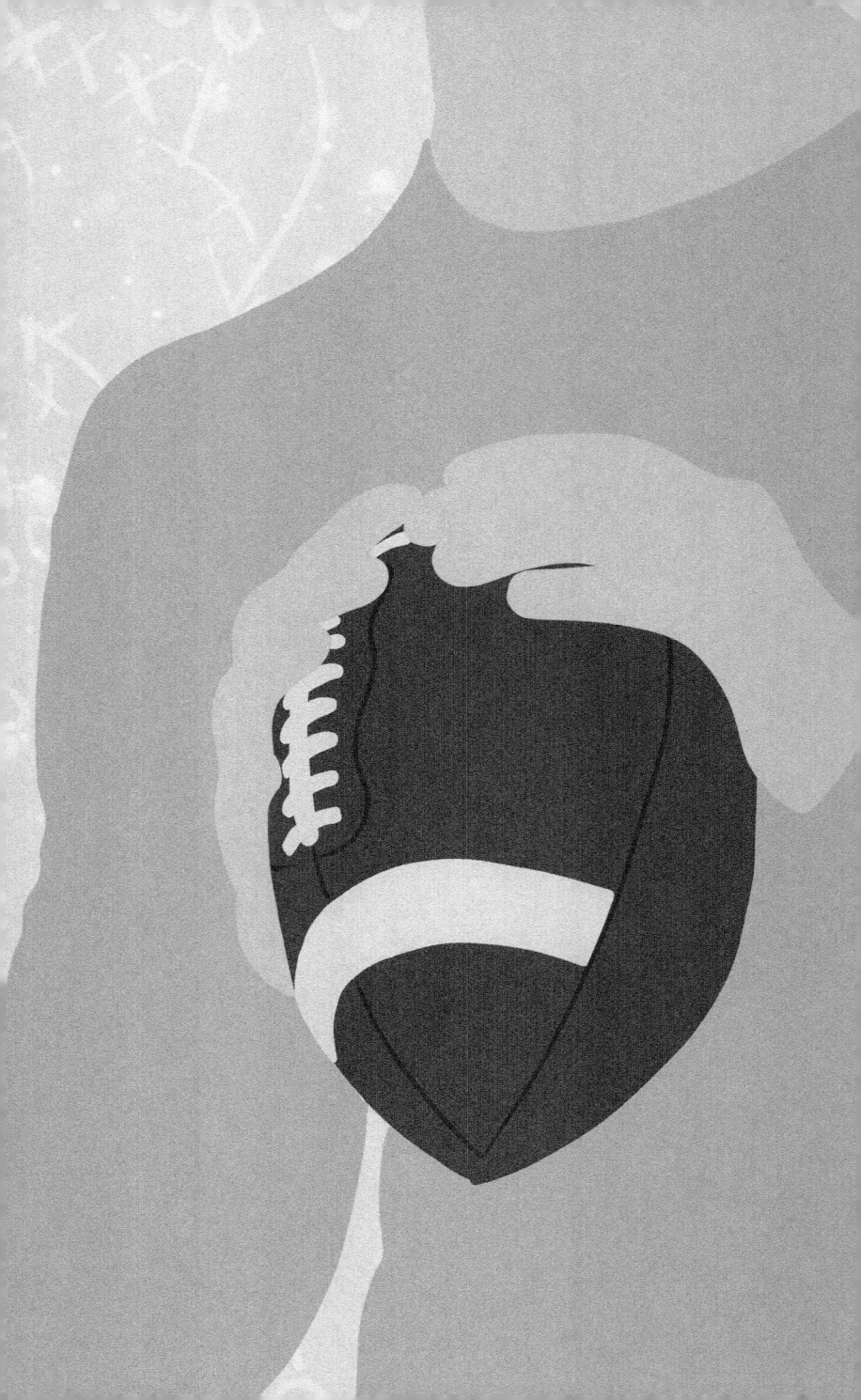

39
OWEN

The trip to New York City wasn't that bad.

I took my Maybach to make sure that Isla is comfortable the entire way there. Plus, although the car sticks out like a sore thumb on our way through Pennsylvania, it fits right in in the city. We'll be fine.

We're probably walking most places, anyway.

We both brought wigs, and I brought a more professional-looking mustache, bought from a local theater store. On top of that, I have sunglasses and a couple of hats to choose from.

If Lois Lane couldn't figure out that Clark Kent was indeed Superman when he wore glasses, I think we'll be fine with what we have while in the city.

Most people there are looking for real celebrities anyway, not athletes from a whole other state.

"You're famous," Isla had told me, not believing that I had said that no one would care. "You're like the first or second best at your position in the entire league. People everywhere know exactly who you are."

But she'd be surprised how many people don't care about football, and the ones who do, don't care about it past their team.

Which is absolutely fine with me.

The drive is only a couple hours, really. About four hours from Baltimore, the drive is pretty easy. We load up on candy and drinks before we're off.

We spend the ride talking about her childhood and how proud of Leo she is. I tell her about mine, too, opening up about how my mom doesn't talk to us much, and therefore my dad doesn't, either.

"Aren't they proud of you though?" she asks, her eyes wide.

I shrug. "I think so. In their own ways. I think they would have been prouder if I followed the path they wanted me to take."

"What did they want you to do?"

"Be a doctor."

"But you're a professional athlete."

"And they're worried about my brain down the road."

Isla nods, understanding. We've talked about this before. The worry about brain injuries is completely legitimate and understandable. I just wish they could be even a little happy for me.

"Have they been to any games at all?" she asks.

"They were at the first one of the season, but they sat on their own. They didn't want anything to do with any of the boxes. Leo had offered."

"That's crazy," she says under her breath.

"It is what it is. They just stay to themselves. My sister talks to them a little bit more than I do but not much."

"Does your sister have a better relationship?"

I let out a laugh. "Absolutely not. She just has a daughter, the one I was watching that day? Well, they love their granddaughter. So she's stuck talking to them more."

We settle into comfortable silence, talking here and there about something she sees on her phone. Later, when we arrive in the city, we find the garage attached to the five-star hotel I booked us for the weekend knowing that no one who works here will say a thing about us. People much more famous stay here without a word.

I leave my car with the valet as someone takes our bags. Checking in, someone gives us our key cards and we head up to our room on one of the top floors with the most perfect view of the city.

"This is so beautiful," she says as she looks out the large window at the buildings outside.

I come up behind her, enjoying the way she instantly curves to me, her back pressing into my chest as her head leans back to rest against me. "Not as beautiful as you," I tell her, kissing the top of her head.

She elbows me. "Stop that," she laughs.

"Stop what?"

"Stop being cheesy."

"It's just true."

Isla wanted to hang out in the hotel for a little longer, relaxing after the long drive. We're there for about two hours, hanging out in bed as we talk about random shit like her favorite breakfast, before we look out the window and realize it's snowing.

Isla's jaw drops as she watches the beautiful snowflakes fall. "There's something magical about snow in the city," she says, her hands against the window.

She's never been here before, and I'm determined to make it the best trip ever. I'm so happy the snow is somehow on my side.

"You ready to get bundled up?" I ask her as I peel off the adhesive on my mustache, applying it to my face.

She turns, watching me do it with the biggest grin on her face. "I can't believe you're actually wearing that thing."

"You're the one who said I'm too famous to not wear a disguise."

She nods. "That's true."

The second we get outside, Isla lights up. She's glowing inside and out, frolicking on the snowy New York City sidewalk is possibly the happiest I've ever seen her.

I won this last week of fantasy, so I got to plan the whole week. Not that I wouldn't let her decide some things to do, too.

But I have something up my sleeve. Something I can't wait for.

"Are you ready?" I ask as we walk through Central Park. I can see the Cleopatra's Needle up ahead, and just past it, covered in snow, sits the glass pyramid structure attached to the back of the museum.

Isla has no idea.

"This place is beautiful," she says as she looks around, gripping her thick hot-cocoa between her mittens.

"I love coming here," I tell her as I follow her gaze, taking in the beauty.

"Have you come here a lot?"

I shrug, pursing my lips. "I've come here enough. My parents used to take my sister and I a lot growing up. Wanted us to see the hospitals we could work in if we became doctors."

"Isn't your mom a nurse?"

"Yeah. And nurses are amazing. But she always pushed us to go to medical school. She wanted to be able to tell people her kids were doctors, you know?"

She nods, and although I know she doesn't totally understand, I know she understands enough.

"We're almost at our first destination," I tell her, pulling her closer. She looks up at me, her eyes wide before she looks around, her eyes squinting through the snow as we cross the street to come out around the front of it.

"You're kidding me," Isla whispers in front of me, her eyes widening as we walk further. "Is this the MET?"

I want to ignore her. To let her think about it until we're right in front of it. But I can't keep the smile off of my face.

"Shut up!" she screams, grabbing my arm as she jumps up and down, pulling me toward the iconic steps.

"Be careful!" I warn. "They're icy."

"If I die here I'll be happy!" she responds without a care in the world.

Running up the steps, Isla takes them two at a time before coming out on top, looking down at the massive amounts of people walking around it in the middle of the day during the week.

"How have I never been here before?" she breathes as I eventually reach her.

"Are you ready to go inside?" I ask.

She looks up at me, her eyes large. "We get to go inside?"

And I can't help it. I double over, laughing my ass off. "You thought I would bring you here without actually letting you go inside?"

"I don't know!" she throws her hands up, her lips quivering on the verge of a smile. "I thought we may just be walking around it."

"I would never do that to you, Peaches. Come on, let's go in."

There were a couple of paintings I thought it was important for Isla to see, and one of them is coming up soon.

We made it through the east wing of the MET, going

through the whole Egyptian wing with wonder in our eyes. I love this wing the most, actually, and the temple room is one of my favorite places in the entire museum. Although there were so many people outside, the museum is a little less packed, making the whole experience so much more amazing.

From there we travel into the American wing before making our way to the second floor. Here, we explore a couple of galleries until we enter one in particular with an incredibly special piece inside of it.

Isla stops in the doorway, and I almost bump into her. The soft light-brown wood beneath her feet squeaks as our shoes slide along it.

"Is that what I think it is?" she whispers, her head whipping to me before looking back at it.

"Yeah," I whisper, nudging her forward.

Isla practically runs to it, her chocolate hair swaying as she goes. She decided against a wig because of the snow, instead opting for her large white hat to go with her brown skirt, black tights, and large oversized sweater.

Her black-rimmed eyes are wild and excited as she looks from me to the painting in front of her. "Did you know this is her sister?" she asks, practically shaking.

"Yeah?" I didn't know that. In fact, I know basically nothing about this particular artist.

"Their family spent a lot of time in Paris. This is a painting of her sister. It's unlike a lot of her other pieces, but she loved the way the sunlight hit her sister's hat."

"Is she sewing?" I ask, looking closer.

"She's crocheting."

I'm not sure what the difference is, but that's okay.

"It's really good," I tell her. It's not exactly my type of art, but I can appreciate it either way.

She beams at it, and I can tell she wants to run her fingers over it but knows she can't.

Her eyes move over to the paintings next to it, realizing that there's more as she finds another image of a lady in front of some tea cups.

And I wonder what the story is. Why she loves this artist so much. So I ask her.

She looks at me as we stand back, looking at the paintings in front of us.

"Marry Cassatt was a badass," she starts, gesturing to the paintings. "She was friends with Degas. She fought for their art in Paris and paved the way for more modern art to come out. She was truly one of a kind and I hate that she doesn't get more recognition."

And it makes sense.

From there I'm careful to keep her moving across the second floor into the other side of the large building, passing through the European paintings wing slowly but surly, stopping at more paintings than I can count as she gapes at them all, her eyes wide and surprised as she sees some of her absolute favorites.

Heading through their photographs exhibit, we finally reach what I really wanted. The 19th and early 30th Century European Paintings and Sculptures exhibit.

I already know exactly where we have to go, so when we start at the entrance, we make our way through the first couple of galleries before going through the next row above.

"Are you *fucking* kidding me?" she exclaims as we enter the room.

Sculptures line the walls encased in glass. So many of them to look at, and Isla takes her time going from piece to piece.

That is, until she sees the sculpture sitting in the middle of the next room over.

And I watch her heart stop, her head slowly turning to mine, and something I can't place glimmering in her eye.

And I swear I see a tear escape.

She walks to it slowly, taking her time as she walks around it.

The bronze sculpture of the Little Dancer.

"I can't believe I'm seeing this in person," she whispers, keeping her hands in the pocket of her coat. I reach for her wrist, pulling one hand out and squeezing it in mine as I stand in front of it, admiring it with her.

If I were here without her, having not spoken to her about the history behind the piece, I would have probably felt differently. Maybe I would have completely overlooked it. But here, right now, with her, it's like it's our entire world.

Like her life so far has been to see this in person, and now she's here, looking at her favorite piece, the one she can't stop thinking about every day, and now she doesn't know what to do.

"Is it everything you've ever imagined?" I ask her.

"It's more."

We spend the rest of our time looking at the other Degas galleries before heading to look at Monet water lilies as well as his other works, and then head to the next gallery where Isla sheds real tears over Van Gogh, filling me in on his tragic life.

It was enough for me to want to shed a couple tears, too.

Later, when she's tired and saw everything she wanted to on this visit, she makes me promise we'll come back one day and see the rest. It's way too much to see in one visit, and she wants to do all the other touristy things while we're here, too.

"I just want you to be happy," I assure her. "We can do anything you want to."

"How did you get us in here under a fake name?" Isla whispers, looking around the restaurant we step into

"If you have enough money you can do anything, Peaches. Most of the richest people in the world aren't widely known. Just flash some money and you're in."

She nods, still looking around the beautiful dark restaurant as we're led to our private table in the back. Since it's dark, I've taken my mustache off. This place is private with no phones allowed.

Menus are put in front of us, and Isla seems super concerned that there are no prices listed. "Don't worry about it, seriously," I tell her as she scans it.

"Can you order for me? I don't think I've ever eaten anywhere so fancy. I have no idea what half of this stuff is."

I chuckle, looking it over myself. I order almost one of everything, going all out.

I'm no stranger to fancy restaurants. Leo and I used to go to them all the time before he found that girls threw themselves at him. When we were rookies the team would go out to one of the most expensive places, and the other players conveniently *left their wallets at home*. The rookies would have to pay for it.

When you're new to money, it comes as quite a shock to the system, no matter how much your contract was for. Eventually you get used to it, but it was hard to hand over thousands of dollars for food and the most expensive bottles of wine and liquor.

I always wanted to use that money on someone I loved, and eventually started bringing my sister and her daughter out for fancy dinners.

And I can still do that. With Isla in tow.

We settle into our private table, talking about everything we can think of as the most immaculate dishes are sat in front of us.

"They're like art," Isla said at one point, and I'd have to agree with her.

When it's time for dessert, we get a mix of everything plus a tray of the most amazing chocolates we've ever tasted.

And when we're done, and she tries to sneak a peek at the receipt, I hide it, crumpling it up and throwing it out before she can find it in a coat pocket or wallet and offer to pay half.

Since the hotel is on the other end of the park, I order an Uber, and as I'm settling into my seat, Isla reaches across my lap, playfully rubbing her hand across me.

In seconds I'm ready to go, all too aware that we're in the back of a car.

I pin her arm down by her side, entwining my fingers with hers as we both sit, stiff and ready to go, in the back.

The second we get up to our room, she's stripping off her outfit.

"Leave the leggings on," I moan into her mouth as I fiddle with the her bra clasps, slipping it off her shoulders and throwing it onto the floor, pushing her into the door. I grab her hands, bringing them above her head as I kiss up her chest, sucking on her neck before capturing her open lips in mine as she pants.

"Why would I do that?" she asks, struggling against my hands.

"I want to try something."

She looks at me, questions in her eyes as I tilt her chin up to meet my lips again, kissing her gently this time. Letting her arms down, I run my hands along her hot skin, enjoying the flush from the cold on her cheeks.

Lifting her, I carry her to the bed as she lifts my shirt. I set her down before helping her take it off of me, pushing her back as I pull her skirt down, leaving her in just her leggings and boots.

I look at them, running my hands down her thighs before landing between her legs, feeling her over her tights.

She moans, her fingers going right to her nipples as she rolls them between her thumb and pointer finger.

"These weren't expensive, right?" I ask.

Her head immediately pops up as her brows furrow, trying to figure out what I'm doing.

"No?"

"Good."

Taking both sides in my fingers, I rip a large hole in her tights, just enough to pull her thong aside and slip my tongue through, devouring her without another word.

Isla yells in pleasure, fisting my hair and tugging me closer as she wraps her legs around me, her boots oddly sexy wrapped around my neck.

"Oh God, Owen," she says loudly without a care in the world, no longer sharing a wall with her brother.

"Are you going to come for me, Pretty Girl?"

"Yes, please Owen," she pants, her head thrown back further.

I travel up further, sucking on her clit before diving in again, no longer trying to be nice. Not trying to be gentle. I roll her clit between my lips as she tries, pushing into me even harder, her body shaking.

"Come here, please Owen."

"I'm busy," I murmur into her, continuing to devour her.

She pulls on my hair, ready for me to be done. "Now!"

Listening to her, I kick off my pants, climbing on top of her before running my fingers over her dripping pussy, bringing them to her mouth.

"Open," I say, and she does as she's told, sticking her tongue out. I thrust my fingers in, and she closes her mouth around them, her tongue cleaning them off. "Good fucking girl," I growl before lining myself up, thrusting inside of her roughly.

With a moan, Isla grips the sheets in her fists, her eyes closed tight as I let her adjust to me for a moment.

"Do you see what you do to me Isla?" I ask her breathlessly as she reaches her peak again. "I swear you're my undoing."

WEEK FOURTEEN

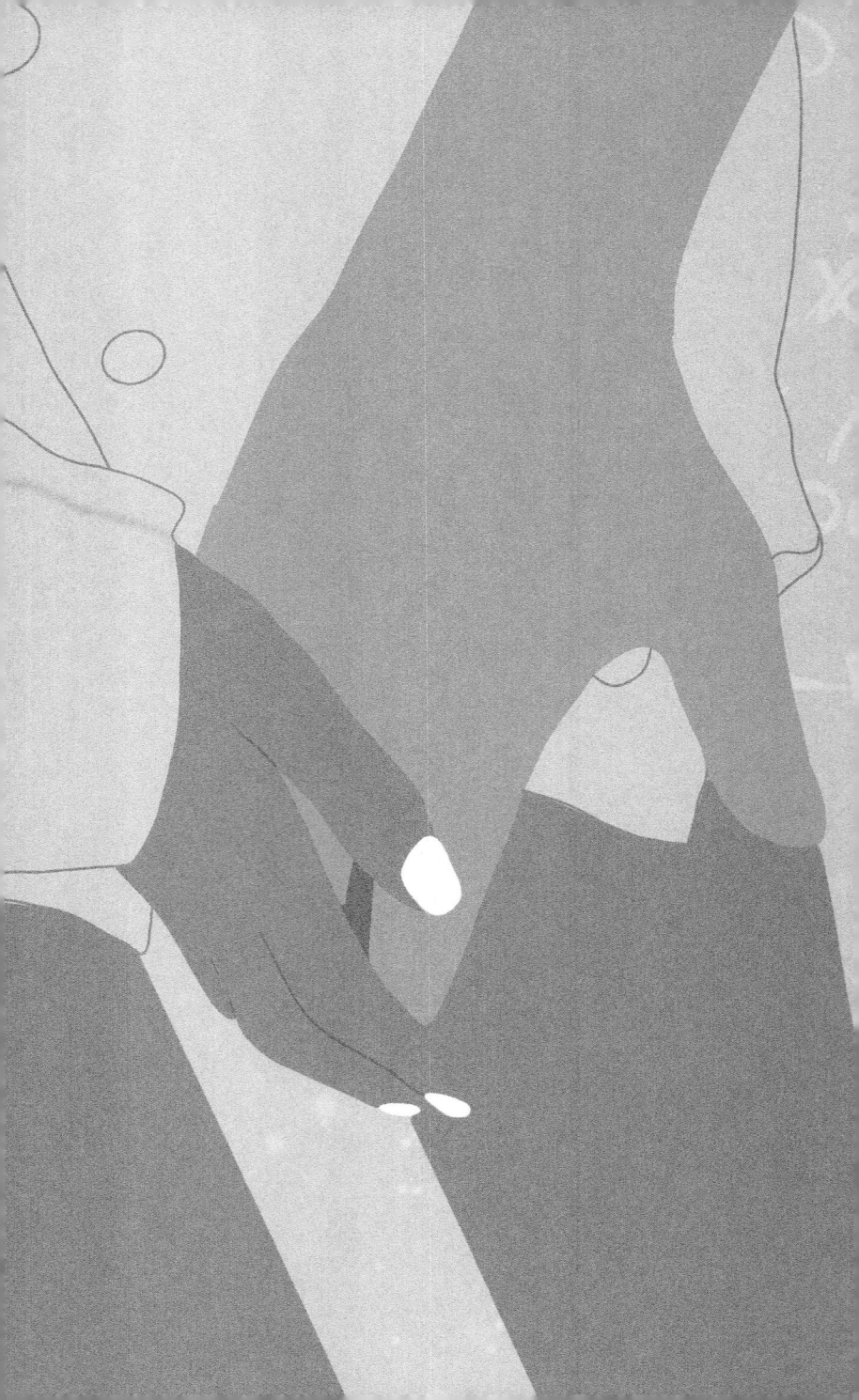

40

ISLA

Bye week flew by, which kind of sucked for me.

I never wanted it to end.

Leo was back by the time I arrived home on Thursday and was really confused about where I went. I told him the truth: I went to New York City with friends, I told him.

But for some reason, he never seemed to question Owen.

Not that I'm complaining.

The last night we were in New York City, Owen took me to Bryant Park to explore all the stands, buying me the most delicious waffles and the thickest hot chocolate I've ever had. Since it's only a few weeks until Christmas now, all the lights were up in the city, Christmas decorations everywhere.

After we were fed, Owen took me ice skating. Something I've never done, but he kept me from falling on my face.

It was a questionable activity, and I had to ask him if it was in his contract that he couldn't, which he wouldn't answer. But I had fun anyway, and Owen's ankles came away unscathed, thankfully.

What was even better about the bye week is that although

we weren't home for it, I won this week, and Owen has to do one thing I want to do.

"You want to do what?" he asks Tuesday morning. He slept here last night, dodging a text from Leo to hang out. I told him he could. His friendship with my brother comes first, especially with how pissed he's going to be when he finds out about us. I'd rather them be solid.

He didn't want to.

"I want to try wax play," I tell him, but he only looks confused. "You don't know about it?"

He shakes his head.

"I've always wanted to try it."

"What do I need?" he asks.

"Wax."

"Well what kind of wax?"

I shrug. "I haven't looked that much into it."

Owen pulls out his phone, searching for what we'd need. "It looks like they say we need low-temperature candles so that you don't get burned," he says.

"Okay, you want me to get them?"

He shakes his head, already adding a set to his cart and checking out.

Training is ramping up for the Cobras the closer they get to playoffs. They're pretty much guaranteed a spot, and they're all so excited.

So when Owen tells me that he's going to be a little late on Thursday, it doesn't come as a surprise.

He had been over a little bit on Wednesday, but he left to spend time with my brother, sneaking out and just going next door.

But when he comes by on Thursday, he has a bag of candles, a lighter, and a silk tie that it came with.

"I'm thinking dessert first," he says as he crushes his lips against mine, making sure the door is locked before picking me up and leading me to the room.

I've been working on paintings all day, cooped up on my living room floor, and a break feels great.

I got a call from the man I sold my painting to at my last gallery showing who told me that he called the owner and got my contact information. He showed my piece to a collector, a friend of his, who talked to someone who owns a bigger gallery. They want me to show my pieces in a couple of weeks.

Just me.

And I was invited.

The gallery would get a percentage of my sales, but I get to keep the rest. No paying to show there, either.

Although excited, I've been stressing ever since, making sure I have enough pieces to show.

I haven't told anyone yet, either.

I just want a night to relax with Owen.

Securing my hands above my head with the silk tie, Owen smiles down at me, ripping his shirt off, exposing his beautiful chest. All I want to do is run my tongue along it as I listen to him moan.

But we have things to do.

Priorities.

"You ready?" he asks.

I nod, my eyes hooded as I watch him grab a candle.

"If it hurts or you want to stop at any point you tell me, okay? One stop and I'm done."

My stomach warms with a now familiar feeling. I can't quite put my finger on it, but I think it's safety.

I feel safe with him.

I feel whole.

I feel loved.

Loved?

I mean, yeah. I feel loved. It's been months, and neither of us have said it, but I do.

I feel cherished and worshipped.

This is how every woman should feel in a relationship.

Owen lights the candle wick, letting the wax warm and melt before holding it high over my body. When the first drip lands on my stomach, I feel the floodgates opening, the place between my legs instantly pooling.

My eyes roll back as Owen watches, and he smiles. "Does that feel good?" he asks, biting his beautiful lips.

I nod as his dark eyes scan me, taking me in. He brings the candle up, dripping some wax over my breasts before holding it over my nipples. The second the warm wax lands on them, I moan.

Owen continues his way back down my torso, down my thighs and back up, bringing the candle closer as it drips onto the inside of them. I resist the urge to clasp them together, enjoying the feeling too much.

At this point my entire body feels over-stimulated, and all I want is to feel him inside of me. But when he drips a bit of wax on the outside of my clit, I can't help the loud moan that escapes me, and he blows out the candle, lowering his head until he captures my clit in his mouth, humming into it.

"Owen please, I can't take this anymore. I need you now."

Instead of arguing this time, he gets off of me, flipping me over so I'm on my front. Bringing my ass back and spreading my legs, he angles himself between my legs before grabbing my hair in his hands, pulling me back to meet him as he thrusts. I yell as he moans, meeting him with every thrust of his hips.

Gasping for breath, I match his tempo, throwing my ass back and hearing it slap his skin as his balls come forward to hit my clit. As I angle myself further down onto the bed and he hits that sensitive spot within, my body hums as I come alight.

Owen groans as I tighten around him, and a few thrusts later, he collapses on top of me, kissing my shoulder blades.

"You liked that?" he asks as he runs his fingers through my hair.

I nod, still trying to catch my breath. "I loved that," I say breathlessly.

"I liked it too," he murmurs into me.

"I should take a shower," I whisper, all too aware of all the wax covering me and now my bed.

He hums into me, immediately standing and heading to the bathroom. Water starts, and a few minutes later he returns, lifting me and carrying me into it.

The first thing I notice is how heavenly it smells, the scent of my coconut soap making my mind numb, and it takes me a moment before I realize that Owen is lowering me into the bathtub gently, the bubbles inside of it covering me.

After I'm settled, Owen climbs in after me, water splashing to the floor as his massive frame fills the rest of it.

I giggle, smiling at him as he tries to get comfortable. This place has the most ginormous bathtubs, and although they're definitely meant to fit two people, most people aren't as big as Owen.

"You don't have to sit here with me," I tell him, running my fingers through the bubbles.

"I want to."

WEEK FIFTEEN

41

OWEN

Isla and I officially made the playoffs, and being the first two teams in the league, we have a bye week as the others battle for a playoff spot.

The last couple weeks with Isla have been nothing short of amazing, and with things being more solid, I feel like I'm playing even better somehow, having less to think about.

We have a one P.M. game today against one of our toughest competitors, and if we win, we clinch a playoff spot. It's serious, and I can't wait.

Practice goes perfect, and when it's time for the game to start, the stadium is alive. I know that Isla is in the box with her parents, and although I can't see her, knowing she's watching adds and extra layer of excitement. I just want her to be proud to be mine.

The first half of the game runs smoothly. I get one touchdown, Cooper gets another one, and Jaire, our running back, even got one for the first time in a bit. He's a great running back, but Leo definitely prefers to throw the ball which benefits me, the other receivers, and Cooper much more.

But this defense has been an issue for us, so we're trying to run the ball a little more.

In the third quarter, Emmett goes down as the other team's tackle runs into him. They bring him to the tent, examining his ankle.

We think he'll be okay, but he's going to be out for the rest of the game.

The other team is catching up to us and I run a whip route as we approach the goal-line, running ahead before spinning, making my way across the field toward the sideline, catching the ball from Leo with ease before dodging their defense, rolling into the end zone.

The crowd roars to life around me as I go up to the stands, handing a kid holding a sign with Leo's number on it. She smiles, exposing her missing teeth as she cheers, turning to show her parents as they wave at me. I turn, pointing in the direction of the Warners' box before running into the group of players celebrating.

The rest of the game goes by without a hitch. One of their linebackers gets injured as well, and we're back on even playing field.

We end up winning the game easily, securing our spot in the playoffs. The whole place roars with applause and screams, and as we go around exchanging jerseys, I'm approached by a couple of journalists.

"Owen! You had such a great game today, thank you so much for talking to us," the woman says as she holds the microphone to her face."

"Thank you so much," I reply as she holds it out to me.

"What are you plans for the rest of the games in the season?"

I shrug, smiling. "We just have to do the best we can. We want to go out with a bang. Just because we got a playoff spot doesn't mean we're not going to try our absolute hardest. We have the best guys in the whole league, and the best defense. I think people really underestimate us, and we're just here ready to prove ourselves."

The woman nods, taking in what I said before bringing the microphone back to herself. "I remember we talked last season and you weren't a man of many words," she smiles, "you've been so happy lately, is there a reason?"

I can't help the smile that creeps onto my face as I think about how I should answer. I decide to answer simply. "I just have a lot to be happy about lately," I tell her, shrugging my shoulder.

She lets me go and I run off toward the locker room, ready to get out of my uniform and talk to my girl.

"I just can't believe that this mystery person is at the top of our league," Emmett mutters under his breath as he changes.

Thankfully, he just rolled his ankle a little, and he should hopefully be able to play next week. They're going to see how he does in practice.

"I keep trying to get answers from Leo but he won't budge. Just keeps saying it's someone who works for the team."

I get changed silently by them, trying to make myself invisible. I don't feel like having this conversation at the moment.

"Do you know what's going on?" Cooper asks me, and I find myself caught.

I turn to him, my lips pressed together as I shake my head.

"Why do you look red?" his eyes narrow.

I sigh. "I'm just tired," I tell him, pretending to yawn.

Apparently very badly.

His eyes narrow further as he grabs my wrist, pulling me away from everyone. When we turn a corner into a private area, he pushes me gently into the wall.

"Spill," he demands.

"I don't know what you're talking about," I say simply, leaning against the wall and crossing my arms over my chest.

"Bullshit Crosby, you know something is up. Now spill. Now."

And because I don't really have any other choice, or maybe because I'm losing my will to care, I do.

"I've been seeing Isla."

Cooper's face is stoic, his eyes looking me over cooly.

Finally, after a few moments of silence, his eyes narrow. "I fucking knew it," he says, punching me in the shoulder.

"What?"

"I knew something was going on between you two. You've been so fucking weird and I saw you two talking at the bar on Halloween. I knew it!"

"It's still a secret. You can't tell anyone," I whisper, hoping he gets the picture.

"You're a dead man dude, but I'm here for you."

"What?"

"Leo is going to fucking kill you, man."

My shoulders sag. "I know."

"No you don't. You know how much he loves her. He's going to strangle you to death."

"I'll be fine."

"Wait, is she the other person in the fantasy league?" His eyes open wide, his lips pursed as he looks down at my naked chest. "I fucking knew those nipples looked familiar!"

"What?"

"Stop saying what, you know exactly what I said. The pierced nipples. You did it for her, didn't you? I knew the nipple looked familiar."

"Why do you know how my nipples look?"

He rolls his eyes. "Owen we see each other naked all the time. I could probably assign a name to everyone's dick pictures."

My jaw hangs open as I try to figure out how to respond to that.

"Okay being completely for real, I think that you two are a good match. I adore Isla and I think that she needs someone like you. But Leo? The big man is gonna be big mad and you need to think about what you're going to do when he finds out, got it?"

I nod, biting my lip. "I want to just tell him already. I think he'll get over it."

Judging by Cooper's face, he's not totally sure.

"I think that he'll get over it eventually maybe, but you need to be braced for impact when he does."

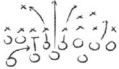

The guys go out after the game, and I go to Isla's. I told them I was just too tired to go out with them. I'm not sure they believed me.

Taking the steps up to her place two at a time, I think about what I'm going to tell her tonight. Whether I should say that I want to tell Leo. To get it out of the way before playoffs.

Although we'd be professional, of course, I don't think it's worth making waves. I'd rather it be out in the open before anything bad happens.

But when she opens her door, all thoughts leave my head.

My girl, standing in the middle of her door, a #4 jersey on… and nothing else.

Not a thing.

She plays with the hem of it, lifting it slightly so I can see she's not wearing underwear.

She bites her lip, her dark hair falling around her in beautiful waves. My mouth drops open, and I swear I'm drooling.

"Holy shit," is all I manage to say as I slam the door shut, locking it twice before turning back to her.

She's instantly in my arms as I pick her up, our tongues dancing as she wraps her arms around my neck, her legs securely around my waist as I bring her to the kitchen island, not even wanting to wait until she gets into her room.

"Congrats on the win," she giggles, bringing my face to hers again. She kisses my jaw before nipping at my bottom lip, and with a growl, I kiss her ferociously, slipping my fingers between her legs as I play with her already wet pussy.

"You were ready for me," I whisper into her. She sighs, not bothering to respond. Instead, she pulls away from me, dropping to the floor where she pulls my pants down, my cock springing to life as she immediately takes it in her hand, placing her warm mouth over it.

She takes me deeper than she has ever before, and I try my hardest not to finish too quickly, but she feels so fucking good it's so hard.

"God dammit, Isla. What are you doing to me?" I manage to mutter as I grab her arm, lifting her up onto the island. I don't take the jersey off. I want nothing more than to fuck her in it, watching as she comes undone wearing my fucking number.

Isn't that everyone's fantasy?

Lifting her leg, I force her legs open as wide as possible as I slam into her, watching her squirm as I bring my thumb to her clit, playing with it as I go.

Her legs jerk, and when she tries to wrap them around me, I force them open once more. "I've thought about this so many times," I tell her. And I have. Every night since this fucking thing started.

"You're so fucking beautiful," I tell her as I watch her squirm.

I can feel her tighten around me, her body shaking, and I follow a moment later.

WEEK SIXTEEN
(SEMI FINALS)

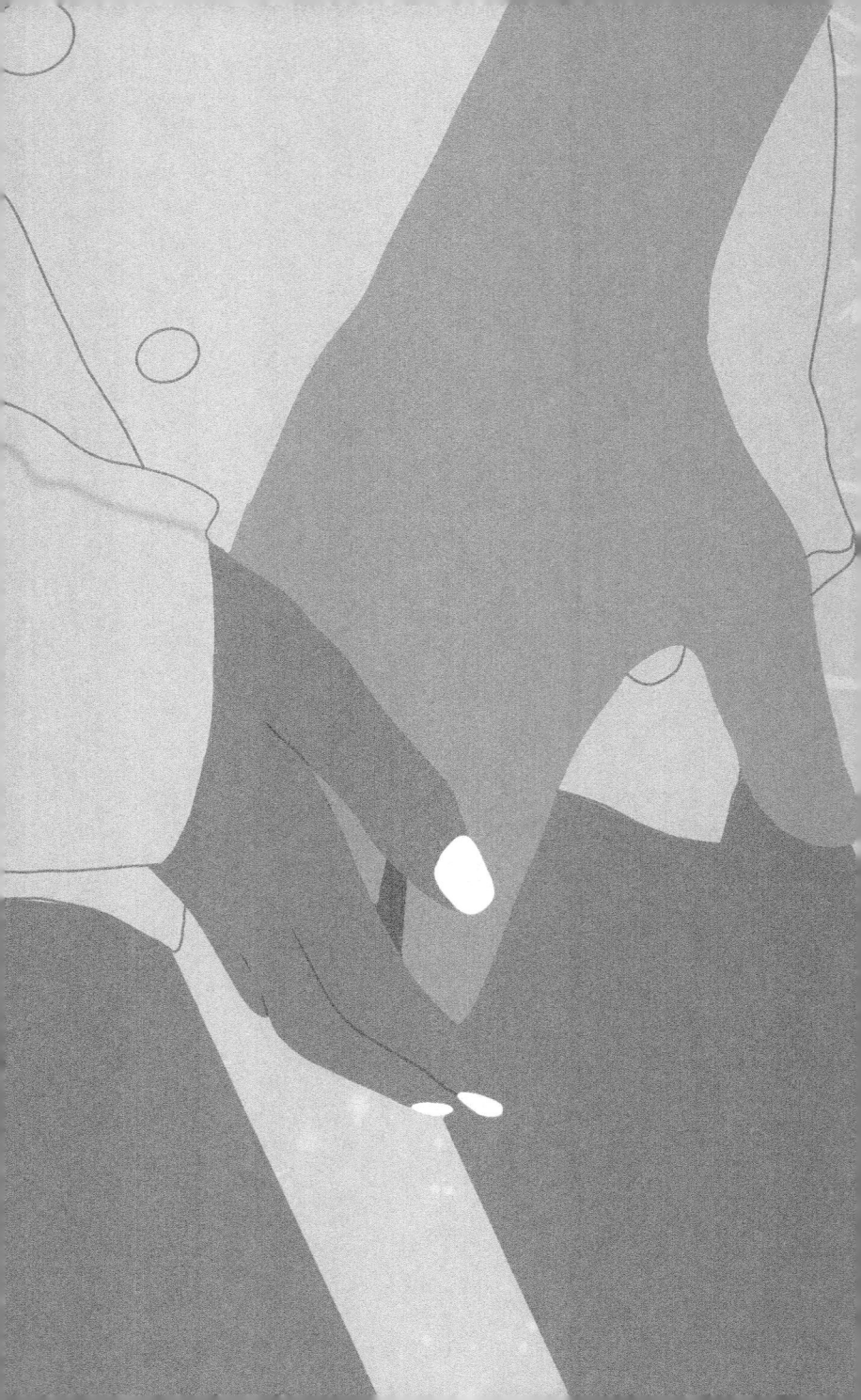

42
ISLA

It's week sixteen of fantasy… and the week of Christmas.

Owen and I play two different people this week, and if we win, we'll be up against each other next week.

Despite me dropping him a couple of weeks ago, my other players have really kept me in the game. I mentally thank them for stepping up.

Meanwhile, Leo has done much better with Owen on his team. I'm happy that I could sacrifice Owen to help the needy.

Wednesday night, Owen turns up at my place as usual with ingredients to make dinner. We sit in the kitchen talking when I blurt out, "I have another gallery showing."

He stops, his caramel eyes meeting mine. "What?"

"I got another showing. I was invited this time. It's in a couple of weeks." I bite my thumb, nervous about what his response will be.

I don't think it'll be bad, but it's no secret that things didn't exactly go as planned the last time.

"Oh my God, Isla that's fucking amazing!" he says, setting down his knife and coming at me for a hug.

He picks me up out of my stool, spinning me in a circle as he kisses my head.

"I assume you don't want us to come?" he says with a sly smile.

My nose wrinkles, my eyes misty at his reaction.

"Umm, it's nothing against you at all, but no. I'm going to tell Leo to stay far, far away."

He nods, understanding instantly. "As much as I want to be there with you I understand," he says.

"Maybe when we're public, and if it's an invite-only showing?" I shrug.

"I'll be there the second you want me there, but like I said. I get it if you want me to stay away."

I nod, smiling as I sit back down.

"Speaking of being public," he winces.

"What?"

"I was thinking. I want you to wear my jersey to the next game."

I still, my eyes wide as I watch him to see if he's joking.

"You're not serious."

He nods.

"Owen, Leo is going to know."

He shrugs. "I want you. I don't care if he knows. He's a big boy. He'll be fine."

I shake my head. "We should wait until after playoffs."

"Weekly loser has to do what the winner wants, Isla. You know this. And I want you to show up to that game next weekend wearing my number."

I pale, my mouth opening but nothing coming out. I want that too. I want things to be out in the open. But I'm not sure I want him to find out like this.

"It's going to be okay," he says, his head tilted to the side as he chops veggies.

"Okay," I say simply, my head down.

"I promise."

It's Friday. Christmas. Owen wakes up at my place before we both set off to spend the day with our families. Leo has already texted me ten times to make sure I'm meeting up with them at the right time, right next door, and I feel guilty every time I think about having to actually face him tonight.

Thinking about next weekend makes my head hurt. Sure, I could win this week. But it's unlikely. Owen has been good. Really good. And although my guys have been satisfactory, they haven't been as good as I would have hoped.

Still better than the others though, and that's what matters.

I can worry about my numbers while playing Owen if I make it to next week.

I asked Owen to help me put up the tree last night while we watched the Thursday night game. It was last minute, obviously, but we had fun regardless. I'm not sure why I didn't put it up sooner, but I'm glad I did.

I had put Owen's gift under the tree before going to bed, and when I wake up, I walk out to a little blue bag under it, too.

My heart flutters in my chest as he follows me out of the room, watching my reaction as I run to it. "Holy shit," I tell say as I grab it. I look at him, practically in tears. "Can I open it?"

He nods, his dazzling smile even more beautiful on his sleepy face.

I carefully remove the tissue paper from the bag, peering inside at the small blue box. Removing it, my heart thuds against my ribcage. I open it carefully, and when I see what it is, my vision blurs, a fat tear running down my cheek.

"I hope you like it," he says, running his hand through his

hair as he watches me. He looks concerned; like maybe my tears are bad.

"This is perfect," I whisper, putting it down on the arm of the couch before running at him, jumping into his arms. He grabs me as I wrap my legs around him, fastening myself to him as close as possible.

"I looked up the exact one Taylor Swift has," he tells me against my cheek.

Climbing down, I grab it, taking it out of the box and holding it out to him.

He brushes my hair out of the way before fastening it around my neck, his knuckles brushing my skin and sending shivers down my spine.

"I realized the other day that I really, really like you wearing my name, Peaches," he says as he kisses my neck, wrapping his huge arms around me.

"I love it so much."

The small circular piece of silver settles between my collarbones, a cursive O sitting in the middle of it.

I turn in his arms, wrapping mine around his torso, my face nuzzles into his upper chest. His chin comes down onto the top of my head as he moves us back and forth, Christmas music on in the background. He must have put it on while I was much too wrapped up in what I was getting.

"Can I open mine?" he asks, and I blush. Mine was much less meaningful, I think.

I nod, and he goes over to the rectangular, flat object under the tree.

Unwrapping it, he just stares.

And I think he hates it.

"If you want something else I can absolutely—"

"No," he interrupts, and when I walk around to see his face, I find tears in them. "It's perfect," he says.

"You don't have to hang it, I just saw the photo you sent

me from the MET and I just loved it so much…" I trail off, not sure what else to say.

After our New York vacation, Owen sent me all the photos he took of me. Of us. I'd never be conceited enough to paint a photo of myself to give to him unless he specifically asked, and even then I think it would be really hard for me to paint, but there was one photo I loved so much I desperately wished I could make it my background. If I didn't have to worry about Leo seeing it, I would.

Owen holds up a painting of us standing in one of the galleries lined with Degas artwork. We were standing back, taking it all in, when a random stranger asked if we wanted a photo.

We posed together for a couple, and then Owen leaned down, placing a kiss on my cheek. His fake mustache had tickled, and my smile was so big it took up half my face. We had erupted into a fit of giggles as the woman handed him his phone back.

And now it's a painting, in my style, fake mustache and all.

"What a mind," he whispers, looking between the painting and me.

I blush, looking down at my hands.

"Isla, I don't think you understand how fucking talented you are," he whispers, placing it down carefully before coming over to me, lifting my chin to look up at him. "You're so fucking talented it hurts."

"It hurts?"

"I'm not sure I deserve you, Peaches."

"You're a professional athlete," I scoff. "If there's one person who thinks that they're under-qualified to date you, it's me."

He shakes his head. "I'm not going to argue with you about that, because I don't want to hear you put yourself down. You're truly exceptional and I wish you saw that in yourself more, beautiful."

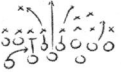

I head over to my brother's around ten in the morning after finding my best sweater. One that I can tuck my necklace into so I don't have to explain it to Leo. I'd rather not deal with that at the moment.

The plan is to spend time with my family before my friends come over tonight to have our own little Christmas together. My parents invited them to Leo's, but I'm not quite sure they're ready for that yet.

Are you kidding me?

Mila had freaked when I sent her what Owen got me. They all had. The second I told them about our New York trip, they were fully on board for Team Owen.

Despite all of my secrecy, they were all happy for me, and that's what mattered.

And that's why we've been friends for so long.

"Are you guys really looking at going back after the season?" I ask my mom and dad as we settle at the table for some Christmas lunch before opening presents.

"Your mom wants to get back to the cows," my dad says with a frown, and I feel like there's something there that I'm not seeing.

"I think they're lonely," she shrugs.

"They're not yours though, right? Aren't their owners taking care of them?" Leo asks from the end of the table.

My mom waves her hand, not bothering with a proper response.

My mom sets food in front of us, telling us to dig in. Leo is the first to listen, not wasting any time.

"How are things going sweetie?" My mom asks as she sits down. I can tell from the glint in her eye that she's secretly asking about Owen.

I look at my plate, quickly stuffing broccoli into my mouth.

She waits for me to swallow, her hands folded in front of her.

I sigh. "It's going well," I assure her with a tight smile.

"Before we go I'd like to have a day with you if that's okay."

"Yeah mom, that'll be great."

We eat in silence for a moment before I realize I should probably tell them at least one thing I've been keeping from them.

"So, I have a gallery showing in a couple of weeks," I tell them, sipping on my wine.

"Really? Honey that's amazing!" my dad says, a huge smile on his face. I blush, unsure about whether they're being serious or they're just trying to make me feel better.

"I was invited to it, too. I usually have to pay to have a show, you know? That's why last time was, well," I meet Leo's eyes and he quickly glances away. "a bit disappointing."

"Don't worry Isla, I'll be out of your hair." He salutes me, his mouth full of potato.

"Thanks, Leo." I smile at him, feeling guilty again for everything.

"I'm just really nervous. I was recommended by someone who bought one of my other paintings, and I can't wait for it, but God, what if no one shows up?"

"Sweetie, your work is amazing. People are going to show up."

I nod, pushing the rest of my food around my plate.

"It'll be good."

Leo and Owen fly out of Baltimore Friday night for their game on Sunday. My parents come over to watch it at my place, and we sit around my living room, pizza spread out on my coffee table as we watch Owen score a touchdown in the third quarter.

The team has been struggling a little bit this game, but they've been doing okay overall. There were a couple of injuries on the defense, including someone else I think is in the fantasy league. Emmett was able to come back and play this week though, so they're still great, forcing turnovers like only they can.

"This is a team that'll make it all the way," my dad says, pizza in his hand as he points to the TV.

I nod. They are. Sometimes you just know.

I grab my phone, swiping through the fantasy app. I'm winning this week, which means I'll likely be facing Owen for finals next week.

I watch as three more touchdowns are scored, and when the clock counts down to zero, the boys celebrate wildly, jumping all over each other. The coach screams, pumping his fists as they come running in.

And I've never been so proud.

WEEK SEVENTEEN
(FINALS)

43

OWEN

One more week of the regular season.

A home game.

And Isla has to wear my number on her jersey.

I thought it was a good idea. Until now.

"I mean they're allowed on the field whenever they want, but I invited them specifically this time," Leo says. "I think all the families should come down before the game. It'll be fun."

My sister and her daughter *are* coming to the game, and I got them passes too before I knew about Isla.

"Oh really?" I ask, pretending like I'm not panicking inside.

He nods, scooping the pizza into his mouth.

"Well my sister is coming with her daughter."

"You know I've never met your sister," Leo says through his chewing.

I chuckle. "She's really cool. Just a little older than me, and her daughter Elara is the cutest little girl alive."

Leo makes a face. "I'm not sure how I feel about kids, man. They scare me."

I sigh. "They scare me too, if I'm honest."

Isla and I talked about it one night after we had sex. What

would happen if something happened? She's not ready to be a mom, and I'm not ready to be a dad. I was relieved to hear that she's not sure she wants kids, much less anytime soon.

We're both so career-driven that it wouldn't make sense for us right now. Maybe after I retire, which, if it were up to me, wouldn't be for a long time.

I want to do this for as long as my body allows me to.

"But Elara really is the best. I'll watch her any day," I chuckle.

"Is your sister's husband coming?" Leo asks.

I grimace. "She's divorced. Her ex will not be coming, that's for sure. He knows I don't like him."

Leo looks at me from the corner of his eye before going back to his phone, shoveling another slice of pizza into his face.

I'm not sure how he gets away with eating so much pizza, if I'm honest. But he's in great shape and the trainers haven't said anything apparently, so he keeps doing what he's used to.

"That's sad," he says simply.

"It is," I shrug. Getting my sister out of that situation was one of the most important things I've done in my life, and I still secretly send her money. She thinks it's her ex, but it's me.

I know she wouldn't accept it from me no matter how much I make. She's too prideful for that.

"Anyway, you should have her sit in our box," he tells me suddenly, looking up.

"No it's okay man," I start, but he glares at me. "No, it's fun. It's warm. Keep the kids warm, Owen. God."

I roll my eyes, smiling to myself as I take a bite of my own food. Chicken. Very different meals.

"Fine," I say to appease him. "She can stay in the box."

With Isla, is what I think. *While she's wearing my jersey.* Should I tell her before she gets there? I'm not sure.

"It'll be a good game," Leo says with a nod.

I hope so.

It's before the game and we're practicing. My heart races as I watch the sidelines for Briar and Elara, but also for Isla. I know that the second Leo sees her he's going to want to lose his shit on me.

Maybe it was best that he find out here before a game. I know for a fact he won't let it hurt his performance, and maybe he'll take his frustration out on other people and not me.

One could only hope.

I run a route, catching the ball from a coach before tossing it back.

Finally, after what feels like hours, the families make their way out onto the field.

Briar and Elara are first, and I smile widely as I see my niece skipping onto the field wearing my jersey, the same as my sister. Her blonde hair flows around her shoulders as she pulls her hat down over her ears, and I'm happy to see that they bundled up so they'd be warm the whole game. The sun is probably going to be setting in half an hour or so, and it's going to get super cold.

But they're also in the box for this game, so if they need to they can stay inside where it's warm.

"Hey you!" my sister calls, waving to me. I wave back, running over to greet them. There's a rope between the sideline and where we are, but I reach over, hugging them both and scooping Elara into my arms.

"Mind if I introduce her to the guys?" I ask Briar.

She shakes her head with a smile, her face glowing as she

looks around the stadium, her blonde hair blowing in the breeze. She's been to quite a few of my games over the years, but she's never actually been on the field.

Taking Elara around to the guys, I introduce her to Cooper and Emmett before Leo. "I love your hair!" she beams, and I pull her away before she can touch his disgusting, sweaty head.

"Thank you!" he beams back, a huge smile on his face as he looks over to the sideline, spotting my sister. "Is that her?" he asks, his eyes flickering to me as his body stills.

"Yeah, why?"

He shakes his head. "She's just not what I was expecting."

I frown. "What the hell were you expecting?"

He shrugs.

Alright then.

Taking Elara back to the sideline, I put her back down on the ground next to my sister, who immediately takes her hand.

"Leo!" a voice calls from down the field. My head whips around, spotting his mother waving at him.

And behind her, Isla.

Wearing my jersey.

My eyes lock on hers just as I watch Leo, standing in front of me, see her too. I watch his neck turn red under our white jerseys—special for this game.

He turns to me slowly, his face a mask of fury.

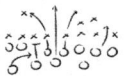

We're up by twenty-four in the fourth quarter, and the minutes are ticking by quickly.

We've been doing great, but mostly because Leo has been ferocious tonight. One of the best games of the season by far.

And I can't help but think it's because he's fucking mad as hell.

I keep thinking about Isla and my sister up in the box together. I didn't have time to tell my sister about her, but she's going to know something is up the second she sees Leo Warner's little sister with my last name on the back of her jersey.

I'm sure her parents had questions, too.

But either way, what's important at the moment is we finish this game out strong.

A minute later coach calls us off the field, substituting some backups for us. We're up enough with plenty of time to go, and he doesn't want us injured for playoffs.

"You okay?" I ask Leo, my hand on his shoulder.

He shakes it off, taking a seat on the bench as he watches the game.

No, he's not okay.

I just hope I don't get my face punched in.

We won the game, and our coach has been giving us a speech for the last fifteen minutes, thanking all of us for a great regular season.

But the vibes are off, considering Leo is standing behind him, his face a mask of anger. Our coach pats him on the shoulder, saying that he's glad that he's fired up for the first playoff game before his eyes find mine in the crowd, realizing that Leo has been scowling at me the entire time.

I'm going to get an earful from him later, too.

It's twenty minutes later as we're getting ready to leave that he blows up, unable to contain his anger any longer.

"What the fuck do you think you're doing?" he hisses, pushing me in my chest as I fall back into the locker.

"What do you mean?" I ask, pushing him back.

"You're going to hurt her, Owen. Jesus Christ, I warned you about messing with her," he practically screams in my face, his fists balled by his side.

"I'm not going to hurt her, Leo. You need to let her live her life."

"I am!" he screams, bringing his fist to the side of the locker next to me. "She has so much going for her, Owen and you're going to fucking ruin it. You should have just left it alone."

I shake my head. "That's not fair," I tell him.

"How long has this been going on?" he asks. Cooper and Emmett come up behind him, along with some of our other friends.

I shrug, trying to find the words. Trying to find the excuses. Trying to find anything I can think of to make this a little better. To at least sound a little better. "It's been going on for a while," I tell him.

"How. Long?"

"We've been talking for the last seventeen weeks," I say quietly, lowering my gaze as Leo seethes, his nose flaring like a bull about to rage.

"I had one rule," he growls, his finger jutting out to poke me in the chest.

I shake my head, surprised. "No, Leo, you had five million rules. For everything. And all of them were so incredibly unfair it's not funny."

His face turns even redder. "Owen, I told you to stay away from her. That's all I wanted from you, and you couldn't fucking do it. How dare you?"

"How dare I?" I wave him off. "This conversation is going around in a circle. You're going to have to get over it at some point."

"I actually don't."

I freeze. "What?"

"I don't need to get over it. And you're going to stop seeing her."

I shake my head.

"No I'm not."

But it's his next words that make me still, and my world collapses.

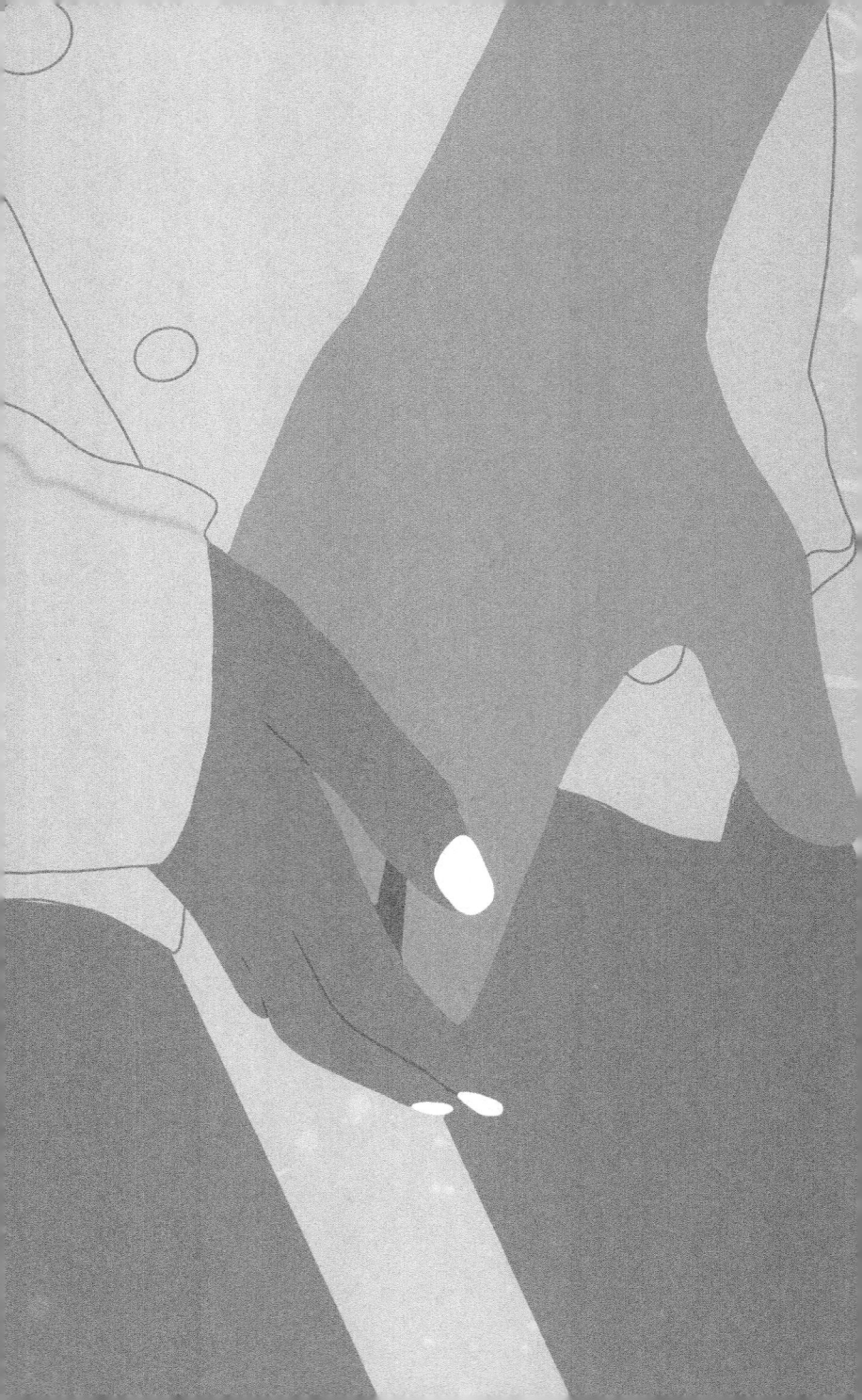

44

ISLA

I won the fantasy season. Not that I feel like celebrating much.

I haven't heard a single thing from Owen since the game, and I can feel myself spiraling.

My brother hasn't spoken to me, either. Not that I want to talk to him at all.

I know that this is about me. I know that Leo is upset. I know that Owen was told not to speak to me.

But I so desperately wish he would at least tell me.

It's midnight, and I finally send him a text, my head spinning. I curl up in bed, trying to keep the tears from coming.

> Can you please just tell me if I did something wrong?

A few minutes later, my phone buzzes.

OWEN CROSBY
> I'm sorry, Isla. I'll explain after the season.
> Please forgive me.

> I just wish you would tell me.

> I told your brother I wouldn't. Just please believe I don't have a choice.

I smack my phone on my bed, covering my eyes with my fists.

God, I hate him. Leo.

He means well. He does. But this? He hurts me every single time he tries to protect me. I can make my own choices. I'm a big girl. I can do it.

But I respect their jobs. I'm not going to go out kicking and screaming. I'm not going to make waves. I get it. This is their job. This is their passion. I just need to get through the next couple of weeks, and maybe, just maybe, I'll get my answers.

Or maybe I won't.

Besides, I'm already overly stressed about my showing in a few weeks. It's coming up fast, and I need to make sure that everything is perfect.

This could be my big break.

45

OWEN

I hate that I'm hurting her more than anything. If I were her, I wouldn't forgive me, either.

She's told me that she hates that her brother comes before her. For everyone. She comes second to everyone but her friends.

I wanted to be someone who put her first. I told her I would. Promised her even.

But when Leo told me that if I didn't stop talking to her and didn't get my head in the game he wouldn't sign his contact, everything came crashing down.

I can't do that to the team.

Sure, it's horrible that he would even use that as an excuse to get me to stop seeing her. It absolutely is. It makes me see him in a new light. It makes me hate him.

But I can't be the reason the team suffers next season.

I can't be the reason the whole city is upset. The whole state.

I can't do that to everyone. Can't have that sort of pressure.

Do I think he would go through with it? Probably not, if I'm honest. But I don't want to find out.

It's definitely an empty threat, but there are also so many teams that really need a great quarterback willing to pay him top dollar. He could have a great team around him and get paid even more than the Cobras would be willing to pay him.

I can't take that chance.

And now it's been almost six weeks since I last spoke to her. We won our divisional round, and we're just about to go play our conference championship. Whoever wins this game goes on to play the other winner of their conference championship in the Super Bowl.

And I'm mad as hell.

Leo is too.

We haven't spoken one on one in weeks, constantly avoiding each other if we can help it.

The other guys have been upset about it, trying their best to get us to reconnect. For Leo to forgive me.

Nothing has worked so far.

The stadium comes to life, the cheers and screams making us even more fired up as we get ready to play the last remaining team in our conference.

We've got this.

It's the third quarter and we're down by thirteen.

Our defense has been okay, but this team is tough. There's a reason they made it this far.

But we can taste victory. We can do this.

Leo has the ball in his hands as he looks around, and I'm running up the field, turning to run up the middle of the field as he throws to me. I jump, but I'm slammed to the ground as a linebacker grabs my legs, throwing me to the ground.

Fuck.

Wincing, I roll to my side, propping myself up as I look at the sky above, listening to all the boos.

But I don't stay down for long. Getting up, I run back to get into formation. A new play is called, and I run up the field about fifteen yards before taking a sharp right, running to the middle of the field. Leo throws, and I catch it perfectly, spinning to avoid a safety as I take off, running into the end zone.

But I don't celebrate. We need to be winning to do that.

Instead, I run back, ready to keep going.

The game goes on, and in the fourth quarter, we're finally up by a field goal.

The clock ticks down, and just when we think that the other team is going to get a touchdown, killing our chances at the Super Bowl, our defense gets a pick in the end zone, essentially ending the game.

Cheers erupt around us, but all I can think about as I stand, watching everyone around us under the lights, my hands on my hips as I breath hard, is how close this game was.

And I hate that.

We have a lot of work to do before the Super Bowl, that's for sure.

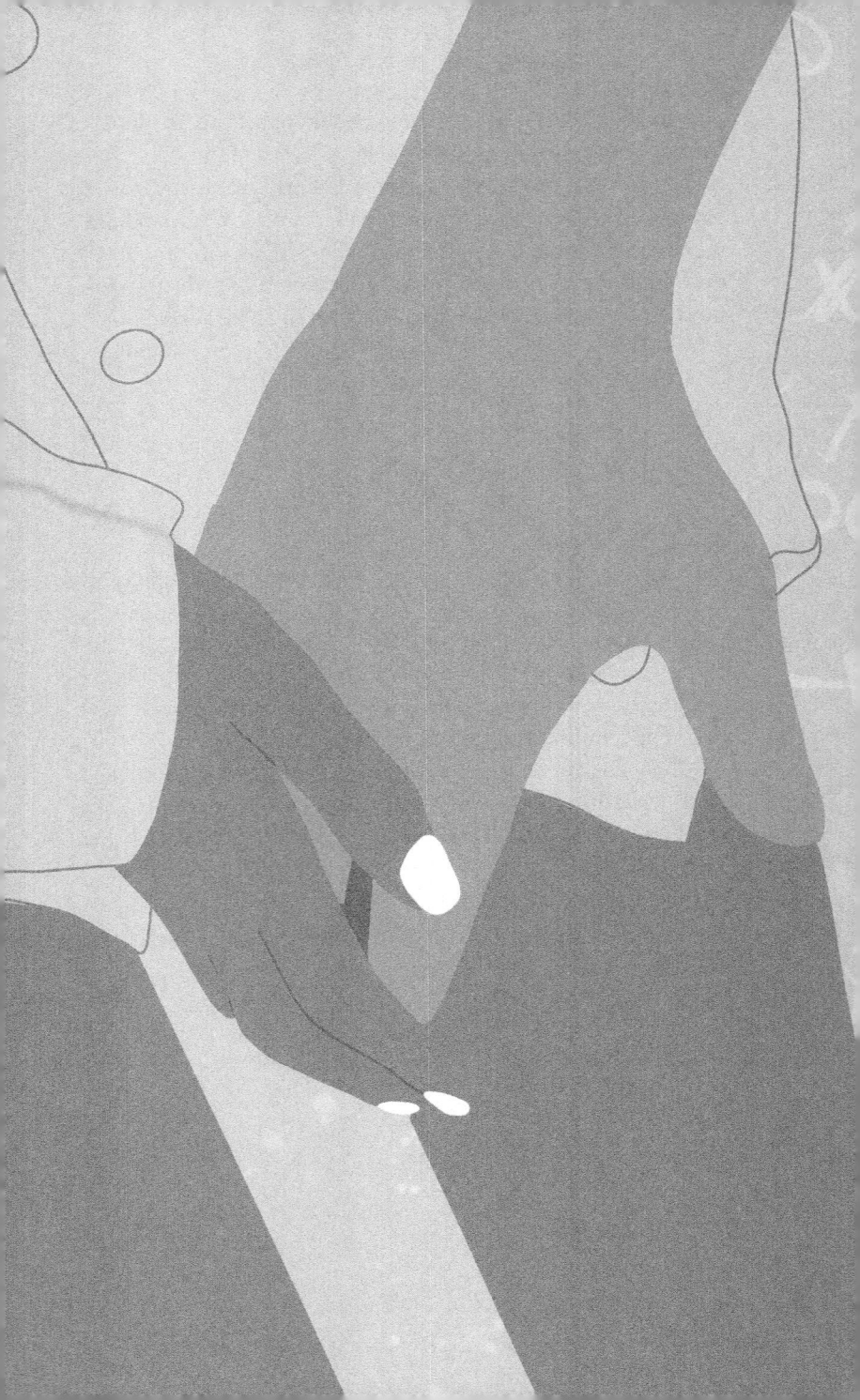

46

ISLA

I don't bother going to their last playoff game.

Instead, I'm sitting on my floor, painting my last piece for the showing when I get the call from my mom telling me my brother is going to the Super Bowl.

And I want to be excited. I do.

But I'm not.

I just can't wait until it's all over. All of it. Every single thing.

I just want answers.

"When is the game?" I ask as I add some blue to the middle of my canvas, highlighting the landscape.

"It's in two weeks," she says, her voice lower now as she realizes what I do.

I know that if I don't go to the game I'm going to regret it. I know that this feeling is going to pass, and at some point, Leo and I are going to be okay again.

And I know that when that happens, this is going to hurt if I don't.

But the game is the very day after my showing.

"I'm going to have to meet you there, Mom."

"I get it sweetie. I'm so excited for you."

Not excited enough to stay and come to it, though, I want to say.

I don't.

God, I just want to scream.

Mila, Amara, and Heidi run around with me as we make sure everything is set up for the showing.

I didn't have to do much this time, instead just making sure everything is in the correct spaces, it's all labeled, and everyone knows what to do and say.

The gallery is beautiful. A giant white room with a lounge on the left, complete with a snack bar that was provided for us. Although Amara enjoyed creating grazing boards for a couple of weeks, she quickly decided that people are much too picky and she didn't want to keep doing it.

"You should go home and change," Amara tells me, her hand on my back.

They've been careful with me since everything went down, making sure that I'm not going to slip into something I can't come out of.

And I've been strong. I slip into those moments because of me. Not because of men.

I know it would be completely reasonable for me to, but I'm just not. I've been so focused on this showing for the last couple of weeks that I've barely thought about any of the men at all, even.

The only thing that reminds me is the plane ticket in my purse for one in the morning. A direct flight across the country to the Super Bowl.

I sigh. "Yeah, I think I'm going to," I tell her.

She smiles at me. "We'll hold the fort down here until you come back, okay?"

I nod, heading out.

My trip home doesn't last long. I'm only there for long enough to throw on my dress, throw up my hair and tie it with a pretty white bow, and throw in some heels. I grab a big bag, packing a pair of slides. I'm going to need them. From there, I grab my suitcase so that I can go straight to the airport. Sweats, a sweatshirt, slides, everything I need is right there so I can decompress and think about what a great night this is going to be.

Because it's going to be great. I demand it. I didn't stress over this for weeks upon weeks for nothing, that's for sure.

Heading back out, I make sure that nothing is left on in my place before driving back to the gallery. I've only been gone for at most an hour, and the showing is going to be starting really soon.

But when I walk into the room, I freeze.

The whole thing is full of yellow and white flowers. Everywhere.

The most beautiful flowers I've ever seen.

My mouth drops as I look around. Mila comes up to me, a huge grin spread across her face.

"What is this?" I ask. I don't remember the gallery owner mentioning flowers would be provided.

"I don't know, I didn't read the note," she tells me, handing me an envelope.

I look at it, turning it over in my hands. The envelope is heavy, and my name is scrawled across it in a handwriting that looks like a man put way too much effort into making something look fancy.

"These were delivered?" I ask, looking around.

She nods, biting her lip as she plays with the hem of her black dress. I look behind her, finding Heidi and Amara in matching black dresses, watching me silently, smirks on their faces as I rip open the envelope.

Hey Peaches

I know I fucked up. I want to start with that. I told you this wouldn't happen, and I let it happen. I can never say I'm sorry enough.

But over the last few months I've fallen in love, and that's not something that I can just move past.

I can't tell you why I stopped talking to you weeks ago. At least, not right now. But just know that I didn't want to stop. I still don't want to stop. But in our time apart I've realize that I really am in love with you.

I love you, Isla Warner, and I'll do every single thing I can do to win you back.

All I've wanted in this life is someone to live it with. I've been picky. I've been stubborn. But I knew from the first day I saw you that there was something so special about you. Something I loved. I didn't know until I had the chance to really talk to you how deep that went. How much I would love you.

> *I think I've loved you for a very long time.*
>
> *I just have to go win this game first, and I know that that sounds stupid, but I promise it's my only option.*
>
> *Afterwards, if you'd let me, I want to be there for you. I want to fix this. I want to hold you every single night, wash your hair in the tub, and watch really bad reality TV.*
>
> *I want you in my jersey every Sunday of the fall.*
>
> *I want you in my bed.*
>
> *I want you.*
>
> *Please think about it.*
>
> *I hate to miss your showing, but I know that I wouldn't be able to come even if I was home. I know you're going to shine, Pretty Girl.*
>
> *Love, Owen*

Tears form in my eyes as I read it over. Nothing, and I mean nothing, could prepare me for it.

"Oh God, Isla honey here." Heidi runs up to me, a tissue covering her finger as she dries my eyes. "The showing is about to start. We got this, okay?"

I nod. It's all I can do at the moment.

A little bit later, the whole room is crowded with people viewing my art, and I can't describe the fear and excitement swirling in my stomach.

"They're all here for Leo," I tell Mila, looking around skeptically.

"He's not here," she says, her brows furrowed. "I think people know he's across the country."

I still don't buy it. Still can't believe it. I'm not sure why, but I feel like they're all here for the team, and not for me.

Well, I know why. It's because the last time was so bad.

"These people are for you," Amara tells me, taking my hand and pulling me into the crowd.

"These are so beautiful," an older woman says as she looks at one of my paintings of the inner harbor.

"Thank you so much," I smile.

"Really. I'm so glad I came today. I saw the posters around the city last week and wasn't sure if I could make it, but I think I'm going to buy this one," she tells me, gesturing to the painting, a glass of red wine in her hand.

I gape at her. "The posters?"

She nods. "Yeah, they were everywhere. I hope you get a good turnout because of them."

My head starts to spin as I look over at Mila, busy talking to another guest.

I don't think we put up posters.

Maybe the gallery did?

But they said they don't do promotions. It was up to me to get people in. They just have people who belong to the gallery who would come, but otherwise? Not their problem.

Did my friends?

I shake my head, trying to focus on what the woman is saying.

I talk to her a little more about the piece and my process before directing her to one of the gallery workers in order to get her checked out. The piece will be marked sold.

As I look around, there are quite a few marked sold, and my eyes widen as I realize that these people really are here for me.

For my work.

Holy shit.

"Isla Warner?" a deep voice says from behind me.

I spin, and my breath catches.

A pencil-thin man stands behind me, a large sweater making him almost look bulky, his slacks loose on his legs. His black hair is brushed to the side, and his eyes are dark, as if he hasn't slept in a week.

Jean Clemment.

Is here.

In front of me.

Looking around the room.

At my art.

I start breathing fast and heavy, my brain not thinking straight.

"I'm Jean," he says as he reaches out.

I get my shit together enough to grab his hand, shaking it once, trying to find my words.

"Your work is impressive," he says as he looks at the wall behind me.

"Thank you so much," I tell him, swallowing roughly. I can't breathe.

"I was in the city and heard from a friend of a friend that I should come check you out. I'm so glad I did," he nods as he starts to walk around.

"I, I um," I fumble on my words, unable to figure out what to say. "I'm sorry," I say as I chuckle nervously. "you've been one of my favorite artists for years. I just love everything you do."

He turns to me, a smile on his lips as he nods. He doesn't say anything else, likely as awkward at taking compliments as I am.

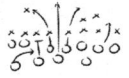

Jean Clemment purchased one of my favorite pieces. A painting I worked on based off of New York City: the parallel between the quiet stillness of the park and the hustle and bustle of everything else.

All dots, short, clear brushstrokes, and beautiful colors, the piece is by far my favorite.

And apparently his too.

"I can't believe that just happened," I say, staring in front of me as I look around at everything.

"Well it did. And you have a plane to catch," Mila says as she hands me my things, practically shoving me out the door.

"I can help clean up a little," I assure her, looking around.

"Nope." She shakes her head. "You go get on that plane. Go get your man."

"I don't even know if I want—"

"Don't even start with me," Mila says as she shakes her head vigorously. "Go get your man or I'm going to kick your ass."

47

OWEN

I didn't hear anything from Isla last night or this morning. Not that I expected to.

Why would she reach out?

I don't even know if she's coming.

But I hope her show went well last night. I really do.

Our time in Las Vegas has been a whirlwind so far, and Leo has been the happiest I've seen him in weeks.

I mean, he should be. We're playing the Super Bowl.

I bought tickets for my sister, niece, and parents to be here, and although I'm nervous about what my parents are going to say—I really don't want to hear about how much work they're missing by being here for their son—I'm happy they made it.

I know that Leo's parents are here, and I'm really happy for him. They'll be flying back to Scotland in about a week, but I'm so happy that they stayed around to watch this.

All I can do is pray for a win and a beautiful woman waiting for me at the end of this. And if she's not waiting for me at the end, I just hope that she forgives me.

That's all I can wish for right now, considering everything that happens reminds me of her.

A fan came up to me last night at dinner saying that he was going to go home and play Wonderwall for his date. I didn't have time to warn against it. He simply told me, hugged me, and ran off, probably about to scar her for life.

I remind myself to ask Isla if I'm allowed to make a post apologizing to every woman in the world for the amount of men playing that damn song.

But from what I hear, it's a right of passage for most women.

I could still be a soundboard to try to protect them from it, though.

Just another thing on my long list of things I have to do soon, apparently.

I was able to see my family briefly before the game, but not for long. We're shuffled off to practice, and our coach gives a speech before we're on our way out the tunnel onto the field, ready to kill it.

Three quarters in, I'm panting on the sideline, ready for the game to be over. We're tied. This team is really good, but I know we're better.

Running back out, Cooper is able to get us close to the end zone, and when Leo passes up the middle, I run from the outside, jumping to catch it. I roll as men jump over me. We get close, but on fourth down we're forced to kick a field goal.

Which is immediately done by the other team after.

Five minutes until the end of the game, we get so, so close.

But their defense stops us in our tracks, sacking Leo.

Less than a minute to go, and we get close again...

But have no such luck.

We're out of time outs and the clock keeps running, giving us no time.

The game ends tied.

Overtime starts.

And it feels like it goes on forever and ever, until Leo throws a pass down the sideline. I catch it, realizing that I have the whole field in front of me, and I take off like a mad man.

Reaching the end zone, the crowd erupts as the lights flash.

The timer ticks down, to zero, and we win.

We win the Super Bowl.

Everything blurs as players run at me, crowding me as confetti rains down on us, lights flashing in my eyes.

I'm lost in a mass of arms, helmets, shoulder pads, and cameras flashing around me.

We won it.

I look around as families make their way down onto the field, greeting their husbands, brothers, and sons, and when I spot the familiar blonde and her kid, I smile.

"Uncle Owen!" Elara screams as she reaches me, jumping into my arms. I spin her around, laughing.

And I feel okay. If this is all I have, I'm okay with that.

My parents come up behind Briar, my dad coming up behind me and patting my back. "We're proud of you, Owen," he says, and I can tell that at least this time, he means it.

My mom has tears in her eyes as she tugs on my arm, forcing me to bend over and hug her. "I'm so proud of you," she whispers, patting me on the back as she smiles.

"Yeah, you didn't do so bad," my sister smiles. "Could have caught a few more of those targets though, butter fingers."

I can only roll my eyes, hugging her, too.

"Owen!" I hear, and my head whips around, watching as a

beautiful brunette bounds toward me before throwing herself at me full-force, almost knocking me over completely. Her legs wrap around me as her head tucks under my chin. I can feel her crying.

"Shhh," I sooth, running my hands over her hair. "I got you, Peaches. You okay? I think I should be the one crying."

"Shut up," she sputters, smacking my back. Her legs loosen as she drops, and when she does, I realize she's wearing my jersey.

And I can't keep the smile off my face.

"You came," is all I can manage to say.

"I wouldn't miss it for the world."

"Look I—" She pushes her fingers against my mouth, silencing me.

"My mom told me what Leo threatened," she says, her eyes narrowing at someone over my shoulder.

I look, spotting Leo watching us, his face calm but sad as he looks around at everyone. A coach approaches him and he smiles, but it doesn't quite reach his eyes. When they're done talking, he turns, throwing us one last glance, and walks over to his parents.

"How did she know?"

"He told them thinking they would be on his side. She kicked his ass."

That wouldn't surprise me.

"I love you, Isla Warner." It slips out before I can stop it. So easily. And I worry for a minute as she stares up into my eyes that she won't say it back.

"I love you too, Crosby. You better not pull that shit again."

I smile. I would never.

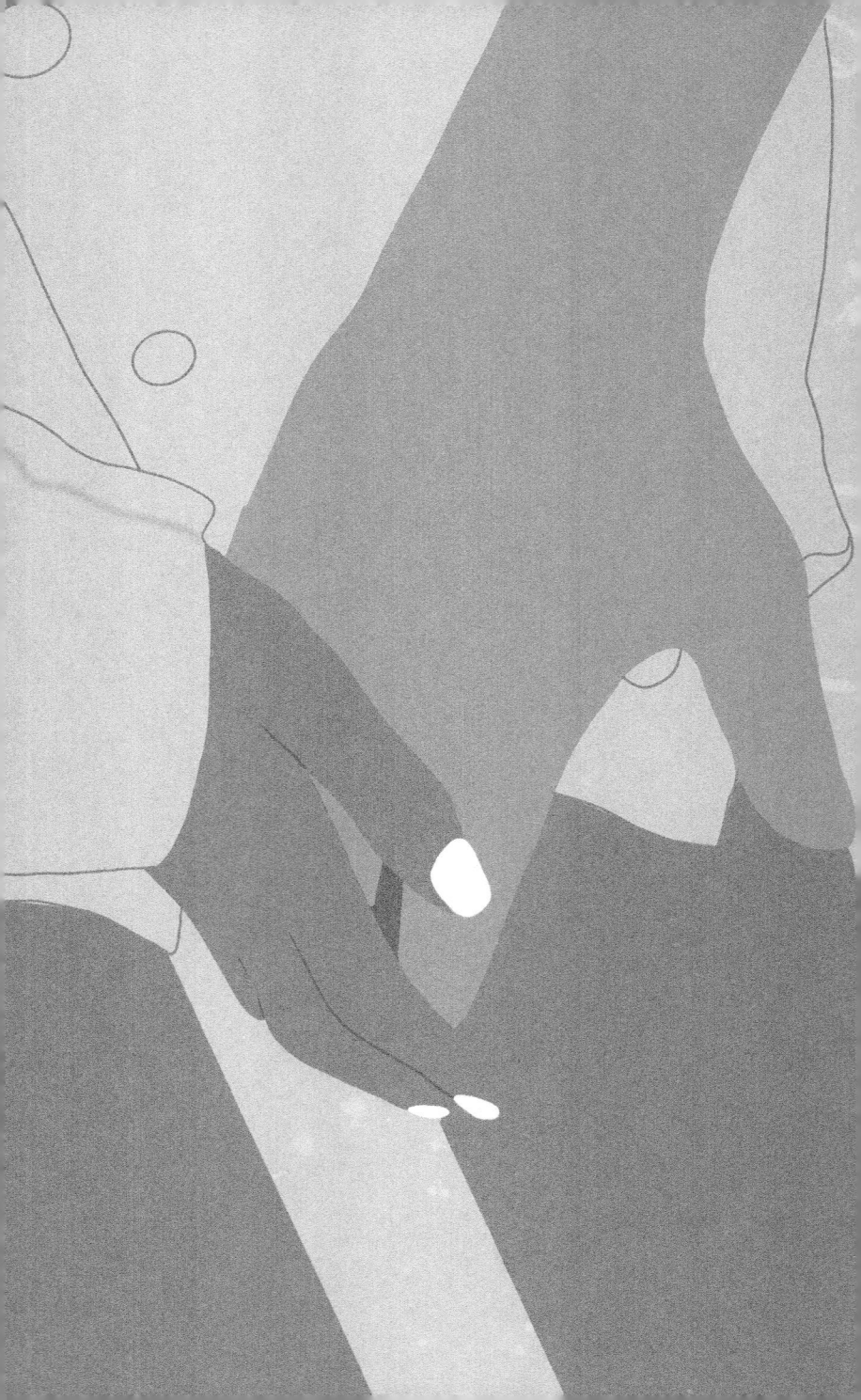

48

ISLA

"What do you mean you bought my place from my brother?" I ask the man in front of me.

"I mean that I bought your place from your brother. So we can live here. Together."

"Why would you do that?" I ask, looking around.

"Because we talked about moving in together like fifty times. We agreed that we'd do it by now. Duh."

"No, I mean why would you buy it from my brother?"

"Because I have no problem just signing it over to you so you can do whatever you want with it."

I look at him, watching him brush his hair out of his face out of stress as he sits on my couch, his giant frame taking up most of it.

"Okay…"

"And I also wanted to be able to make decisions without consulting your brother," he adds fast.

"Decisions like what?"

His lips tighten as he looks around guiltily again.

It's almost the next football season, and Owen has been concerned about our living arrangements after my brother has barged in on us having sex multiple times. Somehow, his brain functions like a gold fish's, and he refuses to learn from his mistakes.

"Well, I may have done something earlier today while you were out." He grimaces.

My brows furrow as I tuck my hair behind my ears.

"You can go check the bedroom."

And I do. I march to the door, swinging it open, only to come face to face with the cutest face I've ever seen in my entire life.

The fuzziest face I've ever seen, too.

The fuzziest little brown puppy runs out, greeting me, their tail wagging with excitement.

"Oh my god, Owen? What is this?"

"That's Peaches."

"Peaches?"

"Yeah, like the peach rings? Like your favorite snack?"

"Yes I know. Why is it here?"

"Because I adopted her."

"We have a dog?"

"Yeah."

My body freezes in shock as I try to process this new information. We have a dog.

A whole dog.

"What?"

Bending down, I pet his furry little head as he runs around me, his little yips warming my heart.

"I just had to. She looks so sweet, just like her mom."

Oh my God, I have a dog.

"So you bought this place from my brother just so that you could get a dog without asking him?"

"Yeah."

"Okay."

But I just can't be mad at him.

I meet his eyes and smile. The second I do, I see his worry

fade away, his eyes filling with excitement as he watches me pet Peaches.

"You know you can't call me Peaches now, right? It's the dog's name."

"You got it, Pretty Girl."

Suddenly there's a loud bang on my door, as if someone is trying to break it down. Owen's face twists in concern as he goes over to it, whipping it open.

My brother stands on the other side, his eyes crazed as he looks at him.

"Owen, I need your help. Right now. Isla, you too."

"What's wrong?" Owen asks, letting him in.

Leo runs his hands through his hair as he tries to calm his breathing.

"I may have fucked up."

"How? Just spill it."

"Well, I was talking to my PR team and they agreed that I had to do something to change my image. It's pretty bad, if you couldn't tell."

Pretty bad is an understatement. He had been caught with strippers in his hotel room a couple of weeks ago and it was a whole mess.

"Yeah?" Owen says.

"Well, I may be entering a PR relationship of sorts."

"Okay?"

"And they may have asked me to send them a list of people I think would be good for it."

"And?"

"And, well, I'm being forced to fake-date your sister. But listen, just listen, alright? It's just for the press, nothing more. She knows what she's getting into."

And I've never seen Owen's face turn so red so fast.

EPILOGUE

Two years later

"I can't believe you just did that." My wife beams at me as the crowd around us screams.

I just won my second Super Bowl, just two years after the last.

But this time, when Isla wears her jersey to my games, it's her last name on the back of the jersey. *Crosby*.

"Isla Crosby, I kind of like the sound of that," she had said.

Isla still goes by Isla Warner for her artwork, considering her favorite artist, Jean Clemment, took her under his wing a couple of months after her show, offering her help to get her name out there. And help he did.

Now her name is known all over the world. Isla paints what she wants, and there's always a waiting list every month on her website as people line up to order prints of her paintings, or more importantly, originals.

"It's been a long road," I tell her, leaning down to kiss her lips.

She moans into me, wrapping her arms around my neck as my family approaches.

And I don't think anything could get better than this.

ACKNOWLEDGMENTS

I think one of the hardest things about writing a whole book is tackling the dedications, but I'm going to try my hardest to make sure everyone is included.

First and foremost, to my grandparents Sandy and Ed, who ignited my passion for football years and years ago. I loved watching games when I was in Maryland, and getting my first Joe Flacco jersey was one of my favorite moments. I wore that thing to school in New York constantly, whether I was called Sacco Flacco or not. I didn't care.

To my boyfriend Alex, who continued to grow my love of football by being one of my only friends for ten years to talk about it with me, and later, once were were dating, taking me to my very first NFL game. To the Ravens, no less. I'm sorry they beat the Vikings, but I'm not *really* sorry, if you get what I mean. Thank you for always being there for me, helping me a bit with this book, and for literally everything.

To Ariana. You're truly one of the best humans and I appreciate you more than you know.

To Jess, one of my favorite humans on this planet for helping me a little bit with some coaching things in this. I really appreciate your help, and no matter what you say, you're an elite coach to me, coach.

To Matt W, who's truly one of the best people on this floating rock, who took the time to explain fantasy to me one night during covid and was ultimately the reason I started thinking hey, this may not be as stupid as I've thought it was.

To Darlene, as always. I wouldn't be publishing this today without you. Thank you so much for the love.

To Aimee, who has become a good friend. I always love listening to you talk about your love of football from across the pond, and as always I adore your cats. I have that scene you requested mapped out in the next book!

To Lily, who is one of the sweetest people you'll ever meet in your life. Thank you for being you. You're the most wonderful person, and I hope you know that your smile still lights up a room.

To Niki. Thank you so much for all the love and encouragement you've given me, and for being so incredibly sweet. I'm so glad that giveaway brought you to me!

To Teri, my resident Orioles fan. I hoped you liked this, but I can't wait for you to hear what I have in store for baseball!

And to the rest of my readers, than you so much for giving this a chance. I'm so excited for you to see what's in store for the future.

FANTASY FOOTBALL TERMS

ADP (Average Draft Position): The average spot in the draft where a player is being drafted. An ADP of 12.0 means that player is being drafted on average 12th overall. It is important to make sure that you are looking for the ADP that applies to your league's scoring (e.g., PPR, non-PPR), because a player's ADP will fluctuate based on those rules.

Bench players: Players on your team who are not in your starting lineup for a given week. Their production will not count toward your total score.

Bust: A player who has not lived up to your expectations. A player can be a bust in a given week or for the season as a whole.

Bye week: Each NFL team takes one week off during the 18-week NFL season. This is called their "bye week." Some fantasy leagues also grant a bye week to their teams.

Ceiling: The maximum statistical upside a player has for a week, season or career. A high ceiling means the player has the potential to score a lot of fantasy points. A low ceiling means he sports little upside. *Also see:* floor.

Cheat sheet: Rankings used for fantasy drafts. May also include other helpful things like injury reports, depth charts, sleepers, busts and breakouts.

Commissioner (Commish, League Manager, LM): The Commish is responsible for creating the league, setting the scoring, determining the roster requirements and managing the league as the season moves along, including settling any disputes.

Cut, drop, release: Each can be used interchangeably to refer to a player who you no longer want on your team. You cut/drop/release the player for a free agent or via waivers.

Depth chart: The hierarchy within each NFL team at a given position -- e.g., starting quarterback, backup quarterback, third-string quarterback.

Draft: How each team in your league builds its respective roster of players. *Also see:* snake drafts and salary cap drafts.

FANTASY FOOTBALL TERMS

Flex: A utility roster spot. Typically, such a spot can be filled by a running back, wide receiver or tight end, though some leagues also include other or fewer positions in their flex spot(s). *Also see:* superflex.

Free agent: A player who is not currently rostered by a team in your league.

Hospital Pass: a pass made to a team-mate who will be tackled heavily as soon as the ball is received

Injured Reserve (IR): For fantasy leagues, this is a roster spot that you can use to stash an injured player. In many leagues, such a player also must be on his actual NFL team's injured reserve list or officially listed as "out" for that week's game.

Mock draft: A practice draft. Helpful for trying alternate strategies and preparing yourself for different circumstances that arise, including draft slots.

Manager: The person in control of all decisions (draft, weekly starters, trades, free agency, etc.) for a fantasy team.

Pickup: A player you add from the free-agent pool or via waivers.

PPR (point per reception): A league which rewards a player one fantasy point for each reception (catch). Many leagues use "1/2 PPR," which rewards 0.5 points for each reception (catch).

Projections: Educated guesses as to what stats a player should produce in a given week or season.

QB1, QB2: In a 10-team league, a QB1 is a quarterback who ranks as a top-10 option, while a QB2 is ranked from 11-20 at the position.

RB1, RB2: In a 10-team league, an RB1 is a running back who ranks as a top-10 option, while an RB2 is ranked from 11-20 at the position.

Roster: The players that make up a fantasy football team. These are the players you see on your "My Team" page.

Sleeper: A player who you think will exceed his draft spot.

FANTASY FOOTBALL TERMS

Snake draft: A draft where the team who drafts first in Round 1 will draft last in Round 2. The team drafting last in Round 1, drafts first in Round 2. This snaking approach in a 10-team league would look like this: 1-10, 10-1, 1-10, etc.

TE1, TE2: In a 10-team league, a TE1 is a tight end who ranks as a top-10 option, while a TE2 is ranked from 11-20 at the position.

Trade: A swap of players and/or draft picks between two teams.

Transaction: Any change to your roster, such as trades, free-agent pickups, etc.

Waivers: A player is on waivers after being dropped by another team. When on waivers, the waiver order of the interested teams determines which roster he joins. Should the player clear waivers (that is, no manager labels him as worth their spot in the waiver line), he is added to the free-agency pool and, thus, available for the first team that wants his services.

Waiver order: The order in which your league's free-agent waivers are processed.

WR1, WR2, WR3: In a 10-team league, a WR1 is a top-10 wide receiver, a WR2 is ranked from 11-20, and a WR3 is ranked 21-30.

Definitions from ESPN.com

ABOUT THE AUTHOR

Anna Noel is an action romance and sports romance writer based in Upstate New York. Getting her start writing when she was only 11 years old, Anna made it her life's mission to build a career around books.

Anna has been writing and selling plots to authors for over 7 years, and went full-time with her freelance writing career in 2020. Since then, she's worked as a copywriter, plot writer, eulogy writer, and ghostwriter.

Anna has been working on her Project Fallen Angel series for years and is looking forward to finally publishing them!

When she's not writing, Anna can be found watching Star Wars, cheering on the Baltimore Orioles and Ravens, cooking, and hanging out with her two cats and boyfriend.

Her website: https://annanoelbooks.com/

Connect with Anna to stay up to date.

ALSO BY ANNA NOEL

PROJECT FALLEN ANGEL SERIES

A series of espionage novels

Reprisal

Read for free on KU

Enemies to lovers, forced-proximity, action romance novel

Harbinger

Read for free on KU

Forced marriage of convenience, forced proximity action romance novel

Penance

Pre-order now. Out February 2024

Second chance western romance novel, lovers to enemies to lovers, forced-proximity, DARK action romance

BALTIMORE COBRAS SERIES

Sports romances

Love on the Waiver Wire

Fantasy football themed sports romance romcom. Brother's best friend, secret lovers

How to Prevent a Fumble

Coming soon

Printed in Great Britain
by Amazon